Daughter of the Most High

ISBN (Paperback): 978-1-7364392-7-2
ISBN (Hardcover): 978-1-7364392-9-6
ISBN (E-book): 978-1-7364392-8-9

This is a work of historical fiction based on historical events and events recorded in the Bible. Scripture may be quoted or paraphrased by characters and historical figures may be mentioned. However, all other characters and events depicted come from the author's own imagination. Any likeness to persons, living or deceased, is purely coincidental.

All scripture quotations unless otherwise indicated have been taken from the Christian Standard Bible®, Copyright © 2017 by Holman Bible Publishers. Used by permission. Christian Standard Bible® and CSB® are federally registered trademarks of Holman Bible Publishers.

Cover design concepts by C. J. Graves.
Paperback and hardcover design by Jenna Van Mourik.
Images licensed through Shutterstock.

Printed in the United States of America.

First edition: November 2024

Jenna Van Mourik, NowGo Publishing
www.authorjennavanmourik.com

PRAISE FOR ANTIOCH'S DAUGHTER

"Jenna Van Mourik has done it again—created a family that draws you in and touches your heart. Van Mourik shines with a powerful story of grace and forgiveness that's timeless ... Libi and Cassius both have hearts to serve the downtrodden, but will their similarities be able to withstand the truth in their differences? Don't miss this family adventure and sweet romance. Saul and Barnabas make appearances as well as Asa from *Jerusalem's Daughter*. Another story that shows the grace and love of the One True God."

— Barbara M. Britton, author of The Daughters of
Zelophehad series and *Defending David: Ittai's Journey*

"Jenna's sophomore novel delivers a moving message of God's redemption that is strong enough to reach even the hardest lost souls. The love story between Cassius, an imperfect man who believes himself beyond redemption, and Libi, a selfless young woman with her own set of imperfections to work through, will both inspire you and cause you to examine your own heart. Wholesome, uplifting, and thought-provoking, *Antioch's Daughter* is perfect for readers young and old alike!"

— Ashton E. Dorow, author of The Royals of Acuniel series

PRAISE FOR JERUSALEM'S DAUGHTER

"I truly believe this author brings a sweetness to Biblical fiction that is hard to describe. These characters have become vivid to me and I have loved seeing the passion week through their eyes. This story has an even moderate pace that slowly allows you to get to know the characters and then brings you to a climax that has forever changed the world."

— Nicole, host of *The Unending TBR Podcast*

"Rich in historical fact, memorably lovable characters, and inspiring reminders of faith. It's an encouraging story of overcoming fear and learning to trust God. This is easily one of my favorite books and I can't wait to see what Jenna has in store for the rest of the series."

— Audrey Bodine, author

"I loved being in Jerusalem during passion week, the crucifixion, and the resurrection!! Jenna did a wonderful job telling that story while still telling us the story of Shamira and her family ... I know so much research, prayer, and heart went into this book and it definitely paid off! It was beautifully done!"

— Alysha, blogger from *For The Love of Christian Fiction*

Daughter of the Most High

JENNA VAN MOURIK

GLOSSARY

Abba — Father
Agora — Marketplace or large open meeting place, Greek origin
Bat — Daughter of…
Ben — Son of…
Dodah — Aunt
Dodh — Uncle
Forum — Large open meeting place, Roman origin
Fuller/Fullery — Launderer/ancient place for doing laundry
God-Fearing Gentile/God-fearer — Non-Jews who believed in the Jewish God and practiced some Jewish traditions, but did not fully convert to Judaism
Himation — Greek draping outer garment
Hosanna — An expression of adoration or praise for a savior, meaning "help us" or "save us"
Imma — Mother
Madder — A type of plant which produces purple dye
Palla — Roman style cloak or shawl
Peplos — Greek sleeveless outer garment
Python — Figure of Greek mythology
Pythoness — A fortune-telling woman believed to be possessed by the spirit of Python
Rabbi — A Jewish teacher
Sabba — Grandfather
Savta — Grandmother
Shalom — A greeting, meaning "peace be with you"
Via Egnatia — An ancient Roman road that connected Rome to eastern territories
Villa — Large residence, typically removed from a city

FAMILY TREE

ELIYAHU
HODIYAH
AHARON
ELISHEVA
ELIANA
MATTHAN
SHAMIRA
ASA
ELIEL
YEMIMA
KELILA
LITTLE ASA
BINYAMIN
DEVORAH
RUT
BENAYAHU
MILKAH
JERIEL
TOVI
AVIGAIL
TAMIR
CHAVA
YUVAL
GILAD
ALETA
LIBI
CASSIUS
SHIRLI
ANNA

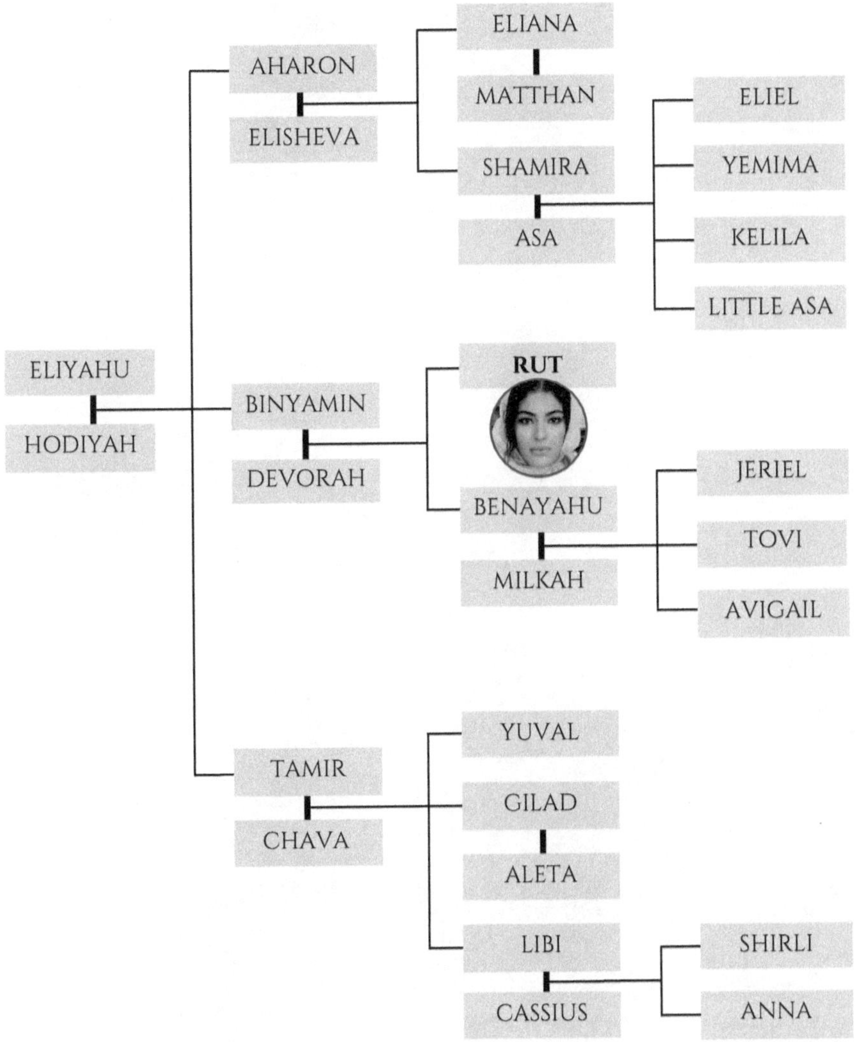

"Rut's Tapestry" Illustration

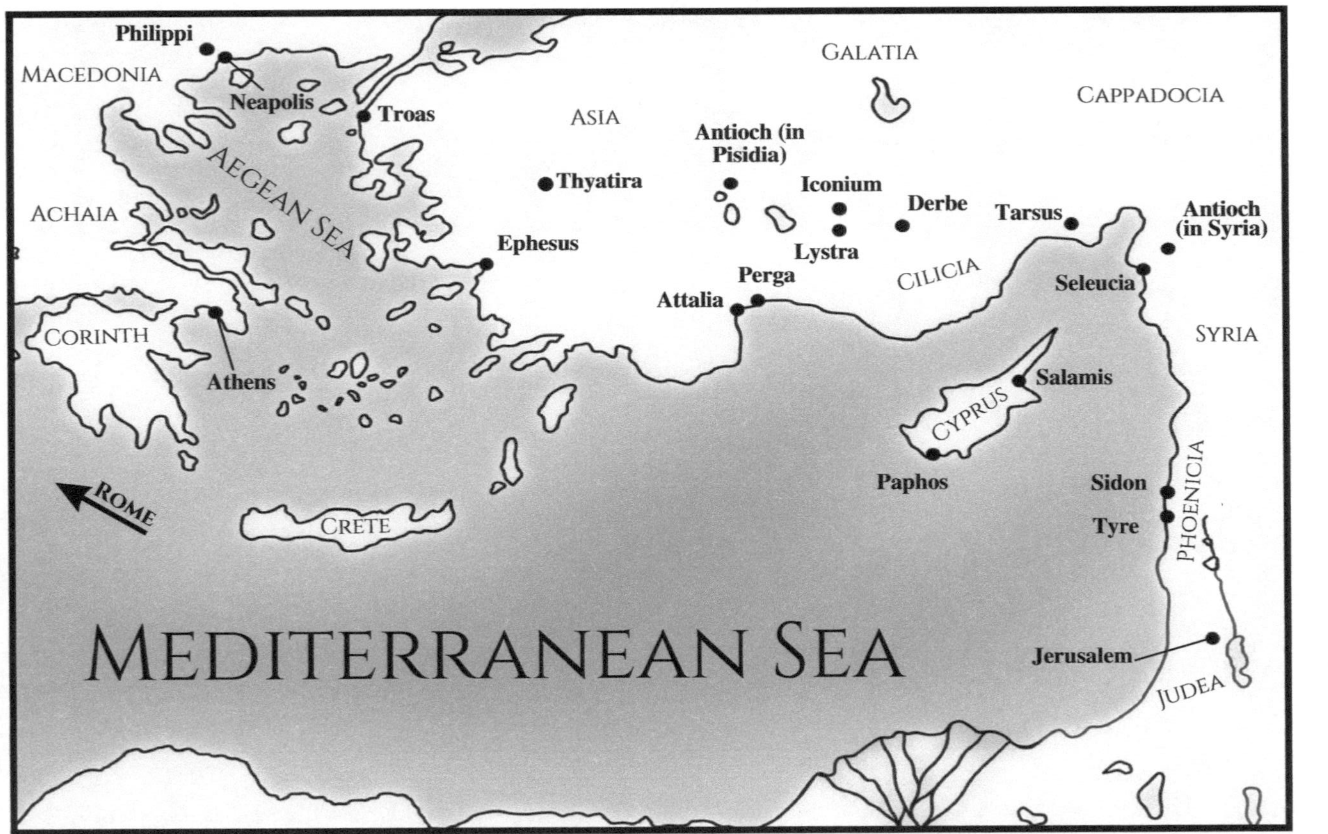

Philippi
MACEDONIA
Neapolis
Troas
GALATIA
CAPPADOCIA
ASIA
Antioch (in Pisidia)
Thyatira
Iconium
Derbe
Tarsus
Antioch (in Syria)
ACHAIA
AEGEAN SEA
Lystra
Ephesus
Perga
CILICIA
Seleucia
Attalia
SYRIA
CORINTH
Athens
CYPRUS
Salamis
Paphos
Sidon
Tyre
PHOENICIA
ROME
CRETE
Jerusalem
JUDEA
MEDITERRANEAN SEA

GOD-FEARING GENTILES

Today, a person who is "God-fearing" is considered to be morally upright and strong in their faith. Did you know that it once meant something different? In the Bible, a God-fearer or devout worshiper of God sometimes referred to a Gentile believer in the Jewish God. These people were sympathetic to the Jewish people and chose to observe many of the same traditions, but did not fully convert. It seems likely that Lydia may have been a Gentile convert to Christianity based on her description in Acts 16:14, which reads, "A God-fearing woman named Lydia, a dealer in purple cloth from the city of Thyatira, was listening. The Lord opened her heart to respond to what Paul was saying" (CSB). She is described as God-fearing, rather than Jewish. Other God-fearing Gentiles in the Bible include Cornelius (Acts 10) and the Ethiopian eunuch (Acts 8).

There are many reasons that Gentile believers may not have converted. Some may not have been ready to fully adhere to every law and custom, including the rite of circumcision; they might have still been holding onto pagan traditions, or unwilling to let go of other beliefs incompatible with Judaism. Alternatively, they might have simply not had the means to learn more and develop a full understanding of God and what Jewish law required. They might not have lived near a synagogue or in a city with a significant Jewish population.

Jesus came so that *all* might have a way to be saved, telling His disciples in Matthew 28:19-20, "Go, therefore, and make disciples of all nations, baptizing them in the name of the Father and of the Son and of the Holy Spirit, teaching them to observe everything I have commanded you. And remember, I am with you always, to the end of the age" (CSB). The Good News of Jesus Christ and the Resurrection would have been life-changing to Gentiles and God-fearers alike, and in this context, it's no wonder that Lydia and others like her would have had their hearts opened by Paul's message.

Note to the Reader

The last time that I put a note addressed to the reader in the first few pages of one of my books was when I published *Jerusalem's Daughter* in 2021. It was my first published book and my first attempt at self-publishing, and I wrote that little note to introduce myself and my story to the world. In many ways, *Daughter of the Most High* feels like the end of a chapter in my author journey; though, to calm your anxious heart, I do not believe that this is the last book with these characters. Many members of this fictional family still have stories to be told! That being said, there are a few things I'd like to share with you before you turn the page.

First, this book is a part of a series with interconnected characters. While you can jump in with either *Jerusalem's Daughter* or *Antioch's Daughter*, if you have not read at least one of the previous books in this series, you may find yourself feeling a bit lost as to where Rut's journey began. I would strongly recommend reading one or both of the previous books before starting this one for the ideal reader experience. Consider yourself forewarned!

Second, as an avid reader myself, I can testify to the truth that more often than not when reading historical fiction, my mind wanders with questions like, "Did that really happen?" "Did that person really exist?" "Would that really be how things were done back then?" "Is that how that was said in that time period?" As a writer, I can also testify that I spend an incredible amount of time following research-rabbit-trails in study books and internet articles. Of course, I am merely a storyteller and not an infallible scholar, so if you do find fault or error, I ask your forgiveness as it was not and is never my intention. If you find yourself with a few questions over the course of reading this novel, I would recommend checking the Author's Note at the end of the book. That is where I share more in-depth details about the research I did while writing this book, and it may be helpful to you if you find those kinds of details intriguing.

On the subject of research, I must also address the secondary subject of words. Writing descriptions and dialogue that convincingly fit a historical time period is no easy task. If you'll allow for a bit of humor here, I have been asked before, "Is that really the word they would have used back then?" My response, as someone who enjoyed historical linguistics lectures in college far too much, has *occasionally* been, "Well, technically speaking, they would not have used any of these words." I write in English, and as my characters would realistically speak another language, my books are already "translations" of sorts. Old English words would still not be old enough for the first century. Trying to find the right word that is both accurate to the time period and still makes sense to the modern reader without causing unnecessary confusion is sometimes not possible. For instance, take the word "butterfly." We *know* that they existed in ancient times, but the English word itself comes from the Anglo-Saxon *"buttorfleoge."* Butterflies were popular subjects for art and myth in the cultures of ancient Egypt, Greece, and Rome, but word substitutes like the Latin *"papilio"* or the Greek *"psyche"* or *"scolex"* may be too jarring in fictional prose and therefore pull the reader out of the story. In such an instance, it may just be better to use the word "butterfly" on its own, and ground the reader in the setting using other means.

Personally, I like to imagine my books like *The Epic of Gilgamesh.* If you did not study literary history, then I apologize for this tangent, but *The Epic of Gilgamesh* is an ancient Mesopotamian story written in the language of Akkadian. It is still studied today, but since not many of us are familiar with Akkadian, translations are widely used and available. When I write, I like to pretend that I am translating the story as though it really were written two-thousand years ago, so that it can be read and enjoyed by the audiences of today. What you read is my "best translation" of these characters' stories, which are so very real to me.

Finally, I must share with you that the bulk of this story was drafted during what was a very difficult, very long, and very painful part of my life. Though many tears were shed due to struggles myself and those close to me were facing, I found comfort in writing and giving words to my pain so that I could process it and remind myself through storytelling of what God's hope looks like. This book deals with themes of anxiety, grief, loss, and depression. The characters struggle in their battles, but rest assured, God remains the victor. Sometimes in life, we can feel like our stories don't make sense or that our lives are out of control and beyond repair. My friends, nothing is beyond God. He weaves every broken thread together, and *that* is the message I pray you will see revealed in these pages. He is God, and He *is* good. Through Him, we can be content in any and all circumstances. By His grace was this book written. All glory and honor go to Him!

DEDICATION

To Maddie and the Mendenhalls, who became like family from the very first day we met. Our family trees may not connect, but it sure feels like it sometimes. Thank you for being such a positive influence on my life and faith.

To all my dear, dear friends… You know who you are. You have encouraged me through some of the most difficult seasons of life, prayed with me through the trials, and rejoiced with me at every milestone and celebration. I thank God every time I remember you!

To anyone who has ever felt alone, know that you never have been. I've felt that too, but it isn't true. God was there, He is there, and He will always be there.

Ultimately, to the One True God, who weaves every thread together into His masterpiece. All glory to Him!

"Come, thou Fount of Every Blessing"

1. Come, Thou Fount of every blessing;
tune my heart to sing Thy grace;
streams of mercy, never ceasing,
call for songs of loudest praise.
Teach me some melodious sonnet,
sung by flaming tongues above;
praise the mount! I'm fixed upon it,
mount of God's unchanging love!

2. Here I raise my Ebenezer;
hither by Thy help I'm come;
and I hope, by Thy good pleasure,
safely to arrive at home.
Jesus sought me when a stranger,
wandering from the fold of God;
He, to rescue me from danger,
interposed His precious blood.

3. O to grace how great a debtor
daily I'm constrained to be!
Let that grace now, like a fetter,
bind my wandering heart to Thee.
Prone to wander, Lord, I feel it,
prone to leave the God I love;
here's my heart; O take and seal it;
seal it for Thy courts above.

— Robert Robinson, 1758
(Public Domain)

Part One

"Charm is deceptive and beauty is fleeting, but a woman who fears the Lord will be praised." — Proverbs 31:30 CSB

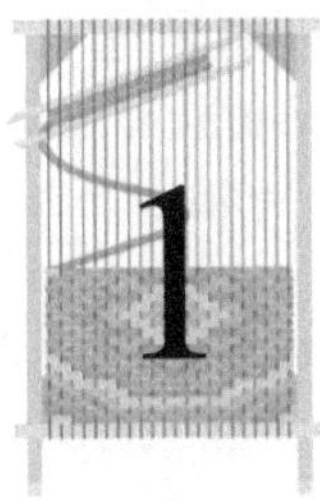

"There is an occasion for everything, and a time for every activity under heaven: a time to give birth and a time to die; a time to plant and a time to uproot; a time to kill and a time to heal; a time to tear down and a time to build; a time to weep and a time to laugh; a time to mourn and a time to dance" —
Ecclesiastes 3:1-4 CSB

41 A.D.

It was early in the morning and well before sunrise. Despite that fact, Rut's back already ached from being bent over her wool projects. The bright pigments of dawn were just barely beginning to dye the billowing clouds beyond her window in shades of blue and orange. Rut stood before her loom, running her fingers overtop the fine threads illuminated by the sun's rays streaming into the room. The work was superb, as it usually was for Rut, whose nimble fingers could traverse the tiny threads both swiftly and delicately to create the finest of weaves. She set to finishing the fabric, pulling the loose threads from their weights and tying off each end with care. When she was done, she folded it neatly. A second length of cloth would have to be made in order to fasten the two pieces together into a single tunic for her husband. *That* would be a project for another day.

Next, Rut turned her attention to the baskets in the corner. Rut knew she needed to start spinning the clean wool into threads if she wanted to finish by the time her *abba* and brother Benayahu returned to the seaside trade ports of Tyre and Sidon. Taking up her spindle and distaff, she sat on a simple wooden stool and began spinning fibers to create threads that would hopefully sell for a good enough price at market to help her family make ends' meet.

This day was like every other morning of the last five years, following a precise pattern like threads in a tapestry; except in life, Rut felt too much like a thread being forced to conform to a design she did not choose. At least when she was seated at her loom or with her spindle, she had control. She felt every movement of the wool between her fingertips, bending it to her will and into patterns of her own making. If only she could have that much control over the rest of her life.

Perhaps then things would be different.

"Who can find a wife of noble character? She is far more precious than jewels," said Shem, Rut's husband. Gently, he reached around and carefully took the distaff and spindle from her hands.

Rut's heart skipped a beat. Though the bed they shared was less than ten paces from where she sat spinning in their simple, one-room dwelling, she had not heard him rise. For a moment, she let herself relax as he held her, closing her eyes to listen as he recited the familiar proverbs, as he did every morning since their wedding. It was his own special tradition, and Rut never protested it.

She focused her mind on the feeling of his hands. They were rough and worn from years spent toiling in the fields, shepherding flocks, and building this little house, but they held her own. As long as they did, Rut was able to forget her troubles.

"She extends her hands to the spinning staff, and her hands hold the spindle. Her hands reach out to the poor, and she extends her hands to the needy. She is not afraid for her household when it snows, for all in her household are doubly clothed. She makes her own bed coverings; her clothing is fine linen and purple…" Shem continued, kissing the top of her head and tugging at her tightly coiled locks of hair, making them bounce up and down.

Rut giggled, briefly transformed once again into a newlywed. "I have never worn purple in all my life."

"You're interrupting me," said Shem with a teasing tone, "but you *will* wear purple one day, my precious jewel."

"Oh, is that so?" Rut turned to face him and take in his smile. Even though years had changed them both, he still seemed to bear the same boyish features as he did when they first fell in love: wide, round eyes, a soft jawline, full lips, and silky black hair that grew in soft waves.

"Someday, when we have more money, I will go with your father and brother to Tyre and bring back vat upon vat of Tyrian purple dye for you so that all of your clothing can be made from it."

Rut shook her head. "That's not very practical for a shepherd's wife."

"But it's what I want for *my* wife. Now, let me finish." Shem turned her back around and began to rub her shoulders while carrying on with his ritual. As he went on, his musical voice lulled Rut into a dream-like state. She'd almost forgotten where she was when she heard a line that drew her back to reality.

"Her children rise up and call her blessed; her husband also praises her: 'Many women have done noble deeds, but you surpass them all!'"

Rut pulled away from him. The reminder that she and Shem had no children together caused new pain to spring forth from an old wound. In the five years they'd been married, Rut never once became with child, and had begun to feel as though she never would. She spoke with her *imma* about it numerous times, yet never found answers. Shamira, Rut's cousin and closest friend, had two little ones of her own. Even Milkah, the wife of her younger brother Benayahu, was expecting.

Her womb remained empty.

A family was all Rut ever wanted. As a young girl, she longed to grow up and be a wife and homemaker, spending every day eagerly learning new recipes and practicing her spinning and weaving skills so that she might be able to manage a house with ease. The four humble walls that surrounded her now, cramped with her small looms and the few possessions she and Shem shared, were not quite the dwelling she'd made up in her childhood dreams.

Shem drew near to her once more, as though he could hear her melancholy thoughts. Tenderly, he whispered, "Everything in God's timing, my beloved."

"That is what you always say," she sighed. She'd heard the phrase so many times that it had lost its meaning for her. The proverbs Shem prayed over her each morning, though they warmed her heart, did little to encourage Rut.

"I always say it because it is *always* true. God is faithful yesterday, tomorrow, and today. We can trust His plan. After all, He brought us together, didn't He?"

"That is true," Rut conceded. Were it not for God taking her family out of Jerusalem, she never would have met Shem. That time was painful for Rut, full of so much loss and change. Shem's family were some of the first people they'd met when they settled in Phoenicia, as they occupied a neighboring farm. Their families quickly became friends, except for Rut and Shem, who'd both been in love with each other since almost the first moment they met. Perhaps it was because Rut's heart had been broken that she'd opened it up to him so quickly. He had wooed her with song, singing often of his love for her and praises to the Lord for the beauty of His creation. Love was uncomplicated then.

"The sun is rising. You should be on your way soon." Rut went to wrap up some food for him and pack his scrip. "Oh, and I meant to tell you last night that the roof needs repair again."

"I'll see to it when I am not so busy," he said, taking the scrip and throwing it over his shoulder.

"You will always be busy, Shem. What if it rains?" Without waiting for an answer, she returned to her seat and picked up her spindle, though she did not begin spinning again.

He laughed, and that only made Rut more frustrated. "I don't think it will rain for some time, Rut. The driest months of the year are upon us. I will have plenty of time to finish the repairs before the next storm comes."

"And if you don't? How long will you be gone this time? A week? Two? Much can happen in a short time, Shem." Rut tucked the distaff into her side and tried to disguise her expression as concentration on her work, but her true feelings were revealed in the sourness of her voice. The tone made her shudder when she heard it; it sounded like when Imma used to scold her and Benayahu as children.

Shem's shoulders drooped as he tied his sandals, and Rut couldn't fault him for multitasking during their discussion. Wasn't she doing the same thing? If only he could stay with her for that one day. *Just one day.* Then the problems they faced might not weigh so heavily on her heart.

But as usual, she had chores to do and he needed to return to the fields.

"I'm sorry, Shem," she whispered. "I shouldn't have spoken

to you like that."

"I'm sorry too," he said, bending down to kiss her farewell. The embrace left her heart racing when it was over. "I'll try to take a look at the roof when I get back, and you can hold me to that. Don't let me cross our threshold until I've made good on that promise, all right?"

Rut shook her head. "No, Shem. You will be exhausted when you return from the fields. I shouldn't have even brought it up until we were closer to the rainy season, and when the sheep can be stabled and fed from stored forage."

"Regardless, I will see what I can do. Better to get started on it as soon as possible, rather than to keep putting it off."

"Are you sure?" she asked.

"If it would put a smile on your face, I'll gladly take a look at it. I know how busy your hands are all day. Let me do this for you."

"All right." Silence fell, but a twinge of guilt compelled Rut to speak again, "If you get home and you really are too tired, please don't feel as though you must. We both work hard for what we have and I don't expect anything else from you that you do not already give me: love when I need it, grace when I don't deserve it, and a home that I get to share with you."

"Beloved, you must understand that I only work so hard because I want to make our lives better in the future."

"Better in the future, but not now." Rut regretted saying the words as soon as they tumbled out of her mouth. She had inherited her sense of humor from her father, though it did not come without the sometimes-sharp tongue of her mother. Years ago she never would have dared to voice such an opinion, but present circumstances had weakened her resolve. When had she let her heart become so bitter? She never used to be this way.

"Rut…"

"No, you do not have to say anything. I'm sorry again. It is my own discontentment that makes me say such things, and I know that is something I need to pray about. You are a wonderful husband to me."

He smiled down at her. "I am glad you understand. You have woven circles around my heart like a grand tapestry, Rut."

She laughed anxiously. "Well, we will likely be unable to afford grand tapestries for a very long time."

"But you will make them for us!" Shem winked at her.

"That will also take a very long time."

"So will many other things, but it will teach us patience, Rut. We will wait upon God's timing in this and in everything."

"In everything," she whispered, echoing the sentiment and praying it would take root in her heart.

"Charm is deceptive and beauty is fleeting, but a woman who fears the Lord will be praised." Shem kissed her again on the lips. Then, all too soon, he left.

Rut stood in the doorway and watched as Shem walked across the valley where her family lived. She smiled seeing her brother join him with the rest of their sheep at the top of the hill. Rut kept watching until every last lamb disappeared from her sight, replaced by the glint of the morning sun as it rose in the sky. She already missed him, yet she knew he was right. Someday their circumstances would not be so difficult.

Perhaps by then they might even have children, and it would be easier too; they would be able to provide more than enough food for them, put clothes on their backs as they grew, and raise them in comfort. As much as it hurt to let go of her expectations, she would try her best to be patient for Shem's sake and for the sake of their marriage.

God knew what was best.

He always did.

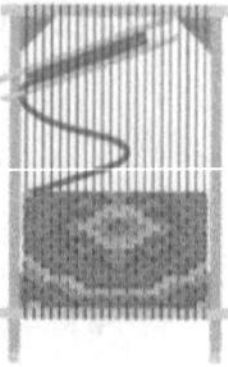

The first day after Shem departed, Rut set herself to the task of cleaning every inch of their house, knowing that in doing so it would become easier to focus on other projects. She ate a vegetable stew for the midday meal and for dinner. Later that night, she stayed up too late spinning wool. The next day, Rut began weaving the second length of cloth for the tunic she'd started. She wanted to have it finished by Shem's return so that it could replace the tattered one he wore. She made a good start on it before her back grew tired and she had to rest.

The third day would have gone much the same as the previous two—full of work and little else—if not for a knock that sounded on the door frame. "Ru-ut!" Shamira, Rut's cousin, called from outside, "Milkah and I have come to see you, and we brought two little helpers with us!"

Rut pulled open the door at the sound of their laughter. "Shamira, Milkah, Eliel, *and* Yemima? I had no idea to expect such a crowd," she teased. "*Shalom*, Milkah. It is good to see you too," Rut addressed her sister-in-law.

"We won't be an imposition, will we? Just say the word and we'll be on our way as quickly as we came." Shamira held her daughter on her hip, and kept a firm grip on her son's tiny, squirmy hand.

"Never! I am always happy to see my family, especially as it gets far too quiet around here when Shem is gone. At least you two have people around who can keep you company."

When Rut and Shem were first married, she appreciated the

privacy their home afforded them. Now she disliked being so far from other people, even if the only thing separating her from her family were the fields of crops they shared. Milkah lived with Rut's parents and Benayahu, so even when Benayahu left for the fields with Shem, Milkah had people around her. Shamira's husband Asa tended the crops alongside Rut's *Dodh* Aharon, planting seeds and making sure they grew enough to sustain their families. Shamira never had to sleep alone at night. Her husband always came back to her before sunset.

"Keep us company, yes," said Shamira, letting go of Eliel briefly to brush Yemima's curls away from her face, "but allow me to get things done? Not always."

"It isn't fun being by myself *all* of the time, you know." There it was again. No matter how many times she coaxed herself into believing she was at peace with her circumstances, a little bit of frustration always made its way out. Rut and Shamira had always been close, in age and in heart. They shared everything with each other, from their first steps to the joys of first love. She always thought that they would share the joys of motherhood together too, raising their children side by side, but that was not the case. Even though they were still close, things were not the same between them now.

Shamira smiled, but Rut knew that there must have been pity in her heart. "I didn't mean it like that, Rut. I wouldn't trade my little Eliel and Mima for anything in the world."

"Mima? Is that what you're calling her now?" asked Rut.

"Sometimes. It's all Eliel can say of her name at the moment." She laughed and Rut admired how she glowed from within. Motherhood brought out a whole different side to Shamira. She was the same fiercely loving and fiercely loyal person she'd always been, but somehow more. Rut wondered what change motherhood would have brought about in her, then banished the thought. Shamira turned to her little son. "Eliel? Can you say

'Yemima?'"

"*Mm*... Mima! *Mm*... Mima!"

All three of the women laughed. Eliel's adorable mispronunciation made Rut instantly forget about her own yearnings. Shamira continued, "Just you wait, Milkah. Soon you'll be chasing your own little one around and delighting in their laughter, their first sounds, their first steps... Savor this time in your life—it is precious."

Milkah blushed as she cradled her growing midsection. "Ever since I came to live with Benayahu and your parents, Rut, your mother has been so attentive to me, and especially now that I am with child, but I don't mind. I never had a very big or close family, and I am so grateful to be a part of yours now. All of you have been so kind."

Shamira instantly took Milkah's hand in hers and gave it a tight squeeze. "Rut and I have always said that we are cousins by blood, but sisters by heart. You are a sister to us as well, Milkah."

"Really?" said Milkah, eyes glistening.

"Of course," said Rut. "Even if I can't understand why you would marry someone like my brother."

Laughter overtook them yet again and it was a while before they could all settle down. Milkah eventually opened up a basket of food that she had carried with her, and the three women ate the midday meal together. After she had her fill, Rut decided to work on some spinning with Milkah's help. Shamira tried to clean up the food while playing little games with Eliel and Yemima, until both children succumbed to sleep. While the little ones napped, the three women kept working, whispering softly about their lives and praying together.

Rut needed this. She knew she did. Her heart yearned for companionship and fellowship. This visit reminded her that even if she wasn't going through the same things as those around her, she was never truly alone. She could lean on others for support, as well as on God. Why was it so easy for her to forget?

Sometime in the late afternoon, when Rut should've started heating up her evening supper, and Shamira and Milkah should have been leaving, the women jumped in unison at the sound of shouting outside the door. With only hills and trees for company in the isolated valley they called home, the sound of so many voices raised all at once was more than enough cause for alarm.

When Yemima began to cry, Shamira lifted her little girl close to her chest and reached for Eliel. "What could that be?"

"I'm not sure," said Rut, carelessly dropping the wool and her spinning tools.

The door swung open and a shadowy figure appeared in the frame, lit from behind by the falling sun. She could tell right away that it wasn't her beloved Shem. "Abba?" said Rut.

"Rut… It's…" Her abba struggled for words. Shamira and Milkah waited in silence for an answer as to what he was doing here. He should have been on the other side of the valley.

Rut didn't wait any longer for an answer. She heard a cry from outside. A painful cry. One that twisted her heart into a thousand tiny pieces. *It was Shem.*

"Abba! No!" She just managed to choke out the words as sobs overtook her.

"Beni and Asa are outside with Shem… There was…"

Rut pushed past him before he could finish. She was followed closely by Milkah and Shamira, who kept the children facing away from the horrific display before them.

When her eyes focused, she saw her husband's body lying on the ground, pale and convulsing. He was alive, and all Rut could think about was how badly she needed him to stay that way.

"Get away from him!" Rut screamed, pushing Benayahu aside. It was too early for them to have returned with the sheep.

Asa moved to stand with Shamira. "He was bit by a snake, but I am afraid it may be too late," she heard him say.

"I tried to bring him back as quickly as I could, but…" Benayahu's whispered voice tapered into silence.

Tears flooded Rut's vision, so much so that she could barely see her husband's face as he coughed and writhed in pain. "Shem," Rut sobbed. Her gaze travelled over his body, down to the reddish-purple swelling at his ankle and the bloody fang marks where the snake had sunk its teeth.

"Rut, beloved, I'm home early." Shem tried to chuckle, but the laughter only made his cough worse. His body wouldn't stop shaking long enough for him to catch his breath. She held onto him tightly, willing his muscles to relax and be still.

"Shh… Don't try to talk, Shem. You're going to be all right." Rut decided that he had to be all right. She couldn't imagine waking up the next morning and not having him at her side. That morning a few days earlier could not be the last one they would spend together—not when she spent most of it quarreling with him about the life with which he had blessed her. She wanted another chance. Rut wanted to hear him sing again to her, just one more time.

"I… promised to take care of the roof…" His words came out barely above a whisper, almost indiscernible to anyone except for Rut, who knew the subtleties of his speech better than anyone. Beads of perspiration dripped from his forehead. "I have to take care of the roof."

"The roof will still be there tomorrow," she said, trying to console herself and him into feeling some semblance of peace. Then they could see to treating his injury.

"Rut, promise me…"

"Shem, no." She knew what he was about to do and she rejected it with every fiber of her being. He was trying to say his last words to her before his soul left his body, but she wasn't ready. She would never be ready. "It's not your time, Shem. Try to hold on."

"Everything… Everything in God's timing, Rut." She searched Shem's glistening eyes desperately for a sign of healing, but his gaze seemed far away and distant, and his lips turned an unnatural shade of blue.

"Not this, Shem. Not this!" Rut protested as she watched his chest rise and fall, rise and fall… "Sing for me, Shem. Sing like you used to when we were betrothed, and I'll sing with you."

"I'll try." He nodded, but barely. "It doesn't hurt so much now."

If only Rut could get him to concentrate on something! Surely, God could heal her husband's wounds if it were in His will. In that moment, Rut prayed more fervently for her husband than she'd ever prayed in her entire life. *"Please, Lord!"*

She looked at Shem, waiting for him to sing. His chest rose again, as though he were drawing breath to begin. A feeling of hope stirred within her. This was the miracle she needed!

But no song came.

Shem's chest fell for the last time, and his eyes went black.

"Nooo!" she screamed. "Shem! Shem! Wake up!"

She felt two hands on her shoulders. One belonged to her brother, the other to her father.

"I won't leave him!" she cried, looking over her shoulder at them. "He's going to wake up! You'll see!"

The sheep bleated in the distance, as if they too were in pain.

"Rut, I'm sorry," Asa began, "but he's…"

"Don't. Don't say he's gone. He can't be gone!" Rut shook her head and refused to move from Shem's side, wailing and digging her fingers deeper and deeper into the dirt surrounding her. Shem was her husband and the love of her life. He was the only one with whom she could ever face the most difficult trials. They were to have many years together, full of children and grandchildren and tapestries of purple.

None of that could happen if he was…

"I—I didn't see the snake, Abba," said Benayahu. "When Shem cried out, I threw my knife and killed it, but it was too late. I should have been the one at the front of the sheep, Abba. It should have been me!"

Rut would have been no happier to see her brother succumb to a snake's venomous bite, but his explanation and expressions of grief did nothing to assuage her own.

"We must move him," said Asa, frustratingly calm.

"Stop speaking to me of sheep and snakes! Leave me here with my husband!"

For some reason, Rut's mind began to wander as she remembered various moments from their relationship, which had now been cut far too short. She remembered everything, from the last time she watched him walk out to the pastures, to their wedding when she had been enraptured by her affection for him. Rut recalled the first time they met, the first time he expressed interest in her, and every hushed conversation and stolen glance they shared during their betrothal.

"Rut? Rut?" Shamira quietly called her back to the house Shem built for her. The house that would never be home again. Shamira continued speaking, but Rut did not take her gaze away from her husband's cold, too-still body. She chanced one more gaze at the wound that was so small, yet full of enough poison to take a man's life.

This didn't feel real.

Rut didn't feel real.

She felt weightless.

Rut could still hear Shamira's voice, but she might as well have been a thousand miles away. "Milkah, would you please take Eliel and Yemima home for me? I will return later with Asa."

Milkah must have done as she was asked, though Rut did not notice her leaving. She noticed nothing except for the pain in her heart and the sudden, stark feeling of emptiness in the world.

"Rut," whispered Shamira, now kneeling beside her, "this is not Shem. Hold on to his memory in your heart, but let his body go. Come with me, and I will help you every step of the way, sister of my heart."

Though tears continued to stream down Rut's face, she took Shamira's hand. Shamira helped her to rise and go inside, where together they wept for Shem. Soon, both of their mothers came to join the mourning. Shem was wrapped and prepared for burial that very evening, though Rut remained wholly unaware of time.

It could not have been long since Shem stood beside her and quoted proverbs, saying, *"She makes and sells linen garments; she delivers belts to the merchants. Strength and honor are her clothing, and she can laugh at the time to come."* This was the time to come, and Rut couldn't imagine that she would ever be able to laugh again.

In the weeks that followed, Rut gave herself up to her work. She kept spinning. She kept weaving. She kept doing everything that was expected of her, but she stopped praying.

Rut was no longer sure that the God of miracles listened to her prayers.

PART TWO

"'For my thoughts are not your thoughts, and your ways are not my ways.' This is the Lord's declaration. 'For as heaven is higher than earth, so my ways are higher than your ways, and my thoughts than your thoughts. For just as rain and snow fall from heaven and do not return there without saturating the earth and making it germinate and sprout, and providing seed to sow and food to eat, so my word that comes from my mouth will not return to me empty, but it will accomplish what I please and will prosper in what I send it to do.'" — Isaiah 55:8-9 CSB

"The sun rises and the sun sets; panting, it hurries back to the place where it rises." — Ecclesiastes 1:5 CSB

50 A.D. — Nine Years Later

Rut could hear the sheep beginning to stir in their enclosure behind her parents' home. When she was a child, the city-sounds of Jerusalem would wake her from a dream-filled slumber. Much had changed since then. When she did manage to sleep, she no longer dreamed.

Her family were her only neighbors. Their large flock of sheep that once brought in a comfortable profit each year was now a much smaller flock managed just by the younger boys and overseen by her brother and father. Their food came not from markets, but from fields of crops managed by Asa and her Dodh Aharon. Every day, the women in her family had other chores to tend to before their husbands returned, and without her own husband, Rut helped the others. Yet no matter how busy Rut kept her hands or how helpful she tried to be, she still felt as though she was in the way. She wasn't supposed to be at home, living with her parents at her age. Rut was supposed to be with Shem.

Shem.

Memories of him brought painful longing for what she could no longer have. Things like the early mornings and hurried conversations before he would take the sheep out to pasture and be gone for days, sometimes weeks at a time. The late nights and Shem's singing filling the quiet of the evening with deep, dulcet tones. Time had taken that from her as well; after nearly ten years, she could no longer recall his voice. She knew he'd raised it in song often enough, soothed her to sleep with gentle melodies and woken her with proverbs and poetry, but she couldn't remember the sound of it. Rut could only remember the words, which now rang hollow and cold. Time passed too quickly, and it stole too much.

As was her usual ritual, she pulled her tightly coiled curls back and twisted them into a single knot, securing her hair so that it would be out of the way while she worked. The earlier she could get things done, the better. As Rut descended the steps and turned a corner into the main room of the family's house, she saw her father Binyamin kneeling in the darkness, head bowed in prayer. Instantly, she felt a familiar pang of not belonging. Carefully moving one foot in front of the other, Rut tried to tiptoe past him so that she would not interrupt.

"Rut?" he whispered. Rut cringed. "Is that you?"

"Yes, Abba. I'm sorry if I have disturbed you."

Her father smiled as he shook his head. "Don't be sorry. I am glad to see you! Come and take in the sunrise with me, daughter."

Rut silently acquiesced and moved to his side. "Do you do this every morning?"

"Every morning since the morning you were born."

Her eyes widened. "Really?"

Binyamin nodded. "I remember that first day so clearly. You woke early with a loud cry that probably startled the entire house. Your imma was resting and *Savta* offered to take you, but I wouldn't let her. I was so proud of you, so excited to know you and to raise you. I took you with me and we sat in the courtyard and watched the clouds part with the dawn. While you fell asleep in my arms, I prayed over you and your imma and every member of our household by name, that God would bless you and keep you in His care. It is how I have started each day ever since."

Rut smiled, touched by this secret habit. "I never knew that."

"You wouldn't." Binyamin chuckled. "As you got older, you grew more fond of sleeping later. That didn't stop me, though. I still woke each day earlier than anyone else so that I could begin my day this way. Would you like to join me this morning?"

"Oh, Abba, I didn't mean to interrupt."

"Indulge me, daughter. It will be like old times." He winked.

"All right," she whispered, but in truth she was more than uncomfortable. It had been a long time since she had prayed herself, something no one in her family knew. She remembered when prayer had been a personal time of connection with God; one that filled her cup and left her soul revived for another day. Her father must have sensed some of her unease, because he reached for her hand and gave it a gentle squeeze.

"You don't have to say your prayers aloud. God hears your heart." Her father bowed his head and Rut did the same.

She spent the next several minutes trying to sort out her feelings. She really wanted to, for she knew her father was right. God *did* hear the heart. Rut had no doubt of that, but where was His grace when she begged for it on behalf of Shem? Where were His answers?

Her father's voice broke through the bitter thoughts clouding her mind. "Our Father in heaven, I know how much You love us every time I look at my own children and grandchildren, for I would give all I have to keep them safe. Yet even that is barely a taste of your overwhelming love and steadfast care. I pray this morning for my son, Beni, and his family. I thank you for the man he's become. The wisdom he holds in his heart is greater than mine at his age, and I am proud of him and the strides he's taken to care for his family and lead them in Your ways. I pray also for my daughter, Rut, and I thank You for her diligent spirit and determination. I said earlier that I would give anything to keep my children safe, but they are grown now. As painful as it is, I must let them go to build their own lives. Lord, I let them go and I give them to You. I know Rut is fully known and deeply loved by You. Keep Your spirit near to her. Draw her closer to You. Remind her that she belongs to You, and that she never has to walk alone. Amen."

"Amen," Rut echoed, tear-stricken by his prayers. She knew he prayed with wholehearted belief and she longed to believe with the same conviction. Try as she might, she still felt hollow.

That lacking feeling hurt worse than grief. Grief came in waves and she had learned that the waves passed. The emptiness, however, never left. Rut wanted more than anything to find rest in God's presence as she once did, but such things seemed out of reach to her. She lived in fear that they always would be.

Rut chanced a look into her father's eyes, terrified that he would see right through her and admonish her for her thoughts. Would he be ashamed of Rut for how she felt? Would he cast her aside if he knew how she struggled with her faith? Shock filled her when she turned toward him and saw no judgment or condemnation—only affection.

"Rut…" he said, choking back a sob. "I have never been one for words."

"I know, Abba." She smiled lightly.

Though he was always quick with a joke around the dinner table and often first to offer his opinion about nearly every subject, Rut's relationship with her father had always been a quiet one. Rut never doubted that Binyamin cared for her. He just had other ways of showing it.

"I love you, Rut. I wish…"

"It is all right," she said, even though she still felt like so much was wrong. She understood his meaning. "I love you too."

"Never forget how much you mean to me." Binyamin spoke with shaky breaths, his own face equally streaked with tears.

"I never have." Rut knew her parents always wanted the best for her. That was the truth. But was she being truthful with them? "I must be getting ready, though."

"Ah, yes. I forgot today was the day Beni would be leaving for the markets."

"We've had a bountiful season, Abba. I am sure he will turn quite a profit in Tyre and Sidon."

Her abba chuckled as he wiped his face with his sleeve. "No doubt about that. Now go and gather your things. I don't want the two of you to get a late start on my account."

"Yes, Abba." Rut gathered her skirts and made it halfway out the door before her father called out to her one last time.

"And Rut?" he said. "Thank you for praying with me."

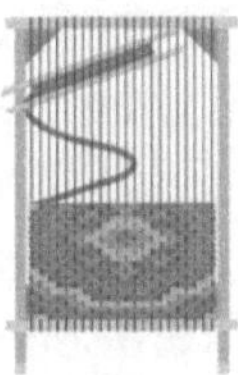

Rut heaved basket upon basket of the finest wool into the cart she and Beni would take to trade. Some wool was woven into lengths of cloth, some was spun and rolled into tight balls, and some remained unspun, but clean. All of it was to be sold. Here in the hills, going to trade was a days-long venture. At least one day would be devoted to traveling between each destination. Upon arrival, they would rent a room in town and stay there for several days as they sold their wares, getting enough money to purchase and bring home whatever the family needed.

When they had first come to Phoenicia following the persecution of believers in Jerusalem, going to trade had been a task shared by Benayahu and their father, since they both had an understanding of numbers and knew how to make a sale. After Shem died, Benayahu began inviting Rut to go with him instead. He told her it was because their father was getting too old to travel and while there may have been partial truth in that, Rut surmised that the invitation came mostly as a result of her brother's desire to help her through her grief.

"*Dodah* Rut, are you leaving for market with Dodh Beni?" asked the beautiful Yemima, Shamira's oldest daughter. The titles of Dodh and Dodah were courtesies for Shamira's now four children, who were not Rut's nieces and nephews by blood, unlike Jeriel, Tovi, and Avigail, who were the children of her brother and Milkah.

"Yes, today is the day we go to trade. Are you here to play with Avigail?" asked Rut. The little girls were as close as she and Shamira had been at their age.

Kelila shook her head. "Mima and I have been practicing our spinning. Can we show you what we've done?"

No sooner had Rut opened her mouth to respond than Yemima and Kelila lifted their hands to reveal tiny bundles of roughly-spun wool. There were some knots in their strands, but both girls showed promise. "Oh my! You two will soon put me out of work!"

"Do you think you could take some of our wool to the

marketplace and sell it?" asked Yemima.

Rut smiled at the two girls and their nearly-identical wide-eyed expressions. "I don't know if we would be able to sell strands of such small length, but why don't the two of you give them to me and I'll carry them with me while I travel? Every time I look at them, I will think of the two of you. In the meantime, you can keep practicing, and when I return I will show you how to weave the strands into something."

"All right, Dodah Rut," said the two sisters in unison, relinquishing their wool into Rut's care.

"Eliel is with Abba planning for the next harvest," Kelila continued, "but Imma is coming with Little Asa to talk to you before you leave. She said to let you know she was on her way."

"Thank you, Kelila. I'll be sure to wait for her."

Kelila nodded.

"There's one more thing…" Yemima swayed from side to side.

"Are you wondering where Avigail is?" Rut laughed lightly. These children were excitable, always chasing after the next thing. "She is around the back of the house by the fire with her imma and savta. Perhaps you can all practice making bread together next?"

"Oh, yes! Thank you Dodah Rut," said Yemima before she and Kelila took off running. Rut's heart warmed at the sound of their enthusiastic giggles and squeals.

Once they were out of sight, Rut returned her attention to the cart, mentally counting her inventory over and over again to ensure that she had everything she needed. Rut realized when she finished that she still held Yemima and Kelila's bundles in her hand. She pulled her satchel from the seat at the front of the cart; the overstuffed bag contained everything she would need for the journey, mainly changes of clothes and extra coin. Rut moved things around until she found a secure spot for the wool at the bottom of the bag, then placed it back on the seat. When Rut turned, she came face to face with Shamira.

"Oh!" Rut placed a hand over her heart. "I didn't hear you approach."

"Little Asa and I came to see you off," said Shamira, bouncing the toddler on her hip. He was the youngest of Shamira and Asa's children, nearly a perfect copy of his father in appearance. While he had the same wild curls, he definitely carried Shamira's childhood streak for mischief.

Rut gave the little boy's hand a squeeze. "*Shalom* to you both. Yemima and Kelila were here moments ago and let me know you were coming. They're off with Avigail now."

"Where are Jeriel and Tovi?" asked Shamira, referring to Benayahu's sons.

"They are helping Abba by the sheepfold," Rut answered.

"I want sheep! I can be shepherd!" said Little Asa. At that, both women laughed.

"Soon, my son," said Shamira, "but first you must be a bit older."

Rut winced. It could have been her sons now begging to be like their abba and herd flocks of their own, if she and Shem had been so blessed.

"Is everything well?" Shamira asked. "I feel like I don't see you nearly enough, and the girls have said they miss spending time with you."

"I'm sorry," said Rut, wringing her hands. How she wished she had a distaff or spindle to hold; something with which she could keep her mind occupied. "I've just been so—"

"Busy. I know," Shamira finished Rut's thought for her. "That's what I told Yemima and Kelila when I gave them the wool to practice with. They woke with the sun this morning because they were so eager to show you their work, and they wanted to say farewell before you left with Beni."

"They're getting very good," said Rut.

"They'd be much better off with your instruction than mine. I've never been able to work wool as well as you have—or at all, really."

Rut smiled awkwardly, unsure of how to respond.

"How long will you be gone?" asked Shamira.

"As long as it takes to sell the wool."

Shamira nodded, though her eyes narrowed. "Do you enjoy the traveling, Rut?"

"Of course." Rut shrugged her shoulders. "I am happy to help Beni how I can."

Rut knew she had given a shallow answer when she saw how Shamira's nose wrinkled. It had been a telltale sign of Shamira's true feelings ever since they were children. "I asked if you *enjoyed* it, Rut."

"I… I enjoy being useful."

"You know you are useful around here. We all care for you so much."

"I know," said Rut. Though she was grateful, how could she make Shamira see that their family's abundant caring was also a part of the problem?

"We cared for Shem too."

Although his name never left her thoughts, it had been some time since Rut heard someone else say it aloud. She assumed others were too nervous to do so, afraid it might send Rut into a flood of tears as it would have in that first year after his passing. "Shamira, it's—"

"No," interrupted Shamira. "If you're going to say it's all right, don't. I know you too well for that. His passing was sudden and unexpected, and your life together was cut far too short. I myself can't help but feel guilty sometimes. When we were girls and our immas were raising us and teaching us, it was you who mastered everything with ease. You could cook a stew that would feed a dozen, and I could barely knead loaves of bread. You could weave lengths and lengths of fine cloth, and all I could do was make messes. I was sure you would marry one day and leave me behind."

"You and Asa were always meant to be together, Shamira."

Shamira whispered, "Are you angry with me, Rut?"

The question took Rut aback. "Angry with you? Shamira, why would you say such a thing?"

"Please do not misunderstand me. You are the sister of my heart and I love you deeply. After Shem's death, you became withdrawn and I understood that. I did not press you because I did not want you to think I didn't care for your grief, but… we barely talk anymore, and I miss you, Rut. I miss walking side by side through life with you. I miss everyday moments and laughs. I miss *praying* together, though I have never stopped praying for you."

"Shamira, I don't know what to say…" Rut looked directly into Shamira's watery, honey-colored eyes. "I have been angry, but *never* at you. I'm sorry if I made you feel such a way, but the truth is… I don't feel like I belong in this family anymore."

"Rut!" Shamira exclaimed in obvious objection.

"No, listen. I am Rut *bat* Binyamin, and I always will be, but you, Shamira bat Aharon… You are also Asa's wife and imma to four children. Beni is Milkah's husband and father to three. The letters that come from Antioch even tell us that Libi is grown up, married, and raising two daughters. You all have families of your own. You are growing older, raising children, moving on with life, and I… I am stuck. I have been since the day Shem died. It's no one's fault that I feel like a burden, but I can't change my feelings no matter how hard I try. Shamira, I adore your children. I love them, and I love watching them grow, just as I do with Beni's children. I couldn't be happier for you and the life you have, but that doesn't mean it never hurts to see and know that such a life will never be mine."

"I'm sorry, Rut. I'm *so* sorry. I didn't realize…" Shamira wiped the tears from her eyes.

"You couldn't have, for I never speak of it."

"You *do* belong, Rut. Please don't feel like you can't share your feelings with me, all right? You have listened to more of my heartbroken speeches over the years than I can count. Let me be the same listening ear for you."

"Thank you, Shamira." Rut didn't know what else to say. This kind of conversation was an unpracticed art for her. If Shamira knew everything Rut had thought, would she be just as ashamed of her as Rut had become of herself?

That was why she could not give up the duplicity yet. As only one member of a large family, she had grown up practicing the art of disappearing in plain sight. She kept up the practice now, making her feelings imperceptible to others. Amid all the other changes that had happened over the years, the changes in Rut seemed to have escaped the notice of others. But what if time was running out?

"Maybe when you come home, you could join us at our house for dinner? The children would love it."

"I would too."

"Good!" Shamira perked up.

"But there's a problem," said Rut.

"What is it?"

"Are you going to be the one cooking this dinner?" Rut quipped, harkening back to those earlier days Shamira had mentioned when she had not yet acquired the skill of cooking food that was actually edible. At last, tears turned to laughter, and Rut was relieved. Soon enough after some more simple conversation, Beni came around with the donkey and they set off on their journey.

3

"She selects wool and flax and works with willing hands. She
is like the merchant ships, bringing her food from far away."
— Proverbs 31:13-14 CSB

Hektor stepped onto solid ground for the first time in weeks, having no trouble adjusting to the still earth beneath him after so long spent at sea. Over the years and by necessity of his job, he'd gotten used to the many pitfalls of travel and learned how to navigate them with ease. He turned and watched as the larger ship they'd travelled on was towed to the coast, before offering his arm to his employer, that she might disembark from the smaller vessel that carried them ashore as well.

"Welcome to Tyre, Mistress Lydia."

"Thank you, Hektor," she smiled graciously, taking his arm. She turned her head over her shoulder to briefly discuss details about their return journey with the man who rowed them ashore. As she talked, Hektor surveyed the horizon. Vessel after vessel rocked on the water in a line, light blue waves crashing against them. On the other side, Hektor could see buildings and columns—the city itself. Not much had changed since their last journey here, though there were certainly more people this time around.

Tyre was famed for its special blend of Tyrian purple, the hue in which Lydia ran her business empire. Every year if possible, Lydia liked to travel to some of the major ports of trade along the eastern coast, stopping at dye-manufacturing epicenters and areas known for their textile goods while constantly looking for new tricks to incorporate into her trade. Hektor would be there at every turn as her personal guard to make sure nothing happened to her or any assets she might acquire along the journey.

This was one of their last stops before they began their return trip to Philippi, where Lydia spent every other month of the year overseeing her business, making and selling purple goods to the nobility of the area. Hers was the most profitable business of its kind in Macedonia, and for good reason. It was not just her savvy that gave her goods superior quality—it was the fact that all those who worked for her were so grateful to her, and genuinely enjoyed being in her employ. Lydia was both a noble giver as well as a sound businesswoman. In addition to jobs, she had given many of them a second chance at life—Hektor included.

"Do you find Tyre to be greatly changed, Hektor?" asked Lydia.

"It looks the same as every other city we've visited," said Hektor.

Lydia laughed heartily. "It is all right to be honest. I am weary of travel, too."

"In that case, I find it all too crowded for my taste, but for your purposes, it will do nicely. Shall we seek accommodations first?" Hektor checked to see that the simple leather armor he wore was secure and that the knife he kept tied to his side for defense remained there, along with the satchel containing Lydia's money.

"I know we should, but I'd like to pass through the marketplace first. I find I have a need to stretch my legs, and I would pay dearly for some fresh fruit after so long of eating the same rations of too-dry bread. Let's start there."

"Very well, then, but I recommend we do not stay very long. It would be best to find shelter before the sun sets."

"What would I do without you as my protector, Hektor?"

"I pray you do not have to find out, Mistress Lydia, for both our sakes." The two of them were used to joking with one another like siblings. Even though he referred to her as 'Mistress Lydia' in public and she referred to him as one would refer to a mere servant in their employ, in truth, they'd become good friends over the years. He'd watched her business grow from a simple but self-sustaining operation to a thriving enterprise. Her business produced lengths of cloth and all manner of textiles in the deepest shades of purple, a color most desired by the wealthy. If there was one thing Hektor had learned while working for Lydia, it was that the wealthy were always in the market for new clothes and finery. There was no better place to get them and no greater price for the quality than from Lydia herself.

"You have been a part of this business for so long, Hektor, that I almost forget you haven't been here from the beginning. I am forever grateful for your loyalty."

"Not half as grateful as I am for yours."

"True... I'll never forget how I found you."

Hektor cringed. "Face-down in a puddle of mud?"

Lydia laughed. "It was not your finest moment."

"And it followed a string of similar moments, I'm afraid." Those were Hektor's 'dark years,' as he oft-called them, before he met Lydia and turned his life around.

"If I'd known then about your streak as a losing fighter, I probably wouldn't have hired you as my guard."

"Thank the Lord you didn't know, then. I would've seemed like a very bad investment."

"Yes, thank Him for that and many other things. I don't anticipate us spending very long here in Tyre, Hektor. I, too, am anxious to return to Philippi."

Hektor nodded as he began to estimate the days left until he could finally sleep in his own bed. "You've been very successful on this trip, Mistress Lydia. It is certain to be a plentiful year."

"Which is exactly why I want to get home sooner rather than later. There is so much work to be done, and I find I have so many new ideas."

In comfortable quiet, Hektor let Lydia muse on about her hopes and dreams for her business as he guided her from street to street. As they turned a corner, Hektor's gaze happened upon a small family—a husband, a wife, and two very young children, a boy and a girl, who toddled along in-between them. The sound of the little ones' laughter, who could not have been much older than four or five years, made Hektor smile. His own upbringing had not been so merry, and he often pondered what it would be like to have a family of his own. The servants and people employed in Lydia's business were close friends, but a desire to find someone to love and with whom to share his heart often surged within him. Given the demands of his job, however, it was unlikely he would find a woman willing to live alongside him. He rarely had the time to look, anyway. Hektor decided that it was enough to have a job, a roof over his head, and a fulfilling sense of duty and purpose in what he did. *"The Lord is my shepherd; I have what I need,"* he reminded himself in his thoughts.

The Psalms always brought him comfort and clarity, helping him set his course in life. They were also one of his favorite parts about being in Lydia's employ, for long ago she had acquired a set of scrolls in her travels and allowed all of her servants who could read to make use of them whenever they wished. Many of the servants taught each other to read using them. It was more than an extraordinary blessing, as there was no synagogue for Jews or God-fearing Gentiles in Philippi. Without a way to learn more, Hektor, Lydia, and others like them clung to the hope for Gentiles alluded to in some of those writings, praying that help would come for them soon.

Turning yet another corner, they at last came upon a cluster of vendors in the marketplace. Most of the sellers seemed to have already gone home for the day or were in the process of doing so, which meant that they did not have much time to browse before they really would need to find accommodations. In a city like Tyre, full of so many transients, finding reasonably priced rooms in well-reputed inns was no easy task.

Stopping at one vendor, Lydia bartered for some fresh fruit— something different than what they were given from the ship's reserves. She graciously offered him a piece and they ate as they walked. Always, Hektor kept an eye on their surroundings as he familiarized himself with this area they only visited once a year.

"That is magnificent work!" exclaimed Lydia, gesturing to a display of wool and woven goods at the end of their path.

"Yes, it is," whispered Hektor, though he was not talking about dyes or spun wool or fine tapestries made by man's own hand. No, Hektor was struck by the most stunning example of God's creation that his eyes had ever beheld: a woman whose beauty was beyond all comparison. Indeed, he'd travelled far and wide, seen every seaside town and port on this side of Cyprus, but he'd never seen a woman as lovely to look upon as the one standing just fifteen paces ahead of him.

Hektor gazed at her in awe and wonder. Her dark, near-black spirals of hair grew far past her shoulders. Her deep-set eyes gazed in deep concentration on the work before her. Her lips, full and soft, parted slightly as she talked to the man beside her. Every part of her came together to reveal a complete masterpiece, and Hektor felt an immediate pull toward her that was deeper than anything else he'd ever felt before.

She looked… sad, somehow.

Hektor couldn't explain it, but he felt like there was a deeper meaning in all of this than a chance connection with another weaver. *"Lord, are you trying to tell me something?"* Hektor prayed in his heart.

"I think I'd like to get a closer look," said Lydia.

"Of course," said Hektor, having nearly forgotten who he was or why he was here. He resumed a confident stance, took the last bite of his food, and offered Lydia his arm. "This way, Mistress Lydia," he said, then led them both exactly fifteen paces forward, though every heartbeat in-between made it feel like a thousand.

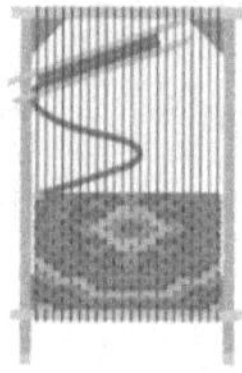

Rut had selected her garments for that day with the utmost care. Whenever she and Beni came to trade, Rut always packed her best clothing. She learned over the years that people were more inclined to purchase wool from sellers who were finely dressed, as opposed to sellers whose attire was more humble. What she wore now was fine in texture and varied in color. Many folds of fabric were cinched by a sash at her waist, completely impractical for wearing near a cooking fire, but wholly effective for enticing customers to browse her family's selection of wool goods.

At the front of their cart in the marketplace, Rut set herself to displaying lengths of cloth she'd woven as samples of the quality of their wool. They already liquidated most of their assets in Sidon, but there was still a sizable amount left to be sold. Rut stretched out the woven cloth so that people would be able to examine it, touch it with their fingers, feel how fine it was, and then be persuaded to buy some of the wool, that their clothes might be equally fine.

That morning while the sun was still rising over the marketplace, Benayahu helped silently. He knew exactly how Rut liked things and had learned to anticipate what she wanted before she could even think to ask such questions. He handed her basket after basket while she arranged everything to be just right. Eventually, customers started to trickle in, and Beni did most of the talking. Rut answered questions when she needed to, but it was Benayahu who closed the deals. She didn't mind; it was the spinning and weaving that she enjoyed.

"These are a bit too small to sell, aren't they?" Beni asked during a late-afternoon lull in business.

"Hm?" Rut turned her head to see the little scraps of wool made by Yemima and Kelila. "Oh, no! Those aren't for sale."

"I should think not." Benayahu laughed, and for a moment, he appeared to be a perfect copy of their father. "What are they?"

Rut snatched them and tucked them in the space between her belt and dress. Though how they managed to fall out of her satchel and get misplaced among the other baskets of wool, Rut had no idea. "Mima and Lila brought them over before we left. They wanted me to take them with me, and I agreed."

"I see," said Beni, crossing his arms and leaning against a table. "Well, they're already well on their way to being nearly as good as you are with a spindle and loom."

"They do show promise."

Another bout of silence stunted the conversation, but Rut did not feel anxious. Benayahu never pushed. A cool ocean breeze made Rut shiver, and she realized how far the sun had fallen. It was nearly time to start packing up their goods so that they could retire to the rooms they'd rented. "Shall we pack up?" she asked, and Benayahu nodded.

"Excuse me," a voice pulled Rut from her routine.

"Yes?" said Rut, turning to address the speaker more directly. When she did, she saw not one but two strangers staring back at her. The first was a woman who could not have been much older than Rut. She was fair skinned, with wide-set eyes, light hair, and a long, straight nose that divided her features. Although she appeared beautiful, there was a certain strength in her gaze that set her apart as resilient and in command of some sort of authority.

The second stranger made Rut blink a few times in disbelief. He looked like one of the sculptures that the Greeks and Romans favored so much. He was tall—much taller than Rut, with broad shoulders, and eyes bright-blue like the sea at midday. His hair was sand-colored, and Rut wondered if perhaps the pair were related.

Both of them were well-dressed, although the woman was considerably more adorned than the man, with layers and layers of deep-colored purple cloth draped across her figure. The man's clothing was more functional than fashionable. Although the weave and texture of the fabric was less delicate, the lines of his muscles could still be seen underneath his armor-like leather garments. Rut realized she had been staring and forced herself to look away, grabbing the nearest thing to her and offering it to the woman.

"Are you interested in" — Rut looked down to identify for herself and for her audience what she was holding in her hands

— "some fine-spun wool? It is the purest white you'll find in Tyre."

The woman smiled at her silently and reached to feel the wool with her fingertips. "Who spun this?"

"I did." Rut shuddered. Even though she was no longer looking directly at him, she could feel the man's blue eyes staring at her. She was horrified at herself for spending so long looking at him. It wasn't proper for a woman to do so, let alone a widow.

"Your work is impeccable," said the woman. "What is your name?"

Rut looked to her brother Benayahu, who nodded with a toothy smile. Brothers, Rut decided, were of no help when one needed an escape from a potentially awkward situation. He knew Rut was not half the salesperson he was; she couldn't fathom why he was not stepping in to take over this interaction. "I am called Rut, and this is my brother, Benayahu *ben* Binyamin," she finally answered.

"Did you spin all of this?" The woman gestured to their display with one hand, handing the spun wool back to Rut with the other.

"Yes," said Rut.

"I told you," the woman whispered to her male companion, "*magnificent* work."

"Yes, Mistress. This work may even rival some of what comes from your business."

Rut blushed at their compliments. The man had called her "mistress," so Rut deduced that he could not be related to her, given that he spoke as a servant. However, she also noticed *how* he spoke to her, with humor and levity in his tone. A servant would never speak to their master in such a casual way, unless there was a considerable degree of familiarity between them.

Rut chided herself for even caring. The only business of theirs she should have any interest in would be if they chose to make a purchase, and as the day was fast approaching its end, she needed to work quickly.

Clearing her throat, Rut continued, reaching for one of her sample lengths of cloth. "This length of cloth was made from this exact same batch of wool."

"It's splendid." The woman leaned in for a closer look. "Did you do the weaving as well?"

"Yes, I did." Rut nodded.

"I assume you made your own garments too?"

Self-consciously, Rut began smoothing her dress. "Indeed, from my loom at home."

"The colors are stunning. Where did you get the dyes?" One by one, the woman whose name Rut still did not know continued to ask questions that overwhelmed Rut—not in their subject, of which Rut was very knowledgeable, but in their volume. She asked more specific questions than any other customer ever had before; things like the kinds of looms Rut had used in the past, how Rut treated the wool before and after dyeing, how it absorbed color… Rut began to wonder if she was revealing too much. Didn't a shrewd business owner keep their secrets closely guarded in order to make their product more desirable?

"That is fascinating! Simply fascinating, isn't it, Hektor?"

Hektor.

So that was the name of the man who bore eyes as powerful as lightning.

"Indeed," he replied.

"Do you live here in Tyre?" the woman asked Rut.

"No, my brother and I travel here a handful of times each year to sell and trade. I do all of the work from our home, a full day's journey from here. We have a farm where we raise sheep."

"You do all of this from your home?" The woman's jaw dropped.

"Well, it isn't just me. Our whole family works together. My imma and sister-in-law help with—" Rut started to explain, before her brother interrupted.

"My sister is being modest. Rut does almost all the spinning and weaving for our family! She has always had a gift for it, since she was a young girl. Nearly everything you see here is a result of her hard work," said Beni.

Rut sighed deeply. All this time she had hoped he would join in the discussion and take the burden of conversation from her, and only now did he choose to speak, drawing further attention to her.

"Will you be here long?" asked the woman.

"We begin our journey home tomorrow, so if you'd like to make a purchase, now is the time," said Beni, obviously ready and eager to close a sale.

"I see." The woman pursed her lips. "I apologize if this seems too forward of me, but I would very much like to continue talking with you. Might I inquire as to where you are staying?"

"Certainly, but if I might ask first, what is your name?" asked Benayahu, his stance shifting from salesman to protective brother.

The woman's cheeks reddened. "Oh, how rude of me! I am called Lydia, and this is my guard, Hektor. To be completely honest with you, I myself am a seller of textile goods, though my business is in Philippi and my specialty is in cloth dyed purple. I am on my way back there after traveling to see what other sellers like me are doing in this part of the world."

Rut hoped no one would notice how her brows moved closer and closer together with each shocking revelation Lydia shared. A working woman? That wasn't too unusual. Many women worked. Rut herself spent every waking hour spinning and weaving to help her family make ends meet, but Lydia spoke of her *own* business. Clearly it was also a profitable business, given not only the presence of a guard, but also the fine texture of her clothes. Despite being made for travel, they still held an element of extravagance in their color and the sheer volume of luxurious material draped over her shoulders.

The hue of her garments put Tyrian purple to shame. Rut wondered how she managed it—not only the dye, but *all* of it.

"We are staying at the inn on the northern edge of the city—the one marked by the olive tree growing out front. Do you know it?" asked Benayahu.

Lydia looked to her guard who gave an affirmative nod. "We know it well," said Hektor. Then, with lightness in his tone, he added, "It is possibly the only reputable inn within walking distance."

Benayahu laughed, clapping his hands in amusement at Hektor's quip. She looked between the two of them, her brother and Hektor, and recognized the same mirthful glint in each of their eyes. Although they were different outwardly in almost every possible way, in that regard, Rut could see them as two separate pieces cut from the same cloth.

"You are quite right," said Beni. "I believe they have more rooms available if you are seeking accommodations for this night. There was another group there, but they departed this morning."

"We will head that way," said Lydia. "Perhaps we may speak this evening?"

"I don't see why not," said Benayahu. Rut wondered if and when he would choose to ask her opinion on the matter.

"Wonderful!" said Lydia. "Oh, there is one more thing."

As the conversation had gone on, Rut had gradually returned to her earlier task of packing up their goods and was only half-listening to what they were saying now.

"What is that?" asked Benayahu.

"How much would you take for everything you have?" said

Lydia. Rut stopped what she was doing immediately to look up and see if Lydia was being serious, and she was. Lydia had already drawn open the strings of her purse to begin counting out the coin for her payment.

*"She makes her own bed coverings; her clothing is fine linen
and purple." — Proverbs 31:22 CSB*

Rut could see it plainly on Benayahu's face. He had been
equally surprised when Lydia purchased every last bit of wool—
both spun and raw—and paid extra to have it taken back to
where the rest of her belongings were stored. Benayahu never
shied away from a good sale, but from his reaction it was
obvious that even he hadn't expected to make *such* a good profit
this season. Rut couldn't recall a single time in all of their trips
to Tyre and Sidon when they'd sold out completely.

Now, back at the inn, Rut, Benayahu, Lydia, and Hektor
lounged on cushions in the common room, which was dimly lit
by the faint glow of oil lamps in each corner. As expected,
Benayahu continued to monopolize most of the conversation
while Rut took in every detail as it was told. Every so often her
gaze drifted toward the olive tree swaying in the breeze just
outside one of the larger lattice windows, but her attention
always returned when Lydia added to the conversation.

"I am originally from Thyatira," said Lydia. At the mention of her place of origin, everything suddenly made sense to Rut. While Tyrian purple was made from sea snails and therefore costly, she heard that in Thyatira, the root of a certain plant was used for creating purple dye. Frustratingly, Rut couldn't recall the name. Evidently, Lydia had found the perfect formula since Rut did not notice any significant difference in her garments.

Inquisitiveness compelled Rut to interject in the conversation, finally asking the questions that had been swirling around in her mind since they'd met. "Is that where you learned the art of dye-making?"

"It was my family's business before it became mine. My father died long ago without any sons, you see," Lydia explained, smiling graciously.

"I am so sorry for your loss," said Rut.

"Thank you." Lydia nodded. "You speak as someone who knows that kind of pain personally."

Rut swallowed. "My husband died many years ago."

Lydia reached out and gave Rut's hand a small, gentle squeeze. "I am sorry for your loss as well," she whispered, and the gesture unexpectedly touched Rut's heart.

Straightening on her cushion, Lydia continued, "Before my father died, he worked so hard over the years to build vat after vat, plant row after row of *madder*, and perfect his formulas, that it seemed an impossible task to move his operation anywhere but Thyatira."

Madder. Rut tried to commit the name of the plant to memory so that she would not forget it again. "But you live in Philippi now?"

Lydia grinned. "Indeed, though I still travel every year to source supplies and look for new inspiration. That is how I ended up here."

"That is most impressive," replied Rut. Her mind's eye could hardly begin to fathom it. What would it be like to lead such an enterprising life? To manage it all with Lydia's confidence? Although most of it shocked, bewildered, and even terrified Rut, a part of the idea thrilled her. If Rut were like Lydia, she wouldn't feel as much like she was in the way of others. She could make her own way.

"My servants in Philippi are very talented," said Lydia, awakening Rut from the dream-like state into which she had fallen. "Spinners, weavers, those who work in the *fullery…*"

"Fullery?" asked Rut.

"Yes, because of the unique dyeing process, we offer a special washing service to our customers so that the longevity of their goods might be prolonged," Lydia explained.

Rut had heard of fulleries but had never seen them, even in Jerusalem. Some women earned an income by doing laundry for others, though most washed their own clothing.

Lydia leaned forward and clasped her hands together. "I know that what I'm about to say may sound absurd, given that we've only just met, and I'm sure your first reaction will be to say no, but… Oh, I think I would regret it for the rest of my days if I didn't at least try."

"I don't understand." Rut glanced back at her brother to see if his expression was readable.

It was not.

"I'd like to invite you to come back to Philippi with me."

At that moment, Rut locked eyes with Lydia and it felt like the earth had fallen out from beneath her.

"Me?" Rut gasped.

"I've never seen anyone with your level of skill at spinning and weaving. Even from the opposite side of the marketplace, I could see that your work was impeccable and I had to learn more."

Rut coughed to clear her throat. "I am sure that can't be true.

I have but one small loom, and everything I know was taught to me by my mother. I know nothing special about the trade."

"Rut," Benayahu raised his voice in protest, "your humility is admirable, but you have a natural talent. Everyone is always saying your skill is unmatched."

"Beni, please." Rut forced herself to smile.

"I only want what's best for you, sister. You should at least hear what she has to say." Rut had a strong urge to swat at her brother's arm the way she would have when they were very small children. Why was he so eager for Rut to hear Lydia's offer in full? Did he truly think it was a good idea? Or worse, as Rut was beginning to fear, perhaps he wanted to be rid of her.

She stopped herself from pursuing that line of thinking any further, knowing it was unfair. Benayahu was her brother, and he could never think of her like that.

Lydia began again, though she spoke at a much slower pace. "First, I want to make it clear that you do not have to decide right away, but I would very much like to host you as a guest in my household, as well as perhaps have you consult on my business."

"Me? I'm not sure what I would have to offer," said Rut.

"You could pass on some of what you know to my own weavers and spinners. As I said before, I try to travel every year, so you would be able to return, or you could decide to stay longer. You would have your own room and would want for nothing while you were under my roof. I would compensate you for any work you did, of course. I've thoroughly enjoyed speaking with you, and, even if this is rather sudden, I'd love the opportunity to get to know you better."

"I… I don't know what to say. My family needs me here."

Lydia's eyes widened emphatically. "Certainly! I hope you'll pardon my enthusiasm. I know I can act impulsively—sometimes too much. When I see something that inspires me, I know I must go after it with all of my heart or regret it the rest of my days."

"I understand," said Rut, laughing nervously. In truth, those qualities reminded her of Shamira. How many scrapes did they find themselves in as youths because Shamira got an idea in her head that she couldn't let go? Too many to count, and Rut always went along with her, if only to try and provide a voice of reason.

"I hope you know that I already consider you as a friend. We don't know each other well, but I sense that we share a kind of sisterhood beyond only being in a similar trade."

"You are very kind," said Rut, though she truly did not know how to respond.

Another awkward silence befell them and Rut found herself looking back and forth between Lydia, her brother, and Hektor. The second time her eyes met with his, she couldn't help but feel that there was something in his ocean-like gaze urging her to respond to Lydia's request affirmatively. His head seemed to slightly nod as he cracked a half-smile. What was he trying to say to her?

"Our ship is to stay in these waters for one week so that the crew can rest and resupply. Then we will be continuing on in our return voyage. I will remain at this inn during that time. If you do not return, I will take no offense, but if you do; you will be most welcome."

Rut breathed in shakily, preparing herself to decline so that she would not leave Hektor and Lydia under any false pretenses. "I am flattered by your offer, but I don't think—"

"Don't say it!" Lydia laughed lightly. "I think it will be easier to handle the loss if I never actually have to hear you speak the words aloud. At least this way I can live with hope."

"All right," said Rut, resigned. She raised her eyebrows at her brother, pleading with him to say something, *anything* that would get her out of this situation.

Benayahu clapped his hands together after what felt like an eternity. "Well, Rut and I must leave early tomorrow morning if we are to make it home in a timely manner, so I am afraid we will have to retire now."

"I hope we haven't kept you talking too long," said Lydia.

Benayahu shook his head. "Not at all. It has been most wonderful getting to know you both, though I hope you will understand if I don't seem too enthusiastic, given the topic of conversation has revolved around you taking my sister to the other side of the sea. I can't blame you though—I don't know how we would manage without her!"

Benayahu laughed heartily, exactly like their father. How she wished she could be as blithe.

"Thank you for indulging my curiosity," said Lydia, rising from her seat with Benayahu and Rut. Hektor did the same. "I hope our paths will cross again, perhaps next year if not sooner. I'd love to purchase more of your wool."

Benayahu lifted his hands and shrugged his shoulders. "We're here often. You never know."

"And Rut," said Lydia, leaning closer so that only Rut could hear what she would say next, "I apologize if I made you feel uncomfortable. I never mean to, but I know I can come across as too forward. I hope you will still consider me as a friend too?"

Rut nodded her head and smiled in return, finding it impossible to resist Lydia's positive demeanor. "We are friends, indeed. Thank you again for your purchase of our wool. I know it will mean so much to my family."

"Do not consider it any kind of favor or bribe. I know good quality when I see it, and I saw it in you and in your family's wool. Safe travels."

"Safe travels to you, too, Lydia." Turning to Hektor, Rut added, "Farewell, Hektor."

"Farewell," Hektor echoed, bowing respectfully.

As she made her way to the room Benayahu had rented for her, she wondered if she would ever see either of them again.

Hektor sank backward into his cushion and took a slow sip of the water in his cup. One by one, people took their leave of the inn's common room as the hour drew late. He and Lydia remained, neither of them feeling particularly eager to retire to yet another confined space.

"You seem to have a lot on your mind," said Lydia, with a pointed gaze and a tight-lipped grin as she leaned on her cushion.

Hektor shook his head and smiled. "Why did you make that offer to her?" he asked, though he already knew the answer. Now that their company was gone, Hektor and Lydia could once again converse more casually.

"Because she is the most talented weaver I have seen in all my years of being in this trade. Some practice the art for decades before coming anywhere near her level of skill. It would be an honor to have her as a guest."

"I presume that was always your plan, then? From the first moment you saw her in the market?" Hektor raised an eyebrow, setting his cup down beside him.

"Perhaps," said Lydia, matter-of-fact. Hektor laughed, knowing full well about Lydia's proclivity for rash decisions. Like a ship with all of its sails loosed, nothing could stop her once she was set on a course.

"Well, I think she would enjoy it as much as you would." Hektor sighed. "It's clear that you two share many things. You're both very gracious and knowledgeable in your trade."

"Do you think she would like it in Philippi?" asked Lydia, pulling a grape from the leftover cluster on the table before them.

"I cannot speak to that. As you know, to me, no city is different than any other. I was more so speaking about your friendship. You are able to make people from all walks of life feel welcomed and encouraged. I am sure everyone who crosses paths with you would say the same thing: that they owe you for helping them through a difficult time in their lives."

"No one owes me anything, Hektor." Lydia raised her eyebrows at him.

"I do." Hektor tapped the rim of his cup with his finger. He took the last sip before setting it back on the table, this time a little too hard. "I would have destroyed myself if you hadn't stopped me and given me something to live for after—" Hektor stopped himself.

"Tell me something else about her. I want to hear another one of your stories."

Hektor breathed deeply once, twice, and three times. As the years went on, Hektor had forgotten more and more details about his younger sister. The exact shade of her eyes, the specific lilt of her voice when she asked a question, or the way her face looked when she smiled. Hektor blamed part of that forgetting on his excessive drinking in the wake of her loss. Certain things, odd things, remained in his mind perfectly clear. Hektor chuckled; his memory surprised himself.

"What is it?" asked Lydia.

"Karis did most of the cooking after my mother left, and all of the cooking after our father died. She was very good at it." Hektor stopped briefly to suppress more laughter, before continuing. "But one time she wasn't. It was only the two of us, and money was becoming increasingly scarce. It had been weeks since I'd won a fight, and I was coming home emptyhanded after yet another loss. Karis knew what I was doing and she didn't like it, but never said anything about it either. I returned to find a stew she had made waiting on the table."

"What was in the stew?" Lydia asked.

"Well, that's the thing… When I walked into the house, I was instantly hit by the most vile, pungent odor I'd ever encountered, but Karis acted as if there was nothing amiss, so I did too. In silence, we both sat down with our bowls in front of us. I didn't want to eat whatever it was, but I was starving and I also didn't want to hurt her feelings. With my eyes burning from the smell, I forced one mouthful down my throat, then another, and then another."

"It was that bad?"

Hektor nodded. "Karis did the same. Afterward, as she cleared the table, she asked, 'How bad was it, Hektor?' I didn't answer at first because I thought she was referring to my less-than-honorable work that resulted in one-too-many bruises on my face. 'Well, brother? How bad was it?' she asked again, only this time with more irritation in her voice. 'The fighting?' I asked, trying to avoid her ire. 'No, you fool,' she teased, 'the smell when you walked in. I was sure that being hit by that odor would've hurt worse than any other blow you suffered today.'"

At that, both Lydia and Hektor erupted into uncontrollable laughter. From across the room, the innkeeper gave them a stern look, no doubt due to the lateness of the hour—though that only made the laughing fit worse. They did their best to muffle the sound with their hands.

"She knew the whole time how bad it was," said Hektor, through bittersweet tears. "It turned out, the only things we had left were onions and garlic. We sustained ourselves on that garlic-onion-broth for days, until even the neighbors began to complain of the constant smell drifting out and into the streets. Eventually I won another fight, and we had food again for a while, but the smell never left our house! It seemed to come back in waves, and whenever it returned, it always gave us something to laugh about… Even toward the end."

"Oh, Hektor, how I wish I could have known her," said Lydia.

Hektor nodded, once again serious, but no longer sad. It was good to be reminded of the happy times. "She would have liked you, and especially how you never let me get away with anything after you found me. When Karis died, I was on my way to becoming just like our father. If you hadn't stopped me, I might have drunk myself to death just as he did."

"I didn't know any of that when I found you. I only knew that you were injured and needed help, so I offered you food, a place to recover, and a roof over your head."

"It was your patience and hospitality that opened the door for me to not only get back on my feet, but also to become a *God-fearer* like you. Hope like that is no small gift, Lydia."

"You still don't owe me anything, Hektor. It was not me, but the One True God who restored you. I only do what I can, where I can, and how I can. You never know what doors God might open if you don't knock on them first."

"And that's why you made the offer to Rut?" asked Hektor.

"That's why I made the offer to Rut," Lydia repeated.

When the innkeeper poked his head in their direction another time, Hektor became aware of the lateness of the hour. "Perhaps it would be a good idea to get some rest."

Slowly, Lydia rose. "You're right. We have been talking for far too long."

As Hektor stood, one more question came to his mind.

"Lydia… Do you think there will ever be a way?"

He didn't specify what he meant, for he knew that she would understand. There was no synagogue in Philippi and no true place where they could worship the Jewish God or learn how to keep His commands. As Gentiles, they were still separate from those who called themselves His people. They had hope, as Hektor had said earlier, but there were times it felt like an impassable sea still separated them and they would forever be searching for a way to cross.

"I think in times like this… There is a certain psalm I like to remember," Lydia murmured.

"Which one?"

"Do you recall the psalm of David that begins, 'My God, my God, why have you abandoned me?'"

Hektor nodded in earnest. "It is one of my favorites." As one of the first psalms Hektor had read after he joined Lydia's household, it had a profound impact on him from the very first day. The words of pain and suffering in the beginning spoke so deeply to Hektor's grief, and the hopeful message at the end always brought him to tears.

"Do you recall how it ends?"

Hektor quoted, "'All the ends of the earth will remember and turn to the Lord. All the families of the nations will bow down before you, for kingship belongs to the Lord; he rules the nations. All who prosper on earth will eat and bow down; all those who go down to the dust will kneel before him—even the one who cannot preserve his life. Their descendants will serve him; the next generation will be told about the Lord. They will come and declare his righteousness; to a people yet to be born they will declare what he has done.'"

"David speaks of all the ends of the earth. All nations bowing down before the Lord and serving Him." Lydia sighed, her gaze far away from Hektor. "*That* is what I pray for every day, Hektor. Every day."

Without another word, Hektor followed Lydia to the room she had rented as they both presumably pondered the same thought: salvation for Gentiles. When they arrived, she went inside and Hektor took his place in the hallway outside her door. It wasn't the most comfortable of quarters, but it was certainly better than rocking on a ship.

Hektor knew it would be some time before he succumbed to sleep, finding himself too full of energy despite the lateness of the hour. It was a usual side effect of travel, but, in truth, it was not the only thing keeping Hektor awake. He hadn't been able to stop thinking about Rut, the immediate pull he felt when he first laid eyes upon her or the sense that God might be urging him on toward something, though he didn't quite know what yet.

"Did I misunderstand you, Lord?" Hektor prayed. Rut did not immediately accept Lydia's offer, and, for all Hektor knew, that might have been the end of their experiences together. Hektor could resign himself to that idea, however, he couldn't help but wonder if perhaps the Lord was beginning a much grander plan for them. Whatever the outcome, whether this meeting was of little or large significance, all he could do was make himself a vessel willing to go wherever he was led. With that in mind, he prayed one last prayer before drifting off to sleep.

"Lord, make me ready for whatever comes next."

"Rejoice with those who rejoice; weep with those who weep."
— Romans 12:15 CSB

Rut had always found comfort in rhythms and routine. She liked knowing what was expected of her and what to expect from the world around her. There was a rhythm in spinning wool on a drop spindle. Likewise, there were rhythms and patterns in weaving row by row until a length of cloth was complete. Rut sought just as hard to establish patterns in her life. Was that not why she strived to be the perfect daughter? The perfect wife? She always followed the rules, always did what was asked of her, and always tried to do only the best work. Even as a girl, Rut knew that she wanted a normal, steady life, following the patterns of her parents and grandparents before her. Marriage, children, grandchildren…

Life had other rhythms in mind; less comfortable ones, like the rhythm of the rocking motion of their cart. Rut and Beni left before dawn, just as they told Hektor and Lydia they would. As the sun moved higher in the sky and they moved farther away from the coast, the cool breeze coming off the water began to dissipate. Although they hadn't been traveling long, Rut already felt the strain of travel in her back and shoulders. The journey home was Rut's least favorite, because, it always felt much longer.

"I don't know if Abba will believe me when I tell him we sold all of the wool," said Beni.

Rut's gaze remained affixed on the familiar mountainous horizon. "He'll have to believe you when you show him your earnings."

"*Our* earnings, sister," said Benayahu. "This is a family business. I couldn't do this without you."

"Really, Beni?" asked Rut, a hint of disbelief in her tone. She wasn't facing her brother, but if she had been, he would have seen how she raised her eyebrows at him.

In her peripheral vision, she saw Benayahu shake his head. "You think I only ask you to come with me because Abba is too old to make the journey?"

"I assumed that was your reasoning." Rut shrugged. "That, and because you wanted to get me out of the house."

"That's my sister you're talking about, and I would appreciate it if you didn't try to diminish her importance to me."

"What is your reasoning, then?"

Benayahu sighed. "A very small part of it was because of Abba's age. I will concede to that point; but Rut, you're the one who knows the most about the wool we sell. No one in the family handles it as much as you do. No one else understands how it weaves, how it holds dyes... You're an expert. We should've always involved you in the business. You're talented and shrewd, and at the end of the day, I like having you around."

Rut let out a singular laugh, bordering on a cackle.

"What's so funny?" asked Benayahu. Even the donkey pulling their cart slowed its pace.

"I was recalling another younger version of you who felt decidedly opposite."

Benayahu shook his head. "I was a child then."

"But you wanted all of us to call you a man!" At the memories of simpler times, both of them laughed. Rut had forgotten how good it felt to share that kind of feeling with her brother.

Things hadn't really changed that much since they were children. She was still Rut and he was still Beni. They still had the same eyes and hair, and most of the same memories, though their perspectives might have differed.

"I miss how easy it used to be for us to talk," said Benayahu, breaking the silence that had fallen between them.

"Me, too."

"I know things aren't the same as they were when we were younger."

Rut threw a pretend jab at Beni's arm. "I still can't believe Milkah ever agreed to marry you."

Benayahu laughed again. "Neither can I, sometimes. She's given me more than I ever knew I needed in life. I thank God for her every day…" Benayahu's voice trailed off as though he were falling into a distant dream. Later on, he continued, "What did you think of Lydia?"

Rut's brows furrowed. This was a sudden and abrupt change of subject and Rut struggled to see how they connected. "I… I thought she was a very kind woman. She is clearly very successful at what she does, or so it would seem."

"What did you think of her offer?"

"Me? Go to Philippi?" Rut lifted her hand in the air, waving the idea away. "It doesn't make any sense."

"I didn't ask if it made sense. I asked what you thought of it."

"I thought nothing of it," said Rut, bringing her hand swiftly back down in exasperation.

"Rut, please," Benayahu pleaded. "Talk with me like we used

to. Don't hide anything from me."

"Beni, I'm not trying to hide anything. How could I ever realistically leave everyone and everything I've ever known, to go and spend a year in a foreign city with someone I just met?" Rut was trying to convince her brother as much as she was trying to convince herself that it was a nonsensical offer made by an impulsive woman, no matter how pleasant of a dream it may have been.

Benayahu pulled the cart to a stop.

"What are you doing? We'll never get home before nightfall if we stop now!" Rut turned to face her brother.

"Is it home?" asked Benayahu, now staring directly into her eyes.

Rut's breathing hitched. "What?"

"The fields of crops, the little sheepfold, our tiny house in the valley... Is that land your *home?*"

Something about the way her brother looked at her tugged at Rut's heart. She was transformed back into a frightened little girl, uncertain of the world before her and the unpredictability she knew was inevitable. Benayahu may have been her younger brother, but there were times she looked up to him for his bravery, boldness, and decisiveness. He was and always had been so sure of himself, even to a fault at times, though maturity had tempered such impulses. Rut wished she could've had a fraction of his confidence. Her lips quivered, but she couldn't reply.

Benayahu continued, "I'd be lying if I said sometimes I didn't still feel like a stranger in a strange land. We left Jerusalem in such a hurry, stopping in Damascus for only a short time before Abba and Dodh Aharon decided to settle land in Phoenicia. Though I am happy here with our life now, we never really got to say goodbye to the city that raised us, so I'll ask again... Is Phoenicia your home?"

"No," said Rut, now unable to stop the tears from falling. "Jerusalem was home for me. I don't think I ever felt like I truly had a home here except for…. Except for the home I shared with Shem."

At that, Benayahu pulled her close. She wept into his shoulders, the memories of all she had lost over the years still painfully fresh as the days in which they were made. She hadn't been able to cry when they left Jerusalem; she had to be brave. When Shem died, she decided quickly that things were better if she continued to hide her emotions. It struck her that this was possibly the first time she'd cried in the presence of another person since then. Her heart was filled with so much pain, yet it felt so strangely good to finally share it with someone.

Benayahu held her until her breathing settled. When it did, she straightened in her seat and wiped the tears from her face. Rut took a moment to focus her gaze on the landscape, counting the colors that painted the land and sky. When she looked back at her brother, Rut was surprised to see that he was crying, too.

"Shem was like a brother to me," he cried.

"Oh, Beni. Please don't—"

"No, Rut." Benayahu cut her off. "He *was* my brother and I have grieved his loss alongside you, though I know it is not the same. How I wish… How I—"

Benayahu lowered his head to his hands, overtaken with sobs of his own. Rut extended her arm toward him, recognizing exactly what thoughts must be going through his mind. Hadn't she spent years doing the same thing? Wishing that she had done something, *anything* differently?

"Beni… It was an accident. A snake bite. There is nothing we could have done to change the outcome." Rut knew that much was true.

"But I could have done something differently, Rut," Benayahu argued. "We always took turns when it came to who led the herd and who stayed at the rear to make sure no sheep were left behind. On the day the snake bit him, it was my turn to lead from the front, scouting ahead for green valleys and watching for any danger… Shem wanted to trade places with me."

Rut realized with unyielding clarity the great weight her brother had been carrying silently all these years. "Oh." She shuddered as she relived that day's events in her mind's eye.

"Shem said he knew where we could find good grazing land. He'd seen a plant there that he knew you could use to make dyes. He wanted to gather some for you, and offered to lead the way."

"*Shem,*" Rut whispered as though he were sitting right beside her. Even though she'd been distant and discontented toward her husband when he left, Shem only thought of her happiness. Despite having so many other things to worry about, he cared for her before anything else. How underserving she had been of his love…

"We were coming over a hill when it happened. Shem gave the signal that it was safe to follow, and I did. We gathered the sheep in the valley and let them rest. It all happened so quickly after that. I watched Shem approach a cluster of plants, and in the seconds before the snake bite, I saw something moving in the grass. It all happened so quickly after that. He shouted. I ran toward him. The snake bit. I fumbled for my knife."

"You did what you could, Beni," she said in an attempt to comfort him, though it hurt her to say the words.

"I threw my knife and struck the snake, but by then it was too late… Shem was already wounded. I suggested we turn back, but Shem said the pain would wear off. He didn't think the snake was poisonous. By the next morning, when Shem was too ill to stand and his ankle had swelled to twice its normal size, I knew it was too late. He was barely strong enough to walk, and it was all I could do to shepherd the flock and carry him back."

"Beni, you can't blame yourself. I've fought that battle in my own mind enough times to know that it does no good."

"But maybe if I'd insisted we turn for home immediately, or if I'd suggested we go a different way… If I hadn't let him take the lead, maybe that snake would've been gone by the time he came down the hill?"

"And maybe the snake would have bitten you. Please, Beni. I would give anything to have my husband back, but if it had been you in his place, then who would've looked after Milkah? Jeriel would never have known his father, and Avigail and Tovi would have never been born. Yes, I wish Shem was here, but I would never sacrifice my brother or the happiness and welfare of my niece and nephews, and sweet sister-in-law. This grief is a heavy burden, and I wouldn't wish it upon anyone."

Beni's shoulders heaved up and down as he breathed deeply. "Rut… do you forgive me?"

Rut swallowed hard. "There is nothing for me to forgive, Beni. It happened the way it happened. No amount of wrestling with our memories will change that." As Rut said the words aloud, she realized they were as true for her brother as they were for her. Painful as it was, they had to keep going, even when it seemed like the world had stopped a long time ago.

"Then you must tell me, what did you truly think of Lydia's offer? You seemed to get along well with each other."

"Beni, it still doesn't make any sense," Rut tried to explain. She'd never thought about doing anything like this in her wildest imaginings, and she had no idea how anyone else would respond to such an idea.

"What if it did make sense? What if you didn't have to worry about us, or Abba or Imma, or any of it? If there was nothing holding you back, would you go?"

"I could never—" Rut stopped herself. After everything Benayahu shared, he deserved her honesty and she owed it to herself to be honest, too. All this time, she had no idea how guilt-stricken her brother felt over Shem's death. They'd been mourning him side by side, yet separately. She couldn't go on that way. She opened her mouth to speak again, this time giving an honest answer.

"Yes, I think I might."

Rut squeezed her eyes shut, scared to see Benayahu's reaction. Would he hate her for it? Would he be able to understand?

"Then I will help you."

"What?" said Rut, eyes immediately opened wide. She couldn't trust her own ears.

"I couldn't fight to save Shem that day, but I can fight for you, and I will. If this is what you want, just say so, and I will see to it that Abba and Imma understand."

"You would do that for me?"

"I would do anything for you, sister."

Rut blinked back more tears, forcing herself to remain composed. Her eyes already burned from crying too much. "You don't think it's wrong of me? To want to leave?"

"I have watched you live half a life all these years. I know you love us, but I also know that it can't be easy for you. Sometimes, even when we're surrounded by ten or twenty or a hundred people that we know care for us, we can still feel totally alone. I trust Lydia and, for what it's worth, I feel peace about this. If this is what you want, then I'm with you. We may not have always been on the same side as children, but when it comes to facing the rest of the world, I will always be on your side."

"Oh, Beni... Lydia did say I would be able to return next year, didn't she?"

"She did."

Rut weighed the options in her heart. She could stay in

Phoenicia for the rest of her life, knowing she could find some kind of contentment. However, Rut also knew that despite her happiness with her family, there would always be an air of sadness. A cloud of mourning would forever float overhead and she would constantly feel the weight of her situation. Perhaps it would be better, at least for a while, to wake up somewhere that did not have reminders in every direction of Shem's absence.

It would be hard, but maybe the time away would allow her to finally put the past behind her and go where she would be known as "*Rut, the weaver,*" and no longer "*Rut, the widow.*"

"Beni?"

"Yes, Rut?"

"I think I would like it very much if you spoke to Abba and Imma with me."

Benayahu smiled. "Then we'd best get going. We'll need to hurry home so that you can start packing again." With a click of his tongue and a quick motion of the reins, Benayahu urged the donkey forward. This time, the rhythm of the cart's motion was much less painful to Rut. She was nervous, yet for the first time in years, she was excited for the future. This change would be good for her.

At least, she hoped it would be.

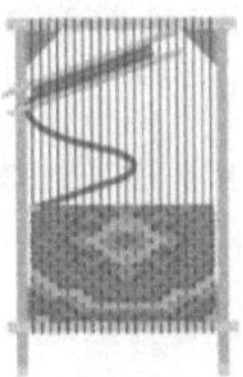

"It is only for one year, Imma," said Rut, packing a small wooden chest with what she thought she would need—which was nearly everything she owned. It felt strangely similar to packing up her things just before she'd been married, except instead of building a life with Shem, she would be building a life all on her own. "Whatever I learn, I can bring home with me, and if I manage to do any work, I will be compensated well for it. Think of what that could mean for our family. Please don't cry."

"How can I do anything else?" said Devorah, Rut's mother. Devorah had never been a very effusive woman when Rut was a child. Becoming a grandmother brought out a new side in her, and one to which Rut did not always know how to respond. "The last time I said goodbye to you like this was—"

Rut closed her eyes, knowing the reason her mother stopped short of voicing her thought was because she was afraid, like so many others had been, of bringing up painful memories. If only she could make them understand that everything since Shem's death had been somewhat painful. Not only the sound of his name, but every breath she took in a world in which he did not exist.

There was no sense in trying to coat with honey what was soured by vinegar. The bitter taste would always remain, no matter how much sweetness you added to it.

"The last time you said goodbye to me like this was when I was going to marry Shem," Rut finished the thought for her mother. "That's what you were going to say, wasn't it?"

Her mother nodded. "You were only going to be a short walk away from me then… Now…"

"Now," said another voice upon entering the room, "our Rut is off to start her own adventure, and we must be proud of her, Devorah." It was Binyamin, Rut's father. He walked toward Devorah, taking her hands in his own and smiling warmly.

"I am proud, *husband*, but can I not also be concerned? What of these people? We don't know them!"

"Beni said he trusted them."

Devorah sighed. "First impressions can be deceiving…"

"Imma, please. It is only for one year at the least, and then I shall likely return."

"Likely?" Devorah repeated, her fears clearly not assuaged. "Binyamin, please! Can't you talk your daughter out of this?"

"I could," said Binyamin.

Rut's heart skipped a beat. Benayahu had kept his word when he spoke to their father with her and she believed him to be an understanding man, but would he change his mind if provoked enough? Did he see the unconventionality of what she was going to do as an impossible plan?

Binyamin continued, "As the head of this household, I could forbid it, but as her abba, I cannot."

"Oh, Abba," Rut whispered, grateful for his understanding on this matter.

"Please, Devorah, let me have a moment alone with my daughter."

Devorah stopped to give Rut a firm embrace, likely only one of many more to come before she and Benayahu began their journey back to Tyre. Then she obliged Binyamin's request and left them in the room alone.

"What is it you want to speak to me about, Abba?"

"Tell me again, is this truly what you want?" His voice broke as he asked the question.

"It is, Abba." At least, she thought it was. Rut still wasn't sure, but knew she needed some kind of change. Whether this was the right path or not was a question that could only be answered over the course of time. If it wasn't, Rut would return in one year and that would be that. It would all be only a memory.

"Then can I ask why? Have we hurt you in some way?"

Rut emphatically shook her head, loosening her curls. "No, Abba! You are all my family and I love you dearly. It is only that I can't—I don't *feel* at peace here. Everywhere I look there are reminders of the past and it makes it difficult for me to move forward."

He looked at the ground, and Rut winced, knowing that these words were hard for him to hear.

"It is unfair to expect you would have been able to live as if nothing happened, I know, but I had hoped... I hoped that you would find happiness with us again."

"That's just it, Abba. I have had happiness." Rut stepped closer to him, wringing her hands repeatedly. "There have been many happy moments, but even in those moments, there has still been pain. It is as if I am constantly bearing this weight around my shoulders. There are moments where I find rest, but the pressure always returns."

Her father's face, which normally bore a mischievous expression as though he were holding back a quip, was now red and streaked with tears.

"My daughter... I didn't realize."

"I don't even know if I realized the fullness of it until the idea of going away for a time presented itself. I know it's frightening and that it's not the way of things, but I think I need this, and I need to be able to do it with your blessing."

"I always knew you were destined to do great things." While Binyamin's smile seemed forced, Rut saw through the tears that the jovial spark in his eyes was still present. "It may not seem like it from my expression, but I am truly proud of you. To think that your talents are not only noticed by me, but by others coming from different parts of the world? You bring honor to all of us, Rut. You have always had my blessing."

"Oh, Abba, thank you!" Rut threw her arms around him and held onto him with fervor, in a way she hadn't done since she was a little girl. "Thank you!"

"I hope you are able to find what you are looking for in Philippi, Rut. God goes before you, and He will be with you wherever you go. Know that I will still pray for you every day, maybe even every hour. As long as you are gone, I will leave a lamp lit for you so you can always find your way back home."

Unexpectedly, the promise brought tears to her eyes. She still didn't know what she believed, and in truth, she had not prayed about this decision or any decision in many years. Rut continued to wrestle with doubt and there were times she despised herself for it. She knew God was real, but sometimes thoughts crept into her mind that made her wonder if He was still with her.

Did He still hold her in His hand?

If she returned to Him, would He return to her?

A combination of guilt and shame never let her find answers to such questions.

"Now, you'd better finish packing. Beni will take you back to Tyre tomorrow; I'd go myself, but I'm afraid I wouldn't be able to control my emotions, and I wouldn't want to get in the way of whatever it is that God has planned for you. The rest of the family will be here tonight to bid you farewell on your journey. Shall I send your imma back in to help?"

"Maybe wait a little while?" Rut tittered through tears. Wiping her eyes, she carried on, "If I have to stop every time she cries, I'm worried I will never finish."

Binyamin laughed. "Yes, you're right. I will make sure that you have enough time to do what you need to do." As he turned to go, Rut turned back to her folding.

In the end, there really wasn't much to pack. Rut wouldn't need to bring any of her supplies, though she still packed her own little drop spindle. It had been worn down so much over the years that it was practically molded to her hand. She didn't know if she would have use for it, but she packed it just in case. Rut couldn't imagine using any other tools—even if they were better quality or in more pristine condition.

There were other things she left behind, like her loom,

knowing that it would be impossible for her to travel with and that there would likely be larger ones where she was going. Her loom was too small to make a full-sized garment in a single panel and she always had to stitch the pieces together to complete a project. She was certain that in Philippi, things would be done differently. Lydia was wealthy enough to have looms available in all sizes, and no doubt the clients there would not be in the market for simple items fashioned from a simple loom.

By the time she was finished, the rest of the family had arrived, as Binyamin said they would, sharing memories as they shared a meal. One by one, she'd spoken at length and said goodbye to each of them... Dodah Elisheva and Dodh Aharon, Shamira and Asa, each of their children, her own father and mother, Milkah, her niece and nephews... Shamira lingered still after Asa took their children home, rivers of tears running down her face.

"You are in my prayers, sister of my heart," whispered Shamira, wrapping her arms around Rut.

"I know," said Rut, holding tightly to her dearest friend.

Shamira pulled backward, but did not let go. Her eyes remained fixated on Rut's. "Wherever you go, whatever happens, there is nothing that could break the bond we share. You will always be the one who knows me best."

"Even compared to Asa?" Rut teased.

"You know what I mean." Shamira laughed, reaching to dry her eyes with her sleeve. Then, her demeanor once again pensive, she added with a wrinkle of her nose, "Rut, I want so much for your happiness and success. More than anything, I want you to always know and remember that God loves you and He cares for you."

Rut began to breathe a little quicker, wondering if Shamira knew somehow of the way in which her heart had changed over the years. Did Shamira know all that time how Rut's faith dwindled?

"That is my prayer for you, Rut, and it will be my prayer for you every night until we meet again—and I know we will, someday. I have faith in that."

Rut's heart slowed back to a normal rhythm. "Thank you, Shamira."

They embraced one last time before Shamira left to return to her own home and family. Rut glanced up toward the heavens. She was unsure if she'd ever gazed upon the stars with this much intent to commit them to memory. Rut wanted to make sure she had this sight written upon her heart—the last time that she would see the night sky over her family's Phoenician home for at least a year. Had it always been so dark? Had the stars always shined so brilliantly? She couldn't say.

As her gaze drifted downward across the fields, Rut realized that there was one person left to whom she had not said goodbye, and she very much needed to before she left.

Shem.

In the stillness of the night and with no one else watching her, Rut wrapped her arms around herself for warmth and began walking. She didn't go to the place where Shem was buried; that would have been too much. No, Rut walked to the place that had been their home for the five years they were married. When she got close enough to reach out and touch the door, she gasped. She hadn't been back to this place since Shem's death, and a wave of emotions crashed over her. Carefully, she opened the door and peeked inside.

It was empty except for some spiderwebs and a near-decade's worth of dust on the few furnishings left behind after her family removed everything for her. Rut was surprised to see how small it really was. She had recalled their dwelling as such, but to think how they lived here with so little made Rut realize how truly full their life together was.

"Oh, Shem." Rut sighed as she stepped across the threshold, a wave of memories crashing over her. "I wonder what this house would look like now if things had happened differently. Perhaps you would have built an addition. Maybe I would have planted a small garden of my own around the side."

Rut paced the room, convinced for a moment that she could still hear the echo of Shem's laughter off of the walls, though it wasn't true.

She continued, "Well, I have news, Shem. I think I'm finally going to weave some of those grand tapestries like you always talked about... I'm going to spend a year in Philippi of all places, and I don't know if I'll ever return. At least, I won't return the same person. Losing you was perhaps the hardest thing I've ever had to endure, and I think that in many ways, I'm still enduring it. I loved you so deeply, and even if I didn't always say it, I was grateful for every moment we spent together."

This time, Shem's voice did come to Rut's mind, though it wasn't an echo or an audible voice—it was a memory.

"Rut, promise me..." Shem had started to say as his life was slipping away. Rut recalled how she pleaded in vain for him to hold on. *"Everything... Everything in God's timing, Rut,"* he had said. How she wished that she hadn't interrupted him. Though Rut already knew in her heart what Shem would have said, she wished she could have heard it out loud.

"You would have wanted me to heal, I know. You would've wanted me to keep going, keep trusting. That's why I have to leave, Shem. I can't heal here. I've tried, but I feel you everywhere. I am reminded of your zest for life with every sunrise. I hear you singing every time the wind blows over the grass a certain way, and I remember you are gone whenever it stops. I know you wouldn't have wanted me to live like this. I *have* to say goodbye to this part of my life. I have to say goodbye to you."

Rut felt a tear trickle down her face. Moonlight filtered in through the roof that time and many storms had worn down even more since she lived there, and Rut realized the lateness of the hour. It was time for her to return home for one last night of sleep before she started her new life. Although she knew that on their journey she could ask Benayahu to turn around at any moment, in her heart, there was no going back. It was time to move on. So, Rut left their little one-room dwelling, closing the door on her way out, and pausing to whisper only two words.

"Goodbye, Shem."

"The Lord has displayed his holy arm in the sight of all the nations; all the ends of the earth will see the salvation of our God." — Isaiah 52:10 CSB

As Rut stood on the deck of the ship watching Tyre and any trace of it gradually fade into the horizon, she relived her last conversation with Benayahu in her mind. They had already met with Lydia and Hektor to finalize the arrangements. Lydia could not have been more thrilled to see Rut reappear at the inn. Benayahu insisted on staying with them until Rut's final departure. Once Rut's things were taken aboard, the others left them to have one last private exchange by the sea before everything would change for Rut—again.

"Last chance to turn back," Benayahu had quipped.

"I won't," she said, smiling through her nervousness. "You kept your word to me about speaking with Abba and fighting for this by my side. I want to make sure I thank you for that. I cannot express to you how grateful I am to have a brother like you."

He shook his head. "It was the least I could do after all you've done for me."

"Me? What have I done?" asked Rut, puzzled by the statement.

"Everything. You always encouraged me to be better when we were growing up. Even when it did not seem like I was listening, I was always watching you, always hearing what you said to me, and always taking it to heart. I was too proud then to admit that I looked up to you, but not anymore." Benayahu's voice cracked, and she saw tears welling up in his eyes. They both had changed so much since they were children, yet in many ways he was still the same.

"I'm going to miss you, Beni."

"I'll be watching from this very spot until your ship is out of sight, and probably even for some time after that, just to be sure."

"You don't have to do that, you know."

"For my sister, I do."

They were interrupted by a call from Lydia, alerting them that it was time for Rut to board the smaller vessel that would carry them to the ship, which floated farther out at sea.

"God be with you, Rut. I love you."

"I love you, too."

Those were the last words they spoke to each other, and the last words she would speak to any of her family for one whole year. As she stood beneath the ship's square sails, every part of Tyre became a more distant memory in her mind with each wave they sailed over. She wondered if Benayahu was still standing there at the water's edge. Had he seen her tears?

"Have you ever travelled by sea before?" asked Lydia. Rut hadn't noticed her approach.

"Never," said Rut.

"Well, there are a few things you should know," said Lydia, linking arms with Rut. "Never look directly at the water. Always keep your eye on the horizon when you are above deck, if you can help it. It will make it easier to maintain your balance and avoid seasickness."

Seasickness. Was that cause of the churning sensation in Rut's stomach, or was the queasiness a result of all the sudden change in her life? It was a change she had chosen and she thought she knew what to expect, but her imagination barely scratched the surface.

"I'll keep that in mind," said Rut, bowing her head respectfully.

Cheerfully, Lydia continued. "We'll be stopping briefly in Thyatira. I have to pick up some new supplies before returning to Philippi."

"Oh, yes, you mentioned that's where you lived before Philippi. Do you miss it?"

Lydia leaned in and raised an eyebrow. "Truthfully?"

Rut nodded.

"The things I miss aren't there anymore, and I am proud of what I've built in Philippi. The business, as well as the relationships. Sometimes I forget that there was a time before I lived there. What about you? Have you lived in Phoenicia all your life?"

"No, my family… Well, we moved there during a difficult time… If you don't mind, I think I would rather not discuss it right now." She squeezed her eyes shut to avoid seeing Lydia's reaction to her bluntness. Rut had already decided to keep as much of her past to herself as possible. She believed it would be easier to leave it behind that way, rather than dragging it with her across the ocean.

"My apologies," said Lydia. "I'm sure this is overwhelming to you. Why don't I show you where we'll be staying so you can rest?"

Rut sighed, relieved. "I would appreciate that very much."

"Hektor, would you lead the way for us?" Lydia called over her shoulder and instantly the man appeared.

With a courteous bow, he turned to lead them down a set of steep steps that reminded Rut of the cramped quarters in her Jerusalem home. Once they descended, Rut immediately bumped shoulders with a short, angry-looking man. This deck was dark, but some rays of sunlight managed to slip through the cracks above, illuminating the dust floating in the air and casting the space in a hazy glow.

"Oh!" Rut gasped in shock. "I'm sorry."

The man grumbled and walked away, disappearing into shadow.

"The crew are well-paid for their sailing abilities but not their social skills, unfortunately," Hektor explained in a hushed voice. "We'll keep going this way."

Without any more awkward incidents, Rut followed Hektor with small, rapid steps. He opened a hatch in the floor that led to a near-black expanse. Lydia gestured for Rut to go first after Hektor, which she did, though her mind fought against it as she imagined the dark hole to be a bottomless pit that would surely swallow her up. Once her eyes adjusted to the lack of light, Rut saw how much smaller this level of the ship was than the one above. It was cramped, and even Rut had to slouch to keep from bumping her head. Poor Hektor was practically on his knees.

"Is this where we'll stay?" Rut hoped no one noticed the obvious faltering in her voice. She knew that sea travel would be difficult and possibly even dangerous, but hadn't yet considered the lack of privacy.

"You and I will stay here," said Lydia, pressing forward and stopping just beside a kind of curtain. She pulled the heavy cloth to one side and motioned for Rut to step through.

When she did, Rut instantly recognized her chest of belongings, and took note of another chest which she assumed must have been Lydia's personal items. It was ornate and beautifully crafted, despite having such practical use. Like all of Lydia's garments that Rut had seen, the chest was exceptionally detailed in ways that made something ordinary feel extraordinary, while still maintaining its functionality.

"If you're nervous about the crew, you need not worry about them bothering us. Hektor stays on the other side of the partition all night long. It isn't much, but it does provide solitude," Lydia said.

Rut turned and locked eyes with Hektor, who stood behind Lydia. Despite the darkness, his eyes still sparkled like sea waves glinting in the sun. She looked away, feeling another wave of sickness crash over her.

Hektor explained, "Though Lydia has paid well for the space on this ship, the crew can sometimes become restless after so many nights at sea. There is no reason for you to fear, Rut. No harm will come to you while I'm around," Hektor promised.

While Rut wanted to feel confident in his words, she only felt more ill. Instead of responding, she stood motionless in the center of the room, if it could be called a room. What had she been thinking?

"I'll leave you to rest for now. There will be a meal later on, but I am afraid it will only be the ship's rations. Will that suit you?"

"Mhmm." Though she appreciated the effort Lydia was making, Rut could barely muster the strength to keep standing.

"All right... Let us know if you need anything."

"I will." The heavy curtain scraped the deck as it fell. When it did, Rut curled up on the floor, wrapping herself in a blanket in an effort to make the planks of wood beneath her less painful. She tried to sleep off whatever it was that ailed her, but sleep did not come easily. Rut could hear all kinds of noises coming from outside. The crew members joined each other in song from time to time, though Rut could not make out the words to their melodies. Every so often, one deep, booming voice shouted something to another. Footsteps passed back and forth on the deck above her. Always, always, Rut could hear the weight of the water hitting the ship on all sides. Was it supposed to move this much?

Eventually, she heard footsteps draw near. "Rut? Are you well?"

It was Hektor.

Slowly, Rut pulled herself up. "Yes, I am all right," she answered, although it was a blatant lie.

"Mistress Lydia sent me to see if you wanted to join us for the evening meal. Shall I tell her that you are still resting?"

"No." Rut pulled the curtain to the side and stepped around it, "I will come."

Hektor smiled and offered his arm. She took it, giving herself permission to lean on someone else's strength, at least for a while. "Are you feeling refreshed?" he asked as they walked.

"I… It was not exactly…. That is, I wouldn't say…"

He laughed loudly, the sound matching his impressive height and unbelievably strong stature. "I beg your pardon, Rut. I'm not laughing at you, I promise. It is only that I have never liked the feeling of being at sea either."

"Do you get seasick?" asked Rut, though she found it hard to believe someone like Hektor could be brought to his knees by mere moving water.

"No, but I do find that I much prefer being on land. Lydia needs to travel, though, and I go where she goes, which means traveling by—"

"Sea." Rut finished the sentence for him, not bothering to hide the repugnance in her voice knowing that she was with likeminded company. He laughed again, deep and resounding, and the sound comforted Rut. It was the first time all day that she'd felt a moment of peace.

Hektor led her toward the hatch they'd come down earlier that day, where she now saw Lydia sitting before a makeshift table.

"Oh, good! You're here!" Lydia rose to greet Rut with open arms. "I was worried about you."

"Nothing to worry about," said Rut, struggling to make her gaze meet Lydia's eyes. "Just adjusting."

"I hope the transition is a smooth one for you. Come and sit beside me."

Immediately, Rut did as Lydia asked, as did Hektor.

"It looks delicious." Rut smiled politely at the spread.

"You can say what you really think," joked Hektor. Both he and Lydia laughed and Rut let her shoulders fall, continuing to feel more at ease.

"What my uncouth guard is aiming to say is that we are all friends here, Rut. We want you to feel at home with us."

"Thank you," said Rut. "Should we eat then?"

"Please, I'm starved," said Hektor. Lydia raised a hand as though to signal him to hold off.

"Do you pray, Rut?" asked Lydia.

"I…" Rut hesitated. What answer did she want to give? Of course she bowed her head beside her family during prayer, but when was the last time she had prayed herself? Whenever she tried to worship, all she felt was emptiness and it filled her with shame. What did that make her? She did not leave Phoenicia to answer questions like this. She left to avoid them.

"I'm sorry. That was far too direct of a question for me to ask."

"No, it's all right. I am Jewish," said Rut, admitting to her heritage at least.

"Really?" asked Lydia, eyes widened in astonishment.

"Yes… Are you disappointed?" Rut was reminded by Lydia's reaction that not all people were friendly toward Jews, especially those with more Greek or Roman inclinations.

"No! I am in awe of how well God has woven our stories together. You see, though we are Gentiles, myself and Hektor and many others who work for me all worship the Jewish God. I only asked because we follow the custom of beginning an evening meal with prayer, and I did not want to assume the same was true of you."

"You are God-fearers, then?" asked Rut, using the term she'd heard once or twice when they were living in the city of Jerusalem that referred to Gentiles who believed as the Jewish people did, observed the same rites and traditions, but were not full converts. They remained separate.

Lydia nodded. "Because there is no synagogue in Philippi, we gather for worship by the river. Unfortunately, we still lack a place of proper learning. Do you know much about the faith?"

"I…" Rut stuttered.

Lydia blinked several times, straightening her back. "I'm sorry, I am clearly getting distracted. As I said before, sometimes I think too quickly for my own good. Let us pray and eat, and we can continue this conversation later."

Lydia clasped her hands together and Rut did likewise, seeing Hektor do the same out of the corner of her eye. Rut followed the rhythm as she had done every other day since Shem's death, but in the back of her mind the faint voice of her conscience whispered that she was living a lie. Was it a new whisper, or had it been there for much longer? Rut pushed it back, reminding herself that when she'd said goodbye that night at the house she once shared with Shem, she wasn't just saying goodbye to him. She was saying goodbye to her old life. Rut wanted to start over and that was exactly what she was going to do. She had pretended to be someone else before, and she could do it again. It might even be easier this time, too, since these people did not know her as well as her family did.

The meal was simple, consisting of bread and cheese. Lydia and Hektor carried on a conversation throughout almost the entire meal, and Rut noticed again the familiarity with which they joked with each other. Was there something more between them or was she imagining it?

Rut ate to sustain, for while she was not hungry, she hadn't eaten anything that day. Towards the end of the meal, the ship lurched forward with more intensity than usual. Lydia and Hektor both picked up their cups and held on to their food. Rut did the same, but fumbled in doing so.

"What was that?" Her voice shook.

"Seems like the sea has more energy tonight than usual," said Hektor, matter-of-fact. How could he be so calm? Rut's whole body started to shiver and not because she was cold. In fact, she was feeling quite warm.

Lydia set down her cup and reached for Rut's hand. "The crew knows what they're doing. This kind of thing happens all the time."

Except it didn't happen all the time. Not to Rut. She thought she hated the sound of thunder badly enough when she was on land, safe within the walls of her own home. It was even worse now that she was trapped in what was suddenly feeling like a floating prison of cedar rather than a ship that would carry her to freedom from her past sufferings.

"Mistress Lydia," called one of the crew from the top of the hatch. Rut assumed from his commanding voice that he was the one in charge. "I'm going to have to ask that you secure yourselves here due to unexpected winds."

"Of course. Are you anticipating very rough seas?" Lydia inquired.

"It shouldn't amount to much, but I'd rather have all of you out of the way."

"Thank you for giving us the warning," said Lydia.

"Yes, thank you," Rut echoed.

The three of them rose from the table. Rut felt like her legs might give way at any moment. They made their way back to the other side of the cargo hold after that, and Hektor stopped on the other side of the curtain, right where Lydia said he would stay all night. Rut added him to her list of things to worry about. If the worst should happen, what good would it do for him to be out there?

Then again, what good would it do for Rut to be trapped inside?

"Will Hektor be all right?" asked Rut once she was lying down.

"Hektor? Oh, he'll be fine. He's used to this." Lydia carried on making up her own bed.

"Oh." Rut heaved deep breaths. *In. Out. In. Out.* She tried to concentrate on the rhythm of her heart, but every clap of thunder made her body jolt. "How long have you known Hektor?" Rut pushed the words out quickly, trying to do anything to distract her from this horrible weather.

"Many years now," said Lydia. Rut could tell from her tone that the questions did not bother her, and for that, Rut was grateful. She hadn't talked much when they ate, but she needed to talk to someone now or else she might burst.

"How did you meet?" This was the question Rut had been pondering since she'd met them, which admittedly wasn't that long ago.

"Our paths crossed by coincidence, though I think now that it was all a part of God's plan. Hektor was ill then, and I called for a physician to care for him until he recovered. When he did, I offered him a job, and he's worked for me ever since. To tell you the truth, I think of him more as a brother than anything else."

"So you trust him?"

"With my life. By the nature of his job, we've become close over the years. I tell him things I wouldn't tell my other servants. We are like family to each other. I promise you, Rut, there is nothing to fear. Hektor will make sure that we are safe from intruders, and the captain and his crew are more than prepared to weather these squalls. If anything, a favorable wind may help us reach our destination sooner."

"I'm sorry if I'm keeping you awake," said Rut, squeezing her eyes shut.

"It's all right. I want us to get to know each other more." Lydia yawned. "I'll admit that I am rather tired, so if I drift off quickly, don't take it personally."

The ship lurched again and Rut curled her fingers around her blanket. After some time, Rut became certain that Lydia was asleep, but it was all Rut could do just to keep breathing. What if she'd left Phoenicia, only to die at sea? Was this a punishment for her faithlessness over the years? If she died, would her family ever find out? Would they learn the truth, or would Beni be left standing at the edge of Tyre, forever waiting for a return that would never come?

Another crash.

Another jolt.

Rut couldn't stand it anymore. She couldn't breathe, and she had to get out.

She had to escape.

*"You answer us in righteousness, with awe-inspiring works,
God of our salvation, the hope of all the ends of the earth and
of the distant seas." — Psalm 65:5 CSB*

The walls of the ship groaned and grumbled from the pressure
put on them by the wind and the waves. Hektor sat up against a
crate, keeping watch as was his duty. He'd closed his eyes, but
the ship's complaining kept him from even coming close to
sleep. He had been comforted to hear Lydia and Rut conversing
on the other side of the curtain. Though he could not discern
what their muffled voices were saying, he was glad to know that
Rut was talking to someone. She'd barely said a word since they
left Tyre. The dinner conversation had been carried mostly by
himself and Lydia. He didn't hold it against her, knowing how
tired she must have been. After what her brother shared with
him before they left, he hoped that weariness was all it was.

They were about to board the small boat that would row them
out to where the larger ship floated when it happened. Hektor
always walked behind Lydia, and since Lydia was talking with

Rut, there was a brief moment when it was just him and a misty-eyed Benayahu standing by the sea. Hektor felt compelled to say something to him.

"I promise that you will see her again in one year's time," said Hektor, emphasizing each word so that the man might see how much he meant them.

"I hope that this is right for her," Benayahu had said. "She's… She's been through a great deal of difficulty. I want her to be happy."

"I will guard Rut with my life, Benayahu, just as I guard Lydia."

Benayahu nodded. "For some reason, I feel like I can trust you even though I've only known you a short time. Please, protect my sister and if it isn't too much to ask, will you see that she is well in Philippi?"

"I will."

"Thank you."

Those were the last words they exchanged, but Hektor had not stopped thinking about them.

"*Lord,*" Hektor prayed silently as he adjusted his position after another sharp movement of the ship, "*I'm afraid I won't be getting any sleep tonight, so You might be hearing a lot from me. I hope You don't mind.*"

He stopped briefly to laugh at his own quip, then settled back into his prayers. "*Lord, I thank You for another day to live on this earth and see the beauty of Your creation. From the sandy shores of Tyre, to the cedar trees cloaking the land beyond Sidon with their shade, to the vast expanse of clear blue water covering the rest of the earth… Even the thunder tells of Your power. I thank You also for this life You've given me, and that Lydia gave me a chance when she had no good reason to do so, other than that she saw how badly I needed help.*

"*I am not a wise enough scholar to know if You listen to me the same way You listen to the prayers of Your chosen people, but I have faith that You do. That is why I am coming to You now to talk about Rut."* The thought of her made Hektor's mind wander. It was clear that she knew heartbreak. Hektor had been as downtrodden once, but through that experience, he learned an important truth: you could not understand joy without also knowing what it meant to live without it.

"No one knows better than me about being low in spirit. How many mistakes did I make while wallowing in my pain, letting it control me? If I'd known then what I know now about You… Well, who is to say that I might have acted differently? Only You know my heart, and only You know Rut's heart. I don't know what she has lived through, but I pray that You would lift her up as You lifted me.

"As for me, my life has always been in Your hands. Lead me in Your will and mold me to Your plans. Let this storm pass quickly, and make this journey a short one. I don't mind the traveling, but as much as I enjoy being able to see so much of Your creation in this world, there's nowhere quite like home."

Just then, Hektor felt something hit his leg—or someone. "What is—" he began to say as he rose. It was Rut! She had tripped over him and was now running toward the hatch. Hektor wasted no time in charging after her.

"Rut, come back! It's not safe for you to be—"

"I can't breathe!" she cried, climbing up the first hatch, barreling past the captain on her way through the second. Hektor followed close behind, with Rut a mere handbreadth out of reach. Hektor promised Benayahu that he would protect his sister. He would not break that promise on the first night of the voyage.

"Rut!" Hektor grunted as he hoisted himself onto the main deck. Rain poured down thick and heavy, obscuring his vision. Mighty winds blew strands of his hair in his face, the water making it stick uncomfortably to his skin.

"What is she doing here?" shouted the captain. "Get below, both of you! That is not a request!"

A flash of lightning briefly illuminated the deck. Rut clung to the mast. There was a railing around the ship that, in better conditions, would keep someone from accidentally going overboard. As much as the ship was rocking on the surface of the water now, however, he feared the railing would do little good if Rut lost her grip.

Hektor tried to run toward her, but struggled to maintain his balance. Another jolt of the ship slammed his body into the mast opposite of hers. "Rut, we must get below!"

"No!" she cried. "I don't want to drown down there!"

Now standing next to her, Hektor heard how ragged and quick her breaths were.

"I can't breathe, Hektor. *I can't breathe!*" Her voice rasped with desperation.

Hektor reached for her wrist, holding on to her as tightly as he could. "You need to slow down your heart, Rut. Breathe with me." He beckoned her with his eyes to match what he did, taking deep breaths through his nose and breathing out through his mouth.

At first she did not follow. "I can't!"

"Both of you! Get below! Now!" The captain continued to bellow at them.

Hektor ignored him.

His attention never wavered from Rut.

"Breathe with me, Rut. We will get through this together."

She looked at him with unsure eyes. Rainwater matted down her hair, making her curls cling to her forehead. Rut anxiously glanced back and forth between him, the captain, and the thunderclouds overhead. Both Rut and Hektor were soaked, but it wasn't important. "I've got you," Hektor assured her. "You're not going anywhere while I'm holding onto you, but we both need to get somewhere safer. Do you think you can walk with me?"

"Please don't make me go back down there."

The sight of her shattered him and he had to fight off every impulse not to wrap her in his arms and hold her. He'd never seen someone so in pain, and been so helpless to fix it. Never, that is, except for his last moments with his sister—but he wasn't going to think about that now. The same thing would not happen to Rut.

He wouldn't let it.

"Do you trust me?" he called to her over the sound of another thunderclap.

She shook her head, digging her fingernails deeper into the mast.

The ship took another wave to its side and Hektor tightened his grip on both Rut's hand and the ship's mast. The deck was only going to become more slippery and difficult to traverse the longer they waited. Hektor continued with more urgency in his voice, "That's not the answer I need right now, Rut. Do you trust me?"

"Y-y-yes…"

"Good." Another flash of lightning made Rut clutch tightly to his hand. Hektor looked at the distance from the mast to the hatch. It wasn't far, but the winds would make it difficult to cross.

Difficult, but not impossible.

"Follow my lead and move when I move," Hektor instructed. "When I give the signal, you *have* to go with me."

"I will!" she cried.

Hektor waited. More thunder made his bones rattle, but he did not fear. The ship lunged forward, backward, then—

"Now!"

The movement of the ship propelled them to the hatch. They slipped toward the end as water came crashing over the sides of the ship, forcing Hektor to practically push Rut through. He followed her quickly before pulling the hatch closed and securing it.

"One more time," said Hektor, guiding her down to the lowest level, ignoring the disgruntled comments and choice language used by the crew members who had witnessed the scene. Once they were back in the lower cargo hold, Hektor led her to an area occupied mostly by crates and sacks. He shuffled some things aside and motioned for her to sit down opposite him.

"I'm sorry," she said, ringing the rainwater out of her curls. "I don't know what I was thinking."

"It's what I'm here for," said Hektor.

"To get into trouble on account of my own foolishness?"

"To keep you safe." He leaned up against a crate. The ship continued to rock, but it was much quieter.

Another low clap of thunder set Rut back on her feet again. "I can't do this."

A psalm came to Hektor's mind; one most appropriate for their situation. Without thinking, he began to speak it aloud. "You silence the roar of the seas, the roar of their waves, and the tumult of the nations. Those who live far away are awed by your signs; you make east and west shout for joy."

"W-w-what did you say?" For a moment, Rut's body stilled as her eyes searched his for answers.

"I was quoting a psalm of David—one of my favorites, actually."

Her head tilted. "You know the Psalms?"

"Lydia has a set of scrolls containing some of them. She picked them up somewhere in her travels, and she keeps them in Philippi for everyone in her household to read. Some of those writings have been a great comfort to me in difficult times."

"That's… very interesting to know. What is it about that particular passage that you enjoy?"

"Well" — Hektor crossed his arms and made himself comfortable — "there are the beautiful descriptions of creation woven throughout, but I suppose my favorite lines come near the beginning of the song. It talks about being overwhelmed by our own iniquities, yet finding atonement and salvation through God, describing Him as the salvation and hope of all the earth."

The ship lurched again and Rut's face twinged.

"Sit back down," he suggested. "Why don't you talk to me about something?"

"What?" she asked, her bold brows moving closer together.

"Talk to me about something else to get your mind off of the storm. It will help, I promise."

She sat back down very slowly, but she did not speak. It became evident to Hektor that she would need some help getting started.

"If you'd like, I can tell a story," he suggested.

"What kind of story?"

Hektor shrugged. "Is there anything you'd like to know?"

Rut wrapped her arms around herself, still shivering. "Do you like traveling by sea?"

He couldn't help but laugh. "Not in the slightest."

"Then why do you do it?"

"Because it is what Lydia asks of me. The sea does have a beauty of its own, though."

"Not from what I've seen." She turned her head and narrowed her eyes, staring intently away from him. Hektor concealed a smile. She was afraid, but that didn't dull her sharp wit. "You and Lydia seem very close."

"I am forever in her debt," Hektor admitted. "Though she denies it vehemently."

"That sounds like an interesting story."

The way she said it made another smile spread across Hektor's face, though this one was more obvious than the first, and therefore more difficult to hide. She was wary and suspicious, as she should be of two near-strangers, but that did not stop her from going with them willingly and leaving the land of Phoenicia behind. Whatever her brother alluded to being in her past, she appeared determined to leave it behind her.

"All right, I'll tell you the whole of it, if you promise to tell me a story of yours in return."

She laughed and shook her head. "You'll never sleep."

"I wasn't planning on it anyway."

"Fine. I agree to your terms, but don't expect any embellishing details or exciting verbiage from me. I'm a weaver of threads, not words."

Her sense of humor intrigued and delighted Hektor, and he hoped there was more yet to come. "I must warn you: the beginning of it is not a happy story. I grew up in Philippi with my father and sister."

"That doesn't sound so bad," Rut interjected.

"Well, it might not have been if circumstances were different. You see, my mother left my father. We were never told where she went, and we were never permitted to speak of her in my father's presence. It was a rather interesting rule, now that I think of it."

"Why is that?"

"Because while we were never allowed to speak of her, my father spoke of her all the time. His descriptions of her are not words I would repeat to you, however, even in the pursuit of telling this story in full."

Her eyes turned downward to the edge of her sleeve, which she was actively engaged in folding and unfolding between her fingers, each time in smaller increments. "I understand," she whispered. The sound of thunder made her shudder but not jump. Hektor took this as a sign of progress.

"He would come home late, his breath wreaking of fermented drink. Always, he would find something to shout at me and my sister about. Eventually he drank himself to death, leaving me and Karis alone."

"Is that your sister's name?"

Hektor nodded.

"It's very pretty." Rut smiled softly.

"She was," said Hektor, letting his eyes lose focus on what was in front of him while he imagined what was long gone. "Nothing like me."

Rut laughed again.

"Karis was beautiful inside and out. I'm not sure where she got it from, considering the company she was raised with, but she made me want to be better, *do* better. Alas, we were struggling for money and for food, and I was becoming desperate to take care of my sister."

"Is that how you started working for Lydia?" asked Rut.

"I'm flattered that you think so, but my hands are unfortunately not well suited to weaving." He raised them in the air and she laughed again, this time a little harder. Hektor found that he was beginning to crave the sound. "No, I walked a different lifestyle for a time. I was always bigger and stronger than other boys my age and even some men. I quickly learned that the fastest way for me to make money was fighting for sport, and that's exactly what I did."

"You fought? In contests?"

Hektor nodded. "Anywhere in the city that would let me, against anyone who would accept my challenge."

Rut's eyebrows moved closer together as she leaned forward ever so slightly. "Were you any good?" He pretended not to notice how she looked him up and down.

"Why, you're looking at none other than Macedonia's very

own champion… The Fighting Lion of Philippi!" He raised two fists in the air in a mock-fighting stance.

"*Really?*"

"No."

This time she laughed so hard that she made a sound through her nose reminiscent of a small piglet. Both of her hands shot up to cover her face. Hektor found it endearing, and soon both of them were in hysterics.

"I'm sorry, I couldn't help myself." Hektor chuckled, still struggling to catch his breath. Once he did, he carried on, "I *was* called the Lion, but I was no champion. What's important for you to know about fighting for sport is this: while it is the fastest way of making money, it is not the most reliable."

"Did Karis know that you were a fighter?"

"I never told her, but she knew. She was perceptive like you."

"You think I'm perceptive?"

Hektor nodded. "You agreed to travel to a far-off land with two people you barely knew. You must have some sense of discernment to make that kind of decision with such confidence."

Rut groaned. "It is a decision I question with each movement of this ship."

"Ah, ah, ah," said Hektor, waving a finger in the air. "This story is supposed to distract you, remember? We can have no more talk of ships or travels or questioning decisions."

"I'm listening." Rut rolled her eyes, but Hektor could see she still suppressed a smile.

"Karis knew about the fighting, but neither of us talked about it. She was my little sister and I wanted more than anything to take care of her the way our father never did. She was the only family I had left."

"What happened to her?"

"It goes back to some of what I said before. Fighting is not the most reliable way of making money, nor is it the safest. There were times of plenty, and there were also times of very little. I would inevitably suffer injuries, or simply lose too many times in a row. We'd go without food for a while, but Karis never complained. She carried on, making do with whatever we had and making feasts out of mere scraps. One day, Karis got sick."

Tears welled up in Hektor's eyes as he spoke the words aloud. He felt a lump in his throat, and heard a voice in his mind telling him that it was his fault. Hektor chose to ignore it, knowing that such voices did not speak truth. Like it was said in the psalm he had only just quoted to Rut, though iniquities overwhelmed him, his hope was in the One True God.

"Oh, Hektor…"

He cleared his throat, forcing himself to continue against the naysaying voices in his mind. "I think Karis was sick for longer than I knew, but she didn't say anything because she didn't want to trouble me. We were both stubborn, I suppose, and by the time I realized how serious it was, we didn't have the money to send for a physician and there was nothing I could do to help her."

Rut took in a shaky breath and continued to cry, though he sensed it was not out of fear of the storm or pity for him. The look in her eyes was that of someone who also knew such deep loss. "I'm sorry that you had to go through that. I do not think there are any words known to man that can soothe pain that deep."

"After she died, I lost a part of myself. I was alone and broken, and I remember stumbling upon an inn one night that offered food and drink to passersby. I walked inside without enough money for food, but enough for a drink. I'd never tasted anything so strong, for while my father came home drunk, he didn't keep such drink in the house. If he had, I still would've had no desire to taste it after seeing what it did to him. That night, however, all I wanted to do was forget, and regrettably, I was successful."

"You took the drink?" asked Rut quietly.

"And many more after that. I don't remember much of anything beyond that night for quite some time. Whenever I try to look back on those years, it is like looking around at the world right after you've woken up, before you've fully wiped the crust from your eyes. It's not very clear to me."

"How did you meet Lydia then?"

"I think a part of me wanted to destroy myself, because I did almost nothing except for drinking and fighting, hoping that one day I would be hit hard enough to never wake up. I didn't find Lydia. She found me."

"She *found* you?"

"I was on quite the streak as Philippi's fighter with the most losses. It was the lowest I'd ever been. Lydia found me lying in the *Forum*, dirty, wounded, and sick, and she had her servants take me to her home and tend to me."

Rut shook her head. "But she didn't know you. What reason did she have for doing such a thing?"

Hektor smiled. "That's who Lydia is. She didn't know me, but she saw I needed help. The next thing I remember is waking up in a strange room, writhing in pain. It wasn't just physical pain, but also pain of the mind. Lydia ordered physicians to treat my wounds and called on her servants to tend to me and help me through. I'm afraid those good people saw some of the worst of me during those weeks, but eventually I woke up—truly woke up—and for the first time in a long while, everything was clear. I continued my recovery there and throughout it all, Lydia did not expect anything of me. She merely offered me a place to rest and rebuild my life."

"And you did?"

"Slowly, and with the help of many others. It was hard work training those uglier habits out of my heart, but I fought harder than I ever had before to do it."

"It seems you were successful," said Rut. "I never would have known if you hadn't told me."

"I wasn't successful on my own. It was the Lord's work. Lydia, her servants, and the physicians helped to treat the symptoms, but only God could fully heal me. I read the Psalms while I recovered and began to take delight in the Lord as I learned about who it was Lydia and everyone in her household put their hope in."

"Is that why you are loyal to Lydia?"

"Yes. You see, Lydia sells purple goods to those who want to buy them. I travel with her and see to it that her business is safe and protected from intruders and those who would like to hurt it. Those are our jobs, Rut, but they are not who we are. We are humble servants to the Most High God, the God of the Jewish people. We are willing to step through every door and follow through with every opportunity He gives us in our daily lives. That's my hope, at least."

"That was a beautiful story, Hektor." Rut's voice was barely above a whisper.

"It's your turn now," said Hektor.

"Oh, please, no. I don't have a story like that."

"I'm sorry, but I'm afraid I have to hold you to your word."

She sighed. "What do you want to know?"

"Have you always been afraid of storms?" Hektor asked.

Rut looked downward as she started folding and unfolding the edge of her sleeve again. "A little, I suppose… I never liked them as a child, but growing up I shared a room with my cousin, Shamira. If a storm came at night and I was scared, I pulled my mat closer to hers and slept soundly through the night, so long as I knew I wasn't alone. My husband used to sing during the storms to help distract me. He was so—" Rut cut herself off abruptly, and Hektor wondered what he should do.

"I'm sorry. It must be difficult for you to speak about." Hektor relaxed his arms at his sides.

"No… That is, yes, it hurts, but it's also good."

Hektor could understand that. Even to this day, each happy memory of Karis came with bittersweet feelings, but he wouldn't trade them for anything in the world.

"What was his name?"

"Shem."

"What happened to him?"

"He was shepherding our family's flock of sheep with my brother when a poisonous snake bit him. There was nothing anyone could have done."

"That doesn't make the pain hurt any less," said Hektor.

Her eyes glistened. "No, it doesn't. I think that's part of why I wanted to leave Phoenicia. It just… hurt too much."

"I understand. Some pain never really goes away. Like old fighting wounds that don't quite heal right, we merely learn to live with it."

"Yes," she whispered, "that's *exactly* what it is like."

Silence fell between them and Hektor thought that might have been the end of it and perhaps she would excuse herself. Instead, to Hektor's surprise, Rut raised her voice in question. "Are you afraid of anything?"

"Hm?" Hektor had been too busy thinking about their conversation thus far to comprehend what she said.

"You're not afraid of storms—I know that from experience— and you're not afraid of fighting. Is there anything you fear?"

Hektor made a very serious face, as though he were thinking very hard on his answer. "Butterflies."

She snorted in laughter, and immediately covered her face again. "Butterflies?" she repeated in disbelief.

"I'm terrified of them," he said, shrugging his shoulders. "I don't have a reason. I just am."

"I was not expecting that answer," she said, still laughing lightly. "All butterflies?"

Hektor nodded. "Every last one, and most other small winged creatures. It's my one weakness. I live in fear of the day a butterfly dares to venture into Lydia's home and it becomes my responsibility to fend it off."

She snorted again, and Hektor grinned.

"But in all seriousness, I fear myself," Hektor shared, his voice more solemn then.

"Yourself?"

"I never want to become like my father. I vowed that for the rest of my life, I would never taste such fermented drink again. I never want to go back on that vow."

In a moment that caught Hektor by surprise, she reached out and placed her hand upon his. It was a gentle movement. Her touch was soft, barely there, but he felt it. "I don't believe you would, Hektor. You're a good man."

He looked into her eyes once more, marveling yet again at how dark and completely earnest they were. "I am not a good man, though I appreciate you saying it. I am just like anyone else, but I am able to have strength through the One True God. He'll give us more than enough to weather any storm when we ask it of Him, Rut."

Hektor hoped that she would respond to what he was saying, praying that it would make a difference for her so that she would not have to struggle so much with the burdens she was carrying.

Instead, she scrambled to her feet when the hatch from above opened. "You down there! Are you well?" called the captain.

"We are," Hektor called back. "Everything here is secure."

"Good. The seas may be rough the rest of the night, but the clouds are thinning. The danger seems to have passed."

"Thank you for letting us know." The captain closed the hatch again, then Hektor rose to his feet. "Rut," he began, hoping to finish the conversation they'd started.

"I'm so sorry for the trouble I caused," she said.

"Don't be. I'm here to protect you whether on this voyage, in Philippi, or anywhere else."

"I appreciate that, Hektor, and I thank you for sharing your story with me." She moved to pass him.

"Are you sure you'll be all right?" he asked.

"I'll be fine. I hope you'll be able to get some rest too?"

"Me? There never was a more comfortable hull in these waters." She laughed again at his quip, then quietly disappeared behind the curtain.

Hektor was pleased, though he wished their conversation had not been cut so short. He found that he had enjoyed talking to her. They got along easily with one another, and he'd been able to share memories with Rut that he'd left unspoken for a long time, as everyone he knew in Philippi was already aware of his story. The kindness with which she responded gave Hektor a good feeling regarding the rest of their voyage, as well as the upcoming year.

Whatever was on the horizon, he was eager to see it revealed.

"She makes and sells linen garments; she delivers belts to the merchants" — Proverbs 31:24 CSB

Rut couldn't stop herself from gaping at the sights all around her, from the brilliant blue waters of the sea when they first arrived, to the lush, vibrant green hills they'd passed through, to the bustling and grand city of Philippi. Perhaps it was the weeks spent in total darkness below the ship's decks that made the colors painted on the horizon dance with vibrancy.

On the outside, Philippi itself appeared to be another walled city, but on the inside Rut saw all the ways in which it was unlike anything she'd seen before. Tall structures towered overhead as magnificent works of art made to look pure white in the sunlight, similar and at the same time wholly different from what she'd been used to in Jerusalem. Rut wondered how many cities on this side of the sea looked like this one or if Philippi was truly one of a kind. Some of the buildings' exteriors were adorned with intricate carvings, like tapestries made of stone. Whether they were grand homes or places of business,

Rut could not determine. Everything they passed seemed like a palace to her. Whatever she had expected when she stood on the deck of their ship and watched her brother shrink until he was no longer visible, it could not and did not compare.

"This is the Roman Forum—we'll also pass by the *agora* later." Lydia gestured from side to side as she explained everything in generous detail, though Rut could only half-listen as she took it all in. The Forum itself was constructed in two parts on either side of the road. More accurately, it was *being* constructed, as nearby builders and building materials evidenced that the work was ongoing. As they continued, they passed outdoor theaters, markets with row after row of the most beautiful artisan creations, and so many more structures. Lydia had names for all of them, but Rut couldn't keep them straight.

A thought struck her like a bolt of lightning: what was *she* doing here? She was a weaver who'd spent most of her life in a cramped house in Jerusalem's Lower City, and passed the last several years in relative obscurity with her family in the country. She'd left their valley home in Phoenicia because she didn't belong, but how could she ever belong in a place as grand as this?

"Impressed?" asked Lydia.

Rut straightened her posture. "I've never seen anything like it," she said, struggling to find the right words to describe how she felt. Affluence was painted on every wall, carved into every relief monument. Each person they passed seemed to walk with their head held high, as though they were an important member of society.

"After Philippi became a Roman colony, almost everything within the original Macedonian walls was rebuilt to demonstrate the best of Roman architecture," Lydia explained. "They even made the theatre larger so they could host Roman games, though it was the mines that once brought true value to the city."

"Mines?" asked Rut, unaware of the city's history. Perhaps too unaware. It seemed like all she did lately was ask questions.

"Mostly gold," said Lydia. "That's how Philippi earned its reputation as the 'shining jewel' along the *Via Egnatia.* They're practically empty now, but those who profited from them remain eager to display their wealth."

That was certainly true. It took four full carts to fit Lydia, Hektor, Rut, their belongings, and all of Lydia's acquisitions. They moved at a pace so slow they might as well have been going backward. Rut knew such feelings were extraordinarily exaggerated, but knowing that their journey was so close to an end made Rut all the more anxious to reach their final destination.

As their cart moved through the interminable streets, Rut took note of the women they passed and imagined the lives they must have led. They moved like waterfalls of color in their long tunics and pleated *pallas*. Some had intricate designs woven into their garments; the kind Rut had always dreamed of but never made herself. After all, what use were such clothes among crops and livestock? Others drew attention to themselves with lengths of cloth lined with fringe or beads as even more telling reminders of their position. Were these the kinds of women Lydia counted as customers? What could she possibly have seen in Rut to think that her presence might be able to add anything of value to her business?

"Here we are," said Lydia as the driver finally pulled them to a halt.

"Here?" Rut gaped at what seemed to her another palace, large enough to be its own walled city within a walled city.

Lydia laughed blithely. "Yes, come inside with me and I will show you around."

"What about my things?" asked Rut. "Should I bring them with me?"

Lydia took her hand and pulled her through the entryway. "Someone else will attend to them." Turning her head over her shoulder, she added, "Hektor, will you see to it that it is done? I'm going to give her one of the rooms in the eastern wing."

"Next to yours?"

"That's the one! Now come along, Rut. I'm so excited for you to see everything."

Lydia's pull on Rut's arm nearly made her trip. She was still thinking about how many copies of her family's home she could fit in the courtyard alone when she heard Lydia call it *the first courtyard.*

"There are others?" Rut took note of the colorful mosaic stone floor, so vastly different from the hard packed earth and rough-hewn wood to which she was accustomed. Every aspect of this home had been curated carefully and sparing no expense. Throughout the main courtyard, there were touches of midnight blue, deep red, and vibrant purple, from the meticulously laid tiles to the painted walls. It was an obvious nod to Lydia's business.

"This is where we welcome guests and entertain visitors. We don't do business here," Lydia explained.

"I see." This area was far too grand for business transactions or work. Rut followed Lydia through more chambers. As they went deeper and deeper into the house, it gradually became less and less filled with ornamentation. One room was incredibly large, with grand, looming ceilings.

"This is where we sometimes host gatherings with other God-fearers, and where meals are taken. We have one mid-morning meal and another at the close of day. You can eat here or take the food to your room, though I do hope you'll join us."

"You eat in the same place as everyone? Including the workers and servants?"

"Oh, yes." Lydia smiled. "The only ones who eat separately

are those who work in the kitchen. You're welcome to sit anywhere you like. It's my favorite time of day when we all get to gather together. Some tell stories, and other times we all join together in song."

"That reminds me of my family," Rut mused. Perhaps some things would not be so different after all.

"Do you miss them terribly?" Lydia paused, stepping in front of Rut.

Rut swallowed her emotions back, manipulating her features into a well-practiced, amenable smile. "I am growing used to them not being around after our voyage."

The storm they'd been through that first night had thrown them off course initially, rather than propelling them quicker as Lydia originally suggested it might. Because of that, it took longer to get to Thyatira than the ship's crew intended. Lydia generously purchased more foodstuffs for the crew to replenish their supplies when they stopped in Thyatira, before going the final distance to Macedonia.

The extra nights at sea gave Rut more time to adjust to being on her own, though the transition was still ongoing. She had no idea how she would truly feel until she was finally settled on dry ground, no longer drifting from one location to the next. In a way, Rut found many similarities in her travels compared to life in Phoenicia. In both, she was living only half a life, in between one thing and the next. Now she was finally coming to her destination—or so she hoped.

"The people in this house are like my family." Even though Rut had only seen Lydia interact with Hektor, she had no trouble imagining that Lydia addressed all of her servants with such familiarity. "It is my prayer that in time you will find fulfillment here too, and maybe think of us as a second family."

Fulfillment. That was exactly what Rut wanted.

"This is what we call the worker's courtyard," said Lydia,

pulling Rut into yet another open space, "being that it is in such close proximity to the workshops and looms, and most of the storage rooms are built off of it."

When Rut saw it, she gasped. Somehow it looked just like home. Not her Phoenician home, but the courtyard back in Jerusalem and the way it was before they had been forced to flee. Off to one side, Rut could see into the kitchen and recognized the familiar scent of bread baking. The rest of the area was lined with simple wooden benches. Jars and crates lay around the floor, which itself was made of stone, like the rest of the house, except in this space it was not so polished. It could almost pass for the hard-packed earth on which Rut remembered playing as a child.

Perhaps most magnificent of all, however, was the tree that grew from a bit of raised earth at the center, with a border of rock all around it. It was no date palm tree like the one Rut had grown up with, but it was equally stunning in its simplicity.

"Is my room nearby?" Rut dared to ask.

Lydia smiled. "No, but we'll head back that way now."

She then led Rut through to the opposite side of the worker's courtyard, gesturing in one direction and telling Rut about the fullery, the weaving room, and the supply rooms. They came back to the dining hall from there, and carried on through more decorated passages. In truth, Rut would have been perfectly content to sleep right underneath the tree in the workers' courtyard, but she followed Lydia's lead until they came to an open doorway.

"This is to be your room," said Lydia.

"My own?" As she crossed the threshold, Rut took notice of the bed with lattice-covered windows on either side. When she caught a glimpse of the view, vast and expansive, she stopped in awe of the bright colors that covered the land.

"Your things have already been delivered," said Lydia. Rut

tuned to see her chest of belongings next to the door. She hadn't even noticed it until Lydia pointed it out. How humble it looked in the room that was practically designed for royalty! "I'll leave you alone now to unpack and settle in before the evening meal. Will you be able to find your own way to the dining hall?"

"Yes, I think so, but wouldn't it be more productive if I went back to the workshops? That is why I'm here, after all."

"Rut, you must learn to rest. There will be plenty of time for getting to know the weavers in the months to come, I assure you. For now, relax and make yourself comfortable. You are my guest."

Lydia offered an encouraging smile as she turned to go, but Rut felt unfortunately ill-at-ease. Relax? She wasn't sure she'd ever really known the meaning of the word. After years of doing nothing but working as hard as she could at everything, Rut didn't know how to rest.

"Thank you," Rut called out before Lydia could fully exit. She at least knew how to be well-mannered.

"Thank *you*, Rut. I have a feeling that this year will be my most rewarding yet." With that, Lydia fully left.

Now completely alone, Rut decided to wait to unpack her things and instead laid down upon the bed. The ceiling was so much higher above her than she was used to. The bed, which should've been the most comfortable thing she'd ever felt in her life, was strange to her and she struggled to settle into it. Furthermore, the silence around her only gave her mind more opportunity to fill the void with thoughts of doubt and worry.

She would get used to this.

She had no other choice *except* to get used to it. This was her life now, for at least one year. However it worked out, Rut could always go back to Phoenicia, but she couldn't go back to life the way it was. Something had to change, and it had to be her.

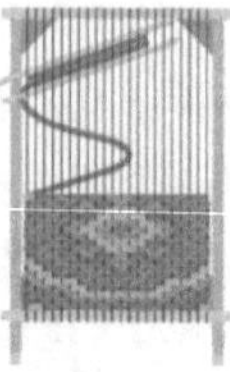

After delivering Rut's belongings to her room, Hektor made his way back to his own cramped sleeping quarters beside the main supply room on the opposite side of the *villa*. His space was more of a closet, really; an annex set aside for him and his few worldly possessions. It was only logical that Hektor stay closest to Lydia's most valuable goods, lest some no-good scoundrel get a foolish idea like trying to steal some of her most precious purple wool in an attempt to sell it off themselves or create a cheap copy. The space wasn't much, but it was enough.

Hektor bent his head and stepped sideways through the narrow doorway, promptly throwing himself down on his mat. How good it felt to finally be still. Hektor craved the feeling of being settled for longer than a night or two. Strangely, Philippi didn't feel the same as he thought it would. Something had changed, or perhaps was in the process of changing within him… But what could it be?

At that moment, Hektor heard the clumsy slipping and sliding of four legs drawing swiftly near. Before Hektor had time to ready himself for the oncoming attack, the old friend pounced upon him, pinning him down upon his mat, licking his face, and making the most amusing and endearing sound, somewhere between a yelp and a whine.

"Hero, my boy!" Hektor bellowed beneath his crushing weight, reaching upward with both hands to scratch the dog behind his ears in his favorite place, and persuade him to move so that Hektor could rise slightly. "How have you been in my absence?" Finally sitting, he pulled back and raised an eyebrow. The dog matched his stance and assumed a seated position, though his tail still wagged behind him, giving away his elated disposition.

Laughing, Hektor continued, "I see the cooks in the kitchen have been feeding you well. You look as if you've gotten more than your fair share of scraps."

Hero barked twice.

"I'm afraid I didn't bring back anything for you from my travels." Hektor reached for the sack he'd dropped on the ground when he first walked in. He pulled apart its ties and began to unpack his spare clothes. "It was certainly an eventful voyage this time. I'm not sure I can recall another like it."

With a whine that seemed to beckon Hektor to continue, Hero laid down completely and inclined his head forward, resting it on his two front paws. Hektor obliged and prattled on, detailing a list of locations, the weather in each, and the constitution of the people they met and with whom they interacted.

"It was mostly the same as every other year. I can't say that I enjoyed it very much, but there is nothing like the smell of the air at sea, or the view of the sunrise as it crests the horizon and makes the whole ocean light up with glittering colors..." Hektor's mind got away from him as he recalled some of those splendorous views. They made all the other less desirable parts of travel well worth it. "Yes, the Lord is quite the artisan."

Hero stood up on all fours and jumped in the air, showing off his abilities with a spin before resuming his previous relaxed stance.

"Glad to see you are in agreement." Hektor laughed. "Although, there was something unusual that happened when we arrived in Tyre."

Hero leaned back and tilted his head as if to say, "*You've been holding out on me!*" He pawed at the ground like he was urging

Hektor to continue talking. Hektor often wondered if Hero really could understand him or if the loving creature simply liked the sound of human voices. Sometimes he liked to imagine what Hero would say if he could talk back.

"Lydia picked up more than wool there. She picked up a new weaver, and a very talented one, too! A woman called *Rut.*"

Bark!

"I think you'd like her, Hero. She's quiet at first—totally unlike you—but once she opens up, it is quite clear that she has a kindhearted nature, and a sharp wit. She has a way about her I struggle to describe… It is as though when I am around her, I can't help but say the most foolish things."

Bark! Bark!

"All right, then, more foolish than usual. Maybe it is because she is so easy to talk to. She is…"

Hektor stopped to allow his mind to recreate the vision of her sitting across from him below the decks during the night of the storm, lit only by a single oil lamp hung in the dark cabin. He remembered with unfailing clarity how the light flickered every few moments, nearly disappearing with each jolt the ship took during the storm. That meager light source lit Rut from above, revealing dark, bronze tones in the masses of otherwise black curls that grew well past her shoulders, trailing down her back and below her waist.

"She's beautiful, Hero. Perhaps the most beautiful woman I think I've ever seen, but I think she might be struggling."

Hero whined.

"Sort of like I was when you and I first met. Do you remember? I was accompanying Mistress Lydia in the Forum when you attached yourself to us, following us all the way home. Of all the households you could've picked, you certainly picked a good one. You were a good friend to me when I was going through a difficult time."

Bark!

"On her first night aboard the ship, she was so frightened by the storm. I think she's still frightened. If only there was a way we could make her feel safe here."

As Hektor pondered the thought, Hero moved closer to him before rolling onto his back and exposing his belly, desperate for the affection and approval of his master.

"That's it!" Hektor shouted, making Hero jump and dash toward the doorway. "Hero, boy, you've just given me an idea!"

Hektor had a plan, and Hero was going to be a part of it whether he liked it or not. "Oh, Lord, thank you for your presence in my life," Hektor prayed aloud, unable to contain his excitement. "Let this plan be a good one!" Looking down at Hero, Hektor clapped his hands. "Come on, my boy, we have to go ask Lydia for help! It may be that I did bring something back for you after all... or someone."

Rut paced the floor of the room, puttering around as she organized her things. She still couldn't call it her own, but as she began to unpack, it started to feel less like the temporary accommodations of an inn, and more like a place she could settle into long-term. When Lydia first left her alone, she'd been overcome by doubts and questions, but she had since pushed those aside, forcing herself to make progress. Her heart still beat a little faster, but hard work was a good distraction. She hung some of her spare work clothes on pegs already affixed to the wall, keeping her more ornate garments tucked away. After that was done, she moved the chest closer to her bed to serve as a kind of table.

Satisfied with the arrangement, Rut opened up the chest again and reached for the few personal items her family sent with her. The first things she retrieved were the little bundles of wool given to her by Yemima and Kelila. At that moment, all her progress at ignoring her feelings was dashed. She knew this was what she wanted, but that didn't make the transition any easier. If anything, it made it worse, because she found herself longing to be in both places at the same time.

Rut held the bundles close to her face and breathed in the scent of home before placing them carefully under her stuffed mattress where they would be kept safe and close to her when she slept. After examining the rest of her belongings—some coin given to her by her abba, her old spindle, her finer clothes, and her satchel—she re-organized them in the chest so that more common things could be more easily reached, and things she would not need as frequently were buried more deeply.

Finally, she walked to the opposite side of the room where there hung a hazy mirror. Standing in front of it, she pulled her mass of curls free from the knot she'd tightened them into at the base of her head and let them fall loose. She shook her head from side to side, letting the strands relax and feeling the relief all the way down to her toes. When she looked back in the mirror, she laughed at the sight of herself, with her hair nearly double the width of her shoulders.

A memory of Shem came to mind. Like the vision of herself in the mirror, it was dim and blurry, but still there in the shadows—the memories of whispered conversations in the dark. "*I love your hair,*" he had said. "*My hair?*" she questioned. He held her face with one hand as he kissed her gently, and tugged at a ringlet that framed her face with the other, making the curl bounce. "*You're so beautiful, Rut.*"

Then, less sweet came the memories of all the times she shirked his praise. There was a time earlier in their marriage that such kind words made her melt into his arms, but as the years went on, Rut found it increasingly difficult to accept a compliment from her husband without her own mind filling it in with criticisms of herself. Why did she have such a stubborn, unyielding predisposition to notice the flaws in something first?

Rut contemplated the answer to that question while entwining her curls into a relaxed braid that would not pull at her scalp quite so tightly. It took some effort, since weaving her own hair required much more strength than weaving thin strands of wool into compliance with her designs. Satisfied with her appearance and realizing by the fiery red cast of the sunlight through the lattice window what time it was, she went to open the door and make her way to join the others for the evening meal. As she did so, she was knocked backward by a strong gust of wind blowing past her with such force that she nearly fell onto her backside.

"Oh!" She scrambled to the back wall of her room, cornered by an unfamiliar four-legged creature.

"Hero!" Another deeper voice boomed. Rut looked to the doorway with pleading eyes, at first unable to see whose shadowy form stood at the threshold. Upon further inspection, it became obvious that the broad-shouldered figure of her would-be rescuer belonged to none other than Hektor.

Immediately, the dog became far less threatening to Rut. With a whimper, he flopped onto his back and raised his paws, and if Rut were not so out of breath from the surprise of it all, she would have giggled at his silly appearance. He had long, gangly limbs and ears that seemed to hang crooked, with a toothy grin that left his tongue hanging halfway out of his mouth. It was clear that this dog was a gentle giant, like his master.

"Hektor, what are you—"

"I'm sorry for Hero's entrance." Hektor whistled and the dog immediately bobbled toward him, sitting at attention by Hektor's feet. "He is always happy to meet new people, but I think that this time I might have said something about you to make him overly-excited."

"You talked to the dog—I mean, *Hero*—about me?" Rut raised an eyebrow.

Hektor laughed. "Oh, Hero and I talk about everything. There's not a better companion on this side of Crete."

Rut relaxed and moved out of the corner of the room, no longer intimidated by the beast. She realized Hero was not the only thing Hektor had brought with him. Held under one arm were a series of wooden beams in varying widths and lengths, but Rut could see that these were not ordinary pieces of wood.

"Is that a…" Her voice trailed off as she realized she didn't need to finish the question.

"A loom? Indeed!" With his other arm, Hektor held up a mallet. "Would you mind if I set it up for you?"

"Are there not looms in the weaving room?"

Hektor tilted his head to the side, failing to conceal half of a mischievous grin. "Yes, but those are for work."

"Is that not what this is?" Slowly, a smile crept across Rut's own face against her will. She found herself unable to resist the charm of Hektor's positive demeanor whenever he was near.

"This is for you alone. For personal use."

Rut blinked several times. "Where did it come from? Does Lydia know?'

"She is the one who helped me obtain it. I asked her if we might be able to find an old loom to give you. I know this place is new and strange, so I thought that if you had a loom of your own, it might feel more like a home."

"Oh, Hektor…. I don't know what to say." Who was this man to show such kindness to her, when she was so unworthy and undeserving of this extra attention? Surely not all who came as guests to Lydia's household were treated so extravagantly? Why was she special to them? *To him?*

"Is it all right?"

"All right? Hektor, I'm thrilled, but this is… I cannot accept it."

"Technically speaking, you can. The question is, will you? And please say that you will, because there's more."

"More?" Rut gaped at him.

"You have to say you accept before I can reveal anything else."

"Fine, I accept." Rut laughed nervously and felt her cheeks blush.

"Good!" Hektor released the wood from his arms, pushing the pile inside of Rut's room. "Because the loom also comes with *this.*" Reaching into the hall, Hektor pulled forth a basket full of woolen bundles.

"Hektor, no!" She hesitantly reached for the basket, daring to move the bundles around and seeing loom weights as well. "It's too much."

"You already agreed, remember?"

"But these are—"

"Gifts. When Lydia heard my idea about the loom, she insisted you have some of these as well. They are small bundles and they won't be missed. We want you to feel at home here, so please don't object again. Just tell me where you would like me to set it up."

"Here is fine," said Rut, gesturing to an empty space on the wall adjacent to the doorway. Immediately, Hektor got to work securing the base and vertical beams. Parts of the process, like setting the weights, were things Rut knew how to do herself.

"Thank you," she whispered, feeling awkward as she watched him work.

Hektor paused from his work momentarily to look up at her, his blue eyes sending cool chills down her spine. "It's what friends are for."

"Well, maybe I'm out of practice at having friends."

"What do you think of Hero?" asked Hektor, turning his attention back to the assembly of the loom.

"He's... large."

"Ah, yes, he definitely has the size of a brave warrior, but I assure you that he's harmless. Have you ever been around a dog before?"

"I knew of those who kept dogs trained to help with the herding of sheep, but we never had any of our own."

"Well, the only thing Hero is trained for is protecting and listening."

"What is he listening for?"

"Not for anything in particular, really, but he listens to me when I talk. The nice thing about talking to an animal is this: they never judge what you say, and they'll always be loyal to you."

Briefly, Rut wondered if Shem ever talked to the sheep. She realized quickly that he must have, for all sheep knew to listen and follow the voice of their shepherd. Did he find the same comfort in sharing conversation with them as Hektor described? What sorts of things would Shem have said if he knew no one was listening but the animals?

"I never thought of it that way," said Rut.

Finally having fastened all the beams of the loom together, Hektor stepped back to examine his work. Silence fell between them for only a moment before it was quickly broken by one short, resounding bark from Hero.

"I'm getting there, Hero," Hektor chided the dog before bending down to scratch Hero's head just behind his crooked ears. "Don't worry, my boy. I wouldn't forget."

Two more barks followed, and the dog began wagging his tail in a back-and-forth motion. Rut laughed again, amused by his silly but endearing mannerisms. Hektor was right; this dog did seem to understand conversation, and he liked to make himself a part of it.

"What did Hero think you forgot?" asked Rut, self-consciously clasping her hands together and holding them beneath her face where the remnants of a smile were probably still evident.

"Well…" Hektor shifted his weight from his left side to his right. Slowly, he looked up at her with his sea-blue eyes and spoke in low tones. "It's about that first night on the ship and the conversation we shared. Do you remember?"

Rut nodded ruefully. She winced at the memory of how she had let her emotions control her. She always tried so hard to keep that part of herself hidden from her family and loved ones, and yet it only took half a day for her to break apart in front of Hektor. "I do, and I'm sorry about that. I shouldn't have—"

"You shouldn't have been frightened by something so wholly new? If anything, we should be apologizing to you for not seeing sooner how overwhelmed you must have been. Do not be sorry for crying out for help."

With every word Hektor spoke, it was as though a great wave came crashing down upon Rut. It was not another wave of embarrassment, but a cleansing wave. How many nights had she tossed and turned, wishing she would have said or done something differently? Behaved in a certain way? Made a different impression? The truth was that she did need help that night on the ship, and she was grateful to Hektor for giving it to her.

"I am thankful to you, more than you can ever know. I realize now how dangerous of a situation I put you in. I just…"

"I am not owed an explanation, but as I told Hero earlier

today, I made a promise to you that night, and it is one I intend to keep. I want you to know that you are safe here. Of course, I won't be right outside of your door, but that's where Hero comes in."

"It is?" Rut looked down at the dog, surprised to see him already staring at her with wide, expectant eyes.

"Hero will be outside of your door tonight, and every night after that. I've charged him with protecting you, and he is fully aware of his duties. You'll likely never find a more faithful servant, and should you ever find yourself in need of someone to talk to—late at night, early in the day, or anytime in between—Hero will gladly listen."

The gesture touched Rut. When Hero seemed to smile at her as he panted for breath, she had a feeling that they would get along just fine. "Thank you, Hektor, and *you*, Hero."

"I want you to know that you need never feel alone here. You've already got friends who are willing to be there for you. Now, shall I walk with you to dinner?"

Rut heaved a sigh of relief. "That would be wonderful."

He offered her his arm, and they made their way to the grand hall together. She took part in the meal, eating the most delicious array of colorful fruits, crisp, green vegetables, savory cheeses, sweet honey, and freshly baked bread, all while meeting the weavers, spinners, and fullers that Lydia employed. She tried to keep their names straight, but knew it would take time before she had them memorized.

Lydia was right; this was a kind of family, and Rut felt no awkwardness in becoming a part of it. After the meal, Rut went back to her room with Hero trailing close behind. As Hektor said the dog would do, Hero laid down beyond her threshold, whining softly as if to wish her good rest before drifting off into his own deep slumber.

For the first time in a long time, Rut rested.

Part Three

"But everything that was a gain to me, I have considered to be a loss because of Christ. More than that, I also consider everything to be a loss in view of the surpassing value of knowing Christ Jesus my Lord. Because of him I have suffered the loss of all things and consider them as dung, so that I may gain Christ and be found in him, not having a righteousness of my own from the law, but one that is through faith in Christ — the righteousness from God based on faith." — Philippians 3:7-9 CSB

"The Lord is near the brokenhearted; he saves those crushed in spirit." — Psalm 34:18 CSB

Three Months Later

"Do you think this will be all right?" asked Rut as she exited from her chamber.

"What did you say?" said Hektor, blinking in wonder and bewilderment. He'd heard the words, but required extra time to gather his wits and come up with a response that would be at least adequate, though he could not think of words with deep enough meaning to describe her beauty.

"Lydia told me that we were going to visit some of her oldest, most well-to-do clients, and that I should wear my best clothing, but I feel rather odd dressing so formally when I am merely a shepherd's daughter. Do you think it is too much?"

Clearing his throat, he responded, "I think you look perfect."

She dropped her hands to her sides and tilted her chin slightly downward, looking up at him with a pointed gaze. The sunset-toned cloth emphasized the depth of her dark brown eyes. "Perfection is a thing I shall never attain, Hektor, but thank you."

Hektor laughed lightly. She was so matter-of-fact and always strong in how she expressed herself. It did not escape his notice that her confidence seemed to grow exceedingly with each passing day. Her personality unfolded like a tapestry, at first appearing small but quickly revealing itself as grand, intricate, and the most eye-catching thing in any room. Rut was just like that. It was impossible to pass her in a room and not stop to look at her, to marvel at every part of her. While her heart remained mostly hidden, every so often, Hektor could catch a glimpse of it in a kind word, a gentle glance, or a wistful smile when she thought no one was looking.

"Do you need me to carry anything for you?" asked Hektor politely. Being that this was Rut's first visit to Xanthe's, Lydia had sent Hektor to make sure Rut was ready and escort them both across town to the place where Xanthe and her daughter lived.

"No, I don't think so. We are just going to speak with them, right?"

Hektor nodded. "How much has Lydia told you about the people you are going to meet today?"

"Not much," said Rut, pulling the strap of her satchel onto her shoulder and tucking some stray curls behind her ears. Hektor was pleased to see through the doorway that a small project hung from Rut's loom. "I don't really understand what I'm meant to do. When Lydia mentioned it to me, I thought she was just letting me know about her plans. I assumed my day would go on as normal and I would keep teaching the other women at the looms and helping the spinners practice, until Lydia told me that she wanted me to accompany her."

"Well, I can't speak for Mistress Lydia's plans, but I can tell you a bit about Xanthe while we walk to meet Lydia at the front of the house. That might give you more of an idea of what to expect."

Rut let out a sigh and closed the door to her room. "I would appreciate that very much. Thank you, Hektor."

"You could say that Xanthe was something akin to a patron to Lydia when she first brought her business to Philippi, or so I've gathered. When Lydia, a woman alone *and* a woman from Thyatira arrived, doors did not open easily for her."

"I always wondered what that must have been like… That is, for Lydia to come to a place foreign to her, where she knew nothing and no one, to build up a business."

"Lydia is confident, and she always has been. I think she would have found her footing even if she hadn't met Xanthe, but from what I've gathered, they found each other and have been close ever since."

"Would Xanthe be considered a friend, then?" asked Rut, looking over her shoulder at Hektor. He felt the intensity of her gaze as they walked.

Hektor shook his head. "Not in the usual way. There is a familiarity between them, but it is a carefully balanced relationship with firmly placed boundaries. They sometimes come close to crossing them, but at the end of the day, Lydia is still the seller of purple goods, and Xanthe is still the buyer. You'll find Xanthe to be…"

"Difficult?" said Rut, bluntly filling in the end of the sentence.

Hektor mulled over the word in his mind, but found it unsatisfactory. "I wouldn't say that. I think Xanthe is a good woman at heart, but she has her own burdens to bear just like the rest of us."

"Did something to happen to her?"

Hektor looked down at the ground, considering each of his

steps as he considered what he would share next. Clasping his hands behind his back, he continued, "I can't say exactly, but when it comes to what your role is in all of this, I think Lydia asked you to accompany her for two reasons. The first and primary reason being to show you off to Xanthe. She is Lydia's most loyal customer, and orders everything to be specially made."

Rut gasped. "I know we spend all day producing purple goods for others, but the thought of having someone else make my clothes and linens for me is still baffling."

"It certainly is a strange world we find ourselves in," Hektor agreed. "In any case, Lydia is likely hoping to help you make connections of your own by displaying your talents to Xanthe. She may make demands of you, but it should give you no cause to doubt yourself. Xanthe is demanding of everyone."

"What do you suppose is the second reason behind Lydia's decision to bring me along?"

"Remember" — Hektor lifted a finger — "this is only my guesswork. I don't know any more than you do, but I suspect she hopes that you will be able to help Xanthe with more than just her textile needs."

"Me? How?"

"Everyone has a story." Hektor paused his speech as he grappled with the few details he knew about Xanthe and her daughter. Admittedly, it wasn't much, but after so many years of accompanying Lydia on her visits, and hearing Xanthe's own servants talk, there were a few things Hektor knew for certain. "Xanthe's is somewhat of a painful one. She masks her pain well and disguises her need for companionship as needs for new clothes and tapestries."

"Holding so much inside... It can eat you alive," Rut whispered. Hektor would've responded in agreement but the whisper was at a volume so low that he sensed Rut did not intend for anyone to hear it. He waited instead for her to speak again. "Thank you for telling me all of this, Hektor," she said as they reached the exterior door.

"Of course," Hektor replied. Then, stopping in his tracks, he held out his hand to signal Rut to do the same. He wanted to make sure that she knew the truth of his heart before they joined with Lydia on the other side of the door. "I will always try to do whatever I can to help you, Rut."

She looked up at him, eyes staring right into his but looking somewhere else entirely. "I believe you. Now," she said, turning, "what shall we do about our mutual acquaintance, here?"

Hero sat behind them, tail wagging.

"He knows when he's meant to stay here and mind things. Don't you, boy?"

Hero settled down with a contented sigh.

"He is a faithful friend," said Rut, before adding, "like you." Stepping outside, Rut greeted Lydia and resumed talking about the day's activities and what was yet to come. Hektor followed his usual two paces behind, keeping a steady eye on them both, as was his job.

Lydia knocked three times on the large wooden door. Rut waited expectantly at her side while Hektor stood behind them, and another one of Lydia's servants waited with a cart of samples in the street. Nervously, Rut smoothed her outer dress as they waited for someone to respond. The choices she'd made today were bold, even for the marketplaces in Tyre or Sidon, but when she looked at her reflection in the hazy mirror, she didn't see a widow. She saw a woman dressed befitting her station as a skilled weaver. She walked the line between artisan craftswoman and modest woman of Jewish birth.

In that reflection, Rut saw *herself.*

"Where did you find these garments?" asked Lydia. "I presume you made them, but I've never seen them before."

"You said to wear my best clothes. These are—" Before Rut could finish her explanation of where each item had come from and how she'd never really had reason to wear them all at once, the heavy wooden door slowly moaned as its hinges struggled to heave its weight. Rut saw how thick the wood was that made up the ornately carved door and once again marveled at the excess of building construction on this side of the sea. As a young girl, the grandest building she'd ever laid eyes on was the temple in Jerusalem. The same amount of detail seemed to be put into every Greek or Roman home they passed when they walked through the streets of Philippi and Rut could not help but wonder why. These buildings were made to house mere men, yet they displayed a level of extraordinary care as though they were made to house deities.

"Good day to you, Mistress Lydia," said the unfamiliar servant.

"And to you. I've come at Xanthe's invitation. I've brought with me some samples, as well as Rut, a weaver whose skills I think Xanthe will want to see for herself."

"It's good to meet you, Mistress Rut." The servant bowed his head slightly in Rut's direction.

"The pleasure is all mine," said Rut politely.

The servant turned back to Lydia. "She is expecting you in the garden."

"Thank you." With that, Lydia passed through the door and

motioned for Rut to follow, walking with as much comfortability as if this were her own home. Hurriedly, Rut jumped forward to be at her side. When she did so, Lydia leaned in to whisper, "Xanthe's not going to be in a good mood today."

"How do you know that?" asked Rut.

"Whenever Xanthe is upset about something, she takes it out on her flowers."

Rut looked over her shoulder to see Hektor. He gave her a reassuring nod, and somehow, it gave her all the confidence she needed. What was it about Hektor that made her feel so secure?

They came to a halt in an open doorway, just before a series of steps leading down. Whatever Rut expected when the servant said 'garden' did not come close to what she found in that space. It was a sanctuary of serenity, protected from intruders of all kinds by high walls covered in curtains of trailing vines. Around its borders were various raised beds of earth covered in blankets of white and purple flowers that contrasted spectacularly with the brilliant greens naturally present.

In each of the four corners of the garden stood a fruit-bearing tree. Rut's eyes were drawn to the pool of brilliant blue water in the center, surrounded by long, lounge-style chairs covered in an excess of patterned blankets and cushions—all made in the same purple.

Lydia's purple.

"Good morning, Xanthe. It's been far too long."

"Lydia! You've finally returned," said a woman, rising from the seat where she had been reclined. If Rut had not seen her move, she would have been convinced that Xanthe was a statue. Her features were nearly too perfect. Even though she was older, she remained a paragon of Macedonian beauty. Rut took note of her narrow nose and lips, high-arched eyebrows, and almond-shaped eyes, accentuated by long, feathery lashes. Her light blonde hair grew long past her waist and was styled in a variety of braids, more complicated and intricate than any pattern Rut had ever woven into her own hair—or maybe even in wool.

"Oh, Lydia! We've missed you so much," said a girl who did not rise, clearly Xanthe's daughter by her looks. She had a soft-spoken, breathy voice—a stark contrast to her mother's lower, more commanding way of speaking.

"Well I hope you got *something* out of your travels. Things were so very dull here for me and Mena without you." Xanthe walked toward them with her hands clasped in front of her. She moved with such poise and precision that she practically floated.

Lydia laughed blithely. "There was much business to attend to when I returned, or I would have come to you sooner. Still, I believe you'll be pleased by the things I've brought."

"I hope so! I have so much to order from you."

"Then we'd better start looking through the samples," said Lydia.

Rut stood still, wondering what she was supposed to do when another servant cleared their throat. Rut immediately jumped out of their way when she realized they were carrying Lydia's samples with them. The servant set them down, and Lydia began going through them with Xanthe. All the while, Rut stood in the entryway still unsure.

"And," Lydia continued after what felt like ages, "I must also introduce you to my latest discovery." She turned to Rut with an expression that bordered on pride. Rut blushed, suddenly feeling quite diffident in the presence of such well-to-do people. "This is Rut, a weaver I found in Tyre. She has graciously accepted an invitation to stay with me as a guest in my home and advise my spinners and weavers."

"Tyre? Where they say some of the best purples come from?" Xanthe raised an eyebrow and looked Rut up and down. Rut stuttered under her scrutiny, but before she could manage to force even one word from her lips, Xanthe continued on. "Well,

I can see you're very talented. Both of you, come and sit in the garden. I want to hear *everything*."

Lydia moved toward a cushioned bench and Rut lifted the edge of her skirt to follow as fast as she could, leaning forward to whisper to Lydia, "What about Hektor?"

"Don't worry, he'll wait just inside. He always stays close enough to hear if we need help, but far enough away to remain respectful and allow for privacy," Lydia whispered back.

"I see," said Rut, still hovering very close to Lydia's side. She was, after all, the only person in the room with whom Rut was well acquainted.

"Sit, sit!" Xanthe commanded, assuming her previous reclined position. Lydia took her seat, and Rut did the same, choosing the one between Xanthe and the girl, who had been called Mena.

Though the accommodations were comfortable, Rut's spine remained stiff as she struggled to relax. For close to an hour, Lydia and Xanthe went back and forth with each other while Xanthe asked a myriad of travel-related questions and Lydia divulged the details of her voyage, both before and after she had picked up Rut.

At no point was Rut called upon to add anything, nor did Mena interject in the conversation, though Rut and Mena shared a few smiles and glances at humorous moments. Gradually, Rut began lowering herself into the opulent colored cushions, becoming as at-ease in her surroundings as Lydia—or at least coming close. As the other women talked, Rut absentmindedly began to pinch the fabric of the cushions together with her fingers, subconsciously taking note of its construction and the weight of the material, dissecting the patterns, and attempting to ascertain how they were achieved. She had nearly figured it out when she once again heard her name spoken.

"And that's how I found Rut," said Lydia, finishing a story

Rut did not hear start.

"Tell me about yourself, Rut," said Xanthe, turning her head abruptly in Rut's direction. Her braided hair swung over her shoulders as she did so, revealing to Rut the exact cut of her dress.

Philippi as a city had Greek origins, but now with Macedonia's status as a Roman province, Rut had noticed most of the Gentile women preferred to dress in the Roman style. Over their tunics, which varied from short to long sleeves, they wore the *stola*—a sleeveless overdress that went all the way to the floor. To accessorize, a palla was thrown over one shoulder. The palla was like any other shawl or veil, but it could stretch all the way to the floor, and was significantly wider than any practical mantle Rut had seen.

Xanthe's personal style was decidedly Greek. Although similar to its Roman counterpart, it was an obvious intentional choice. Rather than a simple stola, Xanthe wore a *peplos* garment, which had added folds of fabric at the top and was cinched in by a belt to accentuate the figure. The garments were fastened together with decorative metal clasps. Over her arms, she also carried a *himation*, a mantle which differed from its Roman counterpart only in how it was draped.

Whatever kind of story Xanthe had, she was clearly trying to tell a part of it with her style of dress.

"I'm not sure there's much to say, really," said Rut, relinquishing the cushion from her grasp and politely resting her hands in her lap. "My family were shepherds—"

"Shepherds!" Xanthe half-gasped, half-laughed. "Lydia, you didn't tell me that she was so provincial!"

Lydia raised a finger. "That is precisely why I was so impressed! She possesses all-natural talent and is completely self-taught."

Rut realized at once that Lydia was trying to soften the shock of Rut's humble background for Xanthe.

"Well, I wouldn't say that," Rut humbly corrected, hoping that she did not come across as rude. She further explained, "All the women in my family worked together to make clothes and other things for our household."

"In any case, it was your weaving that caught my eye in the marketplace. Do you see her dress, Xanthe? It is one of the ones she made herself using only the simplest of looms! She has been instructing my own spinners and weavers during her visit here, but I thought you might want to try some of her work for yourself."

Rut wanted to respond with a degree of modesty, but she sensed that Lydia was no longer speaking as a friend, and instead as a businesswoman trying to sell her skills to Xanthe. Though she was uncomfortable with the lavish praise, she kept her lips sealed and watched how Lydia guided the situation.

"Come closer so that I can have a look at it," Xanthe ordered. Rut did as she was told, surprised by how casually Xanthe gripped her overdress and pulled the hem so close to her face. Rut nearly lost her balance.

"Well? What do you think?" Lydia prompted.

"I think…" Xanthe pulled away and squinted, then released Rut. "I think you're exactly right, Lydia. She is the most talented weaver I've ever seen, and she couldn't have come at a better time. I want to order an entirely new collection of garments for Mena."

"Oh, Mother, I wish you wouldn't," said the girl, her airy voice barely reaching more than a whisper. "The clothes I have are in perfectly good condition."

"Nonsense," Xanthe dismissed her. "You know how the styles for young women Mena's age are always changing, Lydia. I want my daughter to have only the best."

"Well, Xanthe, it is really up to Rut. I can of course supply the materials, but Rut does not work for me. You'll have to ask her if she is willing to negotiate a price for her work."

Xanthe did not ask. She simply raised her eyebrows in Rut's direction, and it took Rut far too long to realize she was meant to respond. "It would be an honor to weave some things for your daughter."

The next words out of Xanthe's mouth were regarding payment. She suggested a sum of money larger than Rut had ever even contemplated earning on her own and she sought Lydia's look of approval before agreeing verbally.

"Splendid!" Lydia clapped her hands. "Now that we have the details worked out, why don't we take another look at the samples I brought? Once you describe some of what you're looking for, Rut can take whatever measurements she needs."

A whole new collection of garments! This would be a challenge for Rut, if she was indeed to be the lone weaver in charge of this task. Even so, the prospect excited her. Rut truly was a weaver now, known by her own merit and earning a wage.

"Wonderful!" said Xanthe. Lydia brought over the samples and Xanthe held each of them up to Mena's face, judging how well they complemented her complexion, testing how they draped, and at no point asking for anyone's opinion but her own. Then, after selecting *her* favorites, she began to describe to Rut the kinds of patterns she was hoping to see incorporated. Most of the garments would be light in color, with threads of deeper purple woven in strategically to create fashionable borders. Xanthe spared no detail in making sure Rut understood exactly what was expected.

"I think three complete sets of garments will be more than enough," said Xanthe after she was finished describing what the first two ought to look like. "Mena can pick out whatever styles she wants for the third, but you must use the shades I chose. Anything else will make her look too pale."

"Why don't I start taking measurements while you describe what you want to me?" asked Rut, finally turning to Mena. In truth, she was eager to hear the girl's ideas. She'd been so quiet, but from their earlier silent interactions, Rut could sense they would share a kinship of sorts. Opening her satchel, she pulled out a cord that measured exactly one cubit long.

"All right." Mena smiled, her whole face lighting up for the first time since Rut had arrived. Slowly, she moved to get up, tossing the blanket under which she'd been curled up aside.

"Mena," Xanthe sighed. "Why don't I send for someone to help you?"

"Please don't, mother. I am well," said Mena, waving her off.

"I'll call one of the servants."

Mena let out a sigh when she was finally standing upright. "There. See? I can stand up on my own."

Rut glanced back and forth between them, and all at once it hit her. There was the breathiness—or *breathlessness*—in her voice, the way she barely moved all day, remaining still even when stifling her laughter, and now the way Xanthe, who had otherwise come across as stern and reserved, suddenly became soft and nurturing… Mena was not well.

Whatever ailed her, Rut did not know, but a pang of compassion twisted and tugged at her heart.

"I'll be quick." Rut smiled reassuringly and set to her task. She measured Mena's height, the length of her arms, the distance from her shoulders to her natural waist. She couldn't help but notice how tiny Mena was, and how cold, even though the garden was quite warm in the light of the sun. Rut took each measurement twice, counting the number of cubits in her mind and ensuring that they would be committed to her memory.

"Very well, then." When Xanthe turned back to Lydia and began to speak in lower tones, Rut realized she had an opportunity to speak to Mena alone and she took it.

"How old are you, Mena?" asked Rut as she worked.

"Oh." Mena giggled. "I've seen eighteen summers."

"You're eighteen?" Rut hoped that Mena couldn't hear the shock in her voice. She was not the young girl Rut first assessed her to be.

She nodded. "I know; I look younger. If you don't mind me asking, how old are you?"

Rut didn't want to answer the question at first, though she knew Mena's intentions were purely out of curiosity. "A bit older than you," said Rut, side-stepping the answer. The years since she had been Mena's age seemed so long as she lived them, but looking back now, they had passed her by in the blink of an eye.

"Does that mean we could be sisters?" said Mena, eyes widening as the corners of her mouth turned up in a soft smile.

"Well, I… Yes, I suppose so." The look on Mena's face made Rut give over to smiles and giggles too.

"Do you have any sisters of your own?"

Rut shook her head. "Just a brother, and many cousins, though I've always wanted a younger sister."

"Then I suppose you should know that my full name is Philomena, though everyone calls me Mena."

"Who is everyone?" Rut asked.

"Mostly just my mother, I suppose, and some of the servants. I don't know many other people, but you may call me whatever you like," she explained.

"Hm… Which do you prefer?"

With a twinkle in her eye, the young woman replied, "Philomena."

"Then that is what I shall call you, Philomena." Rut grinned as she took the last measurement she needed. "You may sit back down now."

"What was it like? Growing up in a family of shepherds?"

Philomena asked the question as though she were searching for an intriguing story and it nearly made Rut snort with laughter. She couldn't imagine thinking her ordinary lifestyle was anything worthy of note, but she indulged Philomena's questions anyway.

"Smelly," Rut joked.

"What were the sheep like?"

"Silly!" At that, both of them laughed, and Rut nearly spilled out the contents of her satchel as she was trying to pack up her instruments again.

"Did you have any dogs? I heard some shepherds keep dogs to help with the herding."

"My family never did, but Lydia's house has a dog to guard the place. His name is Hero."

"Oh, really? I never knew that. What's he like?"

"Well..." Rut paused, feeling a warmth inside as she remembered how Hektor had appeared at her doorstep, arms full of gifts. "He's a very good listener. You can practically have full conversations with him, and he'll look at you as though he is hanging on your every word."

"He listens when you talk? I've never heard such a thing."

"It's true," Lydia confirmed. Rut startled when she remembered the others were still there in the garden.

"Oh, Mother, do you think Rut and Lydia could bring Hero next time they visit? I've always wanted to see a dog!"

Xanthe pursed her lips. "Mena, they are such filthy creatures..."

"Please?" Philomena pleaded anyway. "I think it would be very amusing."

"All right," Xanthe acquiesced, then turned back toward Lydia, adding, "How could I refuse my only daughter?"

"I can't wait to meet Hero, Rut. Do you think he'll listen to me if I talk? I don't have many friends."

"Hero is a friend to everyone, Philomena. Now, let's discuss what you would like for your last dress."

Philomena pulled a blanket over herself, laying down on her side and positioning a cushion so that she could rest her head upon it. Rut knelt down beside her.

"My request is a bit unusual." Philomena's voice was shaky, but whether that was from her mysterious illness or from nervousness, Rut could not tell. She did not yet know her well enough.

"What is it?" asked Rut, shifting her weight.

"I was wondering… Could you make me something more in the Roman style?"

"Of course! Is it because it is more popular?"

"My father is Roman, and I was hoping…" Philomena's voice trailed off into silence.

Rut leaned in, pressing Philomena's hands between her own, giving them a gentle but reassuring squeeze. "Are you not close with your father, Philomena?"

Philomena shook her head, and her eyes filled with tears. She blinked them back, and Rut knew she was being brave. "Were you close with your father? Before you came here?"

If Rut were not so well-practiced at hiding her own feelings, she might have cried with Philomena. How could she answer honestly, without giving everything away? Or without making Philomena feel worse? She sucked in a quick breath. "Everyone's relationships are different, Philomena. My abba and I have certainly had some difficult times in the past, but we've always worked through them. I'm sure you will too."

"I barely even know my father, but I know that he was once a soldier in the Roman Army. I hoped that if I dressed in the Roman style that it might get his attention."

Rut's brows moved closer together as she processed what Philomena was saying. "I thought that Roman soldiers weren't allowed to—"

It was in that moment that Rut's mind caught up with her mouth, making her literally bite her tongue. She winced at the pain, but it was nothing compared to the sting of embarrassment when Xanthe spoke next, revealing that she had unfortunately heard Rut's slip.

"You thought Roman soldiers weren't allowed to marry and have children?" said Xanthe.

Now Rut knew she had truly made a fool of herself! She didn't want to turn, but she forced herself to rise and face the wealthy woman and Lydia directly.

"I'm sorry," Rut apologized. "I shouldn't have—"

Xanthe silenced her with a swift hand raised in the air. "Roman soldiers are *not* allowed to marry or have children while they are enlisted. My husband retired seven years ago."

Rut thankfully had the sense this time not to blurt out that Philomena's age meant that she was born well before his retirement. She supposed that she should have known the kind of people she would meet and come across in Philippi would be different to the friends and family she'd known in the Jewish community of Jerusalem, but it was hard not to be shocked at first.

Xanthe sighed. "Mena, you look pale. I knew this would be too much for you! I shall call for the servants at once and have them take you to your bedchamber immediately."

It was not lost on Rut how quickly her care for her daughter made Xanthe's mood shift. Xanthe clapped in a very specific, very intentional rhythmic pattern, and two servants appeared at once. The first took the blankets from Philomena, and the second lifted her up into his arms.

"Wait!" said Xanthe, leaping toward her daughter. "Take this with you." Xanthe produced a little stone idol from the folds of her dress and pressed it into Philomena's hands. "Place it next to you while you rest so that the goddess will watch over you. Now go.”

Rut's stomach sank. This was the first time she'd seen a pagan idol so close that she could reach out and touch it. It was only mere rock, but it made Rut sick.

“I will pray for you too, Mena,” said Lydia.

Rut looked to see her host smiling reassuringly, and while she tried to emulate her posture and behavior, she couldn't smile as naturally.

Xanthe scoffed dismissively. Turning to Rut, she pointedly asked, “Are you a follower of the lone God of the Jews too?”

Rut nodded silently.

“I should have expected as much. I'll never understand how you can pray to only one deity, Lydia,” said Xanthe.

Lydia shrugged her shoulders. “In the entire pantheon of gods, Xanthe, I never found another who spoke directly to their people and answered their prayers in the way the Jewish God answers His people.”

“Has He ever answered you, Lydia of Thyatira?” said Xanthe, pointedly reminding Lydia and everyone who was within earshot of her Gentile status. “Never mind it.”

Lydia turned away, and Rut saw in her gaze how she, like Hektor and probably everyone else in her household, was still searching, though not for a different deity or idol. As Gentiles living in a city with too small of a Jewish population to have its own synagogue, they searched for a way to belong. A way to pursue their faith.

A lump settled in Rut's throat as she realized the weight they bore alongside with the conviction of their beliefs.

Philomena pleaded one last time, clutching the charm in her fist. “Mother, please let me stay. I'm so enjoying spending time with Rut and Lydia.”

“I am sure they will return many more times as they work on

your new garments. Isn't that right?" Xanthe abruptly turned her head toward them, raising her eyebrows as if urging them to respond.

"Yes," Rut answered quickly, "I'll need to get your approval on the designs as they come together and make sure I have the patterns right."

"You won't forget about Hero, will you?" asked Philomena as the servants took her away.

"I won't," said Rut, waving goodbye.

"We'll be in touch," announced Lydia, "but it is probably best that we take our leave, too. Thank you for your business, Xanthe. You remain my most loyal customer, and I am so grateful for your friendship."

Xanthe laughed. "You know too much of my personal history for me to let you go. Take your leave, then."

"I will keep you in my prayers too, Xanthe," said Lydia.

Rut nodded a wordless goodbye and quietly followed Lydia out of the garden and back through the house the same way that they came. This time, and without so many tense feelings, Rut could take in the interior. She wasn't sure how she had missed it the first time around, but it was covered in purple adornments, more vibrant than even Lydia's home. As much as Rut loved the color, she had to admit to herself that Xanthe's taste was a bit too extravagant when compared to her own. However, as Rut was quickly learning, the buyer was always right in their own mind.

They joined Hektor in the main hall, continuing out the large, creaking doors from which they'd entered.

"That was a good thing you did, Rut," Hektor whispered so that only she could hear.

"What?"

"Showing such kindness to Philomena," he answered, and she realized he must have overheard some of their conversation.

"Do they know what ails her?" she asked.

"Not exactly. Xanthe has summoned practically every physician, diviner, and spiritual adviser in the province, but none have been able to give answers. The only thing they can agree on is…"

"That she's not getting better," Rut filled in the end of the sentence for him.

"She needs all the kindness in the world." Rut turned to see him smiling. "You're a good woman, Rut, and you have a noble character about you."

Noble character.

The words reminded her of Shem and the proverbs about the wife of noble character he used to recite to her every morning. At that time, she believed God answered prayers. She had clung to her faith, treasured fellowship, and chased after joy. Yet when the days of trouble came, she quickly turned away and cast such things aside.

How could she have cast aside that for which the God-fearers in Philippi longed so desperately? How could she have been foolish enough to think that she could forget her faith, ignore what she'd witnessed, and walk away without any repercussions?

Rut thought of the look on Lydia's face when Xanthe had scrutinized her choice to believe in the One True God… She thought also of how they were searching for a way to belong, a way of salvation, and she recalled what they'd heard from Libi and her husband Cassius in Antioch, about Gentiles hearing the news of Jesus' resurrection and being joyfully baptized as new believers. Such things were—as deep as she had been in her grief at the time of hearing them—mere whispers to Rut. Their magnitude did not strike her then as it did now. This faith was no collection of little stone idols like Xanthe's. This faith was real and alive, and Rut had turned away from it.

Hektor thought her character was noble.

How wrong he was.

She thought she was leaving all of her troubles behind in Phoenicia, but it seemed they must have caught a more favorable wind and traveled ahead of her. Rut had never wanted to pray more in her life for guidance or for forgiveness, but she couldn't bring herself to do it. She wasn't worthy. She wasn't the proverbial woman Shem recited poetry to, nor was she a skilled weaver deserving of Hektor's praise.

She realized with searing pain that she was Rut, the lost.

Rather than turn her eyes toward heaven in prayer that night, she once again hid her face under her blankets in a vain attempt to hide her heart. What other choice did she have? She feared that she had gone too far and there was no salvaging the damage, like a garment with a tear so long that it could not be mended.

The threads of her life were broken.

How could she ever be forgiven?

10

"We have this hope as an anchor for the soul, firm and secure. It enters the inner sanctuary behind the curtain." — Hebrews 6:19 CSB

Because Philippi had no synagogue, any Jewish or God-fearing Gentiles among the population gathered by the river and used it as a place of prayer. Each week, Lydia and her entire household, Rut included, made the journey to the riverbank. At the river, they would pray and worship together. At least, that's what the others did.

Rut had tried many times since her arrival in Philippi to join in, but she still felt an emptiness inside that she could not overcome. As a result, she remained disengaged, simply going through the motions like a shuttle passing between threads. With her family, she'd been comfortable to keep up the farce, praying words alongside them but never meaning them in her own heart. Now the lies of omission that she'd swallowed for so long threatened to choke her, and Rut worried she would not survive it. With deep dread, she could not see any way of escape—

especially not after her last conversation with Hektor.

Hektor had called her a noble woman, and though he meant it as an encouragement, his words touched a part of her heart she'd long since thought too calloused to feel anything. Rut realized she wanted to be honest with him, but how could she? Hektor had always been forthcoming with her, willing to trust her with much, but she had never trusted him with anything so personal. How could she start now, when months had passed?

She did not know the answer.

Rut, Lydia, and a small group of other women made up only one cluster along the riverbank. The men had gone farther down and out of sight. Unable to do anything other than feel the war between her heart and her head, Rut sat on a rock some number of paces away from the water itself. In her solitude, she watched the other women. Some talked among themselves. Some prayed silently. Some sang songs of praise to the God they believed in and clung to even though they did not know the fullness of His salvation.

As she observed them, another thought came to her and made the muscles in her stomach contract as though she'd eaten spoiled food. These God-fearers had no means of converting to the Jewish faith—though they observed the rites and traditions—and no formal synagogue where they could go to hear the scriptures taught. They remained devout because hope was all they had.

Rut had been in Jerusalem when the hope of the world rode into the city on a donkey, hailed by songs and palm branches. She heard the news when He rose from the dead, rejoicing alongside her family at this miracle of God—a God many believed to have been silent. In the valley where visitors were scarce, it had been easy for Rut to forget that God had called them to more. Now, even if she wanted to tell Lydia and the others about the miracles she'd witnessed in Jerusalem and the fulfillment of hope for all humankind, she couldn't. Not after what she'd done.

More waves of guilt washed over Rut. Though the morning was brisk, she felt herself sweating. She had once been devout like these women, until she'd turned away. Rut saw now that when she'd turned her back on God in trials, she should have clung more firmly to Him as these people did. It was their hope that sustained them, and Rut would give anything to hold that hope for herself again. One question kept her from claiming it: what if she had strayed too far to turn back?

How she wished she could go back to the very beginning and undo everything. Every argument with Shem. Every time she'd avoided answering her family's questions or cynically turned her head away when prayer was mentioned. If Rut could, she would never have stopped praying. She would never have begun weaving lie after lie together, for that's what they were: lies. The loom she was trying to build her life on was broken. Nothing she wove on it would hold, but she'd realized that too late.

Rut looked up to see Lydia standing over her, and she nearly jumped. "Are you all right, Rut? You look peaked."

Rut self-consciously reached a hand up to smooth her curls away from her face. "I think I'm just tired." It was another lie. How easy it was to start, and how difficult it was to stop.

"Come to think of it" — Lydia lowered herself to sit beside Rut, making her wish that a sudden wave would rise up from the river and sweep her away — "you've been quiet for several days and I've noticed that you haven't been eating much. Should I send for a physician?"

"No, please don't go to the trouble of all that. I'm sure I'll be fine." Rut knew she would not. It would be best, she decided, if she disappeared. But a sea separated her from her family! Even if she could manage to find a ship that would take her, she'd have no way of guaranteeing her safety.

"Well, if you say so, but if you need something from me—anything at all, really—all you have to do is ask."

A chill ran down Rut's spine, making the hairs on the back of her neck stand straight up. She was sure she'd be sick now. Everyone here wanted to help her, and Rut felt so undeserving.

"Lydia, I—" Rut stuttered.

"You there!"

Rut turned toward the wall of foliage behind them and saw the shadows of four men approaching.

"Who are you?" said Lydia, rising to her feet and assuming the stance that Rut recognized as her business-side.

The first, an older, shorter man, came through the trees and called out, "I am called Paul here. We came to this city and found no synagogue, but we were told that there was a place of prayer by this river."

"You were told correctly. This is a place of prayer, but we are only women here," Lydia explained.

"Are you Jews?" asked Paul.

"Some of us. We are all God-fearing."

Paul turned and spoke to his companions, then back toward Lydia. "Might we sit with you and speak for a while?"

"Are you teachers of some kind?" Lydia asked the questions Rut and, she presumed, the other women all wanted to know.

"Something like that, yes," answered Paul. "We bring Good News."

"Come down to the river then and we will hear what you have to say," called Lydia. The other women stirred and muttered hushed remarks. Rut remained on her rock, farthest away from everyone else, while Lydia approached the men directly.

"These are my companions, Timothy, Silas, and Luke, who is a physician," Paul explained, gesturing to the other men with him. Judging by how they stood behind him and by how he spoke for them, Rut could clearly see that he was the leader of the group.

"I am called Lydia of Thyatira. I sell purple goods in the city."

"Thyatira?" repeated Paul. "That is quite a distance from Philippi."

"I came in search of business opportunities. It is easier to sell purple goods in places where they are not as easy to come by, and where the buyers are more eager. What brought you to this city?"

"That is an interesting story." Paul, his companions, and Lydia sat down. Rut kept thinking that she ought to know this man for some reason, but his face was not familiar to her. "My companions and I have been traveling near and far to preach a new message to all those who are willing to hear. Originally, we sought to go from Lystra into Asia, but we felt God leading us in another direction. While in Troas, I had a dream in the night of a man standing before me, begging us to come to Macedonia and help the people here, so we came at once, believing that it was God's will."

"What is this message?" asked Lydia, her brows moving closer together.

As Paul looked around at the assemblage of women, Rut felt his piercing gaze on her. He had a kind of intensity about him that Rut recognized. Water rippled against the riverbank, and Rut's heart pulsed alongside its rhythm. She found herself struggling to catch her breath, though she was doing little more than sitting and listening.

"Please," Lydia urged again, "tell us your message."

Lydia's forthright way of speaking reminded Rut of the day they met. She would give anything to trade places with Lydia, or borrow from her even a minute portion of confidence.

The man called Paul scratched at his chin. "Let me ask a few questions first. You said you came to Philippi from Thyatira for business opportunities. Why?"

"There were many people who dealt purple cloth on the other side of the sea. I came because I was searching for customers," Lydia answered.

Paul nodded. "How is it that you also became a God-fearer?"

"I was… I was also searching for something… Something *more*."

The men with Paul murmured behind him. The way he spoke reminded Rut of the *rabbis* she'd heard in the temple in Jerusalem as a young girl. So often teachers of the Law would begin their lessons by posing a question to their audience. This man did the same thing.

Lydia continued, "I have found the Jewish God and I believe with all my heart that He is the only true God, for He speaks to His people in a way that is different from any other of which I have heard. Yet I am a Gentile, as are those in my household. We have no formal synagogue or place of learning about things pertaining to the Jewish God, which is why I am so eager to hear your message."

"It is not only news that I bring you, but *Good News*, Woman of Thyatira, for I am here to tell you a story of how *our* God— the One True God, as you said—has made a way for *all* to be redeemed, Gentile and Jew."

"How can this be?" asked Lydia.

Leaning backward, Paul spoke loud enough so that all the women who were gathered there could hear him. From Abraham and Isaac, to Samuel and David and beyond, Paul recounted the histories of the Jewish people and God's promises to them. Rut closed her eyes as the familiar narratives of her people's origins washed over her heart anew. These were stories she knew by heart, but had not contemplated for years. Hearing them now nearly undid her. Paul went on summarizing the stories of their faith, right up to Jesus' ministry. Rut was more like an Israelite wandering away from the Lord than she ever realized.

"Since the residents of Jerusalem and their rulers did not recognize him or the sayings of the prophets that are read every Sabbath, they have fulfilled their words by condemning him. Though they found no grounds for the death sentence, they asked Pilate to have him killed. When they had carried out all that had been written about him, they took him down from the tree and put him in a tomb. But God raised him from the dead, and he appeared for many days to those who came up with him from Galilee to Jerusalem, who are now his witnesses to the people."

Tears began flowing down Rut's face, for she was one of those witnesses about which Paul spoke.

He stretched out his arms, continuing on, "And we ourselves proclaim to you the good news of the promise that was made to our ancestors. God has fulfilled this for us, their children, by raising up Jesus, as it is written in the second Psalm: *You are my Son; today I have become your Father.* As to His raising Him from the dead, never to return to decay, He has spoken in this way, *I will give you the holy and sure promises of David.* Therefore He also says in another passage, *You will not let your Holy One see decay.* For David, after serving God's purpose in his own generation, fell asleep, was buried with his fathers, and decayed, but the one God raised up did not decay. Therefore, let it be known to you, brothers and sisters, that through this man forgiveness of sins is being proclaimed to you. Everyone who believes is justified through Him from everything that you could not be justified from through the law of Moses. So beware that what is said in the prophets does not happen to you: *Look, you scoffers, marvel and vanish away, because I am doing a work in your days, a work that you will never believe, even if someone were to explain it to you.*"

Startling Rut from her somber reflection, Lydia abruptly

raised her voice. "Let me not be one of those scoffers. I believe in what you are saying, and I can feel the truth of your words burning in my heart. Who are you and how is it that you have come to be bearers of this message?"

At Lydia's question, Rut waited on bated breath. She was certain she knew this man or must have known of him, though she was unsure of how.

He cleared his throat. "I am a Jew, born in Tarsus of Cilicia but brought up in the city of Jerusalem, educated at the feet of Gamaliel according to the strictness of our ancestral law. I was zealous for God, just as all of you are today. I persecuted this Way to the death, arresting and putting both men and women in jail, as both the high priest and the whole council of elders can testify about me."

Rut's heart burned.

She *did* know who this man was.

Paul was Saul, the very same man whose actions led to the death of her Savta and forced the rest of her family to flee Jerusalem. As if recalling memories from a distant dream, Rut remembered how she had heard Asa and Shamira speak of Libi and their extended family who settled in Antioch, and of Saul's transformation. In her bereaved state, the words had little impact on her. Now her past truly was catching up to her, literally standing before her very eyes, preaching the very message Rut had turned away from.

Paul continued, "After I received letters from them to the brothers, I traveled to Damascus to arrest those who were there and bring them to Jerusalem to be punished. As I was traveling and approaching Damascus, about noon an intense light from heaven suddenly flashed around me. I fell to the ground and heard a voice saying to me, 'Saul, Saul, why are you persecuting Me?' I answered, 'Who are You, Lord?' He said to me, 'I am Jesus of Nazareth, the one you are persecuting.' Now those who were with me saw the light, but they did not hear the voice of the one who was speaking to me. I said, 'What should I do, Lord?' The Lord told me, 'Get up and go into Damascus, and there you will be told everything that you have been assigned to do.'"

Rut didn't need to imagine what it must have been like to live as a blind person. She was all too familiar with living in darkness. After all, she had been there in Jerusalem, too. She had seen Jesus' miracles with her own eyes, yet when her life became nothing like she'd imagined it would be, she no longer saw the light. Worse, she wasn't just surrounded by darkness; she had actively chosen to remain within it, letting it hold power over her. She was letting it hold power over her even now as she listened to Paul's message and silently wept. Rut looked around and saw how others were also moved to tears, though she suspected for different reasons.

"Since I couldn't see because of the brightness of the light, I was led by the hand by those who were with me, and went into Damascus. Someone named Ananias, a devout man according to the law, who had a good reputation with all the Jews living there, came and stood by me and said, 'Brother Saul, regain your sight.' And in that very hour I looked up and saw him. And he said, 'The God of our ancestors has appointed you to know His will, to see the Righteous One, and to hear the words from His mouth, since you will be a witness for Him to all people of what you have seen and heard. And now, why are you delaying? Get up and be baptized, and wash away your sins, calling on His name.' After I returned to Jerusalem and was praying in the temple, I fell into a trance and saw Him telling me, 'Hurry and get out of Jerusalem quickly, because they will not accept your testimony about Me.' But I said, 'Lord, they know that in synagogue after synagogue I had those who believed in You imprisoned and beaten. And when the blood of Your witness

Stephen was being shed, I stood there giving approval and guarding the clothes of those who killed Him.' He said to me, 'Go, because I will send you far away to the Gentiles.' I remain steadfast for this purpose, and here I am today."

Stillness.

When Paul finished speaking, there was only stillness save for the softly-rushing waters beside them.

Then Lydia stood, saying, "Please, let me be baptized also."

From there, time began to pass by in a whirlwind for Rut, as the world seemed to spin out of control around her.

Paul and the rest of his company continued to speak to the women. Except for Rut, they were an eager audience. Paul answered their questions with exceeding detail, elaborating on Jesus' ministry, His resurrection, and His ascension. Lydia and the other women were soon baptized, with Lydia being baptized first.

As the hour drew late, more came and responded to the message, including the men from Lydia's household who had gathered farther down the river. Soon all those belonging to Lydia's household were baptized, Hektor being among them, and Rut watched it all from her rock, unmoving. The joy on his face as he emerged from the water nearly ripped her apart. She was thrilled for them, but she was upset with herself, agonizing over the mess she had gotten herself into. This was no ball of wool that Rut could slowly untangle; these were the fibers of her life all knotted up, and there was no way out by her own hand.

All she could think to do was run away before anyone found out the truth. Whether she would go home or go somewhere else did not matter. Perhaps it would be best if Rut—the woman of Phoenicia, the weaver, the girl from Jerusalem, the widow, every version of her—simply disappeared. The details of her plan yet to be worked out, Rut stood up, ready to run back to the villa if need be, collect her things, and flee.

"Rut? Where are you going?" said a voice from behind. *Lydia.*

Rut slowly turned around to face the woman who had offered her so much, without any expectation of what she could give in return. "I just… I needed a moment."

"I was worried about you. We did not get a chance to finish our conversation earlier, and—" Rut stopped listening to take in how Lydia beamed as though lit from within by joy. Rut recalled feeling much the same once. "Rut? Rut?" Lydia's repetition of her name pulled her back to the present conversation, which she very much wished to escape.

"I'm sorry, please go on." Rut needed to act as though nothing were wrong if she wanted to leave without causing unnecessary pain.

"What Paul has shared… It's extraordinary, isn't it?"

"Yes, it is," said Rut, struggling to make and maintain eye contact with her hostess, her *friend.*

Could she call herself a friend if she'd kept so much hidden?

"What do you think of it?" asked Lydia.

"It's… It's.." Rut struggled to find the words. She couldn't bring herself to say, *"It's something I've heard before, and turned away from."* How could she ever have thrown it aside so easily? Seeing these people and how strongly they reacted only served to make Rut realize how important it was, and how much she had lost. This changed their lives. It had changed Rut's too, and she'd almost forgotten how much.

Lydia took Rut's trembling hand in hers, forcing them to be still. "Rut, I know you're only a guest in my household, but that being said, this message—it has changed and is changing everything."

"Please, stop," said Rut, pulling away. She didn't want to hear the rest. It would only make whatever came next more difficult.

"Rut, you've become like a sister to me, and though I respect your right to privacy and to make your own choices, I want nothing more than for you to share in this indescribable joy."

"I—I'm not like you, Lydia." Rut had wanted to be like Lydia when they first met. She admired the strength and determination with which Lydia ran her own business, managed her own household, and made her own decisions. Rut may have even envied her independence and sense of purpose, but Lydia's purpose came not from purple dyes and business dealings. It came from the strength of her faith and conviction. How could Rut be anything like her, when she had been so weak in her own beliefs?

Lydia's brows furrowed. "Why do you say that?"

"Your faith. You cling to it tirelessly, never letting go no matter what circumstance you are in. I let go once, and I am so ashamed."

"Rut," Lydia murmured. "Do you think I have never struggled? It is only because I have endured so many struggles in my past that I have clung to my faith so desperately. Oh, Rut, I thank the Lord for bringing you here to share in this moment with me. His plans truly are perfect!"

Rut started to shiver, wrapping her arms around herself and backing away in retreat. "No, please. This is all a mistake. I should never have come to Philippi."

"What?" Lydia shook her head. "Rut, I don't understand."

"I'm sorry, Lydia. I'm so sorry!" Rut could stand still no longer. She felt bile rising up from her stomach. Full of regret for everything she had done in years past, she did what she'd been wanting to do all day.

She ran.

"From Troas we put out to sea and sailed straight for Samothrace, the next day to Neopolis, and from there to Philippi, a Roman colony and a leading city in the district of Macedonia. We stayed in that city for several days. On the Sabbath day we went outside the city gate by the river, where we expected to find a place of prayer. We sat down and spoke to the women gathered there. A God-fearing woman named Lydia, a dealer in purple cloth from the city of Thyatira, was listening. The Lord opened her heart to respond to what Paul was saying." — Acts 16:11-14 CSB

The feeling as he came out of the water was unlike anything else Hektor had ever experienced. It anchored him, tethering him to the message Paul preached of salvation. No more would he or anyone else have to live their life searching for a way to be saved; the course was already charted out by the man they referred to as Jesus, the Christ. So long as they held steadfast to this faith, they would never run aground.

A light breeze blew over the river, bringing in dark evening clouds. The dampness of his clothes emphasized the coldness of the wind, but he didn't mind. He was clean, in more ways than one. Every regrettable thing he'd ever done—every sharp word, every fight, every drink—all of it had been washed away. How he wished Karis could see how far he'd come and how far the One True God had carried him!

As Hektor pushed his legs forward, walking slowly out of the river, his gaze fell upon Rut and Lydia standing away from the water. *Rut!* Was she as freed by this message as he was? It was no small thing to know and be truly secure in this gift of grace, bought by one sacrifice and made for all time!

Hektor paused as he drew nearer, his eyes focusing on Rut and the pained expression written across her face. She looked as though she were in total anguish, but why? He couldn't hear what Lydia was saying, but he saw when Rut ran off in a hurry. The hairs on his arms raised in alarm and he bolted to Lydia's side.

"Where is Rut going?" he asked.

"I don't know!" Lydia exclaimed. "She said something about all of this being a mistake."

"I'm going after her." Hektor lunged forward, not giving it a second thought.

"Are you sure that is what is best?" asked Lydia. He knew she was questioning his judgment. In all other respects, Hektor would have listened and obeyed whatever Lydia suggested, but not now. It was more than the promise Hektor had made to Benayahu that compelled him to keep her safe.

Hektor was a ship, and Rut was the tide pulling him in.

"She needs help!" Without another word, Hektor ran to catch up with Rut, pushing his feet off the ground with so much force that he practically flew. "Rut, wait!"

"No!" she cried, dodging through bushes. Hektor made the same maneuver. Once he had cleared through the brush, he came to an abrupt halt at the sight of Rut on her knees in a clearing, head in her hands.

"Rut," he whispered.

He had worried for her that night she'd been upset on the ship, but seeing her now felt different. It stung like a blow during a fighting match, and one that would not heal quickly.

"Please, leave me alone," she said between sobs, her voice muffled.

"I can't. When people are alone, they make desperate decisions. Trust me… I thought I was alone once too." For the first time, Hektor didn't feel the familiar pang of remorse at the mention of his past decisions. That too seemed to have been washed away. "You're not alone, Rut."

Her wild curls flung over her shoulders as she whipped around to face him. "Yes, I am!" Rut practically roared the words.

Hektor stepped back, letting his hands fall to his sides as he forced his breathing to slow after the exhilaration of the chase. It was clear who the lion in this clearing was, and Hektor knew better than to provoke a lion *or* a lioness. She continued, "It is better that I'm alone, because I will disappoint fewer people this way."

"Disappoint people? Rut, everyone here thinks highly of you. Where is this coming from?"

"That's just it," she cried. "You only think that because you don't know everything about me. If you did, you'd be disgraced by me too."

Love her.

Hektor felt the words impress themselves upon his heart, and he knew at once they were from the One True God. *"Oh, Lord,"* he prayed, *"You do have the answers."*

Hektor could stand at a distance from her no longer. Slowly and carefully, he knelt to the ground beside her, joining her in her pain.

"Tell me, Rut. I promise you that I will not turn away."

"I…. I…" She stopped to heave a heavy sigh, and Hektor did not urge her on. He waited with patience, giving her the time she needed to express what he sensed was very difficult for her to voice aloud. "I was baptized with my family when I lived in Jerusalem."

"In Jerusalem? I thought…" Had she ever mentioned living in Jerusalem before Phoenicia?

"Please, let me finish. Once I start, I'm afraid if I stop…"

"Of course. My apologies,"

She nodded. "You know me as Rut, the weaver from Phoenicia, the woman you met in Tyre, but I was once a girl in Jerusalem. A girl who saw Jesus, who was there at the temple when he overturned the tables during the week of His crucifixion. I was there when He entered the city riding on a donkey, and everyone all around praised His name, cried out *'Hosanna!'* and threw palm branches in his path. I was with my family when the earth shook in the hour that He died, and I was with my family again when we heard the news that He had risen once again to life. I was baptized alongside my father, mother, and brother, and when persecution broke out in Jerusalem, I fled with them and others north through Damascus before settling in Phoenicia."

This was it, Hektor realized. This was the story Benayahu had alluded to and Hektor had only guessed at. Rut carried with her more pain than that of a widow. She carried the pain of many losses.

"When our home was taken from us in Jerusalem, I counted it as a test of our faith, but the more hardships I faced, the harder I found it to even utter His name, and I am so ashamed. I was brokenhearted, but I believed we were fleeing for the right reasons, and I believed God would make things right again. My husband, Shem, was my gift in that pain, but then… Then it became clear that the two of us would likely not have children of our own."

Hektor looked up awkwardly at the swaying tree branches and the bluish-gray clouds that floated overhead. He didn't move from her side. He just kept listening, not wanting to do or say anything that might hurt her.

"I prayed for a miracle, but no miracle came. We were married for five years before he died in my arms. Again I prayed for a miracle. I prayed for God to make sense of it in my head, but to me there was no sense in such a tragedy, and after that, I couldn't pray at all."

Rut began to weep again and Hektor remained silent as she had asked him to do, though the feeling of helplessness tore at Hektor's heart. He ached to do something, or say anything that could ease her pain.

Love her.

He felt the message in his heart again, and without thinking, he reached for her hand and held onto it gently. It was in that touch that Hektor realized he did love this woman as much more than a friend. Hektor loved the diligence with which she approached every task set before her. He loved her wit, and the way they could match each other's humor word for word in any conversation. He loved the depth and warmth of her eyes and the curl of her hair, though her outward beauty still paled in comparison to her inward beauty.

Rut spoke of regrettable choices she had made in the past, the likes of which Hektor was all too familiar with, but none of it changed who she was on the inside. The woman Hektor saw within her was still a kind, giving woman, harshest on herself but always full of grace for others. He had witnessed it in how she taught the other spinners and weavers with tender words of instruction, working alongside them with modesty and humility.

Hektor was no textile expert, but it didn't take one to see how her presence had been an advantageous windfall to Lydia's business. More than any of that, however, she saw into people's hearts and acted as a friend toward those in need, as she did to Mena and even to Xanthe. She may have felt alone, but she was always one to make sure that others didn't.

Rut straightened. She pulled her hand away, leaving Hektor's open palms cold. "I still knew in my head that God was real. How could I deny that? But I struggled to believe that He listened to His people. I wrestled with doubt and resentment, and I didn't know how to tell people. My family wanted nothing more than to see me heal, but I couldn't bring myself to share with them the depths of how I struggled. How could they understand? Surely they never doubted like I had, and I didn't want them to look down on me for being so weak. When I came here, I thought that I could leave it all behind and start a new life. The more I interacted with you all, the more I realized it was not possible. You were all so good to me. Too good! I don't deserve it."

"Oh, Rut," said Hektor, wanting desperately to reach across the distance that separated them and wipe the tears from her cheeks. "None of us deserve any of the grace we are given."

Rut shook her head. "When Paul came today, telling stories of Jesus and the salvation offered to all people—stories I knew in my heart were true—I could no longer go along with pretending I knew nothing. Please, let me go and get my things so that I can leave you all and never return."

"Where would you go?" asked Hektor. His muscles tensed at the thought of her alone, defenseless. She could take care of herself in many ways, Hektor was certain, but the world was a cruel and dangerous place.

"I don't know… Anywhere but here."

"You can't leave, Rut."

"Don't you see that I can't stay? I've made such a mess of my life and I can't drag you all into it with me." Her voice was hoarse after so much crying. "How could you ever look at me the same way now?"

It was true that Hektor was surprised by what Rut had shared of her story, but it wasn't his place to judge her—or anyone else's. If anyone tried to speak against her, Hektor would see to it that they thought twice about it.

"Rut, you're not dragging the rest of us into anything, and you shouldn't feel so ashamed. If the hope of forgiveness exists for a man like me, a fighter and a drunk from the streets of Philippi, surely that same hope exists for you." His voice cracking trying to assuage her guilt. "You are no less deserving than any of us, Rut. You just don't see it that way."

"I already had my chance and I threw it away!" She pushed her curls back from her face and wiped the tears from her eyes. "I've made a mess of everything and it's best that I go now before it gets any worse."

"Stop this, Rut." His voice bellowed, and he immediately softened his tone when he saw Rut jump backward. He hadn't meant to shout but in the heat of the moment, he'd forgotten to temper his tone.

"*Lord,*" he prayed with his eyes closed, "*give me the right words. Show me how to love her.*"

He continued speaking when he opened his eyes, though he spoke each word slowly and deliberately, "You are focusing on the wrong things, even now. It's like… It's like when you sit before your loom, working on a tapestry. You see the pattern you're making as you throw the shuttle back and forth, switching colors every so often and gradually creating something beautiful one row at a time. From where you sit, you see the pattern taking shape. You know how each color goes with the next to make up a work of art."

Rut sighed, lips quivering. "What does this have to do with anything, Hektor? My life is no work of art."

"Because if I were sitting on the opposite side of the same loom, I would see only the wrong side, where the different colored threads tangle together and the pattern is indistinguishable. You are looking at the wrong side of the tapestry, Rut. The side with all of the knots and crisscrossed threads. You see only the chaos, but God sees the beauty that chaos has brought."

"Hektor, no… There's no beauty in my life and there never can be."

"Yes, there can," he urged. "You have to choose to look at the right side of the tapestry, where God is weaving every thread together."

"No!" This time she screamed as if with everything she had left. "Leave me alone, Hektor. Just leave me alone!"

It was in that scream, that ear-piercing, world-shattering scream, that Hektor realized an important but painful truth: He could not make her see anything. He could not fix all of her problems as easily as he could fix up a loom. He could not save her from anything by his own strength, any more than he could have saved Karis from death itself. Hektor had always wanted to be the kind of man who could solve any problem. Was that not what he'd done for his sister after their father had died? Turned to fighting, because he'd tried every other means to save them from starvation and ruin except asking others for help? No speech he could ever make, no story he could ever tell, would ever be enough to convince Rut of anything if she didn't want to listen. He did need to leave her, but not alone. She was in God's hands, where she always had been.

The best way for Hektor to love Rut was to let her go.

Though it broke his heart to do so, he backed away, praying with each step for the strength to keep going. No wound from any blow during his days as the Lion of Philippi ever hurt so much, but he knew it was the right thing to do. At least, he prayed that it was, and he clung to that anchoring hope with every fiber of his being.

"Lord, she has always been only ever Yours to save."

Rut kept her eyes closed as Hektor walked away. She didn't want to see the look on his face when he finally accepted that they were all better off without her. She had kept so much from her family and from her newfound friends, going back further than her choice to come to Philippi. She'd started keeping secrets the day that Shem died.

Rut knew from experience that sometimes in a weaving project, a knot could form so tight that the only thing to be done was to cut it out. Rut felt like that kind of a knot, and she needed to cut herself out of the lives of the people she cared about so that she didn't ruin the entire piece.

After a few moments, she started to walk again, though not back to the villa. Instead, she followed the sounds of the river, wandering back to the water. Once there, she peered over the edge to stare at her murky reflection. How could she have held back so much?

It struck her how strangely similar her circumstances were now when compared to that first night at sea. Once again, she found herself crying beside water, desperate to escape. That first night, Hektor came to her rescue and calmed her by talking her through her fears. The water she sat beside now was no storm-tossed sea, but she felt a storm inside of her. Just like last time, Hektor had tried to help her, but he too had given up.

Or had she pushed him away?

Rut thought about his parting words… Was there truth in what he said about tapestries and searching for the hand of the One who weaves them together? Was she the one who'd stopped seeing, stopped looking for the Lord in her life? Rut couldn't believe she was even asking that question of herself; like she'd pushed Hektor away, she'd also pushed her faith away, keeping hope at bay rather than letting it fill the empty spaces in her heart. There had been no gain in any of it; only more loss. She was a failure to herself and to her family, and she probably would be to everyone.

"I can't go on like this anymore," she whispered to herself, raising her hands in defeat. "I need help!"

You are looking at the wrong side of the tapestry.

Rut spun around, thinking that she had heard a voice, only it didn't sound like any voice she recognized. Not Hektor. Not Lydia. Not even Paul.

You are looking at the wrong side of the tapestry.

The second time, Rut realized it is was no ordinary voice. It was a feeling, like the breathing of new life into her lungs, and it felt like it came from God.

"Lord?" Rut's chest burned as her voice broke. How long had it been since she'd prayed, and truly prayed? Years ago, leaning over Shem's dead body, she'd told herself that God did not answer prayers. She'd felt nothing but cold emptiness ever since, but now she felt full and revived.

You have never been alone, Daughter.

The reminder drove out the last chill within her heart, and Rut found warmth and comfort in their embrace. Rut closed her eyes and when she did, she saw a glimpse at the glorious tapestry God had been weaving all along. He had been there in Tyre, leading her path to cross with Lydia's and Hektor's. He had been there on the road with Benayahu, when her brother encouraged her to take Lydia's offer. He had been there when Rut decided to go to Philippi. He had been with Paul and his company, guiding them to Macedonia and even to the riverside. Even in that darkest moment as she wailed for her husband, God had been there. All along, in every good day and every difficult one, His hand had been guiding her to this very moment. How could she not see that then as she so clearly saw it now?

"Oh, Lord, forgive me." At once, she pressed her face to the ground. "You *were* always there! It was me who stopped talking and stopped hearing because I didn't want to hear the answers You gave. But I don't want to stay in this darkness anymore—I want to follow You with my whole heart, for my whole life. I tried to run away from my past once before, hiding my wounds, but I don't want to hide anymore. I want to be made clean."

Rut kept her face downward, shedding a different kind of tears. These were not the tears of guilt or shame; these were tears of gratitude to a God whose goodness knew no end, and whose love knew no limits. She cried thinking of Shem. He would have wanted more for her; Shem knew better than anyone the joy of living in any circumstance so long as one kept the word of the Lord in their heart. Lydia and Hektor had been heaven-sent to pull Rut out of grief in Tyre, just as Paul had been heaven-sent to all of them to preach the joy of salvation and new life; a joy born again within Rut's heart. She wanted to make things right. She *would* make things right.

She rose from the ground, this time rising with conviction. When she did, another peculiar thing happened that she could only describe as coming from God.

It began to rain.

The soft breeze that had been blowing overhead all the day long had carried in clouds that now burst forth, not with heavy rain and terrifying thunder, but with soft light and gentle showers. Rut couldn't help but laugh. She finally felt in her heart what she hadn't felt in a long time. She knew God was real, and she knew He answered prayers. He was answering prayers in that moment, for in that rain, He was washing and restoring her heart, just as she had asked.

She picked up her skirts and ran from that riverbank, running back to Lydia and Hektor and the others to tell them everything, and to celebrate the goodness of God that burst forth like rain from the heavens, bringing water and life to everything that it touched.

"She extends her hands to the spinning staff, and her hands hold the spindle. Her hands reach out to the poor, and she extends her hands to the needy." — Proverbs 31:19-20 CSB

On that memorable day when Paul and his company arrived, Lydia opened her home and offered the villa as a place for them to stay. Since then, Rut saw Lydia's hospitality for the first time as someone on the inside of the home, and home was exactly what this villa had become for Rut. A part of her heart would always be left in Phoenicia with her family, in the same way that a part of her heart would also always be left in Jerusalem with the memories of her childhood; another part of her heart belonged here now.

She treasured this far-off province of Macedonia, with its lush, rolling hills covered in parts by robust trees, and its stone-paved streets lined with bright, white columns. This was the place where God had called her, and where she realized that He had been calling out to her all along.

"Are you ready?" asked Hektor, waiting to escort Rut and

Lydia once again to Xanthe's house. Rut breathed a sigh of relief, knowing that they had returned to their old routines and easy conversations, though there was still so much she longed to say to him after their encounter by the river. More than her heart had changed that day, but like a woven pattern she struggled to replicate, Rut had difficulty finding the words to tell him about it.

"I am," Rut answered. She had already seen to it that the garments made for Philomena would be loaded on the cart with the rest of their things. "But is he?" She gestured to Hero, the mischievous dog who had become quite accustomed to joining them each time they visited Xanthe's to take new measurements or get her approval on designs. He sat at attention, trying to appear dignified and reserved, but his wagging tail gave away his true feelings.

Hektor laughed lightly. "You know, if I were a betting man, I'd be willing to wager that he thinks he's the reason you take all these trips."

"It is highly possible," she replied blithely.

The three of them took several steps through the courtyard in unison, though Hero, having four legs, took twice as many. Still, he matched their pace. A silence fell between them, and Rut wanted desperately to end it. "How are you?" she asked, for it was the only thing she could think to say, despite the wordless feelings swirling around in her heart.

"I am well," said Hektor.

"That is good." She sighed heavily and continued, intending to confront the awkwardness directly, "Hektor, I feel that there is something I must say."

"If it's about what happened by the river, you do not have to say anything, Rut," he replied in low, comforting tones. How was it possible that he could read her mind? She didn't understand it, but she was grateful for it.

"I *want* to. I want to apologize for how I treated you," she explained.

Hektor halted his steps and she instinctively turned to face him. When Rut looked up into his glittering, ocean-blue eyes, she was surprised to see no anger or resentment in them. She didn't know why she even expected such a reaction, knowing who Hektor was. From the beginning of their relationship, he remained consistent. He had never pretended to be someone he was not, unlike Rut.

"If you truly feel that you need my forgiveness, then consider it freely given. I think that the One True God was weaving a great many stories together that day."

"Thank you. I hope there is no hurt between us."

"No hurt at all." While Hektor smiled, Rut still saw a kind of bittersweetness hiding in his eyes. "I just want you to be happy, Rut."

"I am, truly."

"Then I am happy too," he replied.

They stood still and stared at each other for several breaths, time passing too swiftly. Hektor opened his mouth as if he were going to say something else, but he remained quiet. She too tried to speak, but couldn't think of what to say. Looking at him now, she realized how much Hektor meant to her in ways she hadn't thought possible in a long time.

Could she dare to voice such thoughts aloud, or even recognize them in her own heart? Would it betray Shem's memory?

Hektor cleared his throat and began walking forward again. "We should be going or Lydia will wonder where we are."

Rut hurried to follow, brushing the entire encounter aside. Even if she did have feelings for him, it did not matter. When her time was up, she would be returning to Tyre. Hektor would still be a man in Lydia's employ, bound to Philippi by the necessity of his job as her guard. Furthermore, Hektor was a good man. He was kind. She was a widow, who, even when she was filled with joy, would forever be marked by the past.

How could there ever be anything more between them?

"Hero!" exclaimed Philomena, stretching out her arms and reaching as the dog came running.

"Don't excite yourself so, Mena," said Xanthe.

Philomena giggled as Hero sat down on the floor beside her, his tail thumping a steady rhythm against the leg of her chair. "Mother, I'm all right. Really, I am! Today has been a good day."

Rut could hear the truth in Philomena's words, for her voice was the strongest she'd ever heard it. She still rasped some, but noticeably less at that moment. Ever since Hektor told Rut about Philomena's condition, she'd become more aware of instances when her struggles were evident. Rarely did Rut see Philomena engaged in any kind of physical activity. She tired easily, moving without assistance was often difficult for her, and sometimes in very quiet moments, Rut could hear how she struggled to draw breath. Xanthe was always at the ready should Philomena have a sudden dizzy spell or coughing fit, usually producing another stone idol or bag of heavily scented ointments.

Xanthe's expression softened as she stood behind her daughter, brushing the back of her hand against Philomena's long, blonde curls, which were styled identically to Xanthe's in a simple, loose braid trailing over her shoulder. "I only want tomorrow to be just as good, my daughter."

While Rut unpacked the finished garments and made sure every last thread was in its proper place and without imperfection before presenting them to their commissioners, she recognized something in Xanthe's voice: the shadow of her own past. Though Xanthe's words were sweet, there was pain behind them. A heartbreaking sort of pain that one never shared aloud, instead keeping it contained deep within one's heart. It reminded Rut of her life in Phoenicia and how from the outside it appeared as though she were fine, but on the inside, she was slowly wasting away.

"Well," said Rut, standing straight up with an arm full of clothes, "here we have the last of your new garments, made to your exact specifications. Some new tunics and one very beautiful stola." Rut held them out in front of her with a smile, winking at Philomena.

"Oh, Rut! It's perfect! Could you bring the stola closer to me so I could see it?" Philomena asked, with every possible intonation of sweetness in her voice. It thrilled Rut to see her so happy and she complied with Philomena's request immediately, separating the stola from the other garments. "It's so fine!" said Philomena, pinching the fabric between her fingers. "I don't think I've ever felt anything like it."

"I am glad that you are pleased."

"Bring the other tunics to me," said Xanthe, reclining on another seat opposite the low-lying pool of water.

Rut crossed the distance and extended her arm toward Xanthe, offering her closer look at the pattern woven around the edges.

"These will do very nicely," said Xanthe in her own version of a compliment. Rut nodded her thanks, though Xanthe's eyes were likely far too concentrated on inspecting the new pieces of clothing to notice.

"I told you that her skill was unmatched," said Lydia.

"I'm not too proud to admit that when I heard you say you found a skilled weaver in Tyre and that you brought her all the way back here, I questioned your soundness of mind, but you were right, as usual."

Lydia laughed. "I assure you; her presence has done us all good and we are all better for knowing her. We'll be sad to see her leave us next year."

"Why don't you stay here?" asked Xanthe of Rut. "You could work for Lydia, or open your own business. I'm sure you'd be very popular."

Rut's eyes widened. "I…"

"I promise you'll be the first to know if Rut changes her plans—after me, of course," Lydia interjected, saving Rut from having to come up with a reply. "In the meantime, Rut has been generous enough to pass on her knowledge to my other weavers."

"Well, let me get the payment for you," said Xanthe, leaving Rut no more time to ponder the suggestion of making Philippi her permanent home. Xanthe clapped her hands and Rut, anticipating the entrance of servants, stepped backwards to make room for them.

Within the span of a single breath, Xanthe excused herself, and servants arrived to take away the new garments. When Xanthe came back into the garden, Rut took notice of how she dragged her feet across the stone floor. "Here," she said as she practically forced one small but full satchel of coin into Lydia's hands. It clinked and clanged with the force of the action.

With equal effort, she offered another satchel to Rut, and the weight of it made her hand falter. This was the first time Rut had ever made any money on her own and the realization that she could provide for herself astounded her. Lydia had done it. Why couldn't Rut? In Philippi or Phoenicia?

"Thank you very much for your continued support, Xanthe," said Lydia, a pleasant expression never leaving her face despite Xanthe's gruff demeanor. Hektor had been right when he told Rut that the two women were something close to friends; only *true* friends would be so undeterred by the more negative foibles of a person's nature. The fact that Lydia overlooked such things and remained cordial showed Rut that these two women shared a great deal of history with one another.

"I suppose you'll be leaving now," said Xanthe, heaving a dramatic sigh and avoiding eye contact.

"Yes, if our business here is concluded. Is that not what you wish?" Lydia asked, giving Xanthe the opportunity she so obviously wanted to invite them to stay.

"Oh, I just know that something will come to me the moment that you both leave, and then I'll have to send for you again. Why don't you stay a while longer and talk, just in case?" Xanthe spoke in a pleading tone. Rut and Lydia exchanged knowing looks and both took their usual seats in the garden, established on their first visit together.

Philomena tossed a stick for Hero to fetch, beaming as she spoke, "I think I am better with Hero around to lift my spirits." She threw the stick gently over her shoulder again and Hero leapt for it at once. Not watching where he was going, he tripped as he caught the stick in his mouth. Mena laughed loudly, as did they all.

Rut caught her breath after a time, but her eyes began to widen with horror when she realized Philomena's laughter was quickly turning into a ferocious cough.

"Philomena!" Rut jumped to her feet as she saw how Philomena struggled to sit up, choking and unable to breathe clearly.

"Someone, get water!" Xanthe shouted, presumably to the

servants who were ever-present and always waiting for their next order. Xanthe pushed Rut out of the way and moved to sit beside Philomena, lifting her daughter in her arms. "Breathe deeply, Mena," Xanthe whispered.

Rut felt helpless standing beside Lydia as they watched the events unfold. Xanthe continued to whisper and Philomena continued to struggle for air, her face turning from red to blue.

Hero, the dog likely everyone had forgotten about, pushed between them all, resting his head and paws on Philomena's lap.

"Get him away!" Xanthe exclaimed, but the dog did not budge.

Hero pressed even closer to Philomena, turning his head to lick the back of her hand. As he did so, Philomena's breathing began to slow. It was still laborious, but it was not as rapid as it had been. With a whine, Hero once again relaxed his body, laying across Philomena's feet.

"The water, Mistress Xanthe," said a servant. Xanthe snatched the cup and waved them away, pressing it to Philomena's lips, lifting it slowly so that she could take small sips. It took time and effort, but by the time she swallowed the last bit, her whole body seemed stilled. With Xanthe's help, she sank back into the cushions.

"Thank you, Mother." She sighed with her eyes closed. "And thank you, Hero."

"You're thanking the dog?" Xanthe sneered. "That dog caused this. I ought to forbid him from returning to this house after causing such a terrible ruckus."

"No, you don't understand." Philomena's voice was barely above a whisper and Rut had to incline her head forward to understand what she was saying. "Hero *saved* me. I couldn't breathe and I was so scared, but when he came and sat beside me, I was able to calm myself. My chest still hurt, but I wasn't so frightened. You can't forbid him from coming again, Mother.

Please?"

Xanthe pursed her lips. "All right, my daughter," she said. It was not lost on Rut how she blinked back tears. "But no more playing with him like that."

"I won't, I promise," said Mena. "I just like seeing him."

Almost as if sensing that he was no longer needed, Hero scampered away, probably either to find Hektor or to find food, though Rut had no true idea of what Hero did when he wasn't in their presence. He often disappeared while they talked or when no one was around to dote on him. Someday she would ask Hektor about it.

Rut looked to Lydia, wondering what they should do next. Lydia did not move from the spot where she stood. Perhaps she too was waiting for Xanthe to make the next move.

When Rut looked back at Xanthe, she was surprised to see how the woman looked back and forth between the two of them, with a gaze of intense scrutiny. "You've changed."

"What do you mean?" said Lydia.

"You're not as different, but *she* definitely is," replied Xanthe, pointing to Rut.

"I apologize, Xanthe. It must be all of the commotion." Rut blinked in confusion and grappled for some kind of explanation that would not offend.

"No," Xanthe said in rejection of Rut's statement. "I did not say that you changed in a bad way. Only that both of you seem… even more like yourselves. Did something happen that I don't know about? Did someone befall a great fortune? Did the gods bestow their favor upon you in some way? If they did, you must tell me how you managed to sway them so that I might try whatever it was in my own mess of a life."

"No, nothing quite like that," said Lydia, very diplomatically.

"Then what is it? Did your lonely God finally answer you?"

"He did," Lydia answered, firmly and emphatically.

Immediately, Xanthe's eyebrows raised to new heights. "What are you saying?"

"Firstly, He is not a 'lonely' God. He is the *only* God, and the One True God," Lydia explained with a tone of familiarity that only she could use.

"To you," said Xanthe pointedly. "Regardless, I was under the impression that the Jewish God did not associate with 'Gentiles' as your people call us."

The last part was aimed directly at Rut, and something inside of her compelled her to respond, though she might have once brushed off the derogatory remark.

"That's not true," Rut began gently. "Our God's message is for all people, for all time. Why, think of the story of Rahab, among others."

"I do not know this Rahab of which you speak," said Xanthe. "What has she got to do with this?"

Stories that Rut had heard repeated over and over again since childhood suddenly filled her mind. She recalled details she hadn't thought of in years with perfect clarity, as though the words had been etched on her very heart. "After the Israelites came out of Egypt and wandered the desert for forty years, God finally permitted them to enter the land He had promised, but in this land was the city of Jericho. God commanded the Israelites to destroy the city and everything in it. One woman who lived within the city wall helped the Israelite spies—she was a Canaanite, and a prostitute."

Xanthe gasped.

Rut continued, "When the Israelite spies entered the city of Jericho ahead of their invasion, the king demanded that they be turned over. She hid them among stalks of flax, and steered the men who were searching for them in the other direction."

"Then what happened?" asked Philomena, leaning forward and angling her body toward Rut.

"Once it was safe, Rahab went to talk to them on the roof where they were still hiding. She had heard about the other miracles preceding the Israelite people, like how the Lord had parted the Red Sea so that they could cross into safety on dry ground, and the victories in battle they experienced on the other side of the Jordan River. She acknowledged her belief in the One True God, and asked them to swear that when Jericho's day of reckoning came, she and her family would be spared."

"And when that day came, she died along with the rest of her people?" asked Xanthe, her tone flat and her eyes unfocused.

"No," Rut said calmly. Though Xanthe's remark was biting, she did not let it wound her. "The men answered her, saying, 'We will give our lives for yours. If you don't report our mission, we will show kindness and faithfulness to you when the Lord gives us the land.' Then they told her to tie a scarlet cord to the window she'd helped them escape through, explaining that so long as her family remained in her house on the day of the battle, they would be spared."

"What happened during the battle?" asked Philomena.

Rut was delighted by Philomena's interest, but quickly realized that this story was being told to an audience of people who had little to no knowledge of Jewish history or the names of important figures. She quickly calculated the adjustments she'd need to make in her storytelling the way she'd calculate an alteration on her loom before continuing.

"The Lord told Joshua—who was the leader of the Israelite people at the time—to march their fighting men around the city one time each day for six days. On the seventh day, they began marching at dawn, and marched around the city seven times while the priests blew ram's horns. After the seventh time, all the troops shouted as the Lord commanded, and the walls of Jericho crumbled. The city fell to the Israelites as the Lord promised, and Rahab was spared."

"Spared for what?" said Xanthe. "To live impoverished in a city that was destroyed?"

"Rahab received more than her life; she received hope and a place with the people of God because of her strong faith and her bravery. She married and settled with the people of Israel, and through her descendants came our most revered king, David."

Xanthe scoffed, which was not the reaction Rut hoped to see, but admittedly one that she anticipated. "Some lineage of kings."

Rut tilted her head to the side as she pondered the line of broken people. "It is true. Throughout our history, our people have fallen, but the Lord has always been there, waiting for us to return to Him. He waits to lift us up again."

"Is that what He has done?" asked Xanthe, raising her hands from her lap, turning her palms toward the sky in a display of both confusion and disbelief. "Lifted up your people? I heard the Jews are always planning uprisings. Is that what's going to happen? An uprising against Caesar?"

"That isn't what I mean at all. The Lord has made a way for all to receive grace and restoration. He has brought salvation to both Jews and Gentiles, like He did in the story with Rahab."

"That is only one story." Xanthe looked away.

"There are countless others," said Rut, and she knew it was true. There were countless other stories that Rut never wanted to forget again, even if that meant telling them over and over again to herself and to anyone else who would hear.

"I would like to hear more," said Philomena. "Please, Mother?"

Xanthe remained as still as a carved statue. Only fine wisps of her hair moved gently with the wind as she contemplated Philomena's request. "I think that it is time for you to go and rest."

"But Mother—" Philomena started to plead.

"Don't worry," said Xanthe, "Rut and Lydia will return. I have just remembered that I have more business with them. Go and retire now while I discuss the details of what I seek."

While Philomena took her leave, Rut turned to Lydia and was surprised to see that Lydia was already looking at her with a pleased expression. There was more to it than the satisfaction of a new business dealing, and Rut knew Lydia would be bursting with words later. For now, they both listened as Xanthe described the exact specifications of what she was looking for: a new himation for herself.

Rut nodded along as she spoke. Lydia would supply the materials and Rut would do the weaving. As usual, Lydia and Rut would split the payment. When she was finished, the women bid each other farewell, promising to return again to seek Xanthe's approval about the finished garment, which would, of course, be made using Lydia's signature purple blend.

"Well, it certainly took you a long time," said Hektor once they were finally out on the street and headed toward home.

"Oh, Hektor, I think Rut just began something amazing," said Lydia. Rut laughed at her enthusiasm, for it was a perfect reflection of her excitement when they first met.

"Me?" asked Rut, whose mind was still a few steps behind Lydia's, though she'd otherwise grown accustomed to keeping up with the keen, energetic seller of purple.

"Yes, you! I've never seen Xanthe so interested in anything related to faith in the One True God."

Rut bit her tongue to keep herself from uttering a remark about how she had never seen Xanthe so interested in anything that wasn't purple and expensive. "I thought she hated the story?"

Lydia waved a hand in the air. "That's Xanthe's way. She is always overly critical of things she secretly wants to know more about. It's her way of masking how she truly feels until she's made up her mind."

"So," said Hektor, heaving a deep breath, "Rut has finally begun to crack Xanthe's shell, eh?"

"Yes!" said Lydia. "She had Philomena on the edge of her seat and Xanthe doing her best to feign disinterest, but I could tell it was a farce from the way she always kept her ear toward Rut. She told it all so beautifully that it made it impossible for Xanthe to ignore."

"Well, I would hardly say that," Rut argued. She knew there were others out there who were better equipped and far more knowledgeable than she was. As she'd told Hektor on the ship, she was a weaver of threads, not of words.

"I would! I could tell Xanthe wanted to hear more," said Lydia, clutching Rut's arm and giving it a squeeze. Rut hadn't seen her this passionate since she first entreated Rut to come to Philippi. This time, however, Rut was not surprised by her overwhelming sense of initiative. She too was excited by the possibility. "Make your fingers fly, Rut," Lydia continued. "I have a feeling that when we return with that new himation, Xanthe will ask you in her own way to tell more stories. Who knows? Perhaps this will be how Xanthe finally brings her burdens to the One True God!"

"The Lord knows," said Rut, believing it to be true. God knew about Xanthe as He knew about everything, from Rut's wandering heart to the number of stars in the sky. Looking to Hektor and losing herself for a moment in his deep, blue eyes—the eyes of a true and loyal friend that she was grateful to have on her side—Rut added, "We are all mere threads in His tapestry."

That day's events put a different kind of vigor in Rut's steps as they continued their journey. When Rut looked back on it and everything that had happened before, not only since coming to Philippi, but throughout her entire life, she could see how the

Lord was weaving everything together. Since that day by the river, she felt called to live a life dedicated to her faith, and now she felt an even more specific calling to keep working and working hard, giving only her best to each project, and giving her best to others as well.

Xanthe was interested. She was crying out for hope. It was not Rut's storytelling that deserved praise, but God's. Rut prayed her thanks to Him for bringing her to just the right place to be used by Him, even while she had still struggled with unbelief. All her life had been a preparation for this time: spinning wool while listening to her Abba and *Sabba* tell stories, absorbing the words without even realizing it; her talent for weaving that had developed steadily over the years; and her trips to Tyre and Sidon with Beni that led her to Lydia. Even her upbringing in Jerusalem, where she had been one of those blessed to have seen Jesus the Messiah when He was hailed by praises and palm branches, and to have heard the news of His resurrection following the crucifixion.

A memory came back to her, as vivid and bright as though it were happening right before her eyes. It was from when she was still a young girl in Jerusalem, talking with Benayahu and Shamira. Shamira had always been so bold, and after Jesus changed not only their lives but the whole world, she became even bolder. Each of her steps were guided by a desire for others to know the same hope they held, and at the time, it scared Rut.

She had asked her older cousin, *"Don't you worry about what people will say? It's like the disciples said before. This city is dangerous for followers of Jesus. They will all think that we are heretics and treat us like criminals."*

Shamira challenged Rut with her response. *"If everyone in this city could believe what we believe and know what we know, then they would have no room to imprison all of us. Isn't this exactly what Jesus commanded us to do? To spread the good news about his resurrection, and the offering of new life that came with it?"*

"But aren't you scared of what people might think?" Rut had asked again, unable to let go of her fear so easily, for back then she did not understand the full tapestry as she did now.

She remembered Shamira's words—powerful words that Rut was only now beginning to hear with her heart as well as her mind. *"There may be risks and I think that is a question we have to ask ourselves. Is it worth it? Are we willing to lay down our lives for Him as He did for us?"*

Rut was, for she had lived a long time without hope, moving in silence and keeping quiet about all matters of faith. When she'd counted the cost and estimated the risk in the past, she'd counted her pain too great. Now she knew that the cost paid by Jesus was greater still, and that trying to live without faith was like trying to weave on a loom without weights. How could she ever long for more than this: to seek God, and to help others seek Him in any and every circumstance?

*"He gives strength to the faint and strengthens the powerless.
Youths may become faint and weary, and young men stumble
and fall, but those who trust in the Lord will renew their
strength; they will soar on wings like eagles; they will run and
not become weary, they will walk and not faint." — Isaiah
40:29-31 CSB*

Hektor rolled his shoulders forward and backward, pretending to ignore the stiffness that made his movements more rigid than usual. His time as the Lion of Philippi put a strain on his body that lingered still, even after more than a decade had passed since his so-called 'dark years.'

A lamp in hand, Hektor made his rounds throughout Lydia's villa to ensure nothing was amiss and that the perimeter was secure for the evening. He was responsible for the safety of everyone within these walls, so dreams of soaking his aching bones in a hot bath would have to wait.

He remained on guard, listening to every sound and giving every shadow a second glance. A few lamps remained lit in common spaces, though the light waned and the cold night overwhelmed the usually warm interior. All the work rooms and storage rooms had been closed up for the night, doors locked from the outside. All members of Lydia's household and her guests had eaten the evening meal and retired to sleep. As Hektor reached the main hall, something scratched against the exterior door.

He pointed his lamp in the direction of the sound, narrowing his eyes in a fight against the darkness for focus. The flicker of light illuminated the room with soft orange hues, and the scratching began again.

Hektor walked tentatively toward the door; every movement deliberate. Carefully, he pressed his ear up against the wood, and that time he heard not only scratching but whimpering as well.

"Hero?" he whispered, before slowly unlatching the door and opening it wide enough to see through. Sure enough, there stood the pathetic creature, his head hung low in shame. Hektor opened the door wider and lightly whistled for him to come inside. "Where have you been?"

Hero slinked inside, pausing once he was within Lydia's walls to stretch out his scrawny limbs and shake his head with a yawn. When he was finished, Hero dropped his body to the floor and rolled onto his back.

"That's a bit presumptuous, isn't it? Wandering in here and expecting to be treated like a king? I thought I gave you a job, Hero."

The dog turned his head away and whined.

"You're meant to stand guard outside Rut's door. How did you even manage to get outside, anyway?" Hektor hadn't known Hero to be the sort of dog to run off, but perhaps all of the recent trips to see Philomena and Xanthe made him more restless. Hektor bent down to scratch the dog behind his ears, but quickly recoiled when he noticed the stench. "Hero! You need a bath!"

"We'll have to see to it tomorrow," said a voice from the darkness behind. *Lydia.*

"I'm sorry," said Hektor, rising from a kneeling position. "I didn't realize you were there. Is something amiss?"

She waved a hand in the air, holding a lamp in her opposite hand. "Nothing at all."

"Can I get you anything?" Hektor asked.

"No, I was just too restless to sleep. I thought I might check the inventory and go over some of the ledgers while I'm still awake."

"Right this way," said Hektor, leading the way back through the workers' courtyard. With a short, light whistle, he added to the dog, "Hero, go to sleep." At once, Hero scampered away awkwardly in the direction of Rut's room, as though his head wanted to move faster than his legs could carry him.

Lydia laughed softly. "He has become quite attached to her."

"I think we all have," said Hektor, realizing that the brief slip may have given way for Lydia to assume his true feelings—feelings he hadn't given much thought to since that day at the river. The day he realized he'd loved her, and that he needed to love her enough let her go.

Lydia unlocked the door to the storage room and went inside. Hektor followed closely behind. "Look at all of this," she said as she spun on her heel, though there wasn't much to look at. "Rut has taught so much to our weavers here that I don't know if we'll be able to keep up with demand."

"Will that be a problem?"

"We'll have more than enough profits to see us through to next year, but I'll need to find a way to source more supplies if we are to keep up at this pace. I don't know how we managed without Rut, and I don't know what we'll do without her next year."

"Without her?" said Hektor, suddenly very confused.

"She is our guest, remember? Like we spoke about in Tyre, she's only visiting us, generously giving us her time and knowledge. We can't make her stay no matter how much we'll miss her."

He nodded as his mind drifted. How could he have forgotten such a thing? Rut had become such an important part of his life. Letting her go that day on the river had been one of the hardest things he'd ever done, and that had only been letting her go into God's hands. He hadn't yet thought of how it would feel when she returned to Tyre. Though he'd always known it in the back of his mind, he hadn't realized until now what their days together being numbered meant for him.

Just like he hadn't realized how much he loved her until recently.

"She hasn't spoken to me about changing her plans, if that's what you were thinking about," said Lydia. The warm glow of the lamplight cast flickering shadows against the shelves upon shelves of baskets of wool, though it was the knowing look in her eyes that forced Hektor to take a second glance.

"Me?"

"Yes, you." Lydia half-smiled. "Don't think I've forgotten the look on your face when we first met her in the marketplace, or how you couldn't stop staring at her that night we all dined together at the inn in Tyre, or the way you breathed in so deeply when you saw she had returned."

"What... I..."

Hektor was stunned. Had it been obvious to everyone but himself how much he cared for Rut, even from that very first day?

"Magnificent work, remember?" She raised her eyebrow at him, and suddenly Hektor felt his face warm, remembering their initial meeting. He had been struck by her beauty that day, but it was the heart within the woman he'd gotten to know that truly captured his own. No one else he'd ever met was as strong, as witty, as determined, or as beautiful as Rut. Not a single woman in all of Macedonia, Tyre, Sidon, or anywhere else in the world could ever come close.

"All that time…" Hektor whispered, marveling at the realization. Had Rut seen it too? Did she return his feelings, or were they unwelcome to her?

"I should've known it would take you this long to sort it out for yourself."

"You never said anything." Though it was a statement, Hektor's voice lilted up at the end as though it were a question.

"No, I did not," said Lydia, matter-of-fact. "I think we can lock up here once again."

"Of course." Hektor stood aside so that Lydia could exit the storage room first.

When they were both outside, Lydia turned around and twisted the bulky lock back into place. Sighing, she dropped her hands to her sides. "I didn't want to interfere, but I worry about what you're going to do when she's gone. You *are* my most trusted servant, Hektor."

Hektor realized at once what Lydia was truly asking. Though she was not normally one to be elusive with her words, Lydia wanted to know if she would lose more than just Rut when she next set sail for the East. Hektor cleared his throat. "I hadn't really thought that far ahead."

"Do you truly love her?"

"I think…" Hektor shook his head. "I do." From that first day, he'd been in love with Rut, her blackish-brown curls, and her wide, evocative eyes. As they became closer, he'd also grown to deeply admire her gentle but determined spirit, and the way she humbly gave all she had and still sought to give more to others even when her spirit was low.

"Does she love you?"

"I don't know."

Lydia nodded her head. "I see."

"I have not yet spoken to her of how I feel… I do not know what would be the best thing to say, or if I should say anything at all."

"Have you prayed about it?"

"Ceaselessly." In truth, the subject had kept him up talking to the Lord through most of the recent nights.

"What would be next if she did return your feelings?"

Hektor breathed in, hoping Lydia would see how much he respected her and valued the role and place she had given him. "Then I would want to ask her to marry me."

"And if she should *not* return your feelings?"

This was the part in Hektor's prayers where he always struggled.

"Hektor," said Lydia, drawing him back to the present moment, "if she should not return your feelings, could you let her go, without letting go of your faith?"

"Yes," he answered, though he knew it would be painful.

Lydia smiled lightly, reassuringly. "Sometimes when we receive a 'no' from someone else, it is really a 'yes' from God for another opportunity. You just have to be willing to look for it, whatever 'it' is."

Hektor chuckled to himself. "The right side of the tapestry," he whispered. It was true when he spoke the words to Rut, and it was true now as the words returned to him when he needed them most. God didn't form them on his lips just for Rut. He put the thought in Hektor's heart as a reminder for his own life and future.

"I'm afraid I don't know what you mean, but I think it is a good thing?" asked Lydia, raising an eyebrow.

"It is." Hektor pointed his lamp ahead and began walking back to the other side of the villa.

"Good," Lydia said, following his steps. "And Hektor?"

"Yes?"

"If she does return your feelings, you absolutely have my blessing. Though as a selfish employer, I naturally wouldn't want to lose you, I hope you know that as your *friend*, I want what is best for you. I will help in any way that I can. You've come so far, Hektor, and I am proud to know you."

Hektor blinked back tears. "Thank you, Lydia."

"Now," she said, darting in front of him and halting abruptly, blocking his path. "What will you say to her? How will you tell her what you feel?"

"I, uh…"

"Oh, come now, Hektor." Lydia tilted her head to one side. "You must plan these sorts of things out somehow if you aim to be successful, and I do believe you stand a good chance at being successful."

"I think I'll defer to the words of the David, in this instance."

"What words are those?" Lydia's brow furrowed.

"'Wait for the Lord; be strong, and let your heart be courageous. Wait for the Lord,'" Hektor quoted, then side-stepped around Lydia, though she continued to follow at a quick pace as he escorted her back to her chambers.

He would wait on the Lord and he would wait for Rut, as long as it took.

"Once, as we were on our way to prayer, a slave girl met us who had a spirit by which she predicted the future. She made a large profit for her owners by fortune-telling." — Acts 16:16 CSB

"What kind of an emergency did Xanthe say she was having?" asked Rut with short, jagged breaths. She struggled to match Lydia's pace as they ascended the steps to Xanthe's house.

"She didn't—her message only said that she had urgent need of us," Lydia answered, just as desperate for respite. "It seemed frantic."

"What could possibly be this urgent?" Rut asked, though she did not expect an answer. At last to the top of the steps, she stopped to smooth out her garments and right her hair.

Before Lydia could even raise her hand to knock, a servant pulled the door open, and the hinge practically screamed its protest. "You're here! Good!" he exclaimed, with a tired and weary expression writ across his face. With haste, the servant stepped aside and pointed in what was presumably Xanthe's direction, offering no further explanation.

As usual, Rut felt Hektor stop behind them. She couldn't explain it, but it was as though whenever he was near, an invisible thread pulled them together, and that tension was severed whenever they were parted, as though cut by a blade.

They arrived in the bright, sunlit garden before Rut's eyes could adjust to the darkness indoors. She looked around and saw Xanthe pacing anxiously, plucking bloom after bloom.

"The flowers look lovely today," said Lydia.

Xanthe waved her hand, dismissive of the compliment. "They probably only have another fortnight or so before they close up until the next year."

When Rut first arrived, she might have thought Xanthe was being rude. Now, after spending enough time in her presence, Rut knew that her demeanor was not personal, nor directed harshly at any one person more than another.

"What kind of flowers are they?" asked Rut.

"Crocuses," Xanthe answered.

"They're so beautiful." Rut admired the saturated colors of the petals, as deep as wool straight out of a dye vat.

"They only bloom at this time of year, and they close up every night and on very cloudy days," Xanthe explained. "But if I wanted to talk about my flowers, I would have summoned a gardener rather than you."

"We came as quickly as we could. What seems to be the problem?" asked Lydia.

"Problem?" Xanthe repeated, flailing her arms. "*Problem? Isn't it obvious?*"

Rut scanned the garden and found nothing askew, except for the crocuses under attack by Xanthe's own hand. Apparently neither did Lydia, for she continued, "I'm sorry, Xanthe, but I don't—"

"It's everything!" Xanthe collapsed into a pile of cushions

and blankets. "Look at these things! I knew I should have sent them to you to be washed properly, but my foolish servants sent them to another fuller in the city. They *clearly* don't specialize in laundering goods of any kind of real value. The color is ruined!" Xanthe threw her head into her hands. Was she trying to make herself shed tears?

"How long?" Rut mouthed to Philomena, inquiring as to how long Xanthe had been in this state.

"Long," Philomena silently replied with extremely exaggerated facial expressions. Rut suppressed a laugh.

"I know it's the fuller's fault and not yours, since I've never had a problem with your purples fading like this before," Xanthe continued.

Looking around at the same excess of purple blankets, cushions, and decorative textiles that had filled the outdoor seating area of the garden during each and every other visit, Rut could see no difference or change in any of them. She looked at Lydia, who seemed to nod her understanding and agreement with the unspoken analysis of the situation.

"Xanthe," whispered Lydia, gently drawing nearer, "everything looks fine."

"It will all have to be replaced, and you're the only one who can do it."

If the situation had not already been so delicate and tense, Rut would have snorted with laughter. Did Xanthe even realize how outlandish of a request that was? The total cost of replacing every woven thing in this home… Not even Xanthe had that much money.

"That would be very expensive," said Lydia, giving voice to everything Rut was thinking.

"Money is no option, I assure you. How many visits do you think you'll need to make to get the job done?"

"Xanthe…" Lydia chided her as only an old friend could. Rut

stepped to the side, closer to Philomena.

"What?" Xanthe snapped, finally giving up the pretense of being heartbroken over one poor launderer's perceived mistake.

"If this is really what you want, we'll be happy to comply with your request, but if this is about something else..." Lydia's voice trailed off.

"What else could this possibly be about?" Rut noticed how Xanthe's eyes began to glisten, moistened by real tears this time.

Lydia leaned in to Xanthe's ear, speaking in hushed tones that Rut could barely hear. "You don't have to pay us to be your friends."

For the first time since meeting her, Rut saw Xanthe let the carefully crafted veil around her heart slip. Rut could recognize it because she too had once guarded her heart from others so fiercely. It had been strangling, and she could see now how Xanthe was locked in a very similar struggle.

"Mena, would you please give me a moment alone with Lydia and Rut?" said Xanthe, her normally in-command voice breaking.

"But, I—"

Xanthe clapped her hands and in doing so summoned a servant to escort her daughter. "You can come back later, my daughter, but I need to speak with Rut and Lydia on my own."

Philomena frowned taking the servant's hand, but did as she was asked with no further argument. Rut tried to give her an encouraging smile in passing, though it was not returned.

"What is it?" asked Lydia, now sitting down. Rut did the same.

"I'm sorry for my outburst. It was foolish of me, I know, but I didn't know how else to ask you to come."

Lydia smiled lightly. "You were right to call us when you needed us. Now what is all of this really about?"

"I... I have listened to your stories of those outside of your faith who received the One True God, like Rahab and Ruth. I have heard the ones about your God's provision for His people in Egypt, Babylon, and beyond. I have heard about your Messiah and I have even heard how your God forgives what seems impossible to forgive in people like Moses, David, and Samson… Do you think there is a place in your faith for one such as me?"

Lydia exhaled deeply. "Oh Xanthe, you don't know how long I've prayed to hear you say those words."

"Wait! Before you answer, you should know what I have done," said Xanthe, eyes wide with fear. "I will only believe you once I have shared it all. Then you can tell me if I am still deserving of such grace. Though I warn you, my life is a mess of one wrong choice after another… I am not good like the two of you."

"I assure you that we are both very much aware of our own imperfections. Do not compare yourself to us, for there is nothing to compare. But if you still wish to unburden yourself, we are both here to listen."

Rut nodded her agreement earnestly.

Xanthe took in one shaky breath, then opened her mouth to speak. "You know that Philomena's father was once a Roman soldier until his retirement seven years ago. What you have been so gracious as to never bring up, however, is the fact that he still would have been a Roman soldier, unable to marry or father legitimate children at the time when Philomena was born."

Rut's face reddened, not because she was embarrassed to be hearing such intimate details from Xanthe, but because it reminded her of the day she had first met this strong, powerful woman, and how she'd very nearly sent herself packing with her loose tongue.

"You must understand this: I have lived in Philippi all my life. So did my mother and father before me, and their parents, and on and on to the time when this land practically flowed rivers of gold and people believed we would pave the streets with it. So much has changed, but especially the degree of Roman influence. In a matter of decades, those in the governing class were replaced by those appointed from Rome, land was given to retired Roman soldiers to populate the area with more Roman citizens, and Roman soldiers were sent to aid the government. If one wanted to have any kind of status, one needed to be Roman."

Xanthe struggled to continue, squeezing her eyes shut and wringing her hands. Biting her lip, she carried on. "At least, that's what my father chose to believe when he realized his money could only get him so far, which is why he didn't protest when he noticed the way my face lit whenever one soldier in particular was near. What difference did a legal ceremony make? I became his common-law bride, as many others had and have done with other soldiers, and we spent every moment together that we could. Everything was perfect until I discovered that I was with child."

"Was Mena's father unhappy?" asked Lydia, referring to the unnamed soldier in Xanthe's story.

"No… Is that too shocking?" Xanthe looked at Rut.

Rut shook her head. "It is not for any of us to judge another, Xanthe." Her own life experiences as well as the things she'd seen throughout the city of Philippi taught her that.

"My husband was thrilled when I first told him the news. Scared, I think, as all men are, but still thrilled. We were going to have everything we ever wanted. My husband looked forward to having a son, and I… I was just happy to have found a lasting love that would rival any of the stories or myths of the gods. My months of being with child were not easy, but I made all kinds of sacrifices and said all kinds of prayers, doing anything I could do to ensure that my little one would come into the world safely.

Then Mena was born."

"I remember that day," said Lydia, cutting in. "She was so small, and we were all so worried about her."

Xanthe nodded her head. "You never judged me for my actions then, either. You supplied clothes and everything I needed, but I really thought of you as a companion."

"Was your husband upset that Philomena was not a boy?" asked Rut.

"No!" said Xanthe, her expression harsh at first before softening. "No, he loved her when she was in my womb and he loved her just as much when she drew her first breaths, but she struggled with illness from the beginning. She did not grow as fast as other babes, and she was constantly sick with one fever or another. I think my husband blamed himself when he realized the full reality of what we had done when we put our love ahead of all other things, and the consequences borne not only by ourselves, but by our daughter."

"Oh, Xanthe," Rut whispered. She couldn't help but think of her dear cousin Libi, who had been born deaf before Jesus healed her in Jerusalem. They had all felt the shame and scorn of their community, with their neighbors and peers believing Libi's affliction was a kind of punishment for some secret, unconfessed sin in their family. It seemed the Jews and the Gentiles had such beliefs in common.

"My husband had sworn an oath before the gods when he enlisted in the army, and he believed that when he shirked his duty to be with me, he incurred the wrath of the gods. The last time we spoke, all I remember is arguing fiercely about loyalty, honor, a man's word meaning something… I remember some of his last words so clearly, for he said, 'I have spent all this time in Philippi training to defend myself and the Empire against its enemies, not realizing that it isn't just the enemy from beyond who threatens. I am capable of being just as large of a threat to myself.' He made a new vow that he would return to his cohort and spend the rest of his career instilling that same ideal in other soldiers, and that he would never go back on his word again. Of course, I couldn't help but wonder why the promises he made me suddenly meant nothing."

"What of your father? Did he defend you?" asked Rut.

"My father knew no shame because we weren't the only family who had settled for a common-law marriage over a traditional one. I heard shortly after that my husband was promoted and sent back to Rome to find new recruits to train. Every so often we would receive money, but it never came with any letters. He held up that part of his word at least, doing his duty to us, but no more. I devoted my life to Mena, though with every fever and every fainting spell, I wished more than anything that my husband would come back. When he finally did, it was nothing like I expected."

"Did he have a change of heart?"

"No… I don't think it was his plan to come back here, but he had reached the age of retirement and I suspect he had nowhere else to go."

"Oh." Rut shrunk backward.

"He walked into the house one day without any warning and asked me, 'Where are your parents?' 'Dead,' I told him, and that was that. I dreamed of his return, but time had only hardened him. I suspect that he always hoped he would die in battle, but he never speaks to me of anything, let alone what happened in the years we were apart. We share the walls of this home and nothing more."

"We are so sorry that you've endured this on your own, Xanthe," said Lydia, reaching for her hand.

Xanthe blinked, and straightened her spine. "Upon his return, we became legally married, and Philomena was officially declared his child. Hear me when I say this: I don't care if my relationship with my husband is ever restored. I don't even care if there's a way for me to receive this grace and salvation of which you speak in each and every one of your stories. All I want is grace for Mena! No physician or spiritual healer has ever been able to identify her illness, but all say her illness will take her life. I would understand if your God could not give me grace, but she is an innocent. She doesn't deserve to be punished for my own folly. Your God is different than any of the others. He speaks to your people and answers prayers, so I am begging you now—would you pray for Philomena, please?"

A chill went down Rut's spine as she felt a raindrop fall on the back of her hand, only that didn't make any sense, for there wasn't a cloud in the sky. She reached up and realized it was not a raindrop at all, but a tear falling from her eye because of how much this conversation reminded Rut of her own journey of faith, and of the words Hektor had spoken to her that still echoed in her heart. "A very dear friend of mine once told me that God and His grace are like a tapestry… When we look back at our lives, we see tangles, knots, and loose threads, but from where God sits, he sees a beautiful pattern being woven as we are drawn closer to Him. You may see only the chaos now, but God sees everything, and if you look for His hand, you will see that He is still wanting to work in your life."

"He… He is?" Xanthe said, stuttering as she struggled to speak.

"He is," said Lydia. "He has made a light for the nations, that all might be able to see the path toward Him. We will pray for both you and Mena, as we always have, but you can pray too. The One True God listens when we call upon Him."

Xanthe fidgeted with her hair. "After all I've done?"

"Yes," answered Rut confidently, remembering the rainfall that day at the river. There was no way to run so far that God could not hear. "We will show you how."

"Show me, too!"

Rut looked up and over her shoulder, surprised to see Philomena once again standing in the corner of the garden.

"Mena!" Xanthe gasped. "Have you been listening this whole time? I thought I told you to—"

"It's all right, Mother. I heard everything, but it is nothing I did not already know or had not guessed before. It does not change how much I love you, or how much I love Father. You're both still my parents, and there is hope for us yet, even if it doesn't come in the form of healing. It is the deeper hope in all of the stories that we can cling to for strength! The hope of a salvation beyond this world. I want to pray to the One True God, too, so don't send me away again."

Wordlessly, or perhaps because she had run out of ways to express what she was feeling, Xanthe motioned for Philomena to come to her side. Rut and Lydia shared with them the greatest story of all: the story of Jesus. They encouraged them to talk to God as though He were a father, because He was—a good, loving, perfect father, who would always be there for them, waiting with His light to guide them home.

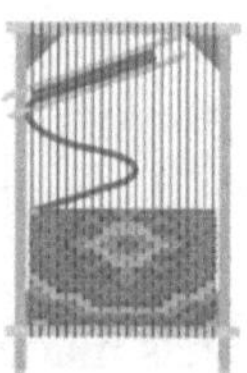

Each week it became more difficult for Hektor to find a place to sit and eat the evening meal. As Paul and his company stayed longer, they naturally reached more and more people with their message—and those people began to gather at Lydia's home to hear Paul speak and ask further questions. Hektor looked at the faces all around, some familiar and some unfamiliar.

That was when his eyes happened upon a woman whose head of dark, black-brown curls faced away from him, though he didn't need to see her face to know that it was Rut. Despite his attempts to wait upon the Lord with patience and trust, Hektor still felt drawn to her. *"Lord,"* he prayed in his heart, *"if she is what You have for me, then test me and strengthen me, that I might be up to the challenge of loving such a rare and remarkable woman. If it is Your will, I believe that You will see it accomplished in Your time, but if it is not, I know what You have planned for my life is even greater, and that is what I long for, Lord."*

Beside Rut at the main table was Lydia. They shared the meal with Paul, Silas, Luke, and Timothy, among a few other guests of honor. It was only right that Hektor also sat at that table as Lydia's guard. There was an empty seat beside Rut, but Hektor had reservations about taking it. After looking around, however, he saw that it was the *only* available space at that table. *"Is this your way of answering my prayer, Lord?"* Hektor chuckled to himself and approached.

"Oh!" Rut jumped.

"I'm sorry. Did I startle you?" asked Hektor, lowering himself to sit beside her.

"A little."

"Apologies—it was the only seat available."

Rut's eyes widened and her lips spread into a wonderstruck smile. "Isn't it incredible? So many have come to speak with Paul and the others."

"Indeed," Hektor nodded, stuffing his mouth with a piece of bread. After swallowing, he called out to the men at the other end of the table. "How have things been for you in the city?"

"Mostly well," said Paul, not without a hint of annoyance in his tone.

Hektor tilted his head to the side, making a quizzical

expression in response as he filled his mouth with some hearty stew. He felt the warmth of the broth fill his belly, partially satisfying an ache he didn't realize was so strong. It immediately made him want more.

"What Paul is choosing not to speak of is the slave girl who harassed us today," said Silas.

"Slave girl?" questioned Hektor as he swallowed back another large gulp.

"We were returning to the place of prayer to see who we might find when we encountered her," explained Timothy. Hektor craned his neck toward the other end of the table where the youngest of Paul's companions sat. The sound of the crowd made it difficult to hear, so Hektor concentrated on the movements of Timothy's face to fill in the gaps his ears could not perceive. "She followed Paul and the rest of us through the city streets, shouting, 'These men who are proclaiming to you a way of salvation, are the servants of the Most High God.' She has continued to do so whenever we are near."

"That is a problem?" asked Hektor, reaching for a pitcher of water in the center of the table and pouring some into his cup.

"She is not just any slave girl, but a *pythoness*," explained Luke. "She tells fortunes in the streets for money."

At that, Paul pushed his plate away, clasping his hands together and pressing them to his chin. "I am concerned about the effect this association may have on our ministry. If people hear the message of salvation coming from a false spirit that is not of the One True God, it could cause confusion. It could also make way for false teachings to spring forth, and I worry that the believers in Philippi are yet too young to be able to discern deception in this way."

Hektor understood the problem clearly now. "Perhaps I could go with you sometime when you pass through the city? I might be able to help fend off any unwanted attention?" Hektor raised an eyebrow in Lydia's direction seeking her approval, though he was certain he would have it.

Lydia nodded her agreement. "That's a wonderful idea, Hektor. I have much too much to do here. You can certainly be spared for a few hours if it will help Paul and his company."

"That would be very much appreciated," said Paul. "Thank you both."

"Of course," Hektor replied. "Anything I can do."

Hektor continued to eat his fill of fruits and cheeses as the conversation carried on to other topics. Lydia discussed how else she could help aid their mission, at one point suggesting that perhaps they might begin dining in the courtyard to accommodate more guests while the weather was clear. Luke discussed his work as a physician, and Lydia shared with him about Philomena and Xanthe, asking if he could discern anything from Philomena's symptoms. Hektor chose not to interject in any of those discussions.

The realization did not escape him, however, that Rut also remained quiet throughout it all. He longed to hear her voice again but was suddenly at a complete and total loss for how to start a conversation with her. What if he said the wrong thing? What if he asked the wrong question? What if he did something foolish to embarrass himself, or embarrass her?

He shook his head.

Such thinking was nonsensical; he had always been able to talk to Rut. No matter what, he still thought of her as a friend. Wasn't that the best basis for any kind of relationship?

Turning directly to her, Hektor asked, "How has your weaving been going?"

She smiled cordially. "Xanthe's orders have kept me busy, but I've finished the last of those, so I've started assisting the spinners more."

Hektor nodded. "That is good, but I was not referring to your work."

"Then what did you mean?"

"Have you woven anything for yourself recently?" asked Hektor. "On your own loom, that is."

"Oh… No, not really. I tried, but…" Her voice trailed off as her eyes traveled to some distant place. Were they traveling back to her home in Phoenicia? Backward in time?

"But what?" Hektor dared to ask.

She turned her gaze back toward him and shrugged her shoulders. "I want you to know I'm very grateful to you for bringing me that loom on my first day here. I did spend many nights sitting before it, and I started several projects, but I always ended up unraveling them."

"Ah." Hektor laughed. "So you're a perfectionist. I should have expected as much from the woman who may one day singlehandedly weave garments for the entire class of Macedonian nobility."

She reached up to cover her face as she laughed heartily. She tried to muffle her snort, but Hektor still heard it, and it warmed his heart. He found the sound adorable, and like everything else about Rut, perfectly unique to her. "I hardly think that's the case," Rut began once she'd regained her composure, "though I'm sure Xanthe alone has enough to clothe at least half. No, no, I am simply here to help share what I know with Lydia's weavers before I—"

"Before you return to Phoenicia," Hektor finished the sentence, and the words hung awkwardly in the air between them for a moment. The thought didn't sting so much to him as it had when he first spoke of it with Lydia, but it didn't thrill him either.

"Yes," she spoke slowly, "to my family."

"Do you miss them very much?"

"I do, but not in the way I thought I would when I first came here."

"How is that?"

Rut began folding and unfolding the edge of her sleeve as she spoke, a habit of hers. "I knew I would miss them in the usual way—that I would wonder what they were doing each day and night, and how the children have grown. I didn't expect that I would change so much while I was gone, and there's a great deal that I can't wait to tell them. Things I should have told them years ago."

"That's wonderful, Rut," Hektor eked out the words. "I'm happy for you."

She smiled up at him, but her eyes lingered as though they were searching his for something—but what? Could it be… *no*. Hektor would not allow his mind to leap to any conclusions. The fastest way to lose was to think the outcome was already won.

"I think you should try to weave something for yourself again," said Hektor, spontaneously declaring the next thing that came to his mind.

"Oh, Hektor. I really don't need anything."

"If it's perfectionism that is your problem, then—"

"It's not that," said Rut, raising her hand. Hektor paused to listen to what she had to say. She pursed her lips, breathing slowly before continuing. "I think in the past, I used weaving as a distraction."

"What kind of a distraction?"

"It's not important," she said, moving to rise.

"Wait!" Hektor reached out with his hand to stop her. "Everything you think is important to me."

She lowered herself back down slowly, calmly, careful to not make a fuss as he had done. "There was a time when weaving was the one area of my life where I felt I had control, and anytime my struggles became overwhelming, I would lose myself to my loom or my spindle. I kept myself so busy that I rarely had time for anyone or anything else, and I liked it that way because I didn't want to engage with others, nor did I want to be left alone with my thoughts for too long. I think I'm scared of that happening again."

While Rut spoke, Hektor began to forget that there was anyone else in the room with them, even though the grand hall teemed with people. There could have been a hundred other conversations going on in that room, and Hektor still would have only heard one voice.

"What if you made something as a gift for someone else?" Hektor suggested. "You could make something for me if you wanted."

Her brows moved closer together, and one stray curl fell down into her face as she tilted her head toward him. "Why do you care so much?"

"Because you possess an incredible talent and I believe God gave you this talent for a reason. You're creative and your creativity should be celebrated, Rut. Is not the One True God a creator Himself, creating the world and everyone in it, including you and me?"

Rut sighed and for a moment Hektor wondered if he had offended her. When he saw her mouth break into half of a smile, his hope was restored. "What would I make for you?"

"Something beautiful," said Hektor. Boldly, and perhaps without thinking, he added in a hushed voice, "like you."

Rut turned away so that Hektor could not see her face. Was it because she did not like what he said? Or because she did?

"I'll think about it," she said, though her tone was not one of disapproval or apprehension. Her voice was soft and airy, like a gentle breeze coming off of the sea. "Mind you, I'm not making any promises."

Hektor could still see the faintest hint of blush on her cheeks when she turned back to him. He smiled looking into her deep brown eyes. "That's good enough for me."

Hektor excused himself from the table after that. He wondered if he'd almost gone too far with his compliments of Rut, but he prayed that it was right. Hektor trusted the Lord, knowing that every good thing came in His timing, but there were moments like when he sat beside Rut and couldn't help but wish that time could pass just a bit faster.

Then again, if Rut was the woman for him, he wanted to be able to treasure each moment waiting for her as much as he treasured Rut herself.

Part Four

"I don't say this out of need, for I have learned to be content in whatever circumstances I find myself. I know how to make do with little, and I know how to make do with a lot. In any and all circumstances I have learned the secret of being content— whether well fed or hungry, whether in abundance or in need. I am able to do all things through him who strengthens me." —
Philippians 4:11-13 CSB

"God is our refuge and strength, a helper who is always found in times of trouble." — Psalm 46:1 CSB

Rut finished twisting the ends of her curls together and securing her hair in a knot at the base of her head, pausing only briefly to check her reflection in the dimly polished mirror. Seeing that everything was in place, or at least as much as she could get it to be, she grabbed her satchel and moved toward the door, taking long, fast-paced strides past Hektor's loom. Was it his, really? No, but after their conversation a few days earlier, she thought of it as such.

Swinging open the door, Rut nearly tripped over a basket left on the floor just beyond her threshold.

"What is this?" she asked herself, bending down to pull it into her room.

When she did so, she saw exactly what it was—a basket full of wool and not just any ordinary wool. These colors were vibrant yellows, greens, and reds—shades Lydia did not keep in her supply. Rut knew immediately two distinct things: the first being that Hektor must have been the giver of this gift, and the second being that he must have purchased this wool at great personal expense, for though they were not as dear as purple, colors this rich were costly.

Rut had partially consented to weave something for him, but could it be considered a gift if he were the one supplying the materials?

"What would I make for you?" she had asked him.

"Something beautiful, like you," he had replied.

The memory of those last two words in combination with the gift brought a warm smile to Rut's face, along with a tingling, fluttery feeling in her heart she hadn't experienced in a long time. Rut shook the giddiness aside—she was too old to have these kinds of feelings, wasn't she?

She wasn't the girl she had been when she met Shem. Rut had changed from blushing young bride to devastated widow in those years. She carried with her complicated memories and experiences that meant she would never see the world in quite the same way again. Like dyed wool, the color of those experiences might fade, but they could never be completely washed away from her mind.

Even so, did that leave room for new experiences?

There was no need to contemplate such things, Rut realized, as Hektor had only ever been a good friend to her. From the beginning, he offered his help and loyalty to her with no question of what he could gain in return. He was still looking out for her, wanting to aid her and see her succeed. Rut realized that she should be grateful for that, and find comfort in such knowledge.

He had also called her beautiful…

In combination with everything else, could it be that Hektor's friendship was more affectionate than Rut assumed?

She had no time left to lazily muse over such things. Rut

closed the door to her chambers behind her and hurriedly made her way to Lydia, who stood alone in the receiving courtyard presumably awaiting her arrival.

"Where is Hektor?" asked Rut.

"It is good to see you too," said Lydia, raising one of her perfectly arched, fair eyebrows.

Rut brought her hands up to her cheeks and shook her head. Could she think of nothing else but Hektor? "I'm sorry, Lydia. How are you this morning?"

Lydia laughed. "I was only teasing, though I am well and I hope the same of you. Hektor is meeting us outside with Hero."

"I hope I didn't make us late," said Rut, adjusting the strap of her satchel on her shoulder.

"Nonsense, but I must ask why you are bringing your satchel? This visit to Xanthe's is a social call. It is not likely that you will need any tools."

Rut shrugged. "I suppose it is a habit. Should I put it back?"

Lydia waved a hand in dismissal. "It's all right this time. We should be going or we will be late."

Sounds of laughter and joy-filled conversation filled the garden and floated out overhead as hearts bloomed with new life. Xanthe had started requesting that Rut and Lydia visit more often to tell news of Paul and his company. They always encouraged Xanthe to join them at Lydia's house to hear Paul speak in person, but she never accepted the invitation. Her polite decline was not because she didn't want to attend; rather,

Xanthe was afraid of what her husband might do if he found out, given that he had not returned to her under the best of circumstances. So, the women continued to meet together in the garden for prayer and fellowship. In her heart, Rut prayed that all of their faith would grow strong here so that when trouble came, they would be able to remain fruitful even in hardship and rooted in God's unfailing love.

"Come, Hero," said Philomena, clapping her hands to get the dog's attention. "Where is it that you're always disappearing to, my friend?"

Rut laughed at the sight of the dog, trotting in with his gangly legs and goofy, panting smile. He sat beside Philomena as she stroked his short, sand-colored fur, his tail still wagging and thumping a steady rhythm against the ground. "That is what I keep wondering as well," said Rut. "It is as though Hero has a life of his own when we bring him here."

"Perhaps he goes to the kitchens to beg for scraps from the servants," said Xanthe. "Isn't that what dogs normally do?"

"Hero is no normal dog, Xanthe," replied Lydia. "I would not put anything past him."

"It's true, Mother," said Philomena, her eyes still focused on Hero, "sometimes I truly think that he understands us when we talk. He surely knows more than just words like 'come' or 'sit' or 'food.'"

"Perhaps he is a philosopher among dogs," Rut jested.

"Or perhaps he has his own business to attend to," suggested Lydia. "Are you a rival to me, Hero? You'd better not be trading away my secrets to any other dogs."

"How is your business doing, Lydia?" asked Xanthe politely, though it was clear to Rut after their many conversations that Xanthe did not have a head for numbers or the technical know-how to understand the complexities of textile creation.

"It is well. We always have a steady number of orders coming in from the governing class, and the victors of the most recent games are eager to display their resplendence as well. Rut's knowledge and advice has made the quality of our goods even more desirable, and I am so grateful to her for being willing to train my weavers."

Xanthe nodded her head. "That is good."

"Indeed," Lydia agreed.

"How are you, Philomena?" said Rut, moving closer to her. As she got closer, she noticed how her lips, normally youthful and rosy, appeared almost blue.

While Rut could see the usual lively sparkle in her eyes, she also saw pain. Why was it that this happened to such a sweet girl, and why was it that no physician could find an answer to treat her?

The longer Rut knew these women, the more Rut understood the depths of Xanthe's fears. Rut lost Shem so suddenly and so unexpectedly; there had never been a time in her young life where she had even considered the possibility of living without him. Philomena, on the other hand, was Xanthe's whole world. She had borne and raised her, protecting her from everything she could. All the while, Xanthe was incapable of protecting Philomena from the sickness that plagued her own body.

While Rut had never contemplated having to say goodbye to Shem, Xanthe contemplated every single day the possible reality that she could outlive her own child. Having Hero around certainly raised Philomena's spirits, and their newfound faith gave them reason to hope for something beyond physical healing, but Philomena's condition was obviously worsening, and fast.

"I am just tired." Philomena sighed. Rut heard the ever-present wheezing in her breath as she struggled to take in more air.

"Perhaps you should go and rest? Lie down for a while?"

asked Rut.

Philomena shook her head. "I would rather be here with you, talking and hearing your stories about Paul, but perhaps you are right. The sunlight seems unusually bright today, and it's making my head ache." Philomena finally stopped petting Hero and raised a hand up to her forehead, closing her eyes. Although Philomena had always been unwell, this was the first time that Rut ever heard her express wanting to excuse herself. Normally it was Xanthe who gave the order in love, not wanting to see her daughter push her own limits.

"Do you want me to call someone to help you to your room?" asked Xanthe.

"No, I think—"

Philomena began to sway and wobble as she stood up, and Rut rose to brace her.

"I'm calling for help," said Xanthe, clapping once again in a very distinct rhythm. Immediately, servants appeared on the opposite side of Philomena from Rut, catching her just as Rut's own strength was about to give way. Philomena's body went completely limp in the servants' arms.

"Take her to her room and summon a physician," said Xanthe. "I will follow."

Rut watched the servants leave, unable to process what had happened. Her arms remained suspended as though she were still holding Philomena, but they were empty and cold.

"Xanthe, what can we do? We can stay with you, or if you need us to leave, we can see ourselves out," said Lydia, clearly thinking much faster than Rut.

"Yes, I think…" Rather than finish her sentence, Xanthe collapsed, weeping.

"Oh, Xanthe, my friend," said Lydia, wrapping her arms around the woman.

"The physicians warned me that this day would come, but I

always thought…"

"We must pray, Xanthe. Mena is in the Lord's hands," said Lydia. "He alone is our strength in times of trouble. There is peace in surrendering our hearts to Him."

"I can't find the words," said Xanthe between ragged breaths. "Please, will you help me to start?"

"Xanthe, do not worry. The Lord hears even our wordless pleas," said Rut through tears of her own, knowing now more than ever how true the sentiment was.

"We will pray, and then we will go with you to be with Mena," said Lydia. Then she turned to Rut. "Will you start?"

Rut nodded and bowed her head, taking the other women's hands. "Our Father in Heaven, Your kingdom come and Your will be done on earth as it is in heaven. We pray as Jesus Christ taught us to—"

"No."

Rut startled at the sound of an unfamiliar man's voice. It was so low, yet it rattled her bones like thunder. She jerked her eyes up to see Xanthe's face, pale and devoid of every other emotion except one: terror.

"Servius!" she gasped.

Rut and Lydia jumped to their feet, and Rut turned to see the foreboding man—presumably Xanthe's husband—standing in the rear entrance to the garden.

"Not you, too," he growled, and Rut felt truly afraid.

"This is a private matter. We should be going," Hektor heard

Lydia say in a clearly distressed voice. Normally, he did not attune his ears to the exact words spoken by the women, but Lydia's tone stood out from the usual quiet, steady hum of conversation. All of his muscles tensed as he inclined his ears toward the garden.

"A private matter, indeed!" a man shouted. The man of the house, perhaps? Hektor had never seen him, but knew he existed. "You should have thought of that before you drew my wife to your sect of agitators and rebels!"

"Servius, no!" said Xanthe. *Servius Arrius!* Hektor recognized the name from overhearing the servants. This was the man of the house!

"How could you be so stupid, Xanthe? How could you fall for their lies?"

"They aren't lies, Servius! I believe them!" Xanthe cried.

"What would you know? Who are these women?"

"Please, Servius—it is only Lydia, the seller of purple, and Rut, a weaver."

"So," the man's speech slurred, his next words obviously infected by the venom of excessive drink that Hektor knew all too well. "You are taking advantage of my wife, selling her dresses with one hand, and superstition with the other. Do not think that I don't know the exorbitant prices she pays for textiles. You are thieves who prey upon the weak-minded."

"I assure you, nothing of the sort has happened—" Lydia began.

"Out! All of you, get out!" Servius shouted, cutting her off.

When Hektor heard the crash of a heavy object followed by the cries of both Lydia and Rut, he wasted no time entering the garden, leaping over the fallen pottery to place himself between the two women he protected and Servius' wrath.

"Stand down," commanded Hektor, his arm outstretched as if to push the man away. "These are honorable women."

Servius' hand held an empty goblet, which confirmed Hektor's suspicions about the man's state of mind. Hektor's mouth went dry as he swallowed back thousands of words he could have said but would not have been effective at assuaging the man's temper.

"You're not in your right mind," said Hektor instead, hoping Servius could still discern reason from mania.

Servius huffed, throwing the goblet at Hektor with a grunt. Hektor knocked it out of the way with his arm, causing it to fall to the floor with a clang. "All of you, get out now!"

"Come on." When Hektor turned to face Lydia and Rut, who was in tears, he spread out his arms as a shield. "Do you have your things?"

Both women nodded shakily. Rut tightened her grip on her satchel, pulling it close to her middle. Hektor escorted them away from the garden.

"Religious scum!" shouted Servius.

"Please, don't—" Xanthe's pleading was cut short by her own wounded scream, which caused Hektor to abruptly turn on his heels with his fists curled. Xanthe had fallen to the ground, though the evidence was clear that she'd more likely been struck.

"Stop this!" said Hektor. "We are leaving, just as you asked. Why treat your wife in this way?"

"In *my* house, I will treat *my* wife as I see fit!"

Unfortunately, Servius was right, and Hektor could do nothing about it. Silently, he continued to usher Rut and Lydia through the doorway back into the main hall, though refusing to take his eyes away from Servius, in case he did something rash in his stupor.

"You will respect me, Xanthe. One way or another, you will learn, and this will be your first lesson: that purple seller and anyone associated with her shall never be allowed in this house again."

"No!" Xanthe protested, though her voice was significantly weaker.

"And they shall likely never do business again—either with you or any other veteran's wife within this city," Servius' threats continued, echoing loudly enough for them to hear even as they stepped out onto the streets.

"Hektor, what are we going to do?" said Rut. "What about Xanthe and Philomena? How can we leave them like this when they need us now more than ever?"

Hektor had not even noticed until now how tightly she clung to his arm. The feeling of it rallied his heart and mind together, making him feel as though he had the strength and wherewithal to tear down the entire wall surrounding the city of Philippi brick by brick. He would build it all back up again in a day if it would somehow make Rut feel safe.

He looked down to see her tear-stricken face, her wide, brown eyes searching his for answers, and her lower lip quivering as she struggled with the unknown.

Hektor didn't have answers about what they would do next. He didn't have answers about what would happen to Xanthe or Philomena. He didn't have answers about what would happen to Lydia's business, whether or not Servius' threats had merit, or what it would mean for all of them. What Hektor did have an answer for was knowing what to do when things were so clearly beyond the control of human hands. They needed to take their burdens and leave them with the Lord. As Hektor had learned— or continued to learn, day by day—to start resting, you had to stop wrestling.

"I don't know what will happen, Rut," said Hektor, placing his opposite hand on top of hers, which still dug into his arm. "but God does. We must leave it to Him now. It is His tapestry, isn't it?"

"Yes… It is," she whimpered, leaning her head against his arm.

Hektor breathed in shakily as he experienced a feeling in his stomach akin to the fluttering of butterfly wings, though strangely and despite his aversion to winged insects, it did not make him recoil. It only made him want to draw Rut even closer to himself and to keep her safe in his arms. Instead, he chose to comfort her with psalms far more eloquent than his own words. "Remember the words of David: 'You yourself have recorded my wanderings. Put my tears in your bottle. Are they not in your book?' The Lord sees our tears and hears our prayers. He will take care of everything, Rut."

All that was left to do was pray. Hektor knew they all would, but as he looked into Rut's deep, brown eyes, he still longed to do more.

"As she followed Paul and us she cried out, 'These men, who are proclaiming to you a way of salvation, are the servants of the Most High God.' She did this for many days. Paul was greatly annoyed. Turning to the spirit, he said, 'I command you in the name of Jesus Christ to come out of her!' And it came out right away. When her owners realized that their hope of profit was gone, they seized Paul and Silas and dragged them into the marketplace to the authorities." — Acts 16:16-19 CSB

Rut sat idle in the weaving room, and she despised the feeling. It seemed that with Xanthe's orders coming to a halt, so halted all the other orders from everyone in her circle—or everyone under Servius Arrius' influence. He had made good on the promises he made in the heat of anger, and Rut wasn't sure why she had dared to hope for anything different.

Rather than a woman seated at every loom, the weaving room remained out of use for two whole weeks. There was no sense in weaving cloth that couldn't be sold, so instead, Lydia's workers sat spinning baskets and baskets *and baskets* of wool. There were no orders pending, no projects to complete, and no real intended purpose for the masses of spun wool that their labors produced. Though she didn't have to, Rut joined in because the busywork kept her hands active. It did not, however, stop her from feeling wholly useless. She was working toward an end goal that did not exist, and it irked her.

While she worked, her knee bobbed up and down with unspent energy. Her eyes lost focus on the world around her as she contemplated all the many things she had to be frustrated about. How could that man—Servius Arrius—speak in such a venomous way to his own wife? Furthermore, what good was Rut's presence in Philippi now? And what would happen to Xanthe and Philomena, trapped in that house?

In a moment of split concentration, Rut dropped the spindle, distaff, and what wool she had managed to spin. "Agh!" she grunted, bending over to pick it up. When she did, her hands brushed with Hektor's, who had reached the messy pile mere moments before her. Her eyes met with his, and their faces were so close they practically shared a breath. Aside from when she had desperately clung to his arm as Servius Arrius threw them out, she couldn't recall being this close to him since that night on the ship when he'd talked to her throughout all of her panic until the storm passed and she could once again rest. However long he'd been standing beside her before she noticed him at this moment, she did not know, but it also did not matter. She was grateful for his calming presence.

She may have even craved it.

"Is it ruined?" he asked as he gathered it back up and placed it in her hands for her.

She shook her head. "Thank you." It wasn't ruined, but the wool that fell to the ground had now picked up a substantial amount of dust, dirt, and debris. Its quality was no longer pristine and Rut's carelessness and anger only added to the work, but in light of everything else, it was of little consequence.

"Anything else I can do to help?"

"No, Hektor. I'm afraid that there is nothing anyone can do." She set the wool and spindle aside with possibly a little too much force, though Hektor did not back away. Rut noticed how some of the other women looked up with concerned glances. Doing her best to put on a calm face, she moved out of the weaving room and into the worker's courtyard for a break. Outside, she felt the warmth of the sun hit her face as she moved to take a seat on a bench and look up at the clouds passing overhead.

"Now I know this isn't just about the wool." Hektor sat down beside her. "What is it that is truly troubling you?"

She turned toward him, raising an eyebrow. "I think you can guess the answer to that without me having to explain it to you—unless you suffered one too many blows to the head in your years as the Lion of Philippi?"

He mirrored her expression, though with an added smile. "I think *you know* that talking about it might help you work it out in the same way that you work out those knots in the wool."

She slid away from him and began to pace, refusing to make eye contact in an effort to keep herself from losing her words. "For the first time in years, Hektor, I was finally able to see God's plan in my pain, and I saw His goodness and mercy in my life. But now there is Philomena's worsening condition, the trouble with Xanthe and her husband, as well as the damage to Lydia's business. Where is God's purpose in this? I am struggling again, and it frightens me… I don't want to go back to the way I was."

"I… I wish I could say," said Hektor.

"Neither of us can answer such questions, I know, but I am so weary of feeling helpless and alone."

"But you're not alone."

Rut turned to look into Hektor's sea-blue eyes, wondering what he meant by his words. Did he mean it in the way of a fellow believer, or did he mean it as something more? What was it about Hektor that made Rut feel like she could share anything with him?

"Rut, I—" He began to say something in a soft, breathless tone Rut had never heard him use before, but other voices cut him off and drew their attention away from each other.

"Hektor," called a male speaker that Rut recognized as one of Lydia's household servants, "someone is at the back door demanding to be let in at once, but we don't know who she is."

Rut realized why the servant had come—Hektor was in charge of the safety and security of all in this villa. If there was a mysterious intruder, Hektor should be the first to know.

"She?" asked Hektor.

More voices approached the courtyard, all saying things like "Please, wait," and "If you'll come this way..." One voice was loudest among them all, however.

"I must speak to Rut and Lydia at once." It was Xanthe, in the worker's courtyard and shouting with as much authority as she would have in her own home, though dressed as a member of the common class.

Lydia rushed out of the weaving room; she must have heard the commotion. "Xanthe!" she gasped.

Hektor turned to the servants who stood around her with gawking expressions. "It's all right. You may all go back to your work."

"Wait!" said Lydia, raising a hand. "Would one of you please bring water for our guest? Xanthe, come with us into another room." Lydia took Xanthe's arm and ushered her to an area more appropriate for receiving guests, and far away from the eyes of the other weavers and spinners—spinners whose tongues, Rut learned, could spin stories faster than their hands could spin wool.

Rut and Hektor followed, exchanging wide-eyed looks of wonder and surprise. All of them sat on cushioned chairs and waited for the conversation to begin. Rut's mind was filled with so many questions, but she waited, appropriately, for Lydia to ask them. This was her household, and Xanthe was her guest just as much as Rut.

"Xanthe, how is it that you have come today?" asked Lydia.

"I stole away but I don't have much time." Xanthe cast aside the heavy cloak she wore, revealing the plainest of garments. She had clearly put thought into her disguise. At a glance, Xanthe could have easily passed as a servant as she left her own house. "Mena is even worse since you last saw her. She has not left her bed since that dreadful day and I don't know what to do."

"Are you well? Is your husband…" Lydia left the half-question hanging in the air as a pair of servants entered, carrying with them some haphazard trays of food and water likely put together in a hurry. They set them down and left quietly.

Xanthe drank some of the water and nibbled at some grapes. Only when Lydia's servants were well out of earshot did Xanthe open her mouth to speak again. "What you saw was the most he has spoken to me in years. After Mena's condition worsened, I summoned servants at once to alert him. I thought it might soften his heart and make him want to *spend time* with her! Instead, he has summoned every kind of pagan healer and spiritual advisor imaginable, each of them bringing with them their own charms, idols, and incense. Will the One True God punish us now because of what my husband is doing?"

Rut leaned forward, projecting to Xanthe a look of sympathy with her eyes. "Keep your faith, Xanthe. God hears our prayers even when we feel He is so far away. We have still been praying for you, too."

"You have?" asked Xanthe, her voice barely above a whisper.

"Of course!" Lydia exclaimed. "And we will *keep* praying until God answers!"

Xanthe nodded in understanding, breathing slowly until gradually her heavy sighs turned into subdued inhalations. Rut looked on at the woman and watched how her eyes darted all around the room, taking it all in. "I've never seen your home, Lydia. Is that not strange in all of these years of us being friends?"

Lydia smiled. "It is more of a business than a home."

"I've barely even left my own house since Mena was small… I had to ask for directions to get here."

"I'm glad you found your way safely," said Lydia.

"I've never seen the inside of a textile business, either, except for what I saw when I arrived. Is it always so busy with so many servants gathered in a single space?"

More than likely, the only reason Rut could surmise that Xanthe encountered so many servants and laborers in such quick succession was because they had nothing better to do than crowd in common areas, but Rut kept her remark in check.

"Sometimes," said Lydia, biting her lip.

"You're lying," said Xanthe, dryly. "I saw the looks on your faces when I entered. I've never seen a textile business, but unless that was a storage room you came out of, I'm fairly certain that there were supposed to be threads on those looms."

Lydia's mouth opened, and Rut too was shocked by Xanthe's shrewdness. "You noticed all of that?"

"Just because I've spent most of my life in relative seclusion within a gilded garden does not mean that I know nothing of the world." Xanthe's voice returned to its usual no-nonsense tone, and Rut was reminded that Xanthe was the kind of woman who could assume command in any environment—even when she would otherwise be considered a foreigner in a foreign land.

"Well, it is true. We have no orders pending, but we are sure more will come in soon. Isn't that right, Rut?"

Rut blinked, unprepared. "What—yes! It is just… slow," said Rut.

Xanthe shook her head. "What you're telling me is that my husband made good on his word, as he always has, down to the exact letter. He has probably told every man he knows to forbid their wives to shop from your wares. Those who had orders pending probably canceled them too, didn't they?"

Lydia did not respond verbally, and Xanthe rubbed at her temples in dismay.

"Xanthe," Rut began again, "trust me in this—things may seem like a tangled mess of threads now, but the One True God is near."

Admittedly, Rut had spent most of the last fortnight struggling with that hard-earned lesson, but seeing Xanthe disheartened—or seeing a reflection in Xanthe of Rut's own feelings—reminded Rut that nothing had really changed. God remained constant. It was people who forgot or turned away, and that was something that they could not afford to do now. They rejoiced in the Lord when things went well; they would continue to rejoice now, for even when things were difficult, the Lord's ways were still good. Still perfect. Still beautiful.

Briefly, Rut chanced a glance at Hektor, whose request of her was the only reason she'd been able to keep practicing her weaving skills. He smiled at her—just smiled—and it filled her heart with an indescribable and immeasurable kind of gratitude.

"I want to believe that, but I still feel so alone."

Rut's heart burned at Xanthe's admission. Had she not just shared the same feelings with Hektor? "Months ago, I too felt alone, and I chose to remain in that feeling even though it wasn't the truth. I would have given up back then, but I know now that neither of us can afford to give up. We must trust that God, like a weaver, is weaving every thread together. He is making something out of this, Xanthe."

"Yes, He is," Lydia echoed.

"Thank you, both, so much," said Xanthe, reaching out for their hands. Rut offered hers and felt Xanthe give it a light squeeze. "I wish I could stay, but—"

"Go," said Lydia with a soft smile spread across her lips, "be with your daughter."

Xanthe nodded tearfully. "You can never possibly understand how much it has strengthened me just to talk with you if only for a short time."

If only Xanthe knew that her visit had been equally as strengthening to Rut as it had been for Xanthe herself.

The three women embraced after that, saying their goodbyes, and Lydia walked Xanthe outside, though this time through the *front* door. Rut stayed behind with Hektor, who had been a passive observer of the short encounter.

"Should we clean this up?" she asked, gesturing to the trays that Lydia's servants had brought in earlier.

"We can take it to the kitchen," said Hektor. "They'll know what to do with it."

"All right." Rut took it in hand and walked beside Hektor toward the workers' courtyard.

"What you said was true," said Hektor. Rut looked up at him and saw the familiar twinkle in his eyes, as though in their brilliant blue color, they contained the stars themselves. "I think we all needed to hear it again. I know it helped me too."

"It did? How?" asked Rut.

Hektor chuckled. "Well, it is only that I too have been struggling with wanting to do more lately. To *be* more. When we were at Xanthe's house and that excuse of a man was saying those horrid things, I wanted to—"

Hektor leaned his head back as though he were physically

restraining himself from voicing the rest of his thought aloud.

"Do some things you haven't done since you were the Lion of Philippi?" Rut whispered.

"Something like that. When it comes to your safety, Rut, I find that I…"

Rut held her breath that time, waiting for what he was going to say next.

"That is to say, when you spoke to Xanthe, you reminded me that God alone is in control of our lives and the directions that they will take. All I can do is pray to Him, and leave my own longings at His feet."

Longings…. Did Hektor long to share his heart with Rut as much as she did with him? She would not likely find out—not that afternoon anyway, for all too soon, they reached the kitchen and parted ways. Hektor went to secure the villa as evening fell, and Rut went back to helping the other women, though she did so with a lighter heart as she contemplated with hopeful prayer the things both said and unsaid between them.

Another day passed with no excitement. Xanthe's visit during the previous day had stirred up some new conversation among the workers and servants, but it quickly died down. Hektor had very little to do but pace the perimeter of the house with Hero, so when Paul told him that he and his company were interested in going into the city to preach that day, Hektor jumped at the opportunity. With the *Python* girl causing trouble for them lately, Hektor now accompanied them as an extra measure of safety and security.

"It's crowded today," said Hektor.

"Indeed," said Luke, the physician. "It must be the cool weather that draws out the people."

"So many people, and yet it is difficult to find those who will listen to our message," said Timothy.

Paul patted him on the back. "That is why I brought you along on this journey, Timothy. You have the knowledge *here*." Paul pointed to his head. "From infancy, you have been taught scripture. That is good! Now is the time for you to learn how to use that scripture inspired by God for the good work of His kingdom."

"I can only hope I do not fail," said Timothy.

"Be at peace, son," replied Paul. "You have presented yourself before the Lord. He will guide you in His plan when the time comes."

"The most important thing," added Silas, "is your willingness to go where you are called. Your earnest desire to serve is a credit to your character, Timothy."

Hektor listened to the exchange with a smile on his face. Timothy was the youngest in Paul's traveling group, and as Hektor observed, a kind of apprentice to the others. Hektor enjoyed listening to their lessons and conversations, as they always taught him something too. He learned from their example the finer points of faith, service, and dedication to God.

A feminine voice wailed ahead of them as they reached the forum. "These men, who are proclaiming to you a way of salvation, are the servants of the Most High God!"

"There she is again," said Silas through gritted teeth.

"The Pythoness," muttered Paul. "Why doesn't she stop?"

Hektor slowed his steps so that he was walking behind Paul and his company, rather than beside them, able to see over them to what lay ahead. "Is she here all the time?"

"She is always somewhere in this area," explained Luke. "She makes a great profit for her masters as a soothsayer and fortune teller."

Something still did not make sense to Hektor. "But what profit do they gain from this? Surely they find it troublesome as well?"

"On the contrary, I think they appreciate how the spectacle draws attention to her," said Luke.

"Well, this is no spectacle. The message we bring is one of truth, not like the heretical tales of Python," said Paul. His eyes narrowed as he looked to the side where the girl waved her arms as she raved and rambled. Paul's jaw clenched and unclenched repeatedly as he seemed to be weighing over his options of how to respond.

"Perhaps if we walk fast enough, we can get to the other side and go—" Hektor tried to suggest an alternate plan for their day, and failed.

"Her madness is hindering our mission!" Paul interrupted, his face reddening.

"These men are servants of the Most High God!" she shouted again, pointing at them. Her eyes were wide, crazed even. Hektor couldn't explain it logically, but when he looked at her, he became overwhelmed with a queasy feeling in his stomach, as though he had taken bad food. "They have come to proclaim a message! A message of salvation!"

At the same time, Hektor could not help but notice how young she was. Had this been the only life she had ever known? The life of a Pythoness?

"How many days has it been now?" asked Paul.

"*Several,*" said Silas.

At Silas' word, the woman began screaming her ravings, overcome with hysteria. Hektor was there to protect Paul and his companions. Since they had nearly passed her, Hektor had not anticipated Paul turning abruptly back toward the slave girl, his finger in the air pointing at her. Hektor spun on his heel, but Paul moved too quickly.

"I command you in the name of Jesus Christ to come out of her!" he shouted.

The whole crowd seemed to hush all at once, Hektor included. The girl's screeching stopped. She fell to the ground unconscious, and her masters rushed to her side.

"Pythia! Pythia!" shouted her masters as they shook her limp body.

Astonishment coursed through Hektor's veins, making his heart race. He continued to watch the scene, and slowly the crowd began to whisper, then mumble about the events playing out before their very eyes.

She groaned softly as though waking up from a long slumber. "My name… is not… Pythia…"

One of the men who held onto her slowly shifted his gaze from her onto Paul, and Hektor felt true fear. The locals in Philippi were fairly tolerant of many religions and faiths, having so many temples and places of worship to their own gods and cults throughout the city. However, even their tolerance had its limits, and if there was one thing Hektor knew how to spot from a mile away, it was a fight waiting to happen.

"You…" The man hissed, dropping the girl's shoulders. Her head hit the ground, *hard*, and Hektor winced. "You've ruined her!"

"*The One True God* freed her," said Paul firmly.

"Seize them!" the man shouted, lunging toward Paul. The other who was with him also abandoned the girl, rushing toward them.

"We need to leave, now!" Hektor shouted, but the people around them were already moving, sweeping Paul and Silas away like a strong sea wave.

Hektor could only reach for Timothy and Luke, pulling them away as the crowd swarmed. Saving the two of them was better than saving none.

"Paul!" shouted Timothy. "We must help Paul!"

Miscellaneous voices in the crowd began to shout and chant, "These men are disturbing the city! We must take them to the magistrates!"

Fighting against the current, Hektor kept pulling Timothy and Luke with him as he pushed away from the danger.

"We have to follow them!" said Timothy.

"No!" shouted Hektor. "If we follow them now, we'll get caught up in it with them."

"But Paul and Silas—" Timothy protested.

"Hektor is right, young Timothy," said Luke. "The slave masters are hungry for revenge. If we follow to see what has happened, we follow at a distance. Can that be arranged?" The physician turned toward Hektor.

Forcing his jaw to unclench, Hektor replied, "I know a place we can go to hear what is happening without being spotted. It is this way." Hektor directed them around the Forum to a less-popular side street.

They needed to find out what was going to happen to Paul and Silas, because it might very well affect what would happen to the entire group of fledgling believers. Hektor thought his days of being so close to fights were over.

He had been wrong.

"The crowd joined in the attack against them, and the chief magistrates stripped off their clothes and ordered them to be beaten with rods. After they had severely flogged them, they threw them in jail, ordering the jailer to guard them carefully. Receiving such an order, he put them into the inner prison and secured their feet in the stocks." — Acts 16:22-24 CSB

Rut took her plate of food to the empty seat beside Lydia, as had become her custom, though there were a number of unoccupied chairs in the usually packed-full dining hall. Namely, the seats belonging to Paul, Silas, Luke, Timothy, and Hektor—whom Rut had not seen all that day—remained empty. "Where do you think they are right now? Should we wait?" Rut asked.

Lydia pursed her lips. "I don't think so. They should be returning any moment."

Rut chose not to remark that they should have returned hours ago. With the change in the season, the sun had begun setting earlier than usual, and all the lamps in the villa had already been lit. Hektor still had not appeared.

"I'm sure they are fine," Lydia added. "Perhaps they are even better than fine? Maybe they met some people who were interested in what they had to say and are presently delayed by conversation. Knowing Paul, I would not be surprised."

"Yes, perhaps," Rut muttered, though the worry did not dissipate from her heart. Something about this evening felt wrong. Was it the smell of the air? The color of the sunset? Maybe it was the mayhem of the past weeks that left Rut in a state of tumult, but she couldn't get rid of the feeling that Hektor and the other men were in some kind of danger.

Rut forced spoonfuls of stew into her mouth, making herself swallow the contents even though the anxious feelings swirling around in the pit of her stomach made all food seem unappetizing. She tried dipping some bread into the aromatic broth and nibbling at it, but she couldn't eat more than a few bites. Rut allowed her mind to wander instead.

Her gaze drifted over other people enjoying their meals. Conversation hummed at a steady pace. The savory scents of spices and herbs, most noticeably garlic, fennel, and mint, filled the room. Lamplight flickered, enveloping the room in a soft, orange glow and giving the illusion of peace.

Without warning, the large wooden doors at the opposite end of the hall swung open, and all conversation ceased. Others jumped, startled by the force with which the doors were opened, but somehow Rut expected this. The entire day she had felt ill-at-ease, but when she saw Hektor standing in the doorway with Luke and Timothy behind him, she knew her worries had not been unfounded.

Heart beating fast and without a thought for how she might appear to others, she leapt from her seat and bolted to Hektor's side.

"Hektor!" she called out as she ran, angling her body sideways to better fit between the tables of people. She felt her side smash into the corner of a table hard enough to leave a nasty bruise, but she did not slow her pace. "What happened? Where is Paul?"

Hektor looked down at her. Unlike that stormy night on the ship when Hektor had been a steadying presence for Rut, she saw no calm in his eyes now. She saw the storm within.

Hektor leaned in toward her face as though to speak only to her, before turning instead to face the rest of the crowd. "Paul and Silas have been taken to jail!"

The room descended into chaos. Women cried and men shouted. Gone were the sounds of goblets and dishes clashing with one another, laughter, and pleasant conversation.

"Is it true? Surely this must be a mistake?" said Rut, speaking only to Hektor as she brought her hands up to cover her face.

"A terrible mistake, yes, but it happened regardless."

"Everyone, please, be still!" Lydia called out. It took several more tries, but eventually the crowd complied as Lydia made her own way to the doorway where Rut, Hektor, and the others still stood. "Hektor, tell us how this has happened."

Once again, Hektor turned to address the whole crowd, and while others took in the meaning of his words, Rut searched his demeanor for answers about how he was feeling. Was he all right? How close had he been to the danger? Did he blame himself for what happened?

"It was because of the slave girl who had been following them. Paul became greatly annoyed and commanded the spirit to leave her in the name of Jesus Christ, and it did, but her owners became enraged. When they realized what had happened, they began to shout that Paul had taken their means of profit, inciting the crowds against them and dragging Paul and Silas off to the magistrates for judgment. Luke, Timothy, and myself escaped the madness and watched from a distance before coming back here."

"Praise God that you were spared," said Lydia, and several others in the room echoed the sentiment. Rut echoed it in her heart and in her prayers.

"We must pray for Paul and Silas, that God would be with them now," said Timothy.

"Timothy is right," said Luke, addressing the crowd, "everyone must pray that God will be with them in that jail cell, and that His way will prevail."

"Hektor, Luke, Timothy," said Lydia, straightening and angling her body away from the onlookers, "let us go into the courtyard. I want to hear more details about what happened today, but I think we should discuss them in private."

"You are right," said Hektor.

Rut followed the group away from the dining hall, keeping a close distance behind Hektor. She remembered the first time she had walked through the exterior doors and taken in this large space; the courtyard alone being bigger than any home Rut had ever lived in and filled with ornamental fixtures made of the brightest and boldest purple hues. It seemed so large and grand then. How quickly she had become at home in this place, yet in light of everything else, how much it now felt like the walls were closing in on them all.

"Are *you* all right, Hektor?" asked Rut.

Hektor shook his head. "I was supposed to ensure their safety."

"Were it not for you, Timothy and myself might have gotten swept up in it all too. Then who would have been able to return and alert the others as to what happened?" said Luke.

"I still regret that I did not do more." Hektor ran his fingers through his sand-colored hair.

"You did everything that you could." Rut stepped in front of him. "Now tell us exactly what happened. Why did they take them to the magistrates?"

Sighing deeply, Hektor explained, "The slave girl's masters told them that they were disturbing the peace. They said, 'They are Jews and promoting customs that are not legal for us as Romans to adopt or practice.' Then the magistrates—well, they had Paul and Silas stripped and beaten, then put into prison."

"The wounds were severe," said Luke, his eyes narrowing in concern like the physician he was.

Rut didn't have any time to react to the horrific shock of those details not shared with the crowd. Sharp banging at the door made them all jolt backward, and Hero came running and howling, his body moving faster than his lanky legs could carry him.

"What now?" asked Lydia.

A chill went down Rut's spine. "Do you think the same people who took Paul and Silas came for us? Could they know he has been staying here?"

Hektor shook his head. "I don't think so."

Bang! Bang! Bang!

"Let me in! Please, let me in!"

"It's Xanthe's husband!" Rut exclaimed.

"Who?" asked Luke.

"He is called Servius Arrius," Lydia explained. "His wife is Xanthe, a woman we used to weave for, and who we told about the message of salvation through Jesus Christ. He was not pleased when he found out, and made threats to ruin my business. Their daughter is the one I told you about—the one who is gravely ill."

"Do you think that is why he has come? Do you think something has happened to Philomena?" Rut felt her eyes widen.

"There is only one way to find out," said Hektor. Turning to face Lydia, he continued, "Shall I see what he wants?"

Lydia nodded her wordless approval.

Hektor took three methodical strides forward. Slowly, he pushed the bolt out of the way and pulled the door open just wide enough to speak to Servius.

Hero continued to bark, but Rut knelt to the ground and called him to her. She whispered, "You'll be my defender now, all right?" Hero responded by sitting right in front of her toes, his tail thumping against her leg. "Good dog."

Rising, Rut inclined her head to see what she could beyond the door. Servius' appearance was not the same as it had been when they first met. Gone were the tell-tale signs of wrath and vengefulness—flared nostrils, narrowed eyebrows, beads of sweat, redness all over his face. This man looked worried, with dark circles under his eyes and mouth agape.

"You must let me in!" Servius said, gasping for air as though he'd run all the way here. Hektor stalled understandably. "*Please!* I would not be here if it were not an emergency!"

Hektor looked over his shoulder at Lydia before opening the door and letting Servius inside. "You must forgive us for being wary," said Hektor.

"What is it you are seeking?" said Lydia.

"You! You are *Christians,* are you not?" Servius' voice shook as his body wobbled back and forth.

Lydia replied, "We serve the One True God, yes."

"I need your help," said Servius. In a moment that could not have been more shocking, Servius fell to his knees and raised his hands, pleading, "I have summoned every healer and made nearly every kind of offering, but they say my daughter will not last the night."

"Philomena!" Rut gasped.

"I've made many mistakes in my life, but I can't make this one now. If I lose my daughter, my wife will never forgive me, nor will I ever be able to forgive myself. This is all my fault."

They all stared at him and each other. As Rut looked around, she saw reflections of her own bewilderment in the eyes of Hektor, Lydia, Luke, and Timothy. When she looked back at Servius, she was surprised by the emotions bubbling up from within her. Rut thought if she saw him again she would feel only resentment, but instead, she felt intense compassion.

"*Oh, Lord,*" she prayed again, "*only you can mend these hearts.*"

"What exactly is it that you want us to do?" asked Lydia.

"Didn't I already tell you?" said Servius, pushing himself up off the ground and onto his feet. "You people are known for performing miracles. The magistrates were saying today that one of you cast a spirit out of a slave girl in the Forum. I am begging you now to come and save my daughter!"

Servius Arrius was a veteran of influential status. For that reason, Rut wondered if he had been present at the so-called trial by the magistrates, or if he had only heard about it.

Lydia responded, "We will go with you to be there with Mena and Xanthe because they are our friends, but we are not the ones who perform miracles. The One True God holds Mena's life in His hands. All we can do is pray to Him."

"Please," said Servius, his voice hoarse, "you're my only hope."

This man was very different from the one Rut had met prior. Xanthe may have wondered about his feelings, but it was clear now that he cared very much for both of them.

Lydia turned toward Luke and Timothy. "Will the two of you stay here with the others? There's no doubt in my mind that more questions will surely rise up before the night is over regarding Paul and Silas."

"If I may," Luke cut in, raising his hand, "I'd like to come as well, as a physician."

"*Of course!*" thought Rut. Servius had said he'd summoned every healer he could find, but he had not yet summoned Luke.

In her heart, she praised God for bringing Luke to Philippi for many reasons, not least among them being this particular moment. *"Lord, be with Luke tonight as he tends Philomena. If it is Your will, guide him toward answers about what ails her, and thank You for sending him to us in the first place!"*

"That would be a good idea," said Lydia.

"I'll get my things." Luke left and returned only moments later with a small bag.

"What about me?" said the young Timothy.

Luke turned toward him, placing a hand on his shoulder. "Remember what Paul said earlier, Timothy. You have the knowledge. Now is the time for you to practice using it for the good work of His kingdom. Encourage the brothers and sisters here until our return."

Timothy nodded, and at once, Rut, Lydia, Hektor, and Luke hurried to follow Servius out the door. Hero slipped through as Timothy shut the door and bolted it behind them.

"Hero, stay!" called Rut over her shoulder, but the dog did not obey, and there was no time to turn back. Even Hero must have sensed what was happening to Philomena, who had become almost as near and dear of a companion to him as those who lived under Lydia's roof.

Hektor was used to waiting in the main hall of Xanthe's house while Lydia and Rut conducted their business in the private garden. He even knew some of the servants in the house well enough to engage in small talk as they passed by. He was quite comfortable in that space. What made him uncomfortable was that he now shared the room with Servius Arrius.

While Hektor sat on the floor, his ankles crossed, the concerned father paced back and forth as the night waned on and they waited for news. Every few moments, Hektor thought of Rut and wondered what she was doing. What thoughts transpired in her head? Was she all right? After all these months of working together and being near each other, it almost pained Hektor to not have her close enough to at least hear the tone in her voice and know that everything was well. The only thing left for him to do in the silence was pray.

Pray, and count how many steps Servius Arrius took each time he crossed the polished tile floors.

The number grew increasingly, and Hektor began to lose track.

"What could they possibly be doing in there?" Servius hissed.

Hektor spoke calmly, actively choosing not to elevate the volume of his own voice. "Whatever they are doing, I am sure they are in good hands."

A servant walked past, carrying in her arms a barrage of idols and trinkets.

"Where are you going with those?" Servius stomped over toward the servant.

The servant's posture immediately slumped as she recoiled into the darkness with wide eyes. In all the commotion, the sun set without anyone bothering to light any lamps in this part of the house.

"Y-y-your w-w-wife told us to t-t-take them away," she stuttered, averting her gaze as she choked out the words.

Hektor looked away so as not to make her feel any more frightened than she likely already did.

"Does she not understand how much those cost me? The healers I summoned and paid for said that—"

"I b-b-beg your pardon, but the physician with her now s-s-said they must be taken away, and Mistress Xanthe agreed."

Servius' demeanor changed once again at the very mention of Luke. He crossed his arms behind his back and straightened. "Carry on then," he said. "You are dismissed."

Hektor felt the breeze on his skin as the servant flew out of the room like a cloud moved by strong winds. Servius returned to his pacing, making several more rounds before speaking again. "What is taking so long?" he snapped.

Hektor weighed all the possible outcomes should he respond or not, ultimately choosing to engage. "Luke is very wise and your daughter is in good hands with him. He is likely doing everything he can right now."

"This is all my fault."

At last, Servius halted his motion and leaned back against the wall, which itself was painted with a colorful fresco depicting a grove of olive trees. From there, he too sank to a seated position opposite Hektor.

"Oftentimes we take on the blame for things that we should not. Things that could never have been prevented simply because they were or are beyond our control. You can't blame yourself for your daughter's illness," said Hektor, continuing in a restrained speaking voice.

He was still unsure of what Servius wanted from him in this moment, and though there was still much happening, he was beginning to fight sleep. He tried to imagine if it were Karis lying in another room what he would have wanted, and he settled on just one thing: someone to listen and to help him see that he was not alone.

"You know nothing of what you speak," said Servius.

Hektor took a long deep breath, leaning his head back as he stretched out his arms and neck. "If you need to be alone with your thoughts, I will keep silent. If you need to be heard, I will listen."

The faint glow of the moonlight filtered in through the windows and open archways, casting the walls and their frescos in overlaying shades of silver and pale blue. Hektor could not see Servius' face clearly as it was shrouded in shadow, so he had no gauge of how the man responded to his offer. Whether he appreciated it or was offended by it, Hektor did not know. So, he closed his eyes and returned to his prayers, until finally Servius spoke again.

"I was young when I met Xanthe."

Gone was the commanding tone of a retired military officer and the gruffness of one embittered with life. There was now a cracking in Servius' voice; a hint of a softening heart. Hektor kept his eyes closed and waited for Servius to continue.

"At that age, I think every young man tends to think of himself as a kind of god. I thought I would live forever and that my name would be carved into history with those of the greatest emperors and conquerors."

"I think we all live with that false sense of security until an experience makes us confront the reality that we won't," said Hektor. Had he not been similar in the days of his youth? How many times had he told himself that he was just one fight away from never having to fight again? How long had he forced himself to endure blow after blow, fooling himself into believing that one day it would pay off in enough silver and gold to make it all worth it, and that he would be able to give his sister the kind of life that she deserved? No more fights, no more onion stew, no more hurt. It wasn't until Karis died that Hektor was forced to confront the realty that no one lived forever, and he did not take it well.

"The gods and their twisted sense of irony had other plans for my life. I was sent here to Philippi to aid the local government. I was so sure that one day I would be striking down enemy after enemy with my sword, that I believed the posting was only a temporary stepping stone to greater glory. I didn't know then that I could be just as great of a threat to myself, which is why, as I patrolled the Forum one day with my fellow soldiers, I didn't hesitate to admire Xanthe from afar."

The room fell silent, and Hektor had to open his eyes to see if Servius was still there. He was.

"She was beautiful then, and she still is now. I was foolish to let it go further, to fall in love with her and form an attachment, but what did I care? It did not matter that I had sworn an oath to serve the empire and remain unmarried until my term was up. Many men took common law wives in the provinces and territories where they were stationed."

"What happened?" asked Hektor.

Servius shifted his weight. "When Xanthe told me she carried our child in her womb, I saw the future so clearly idealized in my mind. I thought I could have it all: my military career and my family. Having my name carved in stone paled in comparison to having 'father' added to my list of titles. I dreamed of a son that I could raise as my own, training him to follow in my footsteps, adopting him formally upon my retirement so that he would carry the status of my Roman citizenship."

"Did things change when Philomena was born because she was a girl?"

"No!" Servius shouted, the flare of anger briefly returning to his voice.

"I'm sorry," said Hektor, immediately apologizing. "I presumed too much."

"You also presumed *incorrectly*. I dreamed of a healthy child more than anything. Even in those first days, physicians were quick to point out that she didn't cry like a normal newborn. Her cries were weak. I felt then that Philomena's illness must have been a punishment from the gods for my arrogance, for there is no pain you can endure that will ever be greater than the pain of watching your own child suffer and being powerless to stop it. I did the only thing I could do. I left."

"You left?" asked Hektor.

"I know. What kind of monster abandons his child and their mother? I'd already been offered the opportunity to go to Rome and assume a commanding post. I took the easy way out and accepted the transfer. I knew Xanthe would bear the shame of being an unmarried mother by staying here, but I believed the best thing I could do for her was die on the battlefield, freeing her from any ties to me. I tried to make up for what I had done by applying the full extent of the law to the very smallest of details with vigor and ardor. I chased after military excellence not for my own glory, but for the glory and honor of being sent into battle to die a true soldier's death."

"Because," Hektor continued for him, "you believed that in death, you would right all the wrongs you'd committed in your lifetime, and the world would be a better place without you in it."

"How did you know?"

Hektor looked across the room at Servius. His eyes had finally adjusted to the darkness enough to see how Servius' brows knit together in confusion.

"Because I once thought the same thing." Hektor winced at the painful memories of his own path toward self-destruction. He remembered the depth of his hurt, like a knife that continued to twist a little bit more with every reminder of what was gone. Still, no matter how deep the pain had been, it was still the wrong path. "It isn't true, Servius."

"There was only one other time I bent the rules…"

"What was that?"

"I… I allowed a boy to enlist. I shouldn't have, but he

reminded me so much of myself, and I thought I could help him. I should have known that I couldn't have been anything close to a father figure to him, when I couldn't even be a true father to Philomena or even a husband to Xanthe. I was sent to lead my cohort not to far off battlefields, but instead to Jerusalem in Judea, where my problems only continued to grow."

"Jerusalem? When?" asked Hektor. Had Servius been there at the same time as Rut? It was highly probable given that Hektor now knew that Rut had grown up there until she'd been forced to leave with her family due to the persecution of believers in the region. They would not have known each other, but it was still fascinating to consider the possibility that even all those years ago, God was weaving their stories together and leading them to this very hour.

"Guess," said Servius sardonically. "It was at the time of the crucifixion of that Jew you call Jesus, the Christ."

Hektor felt his heart begin to race. "You were there?"

Servius nodded, and Hektor saw the movement of his faint shadow on the wall. "And that boy I mentioned? I sent him to guard the tomb. It was all a set up. It must have been! That man's body should've been thrown into a field with the other victims from that day, but instead he was taken to a tomb. When morning came on the third day and the body was gone, the boy had deserted, and the whole ordeal became yet another black mark on my military record. I never left Judea again until orders finally arrived to tell me that I'd reached the end of my service. By a cruel twist of fate, I'd lived long enough to retire and spend the rest of my days facing the consequences of my actions."

"So you came back to Philippi?"

"Not directly, although that is the theme of my life, isn't it? Avoiding one battle, only to run head-first into another? I traveled for a time, only to find that there was nowhere I could go where I would not be haunted by ghosts of my past and memories of another version of me."

"Did you ever find the boy?"

"Yes," said Servius, his voice dropping. "I found him, though he was not the boy I remembered. He had grown into a man, and he was like you—a Christ-follower. He too had been drawn in by the myth that practically destroyed my career and destroyed his life. I wanted to kill him. I should have killed him, for nothing else if not the crime of desertion, but even then, I couldn't do it. I may not be a soldier of renown, but among hypocrites, I am the leader."

Hektor contemplated the entirety of the story Servius had told. It became more clear to him why Servius had lashed out so severely when he'd seen Xanthe praying with Rut and Lydia to the One True God. It was because he had a personal experience in Jerusalem, but not the miraculous, hope-filled experience of which Rut spoke. Servius had been present for that display of God's glory, and yet he had not seen it. Hektor could say the same thing of himself and all those years he'd walked through life blind to hope in things that were unseen.

"Servius," said Hektor, addressing the man with the same familiarity he would use to address a friend, for these were the kinds of trying times in which people dispensed with formal titled and refined speech. "Respectfully, I have to tell you that you are wrong."

Servius grunted. "I *know* that."

"I meant about Christ-followers and the so-called 'myth' of the resurrection. Every word of it is true."

"You think you can fool me? I was there! I was in Judea!"

"So was that boy you spoke of, and he believes it." Hektor stopped to take a deep breath. "I am not trying to fool you, but the One True God is not like the Roman or Greek myths who twist fates and prey upon human emotions, meddling in earthly affairs only to cause pain and inflict punishments. He loves us, and He has a plan."

"For me?" asked Servius, with a hint of incredulity in his voice.

"For all of us."

The dark room went silent again, except for the softest of winds blowing outside, making whooshing noises against the walls of the house. Thinking that perhaps Servius was finished with this line of conversation, Hektor rose from the floor to stretch his back and legs. How long had they been waiting, and how much longer would they be there? He prayed that the length of time they'd gone without hearing anything was a good sign.

With one hand on the wall, Hektor followed it down a passage until he saw light—a lamp, at last! It occurred to him that he had not eaten all day. At least light was a good place to start before searching for food. He took the lamp in hand and retraced his steps back to where he left Servius. When he re-entered the room, Hektor could not have been more astonished by what he saw.

Servius remained seated against the wall, but his face was covered in trails left behind by tears. He had not been crying. He had been weeping!

"I have no fight left in me," whispered Servius. "There is nowhere else for me to run away to."

Hektor hurriedly set down the lamp and allowed the light to burn steadily as he moved closer to Servius, kneeling down beside him. "There is one place left, Servius."

"Where is that?" he scoffed.

"Toward the One True God."

Servius Arrius wiped his eyes as he choked back more tears. "I want to believe that is true."

"You can, Servius. You can!"

"But what about all that I have done? All of my mistakes?"

"Jesus died knowingly for the whole world, that we all might have the opportunity to come to know Him," Hektor explained. "No matter what wrongdoings we have committed."

Servius dropped his head into his hands. "Why would He care for me? I don't have anything to offer. There is nothing I can give Him."

"That is why Jesus gave it all." Just as Hektor was preparing to explain in further detail about their faith and the way of salvation as it had been told to him by Paul, both of them were startled by hurried footsteps coming down the hall. Hektor leapt to his feet as trepidation coursed through his veins.

It was Luke, but Hektor could not tell by his face whether he carried good news or bad news.

"Excuse me, I do not wish to interrupt, but…" Luke clasped his hands together as his voice faded away.

Servius stood and spoke to Hektor, "I want to continue this conversation, but first" — he turned to Luke — "I must know what news you bring of my daughter."

"Your wife has explained to me her history—how she is prone to dizziness, soreness in her muscles, pain in her chest, and attacks of coughing with difficulty breathing. From what information I have without having observed her for an extended period of time, I can only surmise that her most recent attack was so severe that her body now struggles to recover."

"Do you know what it means?" asked Servius, his voice hoarse after telling his story to Hektor.

Luke pursed his lips and continued, "There is much about the body we do not know. Her heart beats fast, yet she is unable to draw enough breath. It's the fever that concerns me the most."

"Will she be all right?" asked Servius.

"I cannot say, but I will say this: if we can reduce her fever, and if she survives through the night, she will likely recover. If she does, I can make a few recommendations about herbs that might help to both ease symptoms and perhaps even prevent them from starting altogether, so that she can learn to manage her condition. However, if her fever does not go down and if her other symptoms do not improve… I cannot guarantee that she will wake to see another sunrise."

Servius nodded slowly and Hektor swallowed hard.

"Lord, please be with us all this night," Hektor prayed. Philomena—like Karis once had been—was too young to leave this world, but Hektor knew they would need to trust in God's plan no matter what, now more than ever.

"Thank you for telling us," said Hektor, breaking the silence.

Luke bowed his head respectfully. "I must return now to my work," he said, excusing himself from the room. Servius did not protest. Rather, he stood as still as a statue while they watched Luke go.

"What would you like to do now?" said Hektor, looking directly at Servius, though his gaze remained unfocused.

With surprising resolve, Servius replied, "I would like you to teach me more about this One True God, that I might understand this salvation for myself, and then I would like you to teach me how to pray to Him, that I might pray over my daughter as I should have begun doing a long time ago."

18

*"And the peace of God, which surpasses all understanding,
will guard your hearts and minds in Christ Jesus." —
Philippians 4:7 CSB*

Rut's eyes burned from exhaustion. She sat with Lydia and
Xanthe by Philomena's side, watching her chest rise and fall,
waiting to hear the almost whistling sound of her breath, and
then waiting to hear it again.

Her spirit wanted to be there for her friends, but her mind
struggled to remain alert. She used what little physical strength
she had to push herself to a standing position, hoping the
movement might trick her mind into thinking she did not need
sleep. Seeing Luke on the other side of the room preparing a
mixture of something, she walked over to him, both to ask if he
knew anything more and if he needed help.

"Have you seen any change?" she whispered, hoping his eyes
which were trained in the field of healing saw some small sign
of improvement she could not.

He looked up from what he was doing and stared at her for a

moment before recognition lit his eyes. It seemed to Rut that even he was growing weary as they waited for something—*anything*. "Nothing yet." He shook his head, and then returned his focus to his task, his eyes squinting at his work. The expression reminded Rut of how she poured all of her mind into her own weaving work, meticulous with every detail.

"What is that you are making?" asked Rut, pointing at the greenish-yellow mixture. She continued to speak in hushed tones so as not to disturb the others.

"It is a decoction of dried olive leaves and boiled water," Luke explained as he methodically stirred the thick liquid, the colors blending until it became a murky brown. If it were a vat of dye, Rut would have thrown it out. "If we can encourage Philomena to drink this, it might make all the difference."

"How much?" asked Rut.

"All of it," said Luke, matter-of-fact. He added, separately, "Though any bit would make a difference."

"I can take it to her," said Rut, holding out her hand. Luke poured the mixture into a cup and gave it to her, and then she took it back to Lydia and Xanthe.

"What is that?" asked Xanthe, her voice hoarse.

"Luke said that if we could get her to drink some—"

Xanthe interrupted before Rut could finish explaining. "Give it to me. I will try." Xanthe took the cup from Rut's hand before she could offer it.

"He said even small sips will help," Rut added.

Xanthe shifted her weight onto the bed beside Philomena, lifting her daughter's head up ever so slightly and pressing the cup to her lips. "Mena? Mena, my daughter, can you drink this for me? Just a little?"

Philomena stirred lightly and made a small sound which tugged at Rut's heart. Xanthe tilted the cup, and Philomena took a small sip, but it made her cough.

Rut turned back to Luke, but he shook his head at her as though he were reading her mind. She cast her eyes back to Xanthe and Philomena, hoping a miracle would come, but Xanthe's attempts continued to be unsuccessful. The look on Luke's face did not bode well for what was to come if things did not change.

Caught between them—stoic Luke, feeble Philomena, desperate Xanthe, and concerned Lydia—Rut suddenly found herself struggling to breathe. Though Luke had called for the immediate removal of all the oils and incense brought in by the previous healers upon their arrival, the air in the room felt thick, and Rut's heart began to race.

"Are you all right, Rut?" asked Lydia, casting a concerned glance in her direction.

"I just—" Rut cut her own sentence abruptly short, unsure of what to say next. She held her hands behind her back as she felt them beginning to shake.

"If you need to step out for a moment, it's perfectly all right," Lydia whispered. Rut saw the kindness in the woman's eyes, and all at once, she recalled how they met, how Lydia convinced her to come to Philippi, and those first nights on the ship when Lydia had talked of wanting them to have a relationship that went beyond business. At the time, Rut did not believe it possible, but this night with Xanthe, she saw how God worked in her heart and in her life to give her exactly the relationships she needed in this moment and this time of her life. They were more than friends now. They were sisters by heart.

"Come and get me if something happens," said Rut.

"We will." Lydia nodded.

"Thank you." Rut walked slowly out of the room, but as soon as she was on the other side of the door and in the hall, she bolted for the nearest open space. She felt her heartbeat accelerate and the muscles in her body tense. It was only when she finally found herself in the garden that she stood still, placing her hand over her heart and forcing herself to breathe deeply. The garden was now wholly devoid of crocuses, just as Xanthe said it would be. Tears flowed steadily down her cheeks, and she sank to the ground, wrapping her arms around her knees.

"Lord," she prayed, *"I don't understand this."* As Rut thought about it, she was reminded of a great many things in her life that she did not understand. She had lost her Sabba Eliyahu, then her Savta Hodiyah. She had lost her home in Jerusalem. She gained a home in Phoenicia with Shem, but she lost that too. She wanted to trust God. She knew that He alone was the one weaving the tapestry, but it was so difficult to trust in Him when all she could see were the loose threads.

Visions of Shem's death filled her mind, of days as black as a moonless night. She squeezed her eyes shut, but she only saw them more clearly. *"It's not your time, Shem,"* Rut had said, desperate for a miracle not unlike she was tonight. Shem, in his unwavering faithfulness had said to her then, *"Everything in God's timing, Rut."* Those were some of his last words to her. How many times had she listened to them over and over again in her mind?

The more she sat alone in the darkness, the more she realized how much pain she had kept locked away in her heart, beyond that of her grief over a life lost—though she had learned you never truly lost something you didn't have in the first place. No, her pain could be traced back much earlier, to the day her family realized that they could no longer stay in Jerusalem.

Things had been so different then, so soon after Jesus' miraculous resurrection and ascension. It had been so *easy* to be faithful in those days. It seemed that the Lord was with them in every sense, at every turn, because He was, until the day that it felt as though He abandoned them.

They were on their way to meet with the other disciples and

believers when they were forced to turn back and flee for their lives after a great persecution broke out against them. Rut remembered linking arms with her mother and brother as they ran faster than Rut had ever run in her life. They made it back to their home, securing themselves beyond the gate in their small courtyard, but Rut knew even then that things would never be the same. The food that had been warming over the fire had been cast out into the dirt. The bench in the courtyard had been knocked over.

Rut recalled looking to Shamira, but Shamira looked only at Asa. That was how it should have been. Even at such a young age, Rut knew that was true, but there was no one to hold Rut's hand or assure her that things would be all right. Instead, Rut's younger cousin Libi tugged on her sleeve and asked Rut what was going to happen next. *"Don't be afraid, Libi. Pray for peace. In fact, why don't we all sit down and pray together? God will hear us and protect us,"* Rut had said as she encircled all of her younger cousins, trying to be the dependable leader that Shamira always had been, and the perfect daughter she had been raised to be. She put on a brave face and prayed for peace then, but soon afterward, her abba emerged from the house with her Dodh Tamir and Dodh Aharon, the three of them supporting Savta's weight as blood dripped from the top of her head.

Libi had run to their grandmother, the sight of Libi crying making Rut cry too. *"It is like your Sabba said, Libi. I think my strength has run out in this life, but I will soon have strength ten-fold in the next,"* Savta had said. Her last words were spoken to Libi, but they were a message to everyone there. *"Never stop singing the Lord's praise. He will protect you as He has always done, and He will give you peace. Take him with you, wherever you go, and never stop sharing His light."*

Except Rut had stopped.

Xanthe's gardens were beautiful even without colorful

flowers blossoming, but there were some days more than others when Rut would've given anything to go back to that simple courtyard, that little rickety wooden bench, and that closeness she felt with her family, so that she could do it all over again. There were so many choices she would have made differently.

Her stomach turned, and she felt a jab at her side.

Not a metaphorical one.

A physical nudging.

She looked down and immediately came face to face with two wide, round, almost-black eyes—Hero's eyes.

"Hero!" she said, reaching out to scratch him behind his ears. "What are you doing here?"

The dog whined and lowered himself to the ground beside her, resting his head on his paws and looking just as distressed as everyone else in the house. As Rut stroked his short fur, she thought of Hektor and how he'd first introduced her to their four-legged mutual friend. Many more memories of Hektor flooded her mind then, of how much they'd both grown and changed, and yet how they had both stayed the same. She thought of Hektor's stories, the way he could tell them so well, make them so real with his choice of words that Rut could forget where she was when she listened to them. Hektor had always been able to remind her of what was important. Hektor was her constant.

"Oh, Hero," Rut whispered, "how did you know to come at this very moment?"

Hero's presence and the memories he carried with him made Rut realize that even if she did have the ability to go back and make different choices, she never would have made it here. She might have spared herself some pain, but she also might never have grown like she did over the course of her life's journey. She likely would not have met Lydia, Xanthe, Philomena, Hektor, and so many others…

She even thought of Paul, whom she had known of in Jerusalem as Saul. He had been the leader of the persecution then, but Rut and her family had heard through communication from her Dodh Tamir about his own miraculous conversion. Who could have guessed that one such as Paul could transform in such a way, and that her path with Lydia would cross with his in Philippi? The answer was clear: only God.

God was weaving, even when it didn't feel like anything good was happening.

God was working, even when things seemed stagnant.

God was mending, even when it seemed like everything was breaking beyond repair.

When it seemed like all hope was lost, Rut knew that God was pulling threads together just as they were meant to be, creating a tapestry so grand and glorious, the likes of which could never be made by human hands.

Like Shem had said, *"Everything in God's timing, Rut."* Tears filled her eyes again, but bittersweet, for she finally understood what he and Savta had meant, and she finally understood what it was to have true peace.

"Lord," she prayed, *"I do trust in You, even though I cannot see what You see and I do not know the patterns of threads like You do. We don't know what is going to happen next. Once, that might have made me want to run from You or try to find answers somewhere else. Help me to keep listening for Your voice, even when I do not hear it. Help me to keep looking for Your handiwork, even when there is so much else on this earth to distract me from it. Most of all, Lord, surround us all with Your peace. Whether Philomena's strength has run out in this life or not, help me to keep my eyes fixed to the right side of the tapestry, and to You, the God who sees both sides of the loom. You are Lord over the beautiful and the painful. You are the one weaving the future, and it is more than enough."*

Rut inhaled slowly and opened her eyes, seeing once again Xanthe's gardens. As she cast her eyes upwards to the stars, she exhaled. A cool night breeze wafted down within the garden walls. She had not forgotten the worries and woes they still faced tonight, but the feeling of peace—*the powerful feeling*—won out over it all.

The Lord won over it all, and when morning came, He would still be the victor.

Hero's ears perked up at the sound of men's voices, likely belonging to Hektor and Servius. "Shall we go to find them, and then return to Philomena?" she asked as she stood.

Hero made a sleepy sound as he stretched everything from his front paws all the way to his tail before rising on all fours. Rut followed the sound of steady conversation to the dimly lit main hall. She couldn't hear what they were saying, but she could infer by the tone of their voices that whatever they were presently discussing, they were serious about it. Hero stole from Rut the ability to be discreet by bounding past her, his claws clicking against the floor.

"Hero, my boy!" said Hektor as Hero pounced upon him, though the force of the dog's weight did not shake Hektor.

"I apologize," said Rut, "I hope I did not interrupt something important."

Servius stood at once and crossed the room in just three long strides. "Do you bring news of Philomena? How is my daughter? And Xan—my *wife?*"

"Luke has prepared a decoction of olives for Philomena and Xanthe is trying to get her to drink it now. I'm sorry I don't have better news." When she looked into Servius' eyes, the change in his spirit took her aback.

"It is all right," said Servius, though Rut could see by the redness under his eyes that he had been crying. "I have peace."

"Rut," said Hektor, rising to stand nearer to them, "there is some good news to be shared."

Rut looked at Hektor, whose face beamed. "What is that?"

Hektor raised an eyebrow at her, but it was Servius who responded. "I have given my life to the One True God, and I serve at His command now."

Rut had to bring her hands up to cover her face as she gasped. "Praise the Lord!" she said. "Oh, Xanthe will be so overjoyed!"

"I'd like to be the one to tell her," said Servius.

"Yes, of course!" Rut nodded quickly.

Servius straightened, assuming a stance more fitting to his military background. "I also wanted to apologize for how I acted when you were last in my home. My behavior was unacceptable. It was only that I was so surprised by what I saw. It seemed like everyone I had ever loved had fallen for what I believed to be a myth, but what I now know as the only truth that makes sense."

Rut couldn't believe what she was hearing, yet she did believe it with all of her heart. "You are forgiven, Servius Arrius." Rut knew she spoke for herself and Lydia as well, for she would react with just as much jubilance when she heard the news.

"But that's just it. I think in the heat of my anger, I may have caused great damage to your business."

"Oh!" Rut exclaimed, realizing what he meant, though business transactions seemed to pale in comparison to all else at that moment. "It is Lydia's business. I am only a lone weaver."

Servius raised a hand. "In any case, as soon as I can, I want to do everything within my power to make things right and undo what I have done."

"I'm sure Lydia will thank you," said Rut, clasping her hands together.

Hektor cleared his throat. "Rut, Servius was telling me that he spent time in Jerusalem."

"Really?" said Rut. "That is where I am from. When were you there?" Briefly, Rut imagined how her younger self would have reacted if she would have known that nearly two decades into the future she would be having a conversation with a Roman soldier—the very kind she feared growing up.

"That is a part of what I alluded to earlier, about my surprise at seeing you praying with my wife and daughter. I was there with my cohort during the conflict involving Jesus of Nazareth. You see, there was a young soldier I was quite attached to then. I thought of him as a son, really, and when there was talk of having guards at the tomb after his crucifixion, I sent him as one of them, yet on the morning of the third day, he deserted. We thought the resurrection was a hoax, so I assumed he fled out of fear of punishment for allowing the body to be stolen."

Servius stopped to look at the ground, and Rut wondered if it was shame that made him pause, but as she studied his face, she saw new tears falling from his eyes, dripping to the stone floor.

He continued, though his voice broke, "I found him years later in Antioch in Syria. He had married and found a family, but I could not let go of the past. I confronted him with anger, but I'll never forget how he responded. He said to me, *I will take whatever punishment God wills for me, but do not harm these people.'* That was when I learned that he had become a Christ-follower. I couldn't understand it then, how someone like him could fall for such an obvious myth. I scoffed when he told me that he would not put up a fight, but he said that he had changed, or rather been changed by his beliefs. When we parted ways, I told him, *'Cassius is dead, and I will no longer spend my time searching for his ghost.'"*

"Cassius?" Rut shouted when her mind registered the name, startling both Servius and Hektor. "I'm sorry." She shook her head. "Where did you say this took place?"

"In Syrian Antioch," said Servius, with a look of bewilderment painted across his face. "Why?"

"You said he was married. Do you remember his wife's

name? Was it Libi?" Rut's hands frantically shook as her mind grappled with the bits and pieces of information—things no one else would have deemed important, but were crucial details to Rut.

"I'm sorry, I don't remember—"

"Were they carpenters?" she blurted out, recalling the trade her uncle had taken up when he took his family farther, while the rest of their relatives had settled in Phoenicia.

At that, Servius' brows furrowed. He leaned backward. "How did you know that?"

That was confirmation enough of what Rut suspected: that God truly was the master weaver of stories!

"My cousin, Libi, who lives in Antioch, is married to a man named Cassius. The same as you described!"

Hektor let out a deep, resounding laugh. "This *is* the work of the One True God!"

"Indeed!" Rut agreed, still taking in the realization.

The feelings of elation could not last forever. Without warning, Hero began to bark with ferocity. "Hero? What is it?" said Rut. She tried to bend down toward the dog, but instead, she fell completely to the floor. "Oh." She raised a hand to her forehead, feeling dizzy. What was wrong with her?

Hero continued to bark and howl until he bolted into the darkness.

"Where is he going?" asked Hektor.

Rut began to shiver—no, she realized it wasn't her shivering, but the room. The floor beneath them. Everything around them.

It was an earthquake!

She struggled to her feet as she saw the furniture around them beginning to slide and the tapestries on the wall shake. The rumbling beneath the ground only grew more intense.

Hektor pulled her and Servius under an archway faster than she could process what was happening.

"Ahhh!!!" Xanthe's ear-splitting scream could be heard from the other side of the house.

Philomena! Forgetting everything else, Rut pushed away from the wall and began to run down the hall to Philomena's chamber.

"Rut, no!" she heard Hektor call out. "It isn't safe!"

She looked over her shoulder briefly until she started to lose her balance, but despite Hektor's warning, she did not stop running. Though the world was literally crumbling around her, only one thing mattered to her in that moment: returning to her friends.

"About midnight Paul and Silas were praying and singing hymns to God, and the prisoners were listening to them. Suddenly, there was such a violent earthquake that the foundations of the jail were shaken, and immediately all the doors were opened, and everyone's chains came loose." —
Acts 16:25-26 CSB

"Heave, man!" ordered Hektor as they pulled apart the rubble that separated them from the other side of the house—from Lydia, Luke, Philomena, Xanthe, and *Rut*. Hektor would have torn heaven from earth to get to Rut. The initial quake caused some of the brickwork in the house to crumble, and though there were two halls that led to Philomena's chamber and hopefully to the others, both were blocked. The stone walls were no match for such strong, violent forces of nature. Even more debris came crashing down in the aftershocks, and it was only when the sun began to rise that they decided it was safe enough to start making a way through.

Hektor had spent most of the time they waited asking himself how Rut could have left the safety of the archway they crouched under, and why he didn't try harder to stop her. His greatest fear was finally pulling the rubble apart only to find Rut's body, limp and lifeless. Hektor clung to the knowledge that God was faithful. He always provided, in ways both seen and unseen.

In the end, trusting God was not only what made sense; it made sense of the senseless. Events that had no obvious meaning—tragedies, deaths, mistakes, accidents, and even earthquakes—had meaning to God. So with prayer, Hektor continued to clear a path alongside Servius, moving brick by brick, stone by stone, and carefully inspecting everything to ensure it was safe to continue. With every bit of headway they made, Hektor felt more assured that the Lord was with them all.

At long last, they saw the light coming from Philomena's chamber.

"Xanthe! Xanthe!" he called.

"We're in here! We are safe!" she answered.

Together, Servius and Hektor pushed aside the last bits of rubble that barred them from the other side of the threshold. As soon as it was clear, both men practically tumbled into the room, sweat dripping from their foreheads.

Hektor looked around in wonder and amazement at how the room remained remarkably intact, as though protected by an invisible shield. Some furniture sat askew and there were obvious cracks in the walls that cut through more painted frescos, but the Lord's hand had been with Luke and these women. *Thank you, God,*" Hektor prayed, careful not to forget Him in that moment.

Never had Hektor felt more relief than when, at long last, his gaze met Rut's, her dark brown eyes holding the same expression of ease. How badly he wanted to tell her he loved her then. What did it matter that others were in the room? Rut was safe, and she had been braver than Hektor had ever before witnessed. She was no timid weaving woman. Rut had a strength about her that words could not easily describe. It was a strength within her heart that shone brilliantly from within—the strength of her faith.

"Philomena!" Servius gasped, at once drawing Hektor's attention to the young woman who lay in her bed, not gravely ill, but *awake*.

"Father," she whispered breathlessly, though smiling. "Is everything all right?"

"All right?" said Servius, falling to his knees beside her, encircling both his daughter and his wife in his arms. "It is more than all right. It is an answer to prayer! Are you.. Is she… Is my daughter truly well?"

"The night was long, but she woke with the morning sun," said Rut, beaming with joy. There were shadows under her eyes, and her curls were frizzy, but she'd never looked more beautiful to Hektor.

"Luke was instrumental. Even when the quake happened, he was quick-thinking and did not let it deter him from his work," Lydia explained.

Luke shrugged his shoulders. "It was God who did the healing. I am merely a tool."

"How great is the Lord our God!" Hektor exclaimed, inwardly dancing for joy as he added this to the mental list he was starting to compile of all the many little miracles that had occurred in the past day.

"I am so glad you are awake, Philomena," said Xanthe, stroking her daughter's golden locks with the back of her hand. "Are you truly feeling better?" It was the softest Hektor had ever heard the woman talk.

"My chest hurts still, but I feel stronger with every breath," said Philomena.

"I'll get you something for the pain, though it should subside on its own soon, time and rest provided," said Luke, before turning back to his jars and tools.

"My husband," said Xanthe, eyes widened, "did I hear you say that this was an answer to prayer?"

"I have so much to tell you, my wife. In fact, there are many years' worth of things I should have told you a long time ago, but I can only begin with this: I was a fool, Xanthe. I was a fool for leaving you alone, but I never stopped loving you or Philomena."

"Servius," Xanthe whispered, tears beginning to trickle down her cheeks.

"I blamed myself for everything that happened between us here in Philippi, and I thought you would have been better off without me. I thought I was doing the right thing, but I was still sabotaging my own life, running from my past and chasing solutions that were never meant for me, when I should have run back to you. In trying to be strong, I became a coward, and it is only now that I see there is only One with strength enough to cover me—the One True God."

"Servius, I don't know what to say," said Xanthe.

"Then say nothing, except that you will give me another chance to make many, many things right between us," said Servius, clasping her hands in his.

"The chance is yours," said Xanthe, through a teary-eyed smile.

Servius turned abruptly to Philomena. "Philomena, I was not the father I should have been, but I—" Servius ran out of words, dropping his head into his hands and weeping at his daughter's bedside.

"You have *always* been my father. You're the only one I ever want to know," said Philomena, reaching for her father.

Luke cleared his throat, and they all looked to the physician.

"What is it?" asked Lydia, walking toward him.

"Yes," said Servius, rising. "Is it payment you need? I must give you something for what you have done."

Luke raised his hands. "Please, I will accept no payment for this. It is God who heals, not I."

"There must be something we can do," said Servius, pleading with the physician.

"There is nothing. It is only what more I can do for you." Luke held up a vial. "I have prepared this. It is a mixture of olive leaf and some other herbs. Your daughter has a weak heart and weak lungs, but I believe if she takes some of this daily, it could help improve her symptoms. This is all I could make up right now, but I can give instructions to your servants on how to prepare more. I can also share with them some instructions about a special diet of foods that I think will help her to become stronger as well."

Luke placed the vial in Servius' hands.

"Thank you," said Servius, returning to sit beside his family—a family restored, though there was still a long road ahead of them. Hektor looked to Rut, who was also already looking at him. Both of them had experienced loss and suffering. Was it possible that their hearts could mend together, too?

Rut had practically fallen into Philomena's chamber during the quake, the tremors of the earth propelling her forward into the safety of the doorway. She wasn't sure, in hindsight, how she managed to make the dash from the main hall to Philomena's chamber in such a short time.

When the earth settled and they all finally had enough time to take stock of the situation, they realized there was no way out of the room. They would not be able to call for servants or anyone else until a path was cleared to them from the outside. Meanwhile, Philomena still laid in the bed unconscious with Xanthe hovering over her as a human shield. It was Luke who held them all together, giving orders, doing everything he could think of, and making use of every herb and ointment he had brought with him.

Only as the sun came up did Philomena's fever break, and she began to open her eyes and speak for the first time in days. Her strength had not run out just yet, and Rut knew that whatever God had planned for Philomena's life, it was sure to be something beautiful and amazing, just like their experiences that night.

Though Rut's prayers for peace had been answered, she couldn't recall ever feeling more relieved than when she saw Hektor pulling away the debris that blocked the doorway—debris that nearly crushed her. He was safe and well! What a life God had prepared for her, so beyond anything she would have planned for herself, yet so exactly right. She couldn't imagine not being here for this moment, not knowing Xanthe and Philomena and Lydia, and not caring so deeply for Hektor as she had come to realize she did.

"We should be going," said Lydia, half-speaking to Rut, and half-speaking loudly enough so that everyone could hear her. "We ought to return home and see if the earthquake did any damage there."

"Of course," said Rut, turning over her shoulder to look upon the family of three, a living reminder that God answered prayers in ways both big and small, expected and unexpected, in His way and in His time.

"I, too, would like to see if anyone else might be in need of my assistance after the earthquake," said Luke, packing his bag.

"I can lead us out of the house," said Hektor, standing at attention like the dependable man Rut had come to know.

A thought came to Rut, making her heart skip a beat. "Do you think Paul is all right?"

"Paul?" asked Servius.

Hektor explained, "He was the teacher you spoke of who cast out the demon. Paul was arrested along with another, Silas, after the incident in the Forum. Perhaps we can find news of what happened at the jail on our way back?"

"Yes," said Lydia, "let's make haste."

Rut instinctively went to gather her things, only to remember that this had not been like any other visit to Xanthe. When Servius came to get them the night before, she did not have time to bring anything with her. Empty-handed, she crossed the room with Lydia to where Hektor and Luke stood.

"I may be able to speak to the magistrates and help clear this up," said Servius.

"Really?" asked Hektor. "Do you think that is possible?"

Servius *almost* grinned. "Though I might be loath to admit it, there are some advantages to being a prominent military veteran and member of society… Speaking of that, in my misguided anger toward you, I utilized my personal connections within the city to cause damage to your business and your reputation, and I must apologize."

"You are forgiven," said Lydia. If anyone else had said it so easily, those listening might have reason to suspect whether or not it was true, but Rut knew that Lydia was genuine. She had always been forthright and direct about what she was feeling, and Rut had never known her to say anything that wasn't the truth.

"I will try to begin undoing some of the damage I've done as soon as I am able," said Servius. "Now go, all of you, and do not worry about leaving us behind. We will see each other again soon."

Their group departed, following Hektor's lead through the pathway he and Servius cleared earlier that morning. On their way, they passed several servants trying to put the grand house back together as much as possible. As Rut continued to walk home with the others, she took note of many of the buildings—the homes she had referred to as palaces when she first saw them. Most remained intact, but there were a few where damage was evident, and some more severe than others. Rut no longer saw any of them as palaces, nor did she find those who inhabited them to be intimidating—they were mere buildings, and the people within them mere human beings like Rut.

They had nearly returned to Lydia's home when Rut looked to Hektor, her heart wrought with concern. "Hero! He ran off during the earthquake!"

"Hero knows how to take care of himself," said Hektor with a reassuring tone.

"What if he is hurt? Or lost? Did you see him in Xanthe's house?"

Hektor shook his head. "Not after he ran off during the initial quake, but I am sure he is all right. He is Hero, after all, and there is no other dog like him."

"Maybe," said Rut, crossing her arms, "but I would still feel better if we knew where he was."

Her statement was met with a resounding laugh, causing Rut to whip her head around to look up at Hektor so fast that her curls struck the side of her face. "What is so funny?"

"Nothing," said Hektor, trying and failing to conceal a smirk.

"Speak, or risk never being spoken to again," she ordered.

"It is only that I was recalling when you and Hero first met. You were so unsure of him then, and now you think of him like family."

"Well, that's because he is like family."

"Fear not," said Hektor. "He eats far too much to stay away for long. He'll find his way home."

Rut looked up at Hektor and saw that familiar twinkle in his brilliant blue eyes. In that moment, the exhaustion of the night's activities finally began to catch up with her. She was so tired and wanted nothing more than to crawl into bed and sleep for days and days on end, but she knew that was impossible. As she looked around at the city of Philippi, she realized that, whether or not Paul and Silas were released, their work for the kingdom of God had only just started. Xanthe, Servius, and Philomena were only one family that had been waiting to be touched by the transformative power of a relationship with the One True God.

Thinking of families led Rut to thinking about her own family in Phoenicia, and how much time had passed since she left. A year no longer felt quite so long, and realizing how soon she would see them made her heart ache with longing. At the same time, it filled her with confusion. It was only a matter of a few short months before her return to Tyre, and she didn't know if she would ever be coming back to Philippi. If she did not, she might never see Hektor or Lydia again, except perhaps when they came to trade. That thought displeased her just as much as the idea of never seeing her brother and parents again, for the people of Philippi had become like family too.

God's kingdom in Philippi was only beginning, but was Rut's time here coming to an end?

20

"When daylight came, the chief magistrates sent the police to say, 'Release those men.' The jailer reported these words to Paul: 'The magistrates have sent orders for you to be released. So come out now and go in peace.' But Paul said to them, 'They beat us in public without a trial, although we are Roman citizens, and threw us in jail. And now are they going to send us away secretly? Certainly not! On the contrary, let them come themselves and escort us out.' The police reported these words to the magistrates. They were afraid when they heard that Paul and Silas were Roman citizens. So they came to appease them, and escorting them from prison, they urged them to leave town. After leaving the jail, they came to Lydia's house, where they saw and encouraged the brothers and sisters, and departed." — Acts 16:35-40 CSB

Several weeks had passed since Paul's departure. They were weeks of spinning, weaving, and worshipping for Rut and everyone else inside Lydia's villa. His last words to the group of believers who had gathered in Lydia's home were, "The grace of the Lord Jesus Christ be with all of you." Yet Paul and his company did not leave without first telling the believers what happened the night of the earthquake.

They had been singing songs of God and praying fervently when the foundations of the jail were shaken, breaking loose not only their chains but all the chains of those who were imprisoned. The jailer who had been assigned to watch them woke sometime later and saw the doors open. Fearing the prisoners had escaped and expecting to be punished himself, he drew his sword in preparation to do the worst rather than face retribution. Paul and Silas called out to him, and he rushed into the jail trembling and asking how he could be saved by Jesus. The jailer was so moved by the message, he brought Paul and Silas to his home where he washed their wounds, fed them, and asked them to baptize him with his family.

Lydia's home had thankfully been spared from severe damage. A few looms and baskets had been knocked over, but since they hadn't had any orders in progress, no projects had been ruined. Lydia's stock remained in perfect condition, ready for when business started back up again—which it already had. God's blessings were more abundant each time Rut tried to count them.

Servius must have said something to the city's officials in Paul and Silas' favor, because later that morning, the magistrates ordered their release. When they learned Paul was also a Roman citizen, they became even more anxious to settle the matter, as their treatment of him was unjust. Though Philippi was a leading Roman colony, as Rut had learned, they were not Rome, and the citizens within these Macedonian walls feared Roman retribution. Paul and Silas were urged to leave the area as soon as possible, which they did right after stopping at Lydia's home to share their tale. Though no one wanted them to leave, Rut had a feeling it would not be the last they would hear from Paul, and she also knew that God would keep them together in His spirit, even if great distances separated them. At least for now, Luke had elected to stay behind in Philippi to provide aid in the aftermath of the earthquake.

In total, Paul had stayed with them for nearly three months before they moved on, and well more than half a year had passed since Rut had left Phoenicia. Now Rut stood in the main hall, as the believers gathered to break bread and pray with one another, which had remained a regular tradition for them.

"It's something, isn't it?" asked Hektor. His voice startled Rut, as she hadn't realized he stood beside her. "All these people here... people we wouldn't have known if it hadn't been for Paul and the others coming to preach their message and teach us what it meant to be saved?"

"It is." This was a bittersweet occasion. There was cause for much joy and celebration as the number of believers only continued to grow, but it was also a reminder of more change yet to come. So much transition had already happened in Rut's life in such a short amount of time; the idea of even more happening before she had a chance to settle gave her cause for alarm. She could almost count the number of weeks left until her return to Phoenicia on her fingers.

All around them, people laughed, cried, talked, and embraced. She wanted to join in, but her heart simultaneously ached to retreat to a quiet place where she could finally catch up with her own thoughts.

"Want to disappear?" Hektor whispered in her ear.

"How did you know?" she turned, looking at him with a surprised smile.

"Because I know you."

"I don't want to be discourteous."

"Come on," said Hektor, motioning with a slight jerk of his head. "No one will notice if you take a little time away. I myself feel a bit of a headache coming on. Perhaps we could find somewhere quiet to rest, before rejoining the group?"

He offered her his arm and she took it, the motion so familiar to her that it was almost second nature. She clung to him and his warmth, and let him lead her to the workers' courtyard. Swiftly, he left and returned with two cups of fresh, cool water, placing one in her hand. Rut sipped it slowly, focusing on calming her nerves. Change was frightening, but it didn't have to be as long as she continued to trust in the pattern God was weaving.

"What is it you're really thinking about?" asked Hektor, setting his empty cup down beside them.

"Nothing... and everything." Rut sighed.

"Sounds complicated," said Hektor, "but I'm sure you can work it out."

"What gives you such confidence?" Rut raised an eyebrow in Hektor's direction. He was so different from Shem, yet he brought out the best parts of her in his own way. Hektor challenged her. He made Rut want to be a better reflection of Christ every time they spoke.

In the time since Rut had met him, Hektor had become her greatest friend, which was why she was so terrified to let him go.

Before Hektor could come up with an answer to her previous question, they were both startled by the sound of barking. It seemed to Rut that they were always being interrupted by something, and this time, the something was the long-lost Hero, bounding into the courtyard, full of energy and excitement.

"Hero! Where have you been?" Hektor knelt down to scratch the animal's fur behind his ears. Hero's barking never ceased. The dog kept jerking his head backward as he stomped his paws. It was more than a happy reunion, for they hadn't seen the dog since the night of the earthquake.

"I'm no expert," said Rut dryly, "but I think he's trying to tell you something." Though what the dog was attempting to say remained a mystery to her.

"Is he?" Hektor lifted both eyebrows in mock-surprise. Turning to Hero, he continued in the higher-pitched voice Hektor used whenever he addressed their four-legged mutual friend, "What is it, my boy?"

Hektor released the dog, and Hero ran from the courtyard as quickly as he came. Rut and Hektor exchanged quizzical looks before following the sound of the dog's paws, through the kitchens and out to the back of the house, where Rut was surprised to see *another* dog with a litter of puppies.

"Hero!" Rut exclaimed. "You have a family!" She knelt down next to the pups, which were smaller, adorable versions of their parents. She couldn't help but giggle as they toppled over each other, fighting for attention.

"So this is what he was up to when he kept disappearing on our trips to Xanthe's house," said Hektor, dropping his arms to his sides in astonishment.

"Who knew Hero was such a romantic?" Rut laughed. "Oh, Hektor, I know exactly who is going to be the most excited about this."

"Philomena?"

Rut nodded enthusiastically. Thanks to Luke's suggestions about food and activity, Philomena not only regained her strength, but grew even stronger. She still had to follow a strict regimen, but Philomena had never been healthier. "Do you think she'll want one of the pups?"

Hektor laughed heartily. "I think the answer to that question is obvious. The bigger question is, will Servius and Xanthe admit such an animal entry into their home? Hero is rambunctious. I can hardly imagine what his offspring will be like."

"I don't think they could say no to anything Philomena asked for, within reason," said Rut, cradling one of the pups. "We should get them all inside, don't you think?"

Hektor nodded and bent downward.

Hero's mate seemed to look at Rut with questioning eyes, causing Rut to whisper to her, "Don't worry. You and your little ones are safe here." At once, the mate relaxed, and Rut and Hektor were able to usher them all inside.

"I think they'll be quite comfortable in this courtyard for now," said Hektor, taking a step backward.

Rut sighed, following him. "Just when I think we are done with surprises for a while."

"At least we know what's next for Hero. He's going to have to adjust to being a father and family leader."

Hero barked twice, though more softly than usual, as though he was adjusting his tone for the sake of the pups.

"What about you?" Hektor asked. "What's next for you?"

"What do you mean?" asked Rut, slowly lifting her eyes to meet Hektor's gaze, though she had a feeling that he was attempting to return to their prior topic of conversation before Hero's interruption.

Hektor took Rut's hands in his—both of them. This was not the same as when he reached for her in a crowd, or offered his arm to guide her through the city. This touch was soft, and his hands shook slightly as he did it. Was he nervous? She inhaled sharply, feeling the roughness of his hands, scarred after years of fighting, but at the same time gentle and tender.

"Rut," he murmured huskily.

"Hektor?" she said, struggling to keep her gaze locked with his as the intensity behind his sparkling blue eyes grew.

"You've been in Philippi for more months now than are left until your return to Phoenicia," he stated, matter-of-fact.

"I know," she breathed out the words she hadn't dared to say aloud because she hadn't wanted them to be real.

"Are you still planning to go back to your family when Lydia returns to Tyre? Back to Phoenicia?" His voice cracked as he finished his question, and the obvious emotion written across his face made tears well up in her eyes.

"Please, Hektor…" Rut shook her head, willing him to slow down. She wasn't sure if she was ready to have this conversation.

"I'm in love with you, Rut." He blurted out the words, then dropped her hands. In that moment, it was as though Rut's heart stopped beating altogether. Was he surprised he said them? "I'm sorry, that wasn't how I meant to say it." He raised a hand to his forehead.

"Is that not what you meant?" she asked, her brows furrowing in confusion.

"No! I mean, yes! I mean—" Hektor stopped abruptly, closing his eyes and taking three slow breaths. Rut felt like she couldn't breathe at all. He continued, "From the moment I saw you in the marketplace, I remember Lydia being astonished over your work as a weaver, but I was stunned not by the beauty of your work. Rather, by the beauty of *you*. You were—you *are* the most incredible woman I've ever had the pleasure of meeting. As I've gotten to know you more, I've fallen in love with your whole heart, Rut. You make me laugh like no one else can. You make me want to be a better man. More than anything, you inspire me with your strength. You work hard at everything you do, and there's no stopping you once you've put your mind to something—even if that something is running down a hall during an earthquake because you *need* to be there for the people you care about. Rut, let me be someone you care about. Let me care for *you*."

"I… I don't know what to say." She struggled to come up with a response, as what felt like rivers of tears fell down her face. This man loved her, knowing all of her flaws and all the mistakes she had made? This man loved her, and was saying it aloud now, after she'd spent so many weeks trying to convince herself that such a love was not possible?

"Rut," he whispered her name again, though it somehow sounded different compared to every other time. "You are my closest friend, and I can't imagine my life without you. Please, say something. I have to know how you feel."

Rut knew she wasn't ready to have this conversation. There was something she needed to do first, before she could respond to Hektor's revelation—a revelation which she had both longed for and of which she had been frightened. Without being able to utter a single word, Rut ran from that courtyard, straight to her chamber.

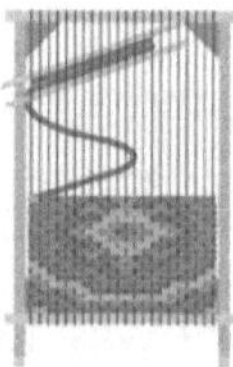

Lifeless, Hektor sank onto a wooden bench—or at least he might as well have been lifeless. She could have taken his heart with him, for his chest felt cold and empty. Though he had imagined over and over again each night how he might finally tell Rut of his feelings, he now began to think that it had all been a mistake, and chided himself for it.

All along he had known she was a grieving woman. Even though it had been years since her husband died, Hektor knew that such pain never truly faded. There were still times when he saw things that reminded him of Karis, or experienced things he couldn't wait to tell her about, only to remember that she was gone and had been gone for many years. Time, as Hektor learned during his days as a fighting man, healed most wounds, but some scars never truly faded. The loss of a loved one left that kind of scar on one's heart. Though he had tried to prepare himself for the possibility of Rut not being able to return his feelings, he was still gutted.

Perhaps he should not have said anything at all. Perhaps he never should have let his feelings for Rut grow beyond mere infatuation. Yet how could he? There was a pull between them. Hektor felt it and he knew she must have felt it, too. The more time Hektor spent with her, the more he wanted to stay by her side just to be near someone so lovely and loving.

Now that she had run, however, Hektor was convinced that he had acted too quickly. He only hoped he could undo whatever damage he caused.

"Hektor?"

He looked up in surprise to see Rut standing in front of him again, her presence just as overwhelming as it had been that day in the marketplace. She clutched something in her hands—a bundle of some sort of cloth.

Hektor stood up at once, his pulse racing. "I'm so sorry. I never should have—"

"Are you taking back the things you said?" she asked, looking as though she might start crying all over again. At that, Hektor became *very* confused.

"No, I meant every word," he affirmed, stumbling forward. "What is that you are holding?"

Rut flashed a hint of a smile at him, and it was enough to put him slightly more at ease. Extending her arms, she unveiled the most intricate tapestry Hektor had ever seen. "This is what I made for you," she explained, her voice soft.

"What you… made… for me?" Hektor reached out to pinch the finely woven threads between his fingers, before pulling his hands back quickly. He looked up at Rut with a questioning gaze, and she nodded at him, signaling to him that it was alright for him to touch the tapestry, though he did so warily. He had never held something so beautiful in all of his life.

"Do you remember when you asked me to weave something for you?"

"Yes," Hektor murmured as he took in the patterns, then suddenly he recognized the colors—they were the colors he had purchased for her using his own wages. He had no idea she would use them to make something so incredible.

Rut continued, "This is what I came up with."

"But how?" asked Hektor. "This must have taken hours!"

"It did," said Rut, "but once I saw the pattern in my mind, it came together easily."

Hektor laughed. "What you think of as easy, some people spend a lifetime trying to learn, and yet still never master. Will you tell me about it?"

Rut's fingers passed over the different colors. Hektor noticed she had used nearly every one. Shades of yellow, red, green, blue, white, and even purple all came together like a fresco made of fabric. "It is my story told in threads. The yellows and greens of Jerusalem and the walls and valleys that surround it. The reds of the dates my Savta used to make for us. The blues of the oceans I crossed coming to Philippi… It's all here."

"It is grand," said Hektor, marveling at all of the delicate lines and shapes she created. Hektor did not have to understand exactly how it was accomplished in order to appreciate how awe-inspiring the work was. He gestured to some white threads that seemed to bulge away from the weave itself, being thicker and rougher than the others. "What about these threads?"

Rut laughed lightly. "Those are threads spun by my nieces back in Phoenicia, Yemima and Kelila. They day I left to trade with my brother, before I met you, they brought me their tiny wool bundles and asked me if I thought I could sell them. I told them I would take them with me instead so that I would always have a reminder of them. It felt only right to weave their wool into this. It is a piece of my family, and a piece of the home I left behind."

"I think it is a perfect touch," said Hektor, and he meant every word. "Is there significance to this pattern here at the center? Made of purple, blue, and white?"

"Those… Those represent my life and yours. The blue is meant to represent you, and the purple is—"

"I think I can guess," said Hektor, running his hand over the pattern. "You are the purple thread."

"I am." She nodded.

"The way you've put them together is extraordinary. It's like they are all holding each other, pulling each other together."

"The white represents God and His light in our lives, always being present in our stories, guiding us and giving us hope."

"This is amazing, Rut," said Hektor, tears forming in his eyes as he took in the meaning of the tapestry and the level of care and detail poured into it. "When you ran off, I thought it was because you did not return my feelings."

"It wasn't that at all," said Rut. "I *was* shocked, but not because I didn't share your feelings. I was shocked because a long time ago, I gave up any expectations of sharing my life with another person in that way, thinking it would never be possible for me again. I wove this pattern for you, secretly hoping that one day you might give me a reason to tell you the story behind it."

"So… What does this mean for us?" asked Hektor.

"Can I tell you something I haven't told anyone else?" She looked up at him with wide eyes, and Hektor would have given her the whole world if it were within his power to do so.

"Of course," he answered.

Rut breathed in a shaky breath. "I think… Before I came here, I, like all of us earth-dwellers at one time or another, forgot that this life is only one short breath in eternity. I went to God, carrying each one of my dark, loose threads with me, and I blamed him for them. It wasn't until someone I care about very deeply told me that I was looking at the wrong side of the tapestry, that I realized the dark threads could be made into something beautiful."

"Like *this*," said Hektor, gesturing at the gift.

"But as I made this, I also realized that from where I sit when I weave, I see not only the order of what I have already woven, but in my mind I see what is to come when the project is complete. In the same way, God not only sees the right side; he sees even the parts that haven't come to be. It was that day on the river that I was finally able to let go of my loose threads, and at last watch for the pattern God was making."

"I don't even know why I said that," said Hektor. "I don't know much about weaving."

Rut smiled. "Then God spoke through you, because it was exactly what I needed to hear. After that, I found purpose in my life, Hektor. There was more to my days than spinning and weaving. There were friends and relationships forming. There was sharing with others who held pain in their hearts about the God who sees both sides of the tapestry. I never want to give that up."

"I'm not asking you to," said Hektor emphatically. He would never want Rut to give up what made her so special in the first place.

"I loved once before, Hektor. Long ago. It was my first love, and I thought it would be my last. I mourned him so, so deeply. The love I had for Shem is not one that I think will ever be replaced, but the love I have for you is something different. I do love you, Hektor."

Those five words were like a seal set upon Hektor's heart, and he wanted to rejoice and be elated that she returned his feelings, but he realized that it was now his turn to share some important things. "You only know me as the man I am now."

"I do," replied Rut.

"I was not always this way."

"I know."

"It was not for nothing that I was called the Lion of Philippi, Rut. I was a beast. Although I have long since vowed never to raise my fists for sport or pick up a drink for any reason, I am still imperfect. I still make mistakes." Hektor wanted to be absolutely sure that Rut knew who he was before he accepted that she shared his feelings, just as it seemed Rut wanted to be sure he was fully aware of who she was.

"I know that too," she said.

"And you'd still have me as a husband?" he asked.

"I would still have you. After all, I am not perfect, either. But… I've been married before, Hektor," said Rut, casting her eyes toward the ground as her cheeks flushed soft-red.

"I know."

"And it doesn't bother you?"

"I don't want to replace the memories of your past, Rut. I just want to be a part of your future." That was the truth. They could never go backward. He could never erase the mistakes he made in his youth, or bring back Karis. All they could do was move forward into the next spaces that God opened for them, trusting in what He had planned.

"What about children?" she asked.

"What about them?" said Hektor.

"I… Shem and I never… I don't think that I…"

At once, Hektor realized what she was trying to tell him, and he regretted his slow-thinking response. He took Rut's hands in his. "God is weaving our tapestry, Rut. Who knows what He has yet to unfold for us? We can pray about it together, and ask for His guidance."

"Then you would still have me as a wife?"

"I would still have you," he answered, hoping things were finally settled between them.

"Good," she said, "but there's one more thing."

"What is it?"

Rut grinned mischievously. "I must return to Phoenicia."

"You… What?" His voice squeaked like an adolescent. Hektor wasn't sure how many more surprises and shocks he could take.

"I must return to Phoenicia, and you must come, too," she said, rocking back and forth on her heels.

"Oh, I must?" he said, raising an eyebrow.

"Yes. To meet my family. *All* of my family."

"Rut!" At once, he picked her up and swung her around in the courtyard, laughing more joyously than he had in years.

"Hektor, you're making me dizzy!"

"Good," he said, setting her down, "as long as you fall into my arms."

"Hektor!" she exclaimed, laughing so hard that she snorted. The sound warmed his heart, and he yearned to hear it more.

"I could kiss you," said Hektor.

"Not until we are married," she whispered. "I want to be married with all of my family around to celebrate with us, and then I want to return here to Philippi."

"Are you sure?" he asked, leaning closer.

"Yes! This is my home now, and I feel called to this place and the people here. I want to continue serving, and maybe even working, if Lydia will have me. I'd be happy to join the other weaving women here."

"Oh, she'll have you." Hektor knew this news would thrill her.

"Good… Then you may kiss my hand, just this once, to seal this agreement." Rut extended her arm toward him.

He smiled at the confidence in her wide, brown eyes. "You speak as though this is a business arrangement."

"Perhaps I've been learning from Lydia."

"You have learned too well, but I agree to your terms." Taking her delicate fingers and raising them to his lips, he bestowed upon her hand the softest of kisses, though his lips admittedly lingered. It was a promise of many things yet to come.

PART FIVE

"Don't worry about anything, but in everything, through prayer and petition with thanksgiving, present your requests to God. And the peace of God, which surpasses all understanding, will guard your hearts and minds in Christ Jesus." — Philippians 4:6-7 CSB

EPILOGUE

"Our citizenship is in heaven, and we eagerly wait for a Savior from there, the Lord Jesus Christ. He will transform the body of our humble condition into the likeness of his glorious body, by the power that enables him to subject everything to himself." — Philippians 3:20-21 CSB

60 A.D. — 10 Years Later

Each day it seemed as though a new thread was revealed in the tapestry of Rut's life. It certainly wasn't the design she would have planned in her youth, but it was somehow even better.

After she, Hektor, and Lydia returned to Tyre, they met with Benayahu who waited for Rut exactly where he said he would be. Rut told him of all that had happened as their whole group rode away from the city to Rut's old family home. There, a light remained in the window just as her abba promised, and the sight of it made Rut weep with joy.

Hektor met her father, and at once they got along as though they'd known each other for years. Binyamin had called him *"an answer to his prayers for his daughter."* They visited for a short time, before they were married in the presence of Rut's family—including her parents, Benayahu and Milkah, Shamira and Asa, and all of Rut's nieces and nephews. Then they returned with Lydia to continue their work with the other believers in Philippi.

"Nessa, come sit beside me," said Rut to her daughter, now eight years old.

"Do I *haaave* to?" asked Nessa, drawing out the sounds of her words as she trotted across the room, hands clasped in front of her.

"Yes, you *haaave* to. Let me braid your hair before we go." Rut turned her daughter around and carefully separated her beautiful sand-colored ringlets.

"Are my girls almost ready?" said Hektor, standing in the doorway.

"Abba!" Nessa ran to her father and he hoisted her up in his arms, her tightly coiled curls bobbing up and down as he threw her up in the air and caught her, making her laugh. Like Rut, she would make little snorting noises when she was especially elated. The sight of them, the family she never thought she would have, never failed to fill Rut's heart with pride—not at anything she had done, but at everything God did.

The life that God had given her was better than any she could weave herself. In Him alone she found peace. In Him alone she found true, redeeming love. In Him alone she found her identity. Where she saw loose threads and knots tangled beyond repair, He saw beauty. Where she would have given up and unraveled the whole tapestry, He never stopped weaving.

"You know, we would be ready faster if I could finish her hair," said Rut, tapping her foot up and down.

"Is that so?" asked Hektor. "Well, then, Ness, we'd better try and sit still for just a few more moments."

"Can you do it, Abba? I like it better when you braid my hair."

Rut shook her head in amusement, for Hektor had never tried

to braid Nessa's hair before. That didn't matter to Nessa, though; she preferred when Hektor did *everything*, and truth be told, Rut didn't mind. Watching their special relationship grow was one of the greatest joys of Rut's life. Hektor was more than a good father to Nessa; he was a good abba.

"I don't think I know how. Besides that, look at my fingers." He held them up to her face. "They're too big to be good at doing hair."

Nessa giggled again. "No, they're not, Abba. Please?"

"I think you should let Imma do it. You'll want to look your best where we are going today."

"All right." Nessa sighed, sitting back down beside Rut. Rut worked quicker this time so that she could finish before Nessa had another sudden burst of energy. "Where are we going anyway?"

"We are going to see your Dodah Lydia and the other believers," said Rut.

Nessa had only ever known Lydia as Dodah, the Hebrew word for aunt. Long ago at the end of Rut's first year in Philippi, she and Lydia were reminiscing about all that transpired between them in that time. She did not know yet about Rut's plans to return to Philippi the following year, or her discussions with Hektor about marriage. Rut recalled Lydia saying, *"I had always hoped we would be friends, Rut, and I don't want to presume too much, but I do consider you to be one of the dearest friends I've ever had."* Rut had smiled and replied, *"You know, growing up my closest friend was my cousin, Shamira. We had a saying: cousins by blood, but sisters by heart. When my brother got married, we told his wife Milkah that she, too, was our sister by heart. You, Lydia, are a sister of my heart, and it is an extraordinary thing to know so many."* From then on, Lydia had been like another sister to Rut, and when Nessa was born, she had never learned to call Lydia anything other than

Dodah. Nessa knew she had other family in Phoenicia and Antioch, and Rut made sure to tell Nessa everyday how she was deeply loved, precious, and priceless to her family and to the Lord.

"Why didn't you say that first?" Nessa squealed. "Oh, Imma! Can you braid my hair faster?"

"Only if you hold still," said Rut, trying to be serious but letting her laughter seep through.

At last, Rut secured the braid, though it was not an easy task with how Nessa wiggled and wriggled. "Abba, guess what I did today!" Nessa exclaimed.

"Hm…" Hektor scrunched up his face as though he were in deep concentration, then released all the tension at once and made his eyes very wide. "Did Imma teach you how to weave something?"

"No…"

"Spin some wool?"

"Abba, you know I'm no good at that." Nessa's shoulders drooped.

"No, I don't," said Hektor incredulously. "I think one day you could be an even better weaver than Imma, with time and practice, of course. You could even make something like *that* one day." Hektor gestured to the tapestry on the wall, which was the one decoration in their otherwise humble dwelling. Despite working with such finery all day, they continued to live quite simply, content with very few physical possessions, because they stored up so many treasured memories in their hearts. It was home for Rut because of the people within its walls.

"I could never make something as beautiful as Imma's tapestry," said Nessa, eyes wide as she beheld the colorful wall hanging that Rut made for Hektor so long ago, presenting it to him on the day they both finally confessed their love for each other.

Rut turned Nessa to face her. "Whatever you want to be, you will be amazing at it, whether that's weaving threads or spinning wool or dying fabrics—"

"Or none of those things," Nessa mumbled.

"Or none of those things," said Rut. "Why don't you tell Abba what you really did today?"

"Oh, yes! I caught another butterfly, Abba! Its colors were like a sunset, all orange and yellow."

Rut pursed her lips as she saw Hektor plaster a smile on his face, though she knew he recoiled inwardly. He despised winged insects, but Nessa adored them, and she loved nothing more than running through the hills and trying to catch them in her tiny hands.

"You did?" said Hektor, feigning enthusiasm. It would have been convincing to everyone except Rut, who knew his secret and had known it since that very first night on the ship carrying them to Philippi. "What did you do with it?"

"Well, I wanted to save it so that I could show it to you, but Imma said I had to let it go," said Nessa sheepishly.

"I think your imma was right, Ness. That butterfly might have had a family somewhere. You did a good thing by letting it fly home. Now are we ready to go to Lydia's?"

"Yes! Yes!" Nessa cheered.

"Very well, then," said Hektor, bending down and letting Nessa climb onto his back to be carried out the door. Rut followed close behind them. Their "house" was really a set of rooms annexed from Lydia's villa. It had been Lydia's wedding gift to them, so that Hektor could still remain nearby and continue his job.

They had their own separate entrance, and it functioned as its own house. When Rut wasn't weaving, she did her own cooking over a fire, and most nights, she and Hektor ate together with Nessa, rather than eating in the main hall with Lydia's other workers and servants. To get to the main house where the believers gathered, they used the servants' entrance at the rear of the building, passing through the workers' courtyard on their way.

As Lydia had made abundantly clear to everyone in the days leading up to this assembly, they had received a letter from Paul, which he had written during his imprisonment. It was to be read that night and Rut was very much looking forward to it.

"Dodah Lydia!" Nessa exclaimed as they turned the corner and joined the growing crowd.

"Sweet Nessa, how are you?" asked Lydia. Hektor bent down to his knees so that Nessa could slide off, which she did at once, running to Lydia.

"I am well. May I sit by you today?"

"Is it all right with your parents?" asked Lydia, looking in Rut's direction.

Rut smiled. "You know she won't sit anywhere else."

"Come on then, and you can tell me about all the different colors of butterflies you've seen since we last spoke." Lydia took Nessa's hand and led her through the crowd.

Hektor, on the other hand, struggled to rise back to a standing position. "What happened to my Lion of Philippi?" Rut teased.

"He got old," said Hektor, wrapping his arm around Rut as he stood. She leaned against his chest and felt him kiss the top of her head. No matter how many years passed, Hektor could always make her feel safe and at ease in any environment with a single touch or glance.

One by one, the rest of the believers filtered in, taking seats in every available space in the room. Their numbers had been large when Paul first visited, and now they were so numerous that even Lydia's robust home no longer seemed as spacious as it once did; but it was still the best meeting place for them.

"All right, everyone. Servius Arrius has volunteered to read

Paul's letter for us, so if you would all quiet down, we can begin," Lydia called out.

The large crowd hushed immediately at the mention of Paul, who was so deeply loved by their community.

Servius Arrius cleared his throat and began, "Paul and Timothy, servants of Christ Jesus: To all the saints in Christ Jesus who are in Philippi, including the overseers and deacons. Grace to you and peace from God our Father and the Lord Jesus Christ. I give thanks to my God for every remembrance of you, always praying with joy for all of you in my every prayer, because of your partnership in the gospel from the first day until now…"

As Servius continued to read, Rut reflected on all that had happened, and the journey that brought each of them to this very moment. Servius and Xanthe became some of the most prominent members of their community, and Philomena had grown healthier than any of them ever dared to hope she would be, thanks to Luke's recommendations. Rut marveled at how God wove their lives together, and she realized as she looked around that it was more than her connections to Servius through her cousin Libi's marriage to Cassius. It went back even further to how the Lord laid the foundations for her faith through her grandparents, Eliyahu and Hodiyah, her parents, her aunts and uncles, her cousins, and her brother. Through that legacy and all of the experiences she had in her life—and Hektor in his own— they were now uniquely positioned to be exactly where the Lord needed them to be to serve and support the believers in Philippi. God was so good and though so much had happened, it still felt sometimes like the very beginning.

Her ears focused again as Paul addressed his imprisonment and present circumstances in the letter. "For me, to live is Christ and to die is gain. Now if I live on in the flesh, this means fruitful work for me; and I don't know which one I should choose. I am torn between the two. I long to depart and be with Christ—which is far better—but to remain in the flesh is more necessary for your sake. Since I am persuaded of this, I know that I will remain and continue with all of you for your progress and joy in the faith, so that, because of my coming to you again, your boasting in Christ Jesus may abound."

Rut pondered the truth of those words. There had certainly been pain in her life along with trials, and there would likely be more. There were also blessings like Hektor and their daughter Nessa, whom Rut had given birth to when she thought she was too old to carry children. Once again, God surpassed all of her expectations, and though each difficult thing she walked through could have given her reason to despair, the good things God brought out of them only made Rut want to keep singing His praises, telling His story, and proclaiming the Good News of the risen Jesus Christ and the life He offered.

"Just one thing: As citizens of heaven, live your life worthy of the gospel of Christ. Then, whether I come and see you or am absent, I will hear about you that you are standing firm in one spirit, in one accord, contending together for the faith of the gospel, not being frightened in any way by your opponents. This is a sign of destruction for them, but of your salvation—and this is from God. For it has been granted to you on Christ's behalf not only to believe in him, but also to suffer for him, since you are engaged in the same struggle that you saw I had and now hear that I have."

It was those words that echoed not only within the high walls of Lydia's home, but within Rut's heart. What did it mean to be a citizen of heaven?

She looked around the room at the multitude of people around her—all people from within the city of Philippi, yet all with different backgrounds. Some Jewish, most Gentile, some Greek, some Roman, and some a mixture of both. All of them were united as children of God. Rut herself had been born and raised in Jerusalem, become a wife and a widow in Phoenicia, and become a weaver, a wife again, and a mother in Philippi.

Oftentimes when she was younger, she struggled with the idea of where and to whom she belonged. She had been displaced, felt in the way, and been a stranger in a strange land. That was when Rut realized she had not been a daughter of Jerusalem, Phoenicia, or even Philippi. Like these people, her citizenship, her true identity and the one she and so many others spent so long searching for, came only from Jesus. She was a daughter of the Most High God. These people were brought together by their Heavenly Father, the One who saw both sides, and wove all of their stories into one. Tears filled her eyes because as she beheld them all, some whose names and stories she knew very well and others she did not know as well as she would have liked, she saw pure beauty.

Like those who had come before her, the seeds of faith planted in this room would only continue to grow from generation to generation. To say that Rut felt blessed to be a part of it was an understatement, for it was still only just the beginning.

This was God's tapestry.

These people and their lives were His masterpiece, and it was still unfolding.

THE END.

FAMILY TREE

ELIYAHU
HODIYAH

AHARON
ELISHEVA

ELIANA
MATTHAN

SHAMIRA
ASA

ELIEL
YEMIMA
KELILA
LITTLE ASA

BINYAMIN
DEVORAH

RUT
HEKTOR

BENAYAHU
MILKAH

NESSA

JERIEL
TOVI
AVIGAIL

TAMIR
CHAVA

YUVAL
GILAD
ALETA

LIBI
CASSIUS

SHIRLI
ANNA

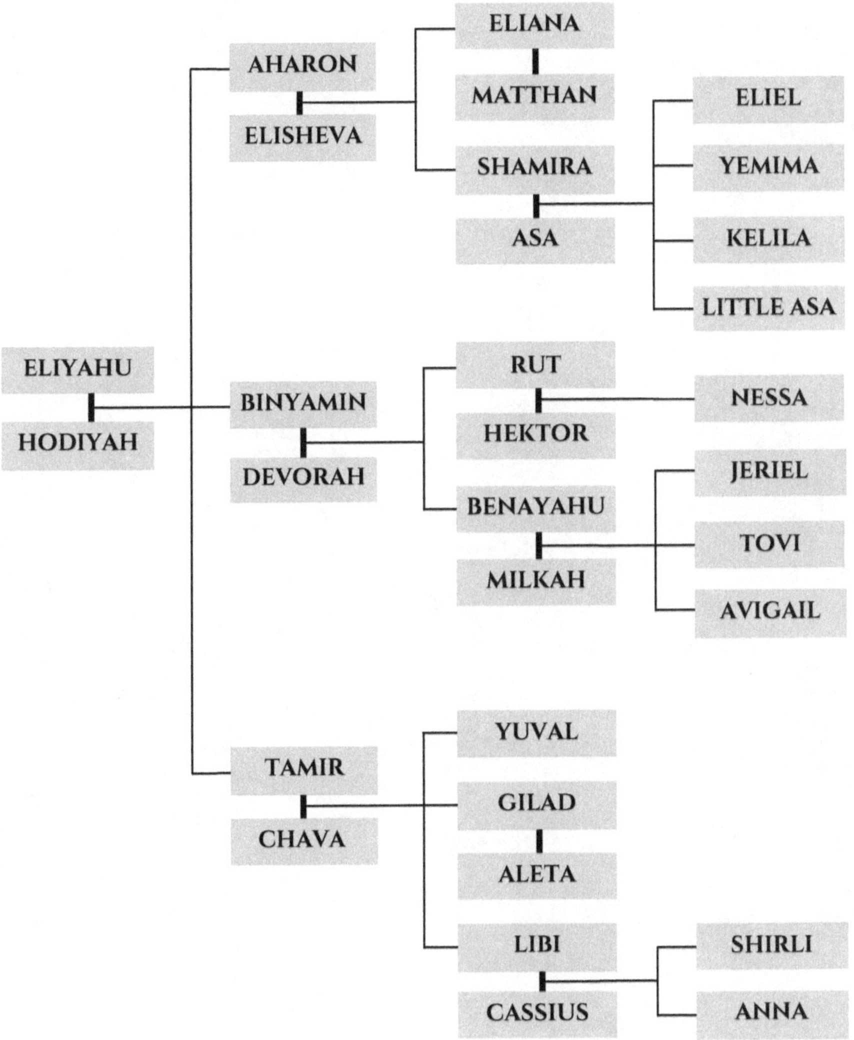

DISCUSSION QUESTIONS

1. In the beginning of the story, Rut wrestles with the circumstances of her life not matching her expectations. Have you ever wondered why something is or is not happening the way you thought it would? How did you respond? We can trust in God's plan for our lives and find peace through praying to Him.

2. Both Rut and Hektor have grieved the loss of very close personal relationships. Have you ever lost someone important to you? How did you handle that grief? What Bible verses can you think of that describe hope for those in mourning?

3. On Rut's journey to Philippi, the ship she is traveling on becomes caught in a storm. Hektor comforts her by reciting scripture. Can you make a list of scripture that would comfort you during a time of anxiety? Consider trying to memorize some of those verses.

4. Lydia is portrayed as a very confident character, bold in her faith and in her actions. How do you think you would have responded to Paul's message if you were in Lydia's position? What do you think that moment would have felt like?

5. In Chapter 10, Rut faces the realization of how she has been ignoring her relationship with God and His call on her life. Similarly today, it can be easy for us as Christians to get distracted by the things of this world. What, if anything, holds you back from going deeper with God? From sharing the Gospel with others? How can you avoid losing track of what's important?

6. In the story, Lydia opens up her home to Paul, his friends, and to others in Philippi. In what ways can you be inspired by Lydia's example? How can you use what you have to serve others and build the kingdom of God?

7. Prior to their conversion, Lydia and Hektor are portrayed as God-fearing Gentiles; people who believed in the Jewish God but had not fully converted. Hektor and Lydia have some knowledge of God and limited access to Scripture, but it is not until Paul's visit that they are exposed to the fullness of the Gospel message. We are blessed to live in a world where the Bible is accessible to so many people in various formats and languages, but many still do not have Bibles of their own. Have you ever considered joining or donating to a ministry that gives Bibles to those in need?

8. *Daughter of the Most High* portrays multiple different kinds of testimonies. Through Hektor and Lydia, we see the perspective of someone with some prior knowledge of faith in God; through Xanthe, Servius, and Philomena, we see the perspective of someone being introduced to faith in God for the first time; and through Rut, we see the perspective of someone who had a strong faith, but struggled for a time with doubt. Which story most closely resembles your own testimony? In what ways is your testimony different?

9. In Chapter 20, Rut presents Hektor with a very special gift: a tapestry that portrays her life in threads and colors. If you were going to weave a tapestry of your life, what colors would you use and why? What motifs or symbols would appear prominent?

10. In the Epilogue, Rut describes her amazement at how God has worked in her life and the lives of others around her. She expresses her gratitude for her family's legacy of faith; a legacy that she will get to give to her own daughter, and hopefully carry on for generations to come. Do you have family members, friends, or mentors who have poured into your life? In what ways? How can you or are you pouring into the lives of others?

Author's Note

I can honestly say that I have never enjoyed researching for a book as much as I did while researching for *Daughter of the Most High*. Unfortunately, as I discovered in earlier drafts, I enjoyed researching a little *too* much, and had to delete paragraphs on paragraphs of historical information that otherwise bogged down the narrative. It's all right, though, since I can make up for it here in the Author's Note.

I don't write stories from the perspective of historical figures. I prefer to write from the perspective of imagined characters like Hektor, Rut, and her family, and explore what historical experiences might have been like from their points of view. I never did figure out how to build a time machine (sorry, eleven-year-old Jenna), but this way of writing has gotten me pretty close. When it comes to portraying historical figures in my novels, I try to imagine very little. Paul's portrayal has not changed much since he appeared in *Antioch's Daughter* in 2023. He brings with him figures like Luke and Timothy, whose dialogue was interesting to explore as I imagined what sorts of things these traveling companions might have discussed with one another. Ultimately, however, I only wrote lines for them whenever it was necessary for Rut and Hektor's fictional storylines.

When it comes to writing for Lydia, I have been itching to write this story for years. The first notions I had of Rut's story came from conversations with friends and family while I was writing *Jerusalem's Daughter* and made a point of showing Rut's skill at weaving. Naturally, connections were made to another woman in the New Testament famed for her connections to the textile trade. We do not know much about Lydia's business. The book of Acts only tells us what is necessary in order to understand the context of her conversion. She is described in various translations only as a "seller" or "dealer" of purple goods. Many scholars have explored what her life might have been like, and made attempts at answering questions such as, "Where did her business come from?" "Was she married, or a single woman of means?" "How and why did she move from Thyatira to Philippi?" On top of that, several other great historical fiction novelists have portrayed her growing and operating her business. Because of that, I deliberately chose not to focus on that in my story; it would've been hard to write about in a way that was natural, since Rut and Lydia's paths do not intersect until Lydia's business has already been well established. Like the book of Acts, I chose to only include what was necessary for the reader to understand the story. For books where Lydia's journey is the main focus, I would suggest *Bread of Angels* by Tessa Afshar or *Lydia: Woman of Philippi* by Diana Wallis Taylor.

As for how and why I portrayed the character of Lydia as I did, I made very specific choices. My interpretation of Lydia is that she is a very impressive woman. She is capable, of course, as she manages her own household. She is firm in her beliefs and her convictions as a God-fearer and follower of the Jewish God. She is even more firm when she is told about the Good

News of Christ Jesus, and is baptized alongside her household after being so moved by Paul's message. Lydia is hospitable, opening up her home to Paul and to the fledgling Philippian church, and she is persuasive in her urgings to Paul to stay as a guest in her home (spending as much as three months there!). Though her account in Acts is short, it leaves a lasting impression! The more time I spent in the Word and in her story, the more I felt I learned about responding to God in the moment, being open to His leading, and faithfully following through with each opportunity He presents. I hope these attributes of her character as I perceived it came across in the story.

Philippi, though a setting in my story, required almost as much research as if it were a character, and in many ways it was. I was fascinated by this ancient city and its rich history. The further I delved into it, the more I realized just how life-changing Paul's message would have been to its inhabitants. Some of this I included or alluded to, but a lot of it ended up getting cut during edits. Philippi of Macedonia was primarily a Greek colony before it fell to Rome. It was a wealthy area, thanks to its rich gold mines, and became even more prosperous after the Via Egnatia was built, connecting the province to the greater Roman world. The area was then populated by Roman veterans and Roman government was appointed and established, though from the people to the architecture, Hellenistic and Greek influence remained prominent. Roman structures were built on top of or around pre-existing ones. More settlers came from all around after either being displaced from their own homes due to other conflicts of antiquity, or because they were seeking some of Philippi's prosperity for themselves.

In this context, it is no wonder that the people there, who may not have felt like they belonged anywhere, would've been so open and receptive to a message that they did indeed belong to God. Those men and women, from Romans and Greeks, to immigrants, refugees, retired veterans, and trade entrepreneurs, might have been deeply moved by Paul's reminder in his letter that as believers, our citizenship is not of this world, but of Heaven, and that our identity is found in Christ alone. In any case, we know from their growth and from how Paul speaks of them as recorded in the Biblical book of Philippians that these early believers certainly comprised a highly driven, extremely generous, and influential church.

I always draw very heavily from scripture when incorporating themes and ideas into my stories. Writing for Hektor was an interesting task, as he is described in the story as a "God-fearer." Many believe that term was used to describe Gentile believers in the Jewish God who were not full converts to Judaism. In the time of the book of Acts, these people were missing out on the "Good News" that Jesus provided a way for all people to be saved. The Bible tells us that rather than going to a synagogue, as was custom, Paul and his company sought out a "place of prayer" by the river outside the city. From this, some infer that there may not have been a synagogue in Philippi. I wanted Hektor to have some kind of a foundation for his beliefs and something to hold onto in his heart, and that is how the idea came to be for Hektor to have access to the Psalms through Lydia. Scrolls of this kind might have been rare. They also would have been expensive due to how difficult they were to produce, though I imagine for those desperately searching for a deeper understanding of faith like the fictionalized versions of Hektor and Lydia in this story, no price would have been too high. If you would like to read and study further some of the psalms that Hektor mentions in dialogue, you can read Psalm 22, 23, 27, 56, and 65.

In terms of other scripture quoted in the dialogue or narrative of the story, Shem reads to Rut from Proverbs 31. Because we don't know exactly what Paul said to Lydia by the river on the day of her conversion, I chose to borrow from other sermons of Paul recorded in Acts, mainly Acts 13 and 22. His style of speaking in such passages is a good reference point for how he might have patterned his ministry elsewhere. Portions of Paul's letter to the Philippians are also included in the very last chapter, though I would encourage anyone and everyone to read the entire book, as it's one of my favorites of Paul's writings. You'll also find the bulk of my inspiration for this story and the Biblical account of Lydia's conversion in Acts 16.

Lastly, in terms of research, and before I go any further with my acknowledgments, I must address the lovable four-legged character who made his debut in *Daughter of the Most High*: Hero. Some of my first ever reviewers of *Jerusalem's Daughter* were my family members, from aunts and uncles to younger cousins. After reading that book, of course, they developed some requests of their own. My young teen and tween cousins at the time wanted things like "more action" and "more dogs." Well, three books later, I hope I finally satisfied your requests! Hero was for you, Goodman family. I hope he bounded in and stole your hearts. For those of you readers wondering about dogs as pets in ancient times, there are numerous references to domesticated dogs in these cultures of yore. While some references portray dogs in a less than favorable light, others show that historical people did have dogs as pets for various reasons. Dogs could be trained as guards, hunters, or sheep dogs as alluded to in Job 30:1. In the account of the Gentile woman asking Jesus for healing on behalf of her daughter, the woman mentions dogs in her impassioned plea as recorded in both Matthew 15:21-28 and Mark 7:24-30. We can also infer from other non-Biblical sources that some may have even loved their animals in a very similar fashion to the way people do today.

Now it is time to give thanks. First, I want to thank our BBC church family. When my husband and I moved across the country in 2023, finding a church to call "home" was a huge priority. I just never expected to find "home" so quickly, and for it to feel so natural! It is also worth noting that when we began attending BBC, they were right in the middle of an expository sermon series on the book of Acts, and in the very same chapters that I was also independently studying for this now-finished book. I don't call that a coincidence. I call that just one example of God being the master weaver of stories! These sermons were as encouraging as they were educating. Sometimes I still have to pinch myself walking into church to make sure it's not a dream because we truly feel so connected to the people around us. It's hard to believe we haven't known you all for our whole lives.

I need to thank my friends—all of you, too many to name. Some old, some new. If you're in my circle of communication, consider yourself thanked! You all know that five years ago, I never would've imagined myself moving across the country with my husband in pursuit of ministry opportunities, now living God's best version of our lives in the Midwest, yet here we are! In the ups and downs of this beautiful tapestry unfolding, "y'all" have held my hand, listened to my tear-filled rants, offered help whenever possible, and been steady by my side whenever I needed you. It could've been easy for me to give up to anxiety and fear, but because of you, I was always able to remember that I was never truly alone. Thank you for always reminding me where to look to find light when the world seems so dark.

Thank you to the Mendenhalls, and the Fig Tree Books & More family for being so encouraging not only of me, but of these little novels. I am so grateful for your prayers!

Thank you to Audrey Bodine, who worked with me as my editor and critique partner for this book. Your attention to detail, level of care and understanding, and willingness to work on my timetable were beyond helpful! Thanks for "writing by light" with me.

Thank you, as *always*, to my family, near and far. Though miles may separate us, I am grateful to always be connected to you. To borrow the words of Paul in Philippians 1:3-4 CSB, "I give thanks to my God for every remembrance of you, always praying with joy for all of you in my every prayer." I consider you all to be my biggest blessings in life.

Thanks especially to my husband, Brandon, for being my greatest inspiration both in writing and in life. I love the way you lead me, the way you pray with me, and the way you and I work together.

Thank you to *you*, the readers, for sticking with me and these characters. This journey is not over yet, and the end of this book is only the beginning. I still find it hard to believe that these words make it into the hands of people all over the world. It is incredibly humbling, and I remain immeasurably grateful and appreciative.

Thank you to my Grandma Graves. It's hard to believe that by the time this book is published and in the hands of readers, you will have been with the Lord for nearly a decade. Grief can change so much in that amount of time, and yet it never really goes away. There's so much to thank you for, that I wish I would've said it more while you were with us on earth. Thank you for being a storyteller and a weaver of words. Thank you for being the kind of grandma who could do or create anything. Thank you for your love of books, and thank you for teaching me how to study, and to love studying. There still exists in this world one of your Bibles, and in that particular Bible there are nearly-blank pages where your fingers lovingly wore the ink off of Philippians. Thank you for loving that book so much that you made me want to delve that deep and love it too. I miss you, but I know I'll see you again, and we'll both stand together in awe and wonder at our Creator.

Finally, thank You to God. By Him is everything possible, and to Him goes all glory for all time. I cannot fully express how much You mean to me, so I'll borrow from the hymn titled "Come, Thou Fount of Every Blessing" that already encapsulates how I feel:

"O to grace how great a debtor
daily I'm constrained to be!
Let that grace now, like a fetter,
bind my wandering heart to Thee.
Prone to wander, Lord, I feel it,
prone to leave the God I love;
here's my heart; O take and seal it;
seal it for Thy courts above."
— Robert Robinson (1758), Public Domain